I hope you will

enjoy!

B.A. Ellison

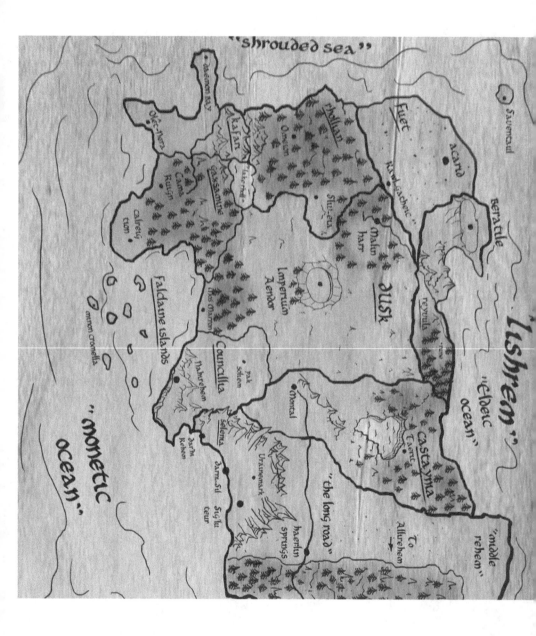

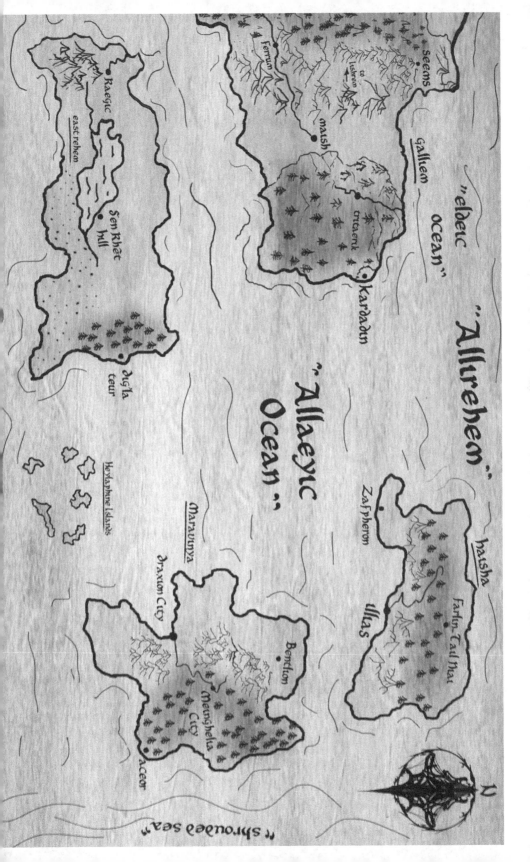

THE DYNASTY OF THE PHOENIX

MINDSTIR MEDIA

Published by Mindstir Media, LLC
45 Lafayette Rd | Suite 181| North Hampton, NH 03862 | USA
1.800.767.0531 | www.mindstirmedia.com

Printed in the United States of America
ISBN-13: 978-1-7356983-9-7
Library of Congress Control Number: 2020922897

THE DYNASTY OF THE PHOENIX

A TALE OF SHADOW & SHROUD

BOOK ONE

B.A. ELLISON

Table of Contents

Acknowledgments

For those who told me that I could,

    I did.

For those who believed in my magic,

    I made it real.

For those who stood at my side,

    The light of our truths will illuminate the darkest shadows.

For those who remain,

    Only the shroud threatens us now.

Our magic will light the dark,

    If we live in the write manner.

Passion, persistence, craft.
Kiszramance, carpdiemce, matterè
B.A. Ellison

A Very Special Thanks

- Paul Martin and Dominion Editorial

- My friend and artist Billy Martin, for listening and delving into my mind so we could all see and have his absolute gem of a cover and the maps.

- My friends and family, who have supported me throughout this journey to its end and the beginning of another.

- To all my readers and fans who truly believe.

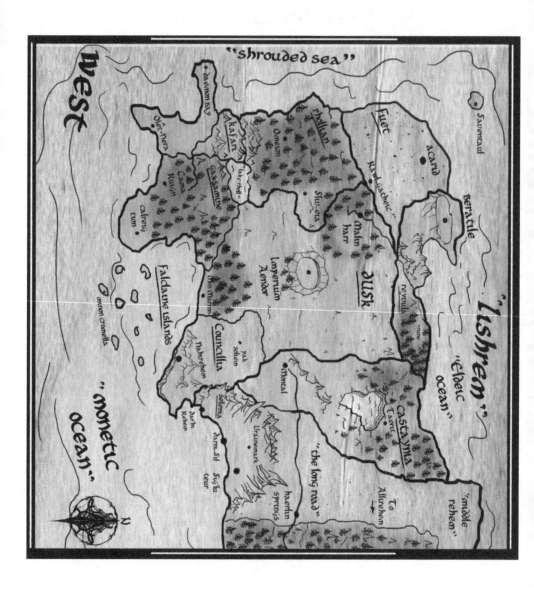

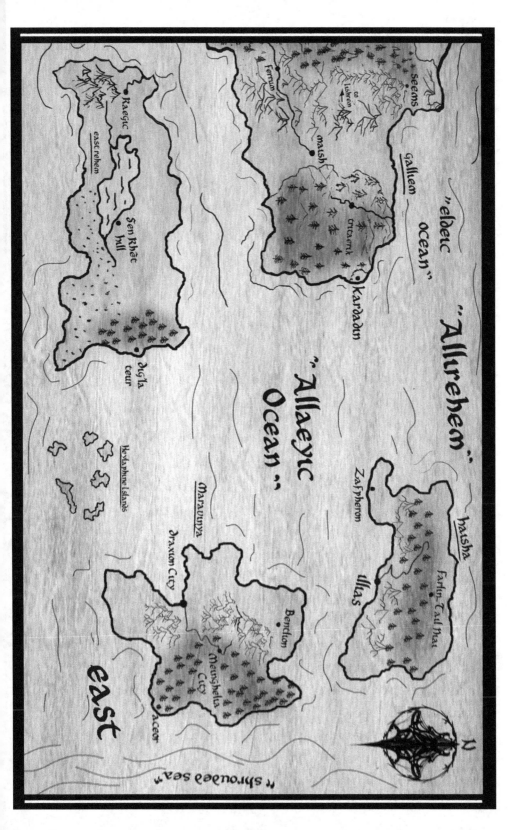

Map Legend

 Forest

 Desert

Mountains

Rivers (unless otherwise noted, some lines used for state boundaries in Iishrem)

Geographic feature or continent

State or Country

• Significant City

A big Round World on a Small Square map

I like this map a lot. It does a great job of bringing what I see in my mind onto a physical plane, which anyone can view, read, and understand. However, as my elementary school principal first told me, all maps have lies. This one is no different. Were this map to be represented on a round globe rather than a square map conformed to print nicely in a book, it would look quite different. I would first say that the most accurate aspect of this map compared to what I see in my mind are the shapes of the land-masses and the geographical features. When looking over the map, readers should be aware that physical features and political features are represented at a certain level of clarity. As this is a small-scale map, it only shows features and cities of according importance. Were I to zoom in, perhaps on a single country like Dusk, there could be many more significant cities and features to show. Yet, this map shows every city of importance thus far and more. Over time, as the series continues, there could, in fact, be more features and cities waiting for the right time to be brought into the story, and thus revealed. On the positioning and sizes of the landmasses, I would say that the supercontinent containing the states aligned with Iishrem, as well as Selenia, Middle Rehem, and Galliem, known as R'hemash, and the island continent of Maravinya are the most accurate—because they're in the center of the map, and therefore there is less distortion. While the shapes of East Rehem and Haisha are also portrayed well, on a globe, their lands further towards the poles would stretch significantly, and there would be more water in between them and the next closest landmasses, although Haisha's most southern tip is not too far from Maravinya's most northern. Thank you.

Content Disclaimer

This book is NOT for children, although I won't define at what age childhood ceases. Older, more mature teens I think can appreciate this book fine. The good news is, everyone grows older.

The Dynasty of the Phoenix has scenes several depicting sex, drug use, violent deaths, and taboos described in moderately graphic, visceral detail. Readers should be aware that some details in these scenes may push their limits, but I am strongly confident that I have towed the line well, to keep myself from going overboard anywhere. I write what's necessary to make the narrative feel colorful, memorable, and authentic, most of all.

All characters, objects, and places are the product of my imagination, and not based on any person living or dead, real or fictional. If you think you're in this book, you aren't. I promise you that! You aren't that remarkable, and not everything is about you. Get over yourself. Seriously. Enjoy!

THE DYNASTY OF THE PHOENIX

Prologue 1

The keepers of the Sword (Gal'gatha)

Another group of darn kids up to no good, the old man just knew it. He approached the corner of a stone-walled corridor inside the dimly lit megalithic superstructure, which housed the museum he curated. He could not quite make out what they were doing yet. However, he had been taking care of his museum for quite long enough to have an awfully good idea of what they were up to—something that they shouldn't have been based on the area they were in.

The area in front of the old man was still crowded with guests, on traditionally one of the busiest days of the year for the museum, he couldn't just force his way through them. It was going to be a challenge to apprehend or call out a handful of rambunctious teens. People knew the old man, but they didn't really know *of* him. The old man considered himself both esoteric and reclusive in that way.

When the old man finally forced his way through the crowd, he found that those who were misbehaving weren't kids but teens. The ages of the participants in these interactions with the old man varied from time to time, and these teens were doing just what he thought they would be. He considered calling out to them— it would take care of them more simply— but as he prepared to yell, he found himself stifled by a troop of small children brushing into him and running around him, even as he had done his best to avoid them. Children are so good at that, after all. So, the old man held off on raising his voice and decided to approach the teenagers more diplomatically.

As he got closer to the four youths, he found that they were all roughly the same age. They had slipped under a marquee rope barrier and approached a raised surface. Shaped like the bottom of an egg with a hole several dozen feet wide in diameter in the center, the hole could be fallen into—if one wasn't careful enough. Hence the ropes.

One wouldn't fall too far though—as there was a net with a high weight capacity—but that hadn't stopped several good scares or been enough to prevent a number of twisted ankles and broken legs over the years.

The museum on this level resembled more the beginning of a cave and descended much farther into the earth than a single level of a museum would normally do. Several stalagmites rose from the cave floor, accompanied by stalactites which descended from above. This was the end of the tour to the public. Far be it so for the old man. He knew that the megalithic superstructure bore much deeper into the subterranean earth than anyone suspected, but all that the public could do was what the teenagers were currently doing—slip under the marquee ropes, lean over the edge to look down, and hope to see something that no one else had before. They couldn't be aware of what esoteric knowledge the reclusive old man really carried with him.

"This is a waste of time," said a short blonde teenage girl with her hands on her hips, standing just behind the marquee ropes. "You aren't going to see anything down there."

Before the old man engaged with them, he wanted to hear a little bit more of their conversation, so he paused in his approach.

"Go on in farther," one boy said to another. The blond-haired one he was addressing currently had his legs up over the edge of the hole. "Perhaps you'll feel the heat of a dragon or see the glare of a raven."

The boy nervously looked in a little farther as the first boy looked like he was considering pushing him in, but then he momentarily decided against it, before folding his arms like a chicken and beginning to screech like an eagle while flapping his arms and running around in a circle. "Be careful not to be swept in by the wind of an eagle," the boy with short red hair and freckles said.

The red-haired boy and a third with square glasses that had remained silent began to laugh, and then even the girl with a ponytail joined in. She picked up a small pebble from the ground and tossed it at the blond-haired boy who still sat with his legs over the edge, hitting him softly on the back of the head. "Perhaps a hawk will hurl a rock at you," she added jokingly.

When they were all having a good laugh, except for the boy with his legs over the edge, and the old man decided he had seen enough. "You know this area is roped off for a reason. Your friend won't fall far if you were to try and push him in, but I wouldn't count on him still being a friend to you afterward if you did."

The blonde girl was the first to turn around, and she quickly reddened at being caught in the act. The two other boys milling around the edge slowly shifted their heads to look at him, probably rolling their eyes first. The boy with his legs over the edge got up quickly, dusting himself off before he also turned around. He pulled his hat off his head and held it over his heart, before walking toward the girl. He looked the most likely to just run off, before any of the others, but the old man would have a word with them all first.

"What is it you expected to see down there?" he asked the blond-haired boy. The red-haired boy who had been acting like an eagle before began to answer for his friend in a patronizing tone. The old man would not hear it, though. He held up his hand to silence the boy and was almost surprised at how well his simple gesture worked.

"I wanted to see something no one else has seen before," the teenage boy with a blond, layered bowl cut began to explain. "I wanted to see fire, light, bones, or magic." The other boys began to laugh and hurl insults at him:

"Geek!"

"Virgin!"

The boy with square glasses added, "Draven!" and both boys burst into laughter.

While the old man had never met this group of teenagers prior to today, he had had this experience many times before during his decades of curating his museum. He had heard all those insults more than once. Even the blonde-haired girl began to snicker lightly, although she had joined in last of all.

Once the laughter had finally subsided, the blond-haired boy looked like he was about to cry. He finished by saying, "I just want to know what it was built for. It's human-made—like everything else in this museum. This structure runs much deeper than here you know. I know there's something down there."

The third boy who had spoken of dragons before made light out of that suggestion. "It's a sinkhole formed by a geological process over thousands of years, just like this entire cave. It's not magic, and it has no higher purpose."

The old man had heard enough. "Alright, that's enough. You shouldn't make fun of your friend just for being entranced by fiction. It's where many of the best parts of our culture and history come from—myth, fiction, and conspiracy. Some of it could even be real. It is certainly nothing to be chided or swept under the rug. Now scram, before I call your parents," he threatened. Three of the teenagers ran off quickly, but the last boy lingered behind for just a moment. "There's some truth to what you say, even if you may never see it. Keep believing," the old man whispered.

The boy looked up at him somewhat spitefully, still a little red in the face from being insulted in so many ways. Some of them were probably true—not that the old man saw anything wrong with that for a boy of his age. "Gal'gatha," said the teenage boy looking at his nametag. "What kind of name is that?"

Gal'gatha stiffened his back. He was not upset, but rather he had heard that question so many times before. His answer was almost always the same. "Well, it's the same kind of name as 'Draven', you know. There were once a lot more of us. Maybe we'll make a comeback someday," Gal'gatha told the boy.

"Even I know that's not possible, for either one," the boy replied, and Gal'gatha couldn't blame him for that. He stood aside as the boy left to go catch back up with his friends.

Before the youth was too far out of sight, Gal'gatha called out, "Hey, kid!" The blond-haired teen turned around to look at him. "Keep your head up. You never know how quickly everything could change." To Gal'gatha's delight, the boy smiled, and just for a moment, Gal'gatha saw the boy's eyes glisten a lighter shade of blue than they had been before. The teen then turned and ran to catch up to his friends who were rounding the same corner that Gal'gatha had just a few minutes ago. When they were out of sight, Gal'gatha took a peek of his own over the edge of the pit. He looked as far down as he could see for a few seconds as his eyes adjusted to the darkness. He knew, in fact, that the boy was quite right. This sinkhole was human-made, and there was *magic* that ran through it, even if no one would ever believe him.

Gal'gatha looked deep into the pit and saw nothing but rock, stone, and darkness, but he knew in his heart that the darkness wouldn't last much longer. The entire world was going to change, and in a few days' time, nothing would be the same again. The days and years to come would shock everyone alive to see them, and they would be fascinating to behold. Gal'gatha stepped back from the edge of the pit, slipped underneath the rope marquee, and headed back into the general section of his museum.

It was near to closing time and many of the guests were beginning to leave on their own accord, but there were some, of course, who would require a gentle prod or poke in the right direction. Gal had nothing better to do while he waited for the museum to empty. He had friends to meet after that, who also helped staff the curation of his museum. In fact, they were much more than friends; they were family.

He began to wander from group to group, attempting to be jovial and affable while he subtly hinted that it was closing time.

Some of them had questions about exhibits, and when they did, it made him happy. There were many interesting artifacts to be explained—even if the guests wouldn't ever have believed their true uses.

A young family milled about near a battle axe with an oak shaft and a head ribbed with red trenches. It *had* belonged to a great hero once, and its unique power was the ability to control the minds of its victims for a time. If plunged into the victim, the victim would not die, and for a brief duration, they would be under the control of the axe's owner. It did not work forever—the victim would always eventually succumb to their injury—but it could temporarily turn an enemy into an ally.

A group of university students circled around a small-scale map of all Iishrem which showed light political boundaries from long ago but also had much more pronounced geographical features. It would show the location of anyone or of several powerful arti- facts—for the right price, of course. Lastly, a couple even older than Gal lingered around a statue of a man kissing a woman in matrimony. In fact, there had once been many weddings within these walls, but they had all taken place over a thousand years ago. Magic ran through the foundations and very construction of this megalithic superstructure. A structure that belonged to a long- dead and long-forgotten civilization. Gal'gatha knew that if the building could have been destroyed by practical means alone, those in the world above who now held power would have surely already done so—and quite long ago as well. Only magic could unmake this structure, as only magic had first created it. The world had long since forgotten and neglected the existence of magic—even though it often stared back at them in front of their very eyes or laid right underneath their noses. Gal'gatha relished the day that would soon come when all of that would change.

Once all the guests from his section of the museum had departed, Gal'gatha took a seat on a stone bench next to a security office and waited to be met by those he knew would soon arrive. Closing his eyes for just a moment, he leaned back against the stoic rock wall and smelled the salty summer breeze of the ocean streaming into the museum from high above and far away. When he listened carefully, he could still hear the faint chatter and murmur of his hopefully satisfied guests as they left.

He hoped he had done his job well today. He always appreciated his guests, but then he thought in his heart about what this structure had become over the last 1,100 years. This museum had been something much more than just a museum long ago. Those who held power in the world above knew this as well, but they had long let it lay in plain sight with their other power in hand. If the House of Lance had destroyed it at any point in the last 1,100 years, they would have already opened a box full of the consequences which he and his friends were about to show them.

While Gal'gatha waited for his companions, he pondered the way things used to be in Iishrem. For this, he needed images in his head; words couldn't quite do it justice. He had only ever imagined them based on the images, until a few short years ago, at least. Gal'gatha rose from the bench and walked over to a stone door that was now softly highlighted by the moonlight, always conveniently after all the guests were gone on this day each year.

His friends would know where to join him when they were ready. This was the night they had all waited for. Gal'gatha made his way over to the door and placed his hand on its center. *Exar Rehem en andme res shrilecc, vendien, ent ramshenk. Du grend sn len shytehd rend rn, du wiel vend ond sond.* Written in an archaic language called Old Calanorian, the words translated as *The world is made of iron, truth, and magic. So long as the sword still is, so shall be all three.* Old Calanorian—a language so esoteric and forgotten only he and his friends could read it. The answers to such questions could only be answered behind this door, and only reclusive men who read Old Calanorian, like him, knew the esoteric magic of how to open it.

His eyes turned orange, and the stone door opened. The tour of his museum did not end here for him. A dank, stale gust of air swept over his body before swirling into the museum behind him. His eyes now glowed a deep red, and he pulled an old torch out of a sconce and struck it against the wall. A staircase illuminated around him, and Gal'gatha descended the winding stairs to the bottom. The light from the moon did not stop at the door when it was opened. Instead, it followed small carved trails within the stone, illuminating several images as he went around. The old man saw images of the four races of the Eedon Rath-ni—ravens, eagles, hawks, and dragons. In the common tongues of the modern world, those words translated into the Lords of the Sky. At least, roughly speaking. There were images of men who had become huge beasts, of witches and wizards, of soldiers wielding magical weapons, and of archers shooting magical arrows. The stairs circled around the sinkhole in a helix. Every hundred feet or so, there were cutouts in the walls with railings, where one could pause and look down toward the bottom of the sinkhole. Gal'gatha continued his descent.

When he reached the bottom of the staircase, it opened at the base of the pit some several hundred feet below the door he had entered through. He was well within the subterranean levels of Rehem now. The pit led into a great hall that was currently enclosed in darkness, but the old man knew how to change that. As soon as he exited the pit, Gal'gatha gently placed the torch into a trench dug within the stone walls on both the left and right-hand side. After that, he just casually leaned against the wall and watched the hall begin to light itself around him. He would never tire of the sight.

"Gal'gatha," said a man's voice from behind. He knew just who it was—one of his friends he had been expecting. Gal'gatha turned around to face his three beautiful daughters and a man whom he very much considered to be the son he had never had. "It's time to begin."

"Ahh, Christian, I'm glad you've finally joined me. Come," Gal'gatha told his son. "And you three, Helga, Talia, and Arlyn, please remain there while I have a word with my son."

"Aye, Father," Talia said, quickly saluting him. Gal'gatha had known she would be first. For a moment, he looked over the expression on his middle daughter's face. Her eyes watched the back of her husband beadily, like she may never see him again. The old man did not believe that would be the case. He watched her look at the back of Christian's head and then saw her gaze travel down his body, her eyebrows rising in appreciation of his form. Christian had married Talia for her long brown hair and medium athletic figure. They would do well together if things went well.

He turned his gaze back to the path in front of them. "I remember when I found you here," Gal'gatha told Christian, leading him over to the bottom of the pit. His family had long since cleared away the last of the bones several hundred years ago, or so he had been told. He wasn't sure he would ever believe it. "One day, when you were young, I found you down here bruised-up, yellow-eyed, and confused. You understood nothing before then, and I opened your eyes. Now *you*, son, are going to open the eyes of the world again."

Gal'gatha recalled the net at the top of the pit. It wasn't prepared for every circumstance. The fact was that Christian had an
essence of strength about him. He thought back to the way that
the teenage boys had chided their blond-haired friend and carried
on about the wind of an eagle. Gal'gatha liked to think it was just
that, in fact, which had brought him Christian in the first place.
The wind of an eagle, many years ago. The net that had been in
service at that point was well taken care of, and it was made to support higher weight and force than Christian at that age could have
possibly provided. Yet the fact that he still ended up falling to the
bottom—and survived without much more than a scratch—confirmed it; there was an essence of strength and magic about him.

"For the price I've paid, I could only hope it to be so. It's what
I've trained for. At least I was there to comfort them beforehand.
I just never wanted to see them killed the way they were and our
name besmirched. I must retrieve them and give them a proper
resting place. For my sake," Christian told him.

Gal'gatha looked over his eyes. He must have been doing exactly
what he had instructed him to do. Christian's eyes had just a hint of
red close to his pupil. His mind was rejecting the influence of the
phoenix, but it would look like he was accepting it to everyone else
but him. Sax Drugren the 12th wouldn't see a damn thing coming.
Yet he was sad at his son's loss. It was a gruesome price to pay for a
chance to change the world for the better, but it all but guaranteed
their success.

Gal'gatha looked over the eyes of the son he had never had.
They were filled with pain. He held out his arms, and a few seconds later, Christian joined him in a somber but warm embrace. A
single tear from Christian hit Gal's shoulder, which he felt through
his shirt. He heard Christian sniffle and then say, "I let them down.

I was their son, and I let that swine murder them in front of the nation, besmirching our name."

Gal'gatha wanted to understand how his son was feeling. "Remember, Christian, they knew what you were fighting for, and they knew our plan. Look over there." Gal'gatha pointed over towards the staircase, where they could still see the bottom of the pit and his three beautiful daughters. "It was a miracle when I found you at the bottom of the pit, bloodied, bruised, and distressed. But the moment I found you, I knew what you were. A Draven. A descendant of Tamil Kun. I saw you with your yellow eyes.

When you fell into the pit, the net never stood a chance. You fell right through it like it was nothing, and when you finished falling and tumbling your way to the bottom of the pit, you were fine. Your parents were proud of you, Christian. Even I had never seen a real live Eedon Rath-ni before yours came to find you. They got to see something no one else has in thousands of years—an Eedon Rath-ni—but not just an eagle, but a dragon, a hawk, and a raven as well. They died knowing you loved them and that their deaths would not be in vain."

Christian walked from the staircase and into the well-lit great hall, and Gal'gatha followed. In front of him was a round table on a platform that overlooked a feudal reception chamber and banqueting hall. On all four sides, there were large open areas within the cave with open ceilings above, revealing the moon and forest several hundred feet above. Not only had the staircase led them below ground, but it also led them away from the outskirts of the city and into the hinterlands, where esoteric and reclusive people like him could slip away more easily.

The two of them took a walk around the entire banqueting hall before Gal paused and addressed Christian. "You've learned everything I ever had to offer, and you have taken it all in your stride. It's taken everything from you now. Why did you say yes? Why did you agree to become the Draven who would bring magic back to the world?"

"Why, I merely played my part. As you said, the world has been waiting for a man like me to change it for the better. It was you who put it all together," Christian told him.

"Mhmm, perhaps that is so," Gal'gatha agreed. He knew he had had help from others as well, and his forefathers had laid the path for everything he had done. "Let us continue our walk."

They walked back into the center of the great hall and stopped just in front of the elevated round table. In a clearing some thirty feet from the round table, there was a well-preserved marble carving of an armored assassin of old. Gal'gatha looked at the front of the statue. The figure was on one knee and looking down while he plunged a sword into the ground. The sword's marble sheathe was quite intricate and seemed to shimmer in the light of the hall.

"Draxion the Bold," Gal'gatha told his son. "Long forgotten by the public, but not by everyone. Not by those who hold power above and cover it up. If they only knew what we held down here."

"But Lance the 1st had believed it to be destroyed long ago. By now, Sax Drugren the 12th must believe that the man and the item were entirely fictional," Christian said, admiring the statue.

Gal'gatha knew he had waited long enough. The night was young, but it would not last forever. "Talia, Helga, Arlyn, come and join us," he called. "There's yet time for one last supper between us before everything changes forever."

They each smiled and came forward into the center of the banqueting hall where a small dinner awaited them. Each of them had prepared a part of the dinner they would share before they would set out on their missions. Gal'gatha himself was most excited for the smoked swine and grilled venison bacon ribs. They would both go nicely with the mixed greens, roasted garlic mashed potatoes, and seasoned tomatoes. Once they all sat down and began to eat, the conversation was light but cherished until they finished the meal.

"I'm not sure we'll ever all be together again after tonight," Gal'gatha began. "And I'm not sure how much longer I have left anyway. This world will be anew when all is finished, and this new world shall have no need for the likes of me. Each of us will be the last of the Keepers of the Sword. Our organization will live on for as long as any of us draw breath. After that, will be no need for us anymore. With that being said, there's something I need each of you to do, now. Please follow me."

Prologue 2
The Eedon Rath-ni (Gal'gatha)

RUINS OF THE COUNCIL OF NATIONS AND DRAVENS,
NAHIREHEM, IISHREM

SUMMER, 1146, FOURTH AGE

Gal'gatha led them back over to the statue of Draxion the Bold, where he paused and looked the statue over again. It was thanks to Draxion and several others that any of this was even possible. He had led the Dravens in the War of the Great Purge against Lance the 1st over a thousand years ago when the House of Lance had first risen out of its ashes and taken over the two weakest nations of Fuet and Rhollian—without much trouble. A great and terrible war had waged over the next thirty years, which razed much of Iishrem to the ground. Draxion and the Dravens who held loyal to a free Iishrem had lost, but not before he had put a plan in place that could one day be taken up by someone such as Gal'gatha. It was a plan to free Iishrem and to show the world that the Eedon Rath-ni were real, magic ran through its veins, and that Dravens waited to be born again.

"You four should stand back now," he warned. "Draxion may not be happy to be woken for the first time in nearly sixty years." Gal'gatha stepped up onto the platform and leaned over toward the statue. He put his lips to Draxion's left ear and whispered, "You won't be angry for the reason I have woken you, Draxion the Bold."

With that, Gal'gatha reached for the sword's hilt. With ease, he drew Draxion's sword from the stone and raised it above his head. As Gal'gatha lifted the sword, he began to feel tremors in the ground. He could hear and see pebbles and stones begin to shake. He could see trees sway in the open air above, but he could feel no wind within the banqueting hall.

He began to hear something more guttural as well. At first, it sounded like the beginnings of an earthquake, but then syllables began to form, and after that, words. The voice spoke deeply, with fluidity, not wasting any time. "Who has taken my sword?"

Gal'gatha did not answer at first. Instead, he got down onto his knees and looked behind to make sure Christian, Arlyn, Talia, and Helga followed suit. When they did, Gal'gatha turned his eyes back to Draxion's statue, now holding the sword level in his hands.

The statue's eyes began to glow a deep, dark blue, and gray wisps began to accumulate around the edges of the statue as if a ghost were contained within it—which Gal'gatha knew from past experience was indeed the case. The ghost of Draxion. "Tell me who has taken my sword, else I will pull down this entire chamber on top of you. You shall never escape," said the ominous voice.

Gal'gatha remained calm while the ground continued to shake around him. He looked up and could feel the gaze of the statue bearing down on him and his children. "It is I, Lord Draxion, Keeper of the Sword of Heroes Passed, your humble servant and curator of the Council of Nations and Dravens, Gal'gatha." He paused briefly, trying to sound composed and unrushed. "You won't be angry at the reason I've woken you. I have wonderful news. It's time for everything to begin. It is time for the world to know of Dravens and the Eedon Rath-ni once again. Will you come forward from your eternal resting place to see us with your own eyes?"

The voice said nothing in response, but as Gal'gatha continued to stare at the statue, its eyes closed. Then, from the statue came a tall male ghost with long, flowing hair, wearing the regalia of an assassin. He was armed with a ghostly curved dagger at his side, and a crossbow was slung across his back. Draxion's ghost walked out of the statue and down to their level where they still knelt. "You may rise, my children," Draxion said, this time in a dry, dull voice. "So, after over a thousand years of resting, it's finally time?"

Gal'gatha had only met Draxion's ghost one previous time. His father had introduced him when he had come of age—just as his father had done for him and so on. Gal'gatha had heard from his father about the way in which Draxion had produced a ghost of himself, and how he had kept his sword safe for all time. Long ago, when the War of the Great Purge had been lost by those who opposed the House of Lance, Draxion had decided the only way to secure a possible plan for the freedom of Iishrem and the return of Dravens to the world was to create a ghost of himself, which could *linger* until circumstances arose where Iishrem *could* be freed, and the world *could* learn of Eedon Rath-ni again.

The process of creating a ghost of oneself was ghastly. One had to make the ultimate sacrifice. You had to be encased within a statue still alive, if only even barely, and then you were left to die with a phoenix feather in your possession. At least, that was according to legend. Gal'gatha pulled himself out of his trance and back to the moment at hand. He wasn't sure if Draxion's quip was a joke or not.

Gal'gatha rose and handed Draxion his sword. "Perhaps you'd like to hold your old sword, once again," Gal'gatha told his ghostly acquaintance. Draxion held out his hand to grasp the sword, but once Gal'gatha let it go, the sword fell right through him. When the sword hit the ground with a clang, they each looked at each other for a second and then burst into laughter. Christian, Talia, Helga, and Arlyn joined in not long after, perhaps still uncomfortable being around the ghost.

Gal'gatha knelt and picked up the sword. "Let us walk," said Draxion, gesturing at the five to follow. "I don't often get to stretch my legs in the physical realm. Not that I wish to be woken more often. Most of the time it happens, it's just an introduction for me to my next curator. If they weren't completely necessary, I would prefer not to do them at all."

They began to walk through the banqueting hall. "How is Hedeth'rehem?" Gal'gatha asked.

Draxion turned and looked at him. "It's all out of whack, my child. There's an ectoplasm shortage, and my ghost stocks are down. But what could I expect? The deathly market is always hard to predict, and poltergeists always have a way of creating problems that they aren't prepared to deal with the consequences of. But anyway, I do believe there are some introductions in order."

"Y-Yes, of course," Gal'gatha stammered. How had *he* forgotten? Gal'gatha had just been caught up in the moment. "My Lord Draxion, may I introduce you to my daughters, Helga, Talia, and Arlyn, and the son I never had, Christian."

Gal'gatha saw each of them wave in greeting, as handshakes were obviously not in order. "It's nice to meet each of you," Draxion said. "Tell me about them," he requested of Gal'gatha.

While the five of them finished walking over towards the hawk statue, Gal'gatha told him about his children, their Eedon Rath-ni, and their plan. His children had a few things to say as well and added their thoughts when necessary.

"So, what do you think? Will this work?" Gal'gatha finally asked Draxion.

He was going to go through with this, with or without Draxion's approval. It was time.

"Christian, you say you're going to assassinate Sax Drugren the 12th? How do you plan to do so?"

"The man is a fat swine and executed my parents as traitors. Yet, over several years now, I have gained his trust and become his favorite guard. Soon he'll be replacing the phoenix feather at the top of the spire in Imperium Aendor. The phoenix will be there with him—to see that it's done. Once the old feather is withdrawn from the feathery, I will throw him from a window to his death far below while my eagle, Anacarin, rips out the heart of his dragon," Christian explained.

Draxion took a moment to stroll about the hall, thinking about the proposal. "Yes." He paused. "Yes, that should work. It will be even more powerful if the phoenix is in sight. More Eedon Rath-ni will be inspired to come out of the Shrouded Sea to your aid, if so. There will, of course, be Eedon Rath-ni who come to fight for Iishrem as well—not to mention it'll break its hold on the minds of men. It should be a good war to watch. One that shall solidify the future of the world, incontrovertibly. You're sure of your abilities to resist its indoctrination, each of you?"

Gal'gatha answered at once, "We are sure, my Lord. They won't know a thing is coming."

Draxion smiled at that and said, "Good. Your effects will be even more powerful then. Now, what of the heir to the House of Lance? What of the days and the war to come after?"

This time, Gal'gatha gave his children a chance to answer first.

"I'm going to take your sword to Reyvula, where, in secret, people still hold prayers and praises to Acentrina of the Stars. The rebellion of Iishrem itself will start there if we're lucky," Arlyn said while she looked deep into the ghost's eyes and drew a strand of her red hair away from her eye.

Gal'gatha noticed that Draxion seemed to grow stiff and sad at the mention of Acentrina of the Stars. At least, as stiff and as sad as he thought a ghost could be anyway.

"I'm an author of fiction, have been my entire life, but I've infiltrated Iishrem Intelligence. While I publish and promote my books deifying Dravens and Eedon Rath-ni, I can siphon intelligence and secrets to whoever so needs it," Talia said next, and Draxion nodded his head.

"I'm a great flyer and can stay out of sight when I need to. I'll be distributing artifacts and histories of the past, so the world can relearn that which has remained lost for so long," Helga told the ghost.

"Good, that's good. What of Allirehem? What of the academy constructed after my passing? I almost feel like I can see it. Perhaps there is another statue of me there, which I could go to one day."

This time, Christian answered. "Once I've assassinated Sax, I'll flee to its location in Allirehem, deep within Maravinya, in the city of Meinghelia. I'll find students and train them in the four arts of Dravenry. Their Eedon Rath-ni will come to them readily. Those students will become leaders in the war or instructors at the academy for future students. Allirehem will fight for us. Gal'gatha and

I have spent the last several years forging alliances with the four major nations of Galliem, Haisha, East Rehem, and Maravinya. They know that they cannot hope to stay out of this. It's going to be a global war—as it was always going to be."

Gal'gatha was pleased with his son's answer. He looked at Christian and smiled at him before putting his hand on his shoulder.

"What of the heir?" asked Draxion.

It was Gal'gatha's turn to answer again. "He's well-protected and well looked after," he began. "A man named Tagros from a long-splintered line of the House of Lance successfully married his sister to Sax some time ago. They produced a single heir to the throne, and they named him Lance the 13th. He will guide him into starting a war with Allirehem."

"He can be dealt with at a later time," Draxion said. "If you kill him now, Tagros or another would only take his place." Draxion looked down at the ground for a moment. "He must not be harmed in this assassination. For a while, he must be allowed to forge his own path in this world—until he can be dealt with for good."

Gal'gatha knew that Draxion was right. "Is there anything else?" he asked.

Draxion turned to look around his home and resting place for the last thousand years. "There's nothing else. I'll be watching over everything, as much as I can anyway. I can already feel myself starting to fade," he told them.

Gal'gatha had a final question. "Will we be able to summon you again while the sword is gone?"

Draxion snared his eyes and wisped his tongue. "You and I both know that the sword shall never return here once it's gone. It's simply not meant to be. I'll be watching over. Perhaps if I'm needed, I could appear," Draxion told them. "It's time for me to go now, though. You each have my blessing: Arlyn to take my sword, Talia to charm the world, Helga to help it believe, Christian to wage the war, and you, Gal'gatha, to guide their way. Goodbye," Draxion told them. He took one last look over his home and then began to fade.

"Wait," Christian said. Draxion stopped fading, but he did not reappear to his full effect either. His deep, dark blue eyes looked into the Christian's yellow eyes. "Don't you have any parting advice or last words? You've waited a thousand years for this very moment."

Draxion thought for just a moment, then answered, "The reason that we failed in the first place, a thousand years ago, is because we weren't prepared to accept the losses and do what was necessary. Don't give up, and don't be afraid to keep fighting. Most of all, don't underestimate the power or the influence of the phoenix. Make no mistake; it's more powerful than any Eedon Rath-ni, and its ability to hold sway and influence over the minds of men is unrivaled. Even after you've killed its master, it will still be unrivaled in that respect. Now go and free Iishrem for the better sake of all men and Eedon Rath-ni." With that, Draxion's ghost finished dissipating into nothing but air.

With Draxion gone, it was time for each of his children to leave and begin their missions. First, each of them would be immortalized within these walls, like everyone else had been in the past. He had a little magic himself, but all his children had much more. They had learned quite well by themselves.

"Are you excited, little sister?" Arlyn, his oldest daughter, asked Helga, his youngest. "It's time for us to immortalize ourselves on these walls. We are joining the Line of Swords, at last."

"I am," Helga began. "I just never thought it would ever happen so quickly." The Line of Swords immortalized Dravens who had been raised within these halls thousands of years ago. Each chamber had a wall containing a subgroup of the Line of Swords. There was the Conspiracy of Ravens, the Congress of Eagles, the Cauldron of Hawks, and the Fury of Dragons. For people like Gal'gatha, the Curators of the Council were immortalized on the walls of the hallway which led away from the pit.

Helga would be the first to be immortalized. When their group reached the open-aired chamber, Gal'gatha took a chance to look over it and imagine what it must have looked like in its heyday. To begin with, there was a well-preserved marble statue of a raven. The crown of its head was level with the top of Gal'gatha's, and it was posed as if it were bowing before them. Its wings were stretched out, and its eyes pierced them.

"Go on, Helga," said Gal'gatha. "Call your raven to you." He stepped away from the statue and turned to his children. Helga stepped forward, and they hugged. For a moment, he ran his hand through her short and wavy blonde hair and looked into her green eyes. Helga was twenty-one and a little shorter than him. When they parted, he watched her step up to the statue while he joined the rest of his family.

Helga stood a few feet from the statue and pulled a short wand out of her coat. She bowed her head, and Gal'gatha could swear that the world became quiet and motionless. When he could feel movement and hear sound again, he looked to see her raising her head and wand. Even from behind her, Gal'gatha knew that her eyes and the tip of her wand would be glowing lime green. "Come to me, Alnor," she spoke to the statue. "It's time."

At that moment, the eyes of the raven began to glow lime-green just like hers. A few seconds later, beams of great light strained themselves beyond the raven, coming from a tunnel in the chamber far behind it, which continued into the mountains. He could see gray clouds far at the end of the tunnel, although he knew if he tried to walk to the end of the tunnel, he would never reach it. Like the eyes of the raven, the tunnel began to glow lime-green and temporarily blinded him. Seconds later, he could hear a screech before him. He knew he could open his eyes again now.

When he did, there was a raven several times his size. Of the four types of Eedon Rath-ni, ravens were generally the smallest, but, of course, there was variation. The raven with eyes matching Helga's stepped forward to meet his daughter and nestled its head against her shoulder. Gal'gatha could feel their magic within his own veins. Now that her raven had joined them, Helga could be added to the Line of Swords and immortalized upon the Conspiracy of Ravens.

Gal'gatha put his arm around his youngest daughter's shoulder and walked with her over to the stone wall at the edge of the chamber. "It's time," he told her. Helga nodded and hugged him one more time, then she held out her wand and pressed it to the stone wall. While the wand began to glow lime-green again, Gal'gatha looked down the wall at the rest of the Conspiracy of Ravens. There were many other immortalizations upon it, but none in the last 1,100 years.

When the immortalization was finished, Gal'gatha looked over the magic-made portrait of his daughter Helga and her raven. Their names were below them. "You will get to see me the most over the years that follow, Helga, but that will not make your task any easier," he told her.

"I know, Father," she returned.

There was something he needed to show her—and only her. This was her task alone.

"A father must say goodbye to each of his children, one by one. The rest of you will stay here. Don't worry, though; we'll rejoin together before I send her off," he told his other children. They each nodded and wandered out into an open-air chamber filled with trees, shrubs, soft grass, and a large open field area where once upon a time ravens would have landed. Gal'gatha took Helga back into the banqueting hall, out towards the staircase, and then behind that where they entered a library.

"You, Helga, have the important task of bringing history back to the world," he told her. The library was as grand and large as the banqueting hall. The entire history of Iishrem until the rise of House Lance and the War of the Great Purge was here, and even some more recent ones which his forefathers—the Keepers of the Sword—had written. The thirty-foot-tall walls of the library were lined with shelves upon shelves filled with histories, tomes, magical books, potion recipes, and appendixes. There were even more rows of bookshelves in the center of the library. "When the world rediscovers its magic in a few days, people will have many questions. They must remember that the world was not always this way. They will look to the people in their communities that they trust the most. You will give those people the answers they will need." Gal'gatha pointed to a large sack full of books he had prepared for her first trip.

"Those are the most essential books, to begin with. There's a list inside with where to take them and whom to give them to. Don't worry; they'll know you're coming. Then you'll come back to me, and I'll have more books ready for you to deliver," he told her. Helga smiled and picked up the large sack of books, lugging it over her shoulder. The two of them walked back out to the open-air raven chamber where Christian, Arlyn, Talia, and Alnor, her raven, were waiting for them.

Over the next few minutes, there were as many goodbyes as there were hugs. The time passed too quickly, and Gal'gatha watched as Helga climbed onto her raven, ready to take off. She looked to him as she ran her hand through her wavy blonde hair. "Fly, and may the truth keep you safe," Gal'gatha told her with a wave.

Helga nodded, and then she leaned down next to the head of her raven. "Let's fly," she told Alnor. The raven reared back and twirled around before he took a few hops forward and glided into the air. Gal'gatha watched them ascend farther into the air, and before long, they were out of sight.

Talia was next, and she too would be immortalized along the Conspiracy of Ravens. For just a moment, Gal'gatha allowed himself to look across the chamber to the other side of the banqueting hall where he could see the intimidating statue of a prowling dragon. When Talia was born, he had thought for sure that the dragons would send one of their own to be her Eedon Rath-ni, but dragons were stubborn beasts. Not one of the five lines of dragons would send one of their own, but the ravens had had no such hesitations. Gal'gatha was not worried. He may not have a child with a dragon that would have completed his set, but the dragons would join the coming war once they were convinced of the importance of their role in it. It would not take long.

Gal'gatha looked over his twenty-four-year-old daughter's brown hair and green eyes. She was almost as tall as him. Talia looked back at him while he stepped towards her, and then she looked longingly at her love, Christian, just behind them. He knew she would do anything for him. He could feel the love between them.

Gal'gatha put his hands on her shoulders softly and turned her back around to face the statue of the raven, where she would repeat the same process they had just gone through with Helga. Talia's eyes glowed a darker, deeper forest-green when she called her raven, Embar, to her. A few moments later, another raven with forest-green eyes appeared from the tunnel. Talia hugged her raven with her arms around its neck, then Gal took her over to the wall to immortalize her right next to Helga.

Unlike Helga, Talia did not use a wand for her magic. Instead, she had a staff. The staff was made of brown oak and was almost as tall as her. Encased by the oak at the top of the staff was a gemstone the same shade of forest green. After the immortalization process, Gal'gatha left Christian and Arlyn to themselves as he took Talia to her room within the structure. The room was below the banqueting hall, and it was accessed via a staircase next to the library.

When they reached her room, it was softly lit by torches, and there were many loose-leaf pages piled up and spread out around the room. "Your sister, Helga, will be distributing the real history of the Dravens and the people that lived around them to Iishrem for us, but you must not doubt the importance of your own task. People will need not just facts, but stories, lore, and canon if they are to accept the new world that we will be living in. You must continue to work on your Eagle Rider books."

Talia's Eagle Rider book series was based on Vorium Galgas. He was a Draven who the Keepers of the Sword had launched as an insurrectionist against the House of Lance more than five hundred years ago.

"Where he failed to liberate Iishrem from the phoenix long ago, you shall now succeed. Your books, when published, will find fame, popularity, and fortune. Now gather your supplies and head for the

Imperium Aendor—and make sure to send me all the secrets you have on Lance and all leaders within Allirehem politics."

His daughter began to tear up when the realization dawned on her how long she would be apart from her husband. "How can you guarantee me that we'll see each other again? That everything will begin as you have planned?" she asked him.

They hugged, and he patted her on the back, attempting to comfort her. "Christian will succeed—I promise you. You will go with him to Allirehem when your books are done and your work spying on the House of Lance is complete. There are two future Dravens deep within Iishrem who are vitally important to everything we hope to achieve and then there are two others in Allirehem. Those in Allirehem will get to the academy to be trained themselves as they won't be indoctrinated or raised within enemy territory, but you and Christian must get our two new recruits from Iishrem there by other means. They will have no other way. Your separation will not last forever, my love," Gal'gatha reassured her.

The two of them walked back out to the raven's chamber and met back up with Christian and Arlyn. Before Talia got onto her raven, Embar, she exchanged several kisses with Christian. They would be the last they shared for a while, but it would not be forever. "I love you, Talia," Christian told her. He kissed her one last time and then Talia climbed onto her raven. A few moments later, she was also out of sight.

With Talia gone, only Christian and Arlyn remained. Gal'gatha looked the two of them over. Arlyn had red hair and blue eyes. She was taller than him, and he was six feet tall. She was twenty-seven, and Christian was a few years older at almost thirty-four. Christian had long brown hair that was gelled back, and he also was several inches over six feet tall. With a simple hand gesture, Gal asked for them to follow him.

Like her sisters, Arlyn would need to be immortalized. Though this time it would be amongst the Cauldron of Hawks. The process was not difficult. Gal'gatha watched his daughter find a hand-sized stone with one sharp side when they reached the hawk's open-aired chamber. At the end of the line containing immortalizations of other members from the Cauldron of Hawks, Arlyn began to chip away at the stone wall with her rock while her eyes turned gray. Moments later, Gal'gatha could see the section of stone wall beginning to resemble his daughter. When Arlyn was done, the three of them smiled together at her carving. Now Gal'gatha knew it was almost time to say goodbye to his final daughter. He watched Arlyn turn away from the wall and approach the bronze carving of a hawk. The hawk looked like it was swooping for the ground, its wings extended to their full span. Gal'gatha turned to his daughter and told her to, "Cast it into the chamber, Arlyn. Your stone."

Arlyn reared back and hurled the stone toward the middle of the chamber. A majestic screech echoed about the chamber a moment later, and Gal'gatha strolled into the chamber and looked towards the night sky. The moon was full this night and directly overhead. Within the moon, Gal'gatha could see the shadow cast by an Eedon Rath-ni growing ever larger. A few seconds later, he felt a strong gust of wind sweep over his body, and then he watched as an enormous hawk landed directly in front of his daughter, several feet from him.

With a loving grasp, she wrapped one arm around its neck. "Rhelg'nar," she said softly.

Arlyn rubbed her head against that of her hawk as she patted its side. When the two of them broke from their embrace, Arlyn sheathed Draxion's sword in a scabbard along the side of her hawk's body. With that done, she turned around and looked back at both. "The sword will be safe with me. I'll take it deep into the mountains to see so," she reassured them.

"It would be costly for them to remove it from there—even if they knew where it was. Ride safe. I may not see you again. Neither of you most likely," he told them. He stepped forward and hugged Arlyn tightly. "Stay safe and promise me that you will outlive the upcoming war."

Arlyn whispered something to him which Christian wouldn't be able to hear—not that it was about either of them. They then smiled at each other, and a moment later, Gal'gatha watched his oldest daughter fly away. When they were out of sight, he turned his attention to Christian and said, "Let's finish what we started."

The two of them walked over to an open chamber on another side of the banqueting hall. On top of the last table they passed before entering the final open-aired chamber, Gal'gatha could see Christian's supplies ready for his mission. The brown-haired man, however, was already dressed in his security uniform for his role in protecting Sax. On the table, there was an assault rifle, a sawed-off shotgun, a pistol, an assortment of various grenades, and then a few other more tactical devices that Gal didn't know the names of.

Outside of that, Gal'gatha had nothing more than a portable computer drive to give his son before he left. Once Christian finished fitting his supplies into his bags and securing some on his person, Gal'gatha handed him the jump drive. "What's on this?" he asked.

"It's not too hard to figure out, is it?" Gal'gatha replied.

"A folder with a dossier on the students in my first class of Dravens to find and teach, and then the coordinates of where to find the academy?" Christian guessed.

Gal'gatha could feel himself smile. "Just so," he told his son. Gal'gatha had never seen the academy himself, but he had heard all about it. There wasn't much written about it within any book he could find in the library, but it had been a secret passed down verbally by his forefathers.

Much like this museum which he had curated—and his father before him—the academy had had curators since the end of the War of the Great Purge. Gal'gatha believed that there would be someone there like him—or at least a small group of people. Perhaps they'd meet in Hedeth'rehem. "With luck, just like the men who have taken care of this museum before him, the academy should be ready and waiting for you too. Open it. Pass on what I have taught you. Change the world," he told his son, and the two of them hugged.

Finally, it was time for Christian to immortalize himself upon the wall which held the Congress of Eagles. Gal'gatha stepped back and watched the young man pull a pistol out of its holster at his side. He slowly took aim, and his eyes glowed yellow. Christian fired three shots in quick succession at the same place on the wall, the impact and sparks of his three shots forming a mural in his image. Christian smiled at himself, perhaps admiring the reflection that he saw before him.

It was time for him to summon his eagle. Below the eagle statue, there was an old wooden bow and a single arrow. While Christian's eyes still glowed yellow, he picked up both and carried them into the open-aired section of the chamber. Gal'gatha followed, watching closely. His son nocked the arrow onto the bow, pulled back, and aimed for the sky. Gal'gatha watched the arrow leap skyward, and they both tracked its ascent for as long as they could.

Just when Gal'gatha had lost track of it, there was a screech that echoed over the night sky, disorientating him. He felt himself shuffle back and crouch down while he covered his ears with his hands. The screech had no effect on his son. Gal'gatha watched trees sway and grass bend as a brown eagle came into view, alighting a couple of feet in front of his son. "Anacarin," Christian said out loud before stepping up to his eagle and nuzzling his head against the eagle's. "How I've missed you." Gal'gatha watched the two of them gaze into each other's eyes. After Christian's initial greeting, he knew the two of them would continue talking to each other within their minds. It was their magic.

When they were finished greeting each other, Christian made ready to leave by handing his duffle bag over to Anacarin to hold with one of her talons. He also loaded his shotgun into a holster on her saddle.

His son would not be with him much longer, and so there was one last thing Gal'gatha had to tell him. "Son," he said slowly. Christian turned to look at him. "There's something I need to tell you before you leave." He walked over to him and put an arm around his back and a hand on the neck of his eagle.

"What is it?" Christian asked.

"Within a few days, the whole world will know your name, and many thousands of people will die because of your actions. You'll be called many things. Some will revere you, and others will despise you. You deserve to know that you're a good man and a great son. I hope you never change for the worse and that you always remember that," Gal'gatha told him, struggling to hold back tears.

Christian didn't seem to know quite how to respond at first. "I'd say I'll do my best, but I'm going to find a way to do even better than that," he said, the corners of his mouth rising. They laughed together and then hugged one last time. After they parted, Christian climbed onto his eagle. Without anything more than a smile, Christian took off into the air and disappeared into the night as Gal'gatha felt a single tear slide down his cheek.

Now all by himself once again, Gal'gatha could finally rest. Before he made his way up to bed, he gave the final chamber a quick glance before walking over and staring at the stone statue of the prowling dragon. His blood felt warm when he was close to it. He could feel the fire in his heart. Why hadn't the dragons sent one of their own to either Helga or Talia? Gal'gatha was sure he would never fully understand. He had read so many stories of their feats and personalities. In short, dragons were unruly, self-centered, and coveted their riches like no other Eedon Rath-ni. Dragons weren't particularly like any of the other races, but then again neither were their riders like the other Dravens. Dragons and their riders were chaos, but if chaos could be tamed, chaos made a powerful ally.

Gal'gatha was sure that the dragons would come forth from their home within the Shrouded Sea to soon join the fight. They just needed to be provoked into action. As Gal'gatha stepped away from the statue to go to his chambers, he knew Christian and his three beautiful daughters would do just that.

Prologue 3
Shadow Theater (Gal'gatha)

When Gal'gatha sent his children off to change the world, he had gone to bed that night believing he had played his part in the story, and that as such he wouldn't have another part to play for quite some time. Yet that night while he slept in his room deep within the catacombs of the Council of Nations and Dravens he had a dream. He stood amongst a crowd of several thousand within the dream, and when he tried to look beyond them, he saw nothing but shadow and shroud.

In the dream, he remained calm, then walked farther into the crowd of people. While he didn't specifically recognize any of the faces, some of them did look more familiar than others. Perhaps they were citizens of his city, or perhaps specters of something much darker. Their faces and features were unremarkable to him, but all races and creeds were represented among the crowd. He approached a fair-skinned man.

"Who are you?" Gal'gatha remembered he had asked the man in the dream.

"Someone you will one day meet because of the changes I will ask you to make," the fair-skinned man told him.

Gal'gatha remembered he had been taken back by that, an answer he certainly hadn't expected. Yet, when he pressed further asking, "What changes? Who are you?" that particular specter disappeared into thin air. His dream continued to linger and so he was provided with an opportunity to talk to more members of the crowd. He approached a tall dark-skinned woman. He did not even need to say a word to her before she began to speak.

"We don't have the time you will wish us to, and that is your fault. You've doomed us all to die, but perhaps in a way you will save us as well," the woman told Gal'gatha with animated expressions.

"What is it you speak of?" he asked her. While in the dream, he tried to think deeper, of what might be causing this. He had certainly had many strange dreams throughout his life living in the epicenter of esoteric magic, which only reclusive men like him understood a glimmer of.

"Show us who we shall all die for," she told him, and then like the fair-skinned man before her, she faded away into nothingness.

In the dream, he remembered feeling the ground quake. The dream was collapsing, he knew, but he had to find out why he was shown this before he woke and lost his chance entirely. He approached one last figure—a young child not too unlike the boy he had spoken to the night before. Perhaps even an intentional apparition of such a character.

"What is it you're here for?" he asked the blond-haired child.

The blond-haired child looked at him in the eyes and spoke quickly. "You want this all to be worth it, don't you? Show us who will represent us in our deaths or decays, then do not waste our remaining time."

Gal'gatha watched the boy's specter fade with each word spoken. By the time he was finished speaking, the boy was entirely gone, and then the rest in the crowd did the same in rapid succession. When all of them were gone, all that Gal'gatha was left with was a place deeper within the derelict Council of Nations and Dravens that he knew he needed to visit when he woke. He woke quickly and with a jump in his step.

When he sat up, the rest of his room lit itself. A dozen bright candles placed strategically about the room that never waxed lit themselves. Gal'gatha got dressed for the day quickly. He *would* show those who observed not *what* they waited for but *who*.

He left his room and walked down a hallway that passed his daughter's rooms and Christian's—now all empty and deserted. The hallway emptied into another, which connected the sinkhole chamber with the stairway to the great hall and Eedon Rath-ni chambers. He took a left and headed up the gentle incline to the sinkhole chamber. The library of the Council laid beyond that, but he needed to take the stairs back up into the premiere level. He began to ascend the circular steps, feeling each step of the journey he had made the night before. When he got to the door that would open to the chamber where he had confronted the teens the night before, he only needed to place his warm hand on its center for it to open. The door shifted open in a grumbling fashion a few seconds later.

A messy gray-haired man close in age named Golmeth waited for him beyond the door. Gal'gatha grumbled at seeing him. He had hoped he had risen early enough for him to slip over to the theater without being bothered by any of the staff beyond his children who helped him curate the Council, but apparently, he hadn't woken early enough.

Like the night before where he had held up his hand to silence dissent from the teens, he did the same with Golmeth. The staffer began to speak but ceased with this gesture. It was no matter to Gal'gatha. He would hear the concerns of his staffer and put his interruption to good use as well. "Walk with me," Gal'gatha told his staffer, and so they did across the lower level of the Council that led to another series of stairs, which would take them up to the main domed level of the expansive, monolithic structure.

"A quieter time of the year than normal," his staffer told him.

"You think our crowds are thinning?" Gal'gatha asked.

His compatriot nodded, adding, "Some, at least. And they all just seem less enthusiastic."

Gal'gatha knew what imminent fate would come for the citizens of his city when Christian's actions were revealed to the world. He wanted to save as many of them as he could. Being inside the Council would save them—at least, in a way. "We'll close for the next eight days, then open on the 9th with a celebration that no one will want to miss!" Gal'gatha told him.

"And not soon forget, I would hope as well," Golmeth followed up.

Gal'gatha turned to him as they rounded the stairs and reached the mostly intact dome. Gal'gatha looked out the circular hole at its apex. "Cursed moon," he said out loud. "Okay, Golmeth, there is a matter I must attend to. Do what you do well and make a flyer for such an event. Distribute five hundred yourself, and then have the others take walks throughout the city as well, or get someone to do that blogging thing about it, I guess? Whatever the youths do these days to spread the word about events they should attend."

Golmeth turned to him and blinked. "Thank you for hearing my concern. I'll see to it right away." He then strode off in another direction. Gal'gatha trusted his compatriot and his staff—they would do as they had been asked, and guests would come for the event as invited. Unfortunately, it would only save a few thousand—the rest of them would be killed or lost to them forever.

Gal'gatha walked through the expansive dome and into the front lobby, then out the front doors. He stepped out onto a stepped, stone plateau that looked out over the sea for as far as Gal'gatha could see. The city sloped downward gradually, with tall skyscrapers all around, but the line of sight to the sea atop the Council of Nations and Dravens was unimpeded by any structure. On his left, at the corner of the platform this portion of the Council's campus stood on, Gal'gatha saw the spire of stone, which rose about fifty feet and curved up in a counterclockwise fashion. It looked like a temple of white smoke to Gal, and then he turned to his right and saw the granite pyramid. That was where he was headed.

The breeze bristled through his hair as he made his way across the plateau. He could open that door the same as the others. Gal felt his eyes turn orange, and the door swayed to the side a moment later. He stepped in and found exactly what he knew he would—more stairs. He sighed and started to descend, slowly. A thick shroud stood two steps before him and only faded as he took a step at a time. He was *old* after all.

There were not many stairs to be taken, perhaps only a dozen, but his old joints felt each one of them. He finally reached the bottom. It was not much farther now, but it was more arduous. He came to another sinkhole. This time he had to take a *ladder.* He approached the pit and looked in—it was pitch-black. Covered in shadow. There was a torch at his side, and so he lit it with his orange eyes and dropped it into the pit, then followed its light down.

When Gal'gatha stepped into the bottom of that pit, he found the Shadow Theater—not even Christian or his daughters knew of this. The knowledge of the theater and ability to use it was the sole knowledge of Gal'gatha alone, as it had been for the reclusive curators who had come before him. He grabbed the torch off the stone bottom and took a few steps into a small, theater, with three rows of stadium seating. There were a dozen chairs made of uncomfortable stone. He knew so from past experience—he had been down here a lot more often since Christian had come into his life, so he would take the seat with a thick, over-stuffed pillow he had left down here for these visits. There was a little dust on it. He patted it off with his hands.

There were trenches for lighting this room like there were in the great hall. So, before Gal'gatha sat down, he lit the trenches on either side and holstered his torch into a sconce. He sat and got comfortable, looking toward the screen of the theater. Of course, there was no actual screen, just a rectangular opening on the front wall of the theater. With the room dimly lit by the fire around him, he could see the dancing shadow and shroud, which could soon show him what those who observed soon wished to see.

The shadow and shroud peeled back to show the inner stone wall behind the screen and what truly powered the Shadow Theater. His magic and knowledge only facilitated such showings. Behind the shadow and shroud hung the eye of a raven, the heart of an eagle, the talon of a hawk, and the fang of a dragon. For a moment, they each glowed, vibrated, and shook, before they were engulfed by the shadow and shroud again, which began to dance more furiously for him. Once his eyes were on the screen, it began to form the figures he needed to see, showing them in colored detail.

The shadow and shroud danced together and illuminated itself for him. It showed him a young boy named Ethan Campbell. When he first saw the figure of the boy, wispy letters denoted his name. He lived with his family in the heart of all Iishrem—the city of Imperium Aendor. The first thing Gal'gatha noticed about the boy was his violet eyes, although they were not always such. The screen danced in front of him again and showed the boy being watched by red eyes, high upon the tall spire of the city from far away.

He could tell the eyes of the spire wished to control the boy's mind like it did the rest of the city, but as great as its power was, the power of the spire was shallow compared to the deep, old roots of the fort whose shadow fell over the home of the boy and his family. The boy had been touched by magic his whole life and believed in it like no one else. Deep down, Ethan knew he was special—even if the world would only ever tell him that he was just like everyone else. Although he had had his struggles, Gal'gatha knew he would keep his faith and fight furiously to one day show others to be wrong.

Ethan had dirty blond hair and a great love of lore, mystery, and art, with a fascination for video games. The Shadow Theater began to show him a memory in the boy's past, which would set the stage for the boy's future. Being ten, he had gone to an arcade within a mall not far from the fort that was near to his home. He went with a close friend, Rich, his parents, and his brown-haired sister, Katie. She was already taller, faster, stronger, and heavier than him, although she was two years younger.

While he tried to enjoy himself with his friend at the arcade, Katie naturally bothered him. She excelled in provoking his magic out of him in his frustration, even if Ethan wasn't able to notice its effects. At the arcade, the boy played a video game called *The Glare of Ravens.* The game was played on a panoramic tv screen about forty percent of a full circle, while the player stood on a square footpad. Ethan sought out the game because not many people played it in the arcade. In fact, the arcade had the only set-up of it in Imperium Aendor. It was made by Saek-a Rehemcast, and all the top scores were owned by the mysterious initials MLK, which Gal knew the identity of.

As Ethan stepped onto the footpad to start his game, the theater showed several had formed to watch him. Talia stood at the back of the crowd, although not as Talia. She had almost silver-blonde hair now and had assumed the identity of the pen name under whom she released her books—Maria Lewis Knowles. She watched him with forest-green eyes and channeled a modicum of her magic into him while he played the game, smiling as she did.

A dozen or two people watched him play in the crowd, including another girl Ethan's age named Kiera. She had lighter brown hair than Katie, and Ethan played the game with a focused look in his eye to impress her. He had played at the behest of a bet offered by his conniving sister Katie -- to break one of the top scores for all of the tickets she had accrued, so he could use them to win a cheap prize offered at an extorted value. If he did not, he would have to reveal his affections for Kiera to her. He did not wish to have to do that, yet.

So, the boy played *The Glare of Ravens.* The footpad had a tract for the boy to walk on. Each step progressed him further into the level, which currently resembled an alleyway filled with dangerous vagrants. As Ethan walked, each vagrant on screen attacked in different ways. To defeat each vagrant, Ethan would have to keep his gaze fixed on theirs while they attacked his character on screen. When the vagrants attacked Ethan's character in the game, a padded pole on the left or right would extend towards him and try to knock him off the footpad. He had to block those with his hands or elbows. There was also a bar at the bottom of the machine, below the screen. Ethan had to jump over that one when vagrants kicked at him.

Ethan progressed through the first four levels of the game: an alleyway, a dark tunnel, a slum, and then a sewer underground. He played the game so furiously well that he defeated all the vagrants and beat all the levels. While he did so, his eyes glowed violet, and his magic radiated throughout the arcade, causing the games to short-circuit and dole out more tickets, even switching some to free play. When he defeated the last vagrant at the end of the game, Gal saw his eyes glow so violet that just after the machine had saved his initials to first place atop the leaderboards, the machine overloaded and shut down... and then every machine in the arcade... and then the entire mall.

Gal'gatha knew his memory with Ethan was coming to an end. As the crowd watching Ethan play gasped at what had happened, they all faded away until Talia with her forest-green eyes was the only one watching him.

Then the theater showed Gal'gatha a dream the boy had had later that night. In the dream, a bald man with scarlet eyes imprisoned the boy's family in front of them with magic and tortured them. "Watch the magic you practice so brazenly, Ethan Campbell, or the phoenix will find you," the bald man told Ethan in his dream. Gal'gatha watched it all from the shadow theater. It was a nightmare for Ethan—one he would not remember in the morning.

The theater would show him Katie next—the eagle's heart would have its time.

Katie's childhood was full of strife and fights. She was almost never the aggressor—except sometimes against her brother. They didn't seem to trust each other, but the children she fought the most were the bullies at school. These bullies were often as tall as her and older, seeking her out because she was different. She was friendly with everyone who didn't get on her bad side, which the bullies did. She was reticent to fight with them, but she was not afraid to. She was good at fighting, and she won many of her fights, but she was untrained, and when she lost a fight it was bad.

The theater went on to show her pleading with her father, Carth—who owned a boxing gym in the lower districts of Imperium Aendor—to train her to fight, one weekend morning while their family ate breakfast together in their dining room. He refused her, saying, "You don't want to fight for a living. You ought to cherish your childhood while you can. When you become an adult, you'll have to spend your life doing something you likely hate, and people will want to kill you." He was polishing the family shotgun.

Ethan laughed at her when that comment from her father broke her and pushed her to tears. She turned and ran up the stairs to her room. The theater also showed the troubles of her father accepting her wish to train. He saw the same talent in her that she saw in herself, but Carth worried about who else would see that talent. What would be the agenda of those who would discover her talent? The House of Lance. Gal'gatha watched Katie cry as she ran up the stairs, striking a nerve within her father. He would train her to fight, and when doing so, he asked her, "Promise me not to get too good?"

She swore but never intend to keep her promise, figuring her father was being facetious – and Gal'gatha knew the fears her father had when first refusing to train her would come true. Katie was different, and the House of Lance *would* be in a war and in need of fighters like her when she came of age. No amount of her father's love could suppress her raw prowess or Draven heritage.

The figures faded, and the tip of the hawk's talon emerged from the shadow and shroud. It was time for Gal'gatha to watch Bailey.

A young girl—younger even than Katie—ran through a forest, chasing birds and kicking leaves with her young mother and father in tow. Gal'gatha could tell Bailey had no fear of dead things. The theater showed her poking a dead Granax with a stick and then lifting a deer skull with her bare hands. Gal'gatha laughed softly as the screen showed her parents scowling at her when she did those things—in particular, her father, Clancy. The man, with his short, spiked brown hair, picked her up and carried her off, while she playfully kicked and punched at his back. Then the theater moved to show Clancy taking long, dreamy glances toward his wife. Elena held a strange-looking device in her hands–to Gal'gatha, at least. The device had a screen with a map of the area on it and short radio antennas that protruded from its end.

She tracked a rare hawk's feather on it as they walked through the forest. As Gal'gatha viewed Bailey's memory, he could see nothing but happiness shared between the three of them. The family eventually tracked the feather to a cliff overlooking a waterfall. Elena would have to repel down and then search a cave behind the waterfall to retrieve the feather.

"Be careful, Mom," Bailey timidly told her mother while she bent one of her short legs behind the other.

"This is my job, my beautiful child. I've been doing this for years," Elena told her daughter while she held her in her arms. Then she went down the cliff, retrieved the feather, and was back with her daughter and husband within an hour. They returned home, and for a second, Gal'gatha believed that was all the theater would show him. Then, however, it showed Elena on another mission this time by herself to recover an artifact for her employer Drev-Tech. She was repelling down another sheer cliff, was about halfway down, and everything looked fine.

Suddenly, Gal'gatha saw her rope and teether begin to strain as several red sparks struck it from an unknown source. The rope snapped, and Elena fell screaming to her presumable death. After a pause though, the theater showed him the bloody place of where she had fallen. Her remains were nowhere to be seen, although there was a considerable amount of blood and brown fur.

When local authorities finally arrived at the remote location, all that linked the scene to Elena was her broken artifact tracker, and some of her hair found in the stool of a she-bear nearby. Gal'gatha was not shown the fate of the she-bear. Next, he was shown was at the *funeral* of Elena, where Clancy lost all his composure, and the loss fractured his relationship with Bailey.

The last scene that the theater showed him of Bailey and Clancy, was of Clancy driving her to an after-school activities fair. The two of them barely spoke, although they often looked at each other and wondered what to say. Clancy signed up Bailey for an outdoor survival group, with a scrawny young boy named Corso who she quickly made friends with. As his vision of Bailey faded, Gal saw the last look that Clancy gave his daughter. It was one of distance and remorse, but also one that had been scarred by the death of his wife, for all time.

For several moments, the shadow theater showed him nothing but shadow and shroud, and Gal'gatha though his viewing was over. Then it brought Brian to the screen—chaos by another name—and showed him many things at once. A grand statehouse of many levels stood at the top of a river. Around the river's path, a grand city lay. Behind the statehouse, however, a darker city lay in ruin. Then Gal'gatha saw Brian in the shadow of the courthouse, his legs over the seat of a Burcgetti chopper motorcycle.

Brian was a tall and lanky ginger-haired boy with scruff. He stood next to two friends, Aelix and Alice, and then before Gal'gatha could see anything further about his friends, the theater whirled around to show him more detail.

Dozens of police cars sat in the parking lot directly in front of the statehouse, but to its sides were alleyways with vagrants and a handful of black sedans. Officers would walk out the side doors of the statehouse, then sit in the back seats of the sedans with their tinted windows. Night fell over the statehouse, and the city began to roil in turmoil. That night, as Brian waited with his legs around his chopper and friends at his side, thousands within the city like him rose late at night to riot. They gathered at his sides and behind him, and several dozen police officers stood a hundred feet from them in front of the statehouse wearing riot gear.

The two sides were agitatedly ready to clash at a moment's notice, and when Gal'gatha looked into the eyes of Brian, it looked like the boy was going to lead the rioters himself. Then the theater showed him more.

Brian came from wealth and had a home with loving parents. It showed him a memory of Brian sitting at breakfast with his mom, and then a few seconds later, he tried to preserve his surprise as if he didn't know the distinct rumble of a Burcgetti chopper. His dad, whose employer made one of the more intricate parts of their engines, was riding a brand new carbon black Burcgetti chopper up the hill to their house.

In the vision, Gal'gatha saw a wide smile crack across Brian's face as soon as he knew what he was getting. He joyously hugged both of his parents for their generosity. Then it showed him riding away to the statehouse and getting into one of the black sedans. The theater did not show him exiting, but it did show him more. It took him back to night again, and he saw the scene on the edge of a riot. Alice stood a few feet away from Brian, holding a lit Molotov cocktail at her side. She lobbed it at the police, and the riot was on.

As the Molotov landed at the feet of the police, they began to fire teargas into the rioters, dispersing them. "Don't run," Brian told the crowd. "All the injustice you've faced and you're as brittle as glass." Brian watched the rioters thin and then handed Aelix another Molotov cocktail. He lit it with his Relnás lighter and then stepped a few feet back. Aelix began his throwing motion, but just before he could hurl his cocktail, a container of tear gas struck the bottom of the Molotov causing it to burst and ignite his friend.

"Oh fuck!" Brian exclaimed. Aelix's horrible screams broke his composure, and he and Alice took off on his chopper, weaving their way through the crowds. The police were too many, and Brian and Alice were later arrested peaceably at a roadblock. Brian spent a few nights in the jail and was later given a trial. The judge wanted to throw Brian into the state penitentiary for five to seven years. Even worse, his parents wanted him to gladly serve it. "It'll teach you a lesson and help you get your life in order. Then once you get out you can get back on track and not make the same mistakes," his father had told him when they had come to visit him, while he awaited bail.

Brian did not want to spend the next few years of his young life in jail. Each night he slept in the jail, Gal'gatha watched how an orange dragon named Alyisay invaded his dreams and told him he was meant for more. He was not meant to rot in and out of a cell for the rest of his life. He was an outlaw and had a code by which he must abide. He would not go to jail, and the next day he was offered a way out. Mr. Macado was a *boss* of his. The man Gal'gatha had seen him visit in the black sedan. The man was tall and thick, with copper skin, black eyes, and black hair. He would defend him if he would continue to work for his associates in Sen Rhêt Hill. Brian knew accepting such a defense would avail him his *freedom*, but he would have to leave Raegic, and his parents would disown him.

Gal'gatha watched Brian's dreams again, as his time in the theater came toward a close.

You are an important life—one that will impact the world. It cannot be spent clinging to your parents, nor behind bars, Alyisay tortured him in his dreams.

Brian had decided by the time he woke up that morning. The theater showed Gal'gatha Brian's trial. Mr. Macado passionately defended his client, and as he was acquitted, Brian's parents, Scott and Kristaine, simply stood up in silence, then bowed their heads and walked out of the courtroom. The next day, Brian rode his Burcgetti chopper to Sen Rhêt Hill and did not look back, although he felt awful about being disowned by his parents.

Quite thankfully, after that, the Shadow Theater had nothing else to show him.

Gal'gatha left the theater quickly, wanting to be above ground again in the open air. He climbed up the ladder out of the shadow, then ascended the stairs and headed out of the Shroud. When he stepped out the door of the granite pyramid, Gal'gatha looked around his city. He tried to remember its beauty, its happy people. The sea below and the mountains that rose far above. He knew those would remain, but he wondered what would become of his city when Christian's actions were revealed to the world. Knowing those who now held power, Gal'gatha did not expect mercy.

Chapter 1

A Boy who Believed in Magic (Ethan 1)

CALANOR STRONGHOLD DISTRICT, IMPERIUM AENDOR, IISHREM

FALL, 1142, FOURTH AGE

*T*he excitement of some of Ethan's fellow classmates died quickly when the bus they were riding came to a stop. They had just arrived at the Calanor Stronghold. Excitedly, Ethan looked out the window and up the rocky hill encircled by the fort. His teacher's voice quickly called his attention back to the front of the bus. They would be getting off now, and the tour would be starting. A pair of students groaned in the row behind him when they realized they would have to get out of their seats and exercise their legs around the fort.

Ethan and Rich got off the bus together and joined the rest of their classmates in the parking lot. "Okay, children, follow me!" boomed their teacher, Ms. Edgarton, from the front. Ethan and Rich smiled at each other and followed the rest of their class. Several chaperones patrolled the edges of the group, to make sure no students wandered away.

Ethan looked ahead at the fort—their group, along with several others and some other general visitors, were approaching up a moderate incline. When Ethan's group reached the outer walls of the fort, he turned around to look back at the parking lot. He could see their bus sitting there, perhaps a quarter-mile behind them and probably about two hundred feet lower than their current altitude. The walls looked to rise about fifty feet above him, and the rest of the rocky hill contained within rose another few hundred feet or so in the air. A tower then rose another hundred feet above the top of the hill. Ethan was already huffing from the walk to the fort from the parking lot, but his legs were not yet tired. He had no doubt they would be, though, when the day was done.

Once they were inside the fort, Ms. Edgarton went to look for their tour guide inside the administrative offices, which were right next to the main gate. She wasn't gone long, but while she was, Ethan had a chance to look around. The walls which protected the fort went around the rocky hill at relatively the same height all the way around. The insides of the walls were lined with stairways, each leading to the top. Beyond that, the rest of the fort tunneled inside the rocky hill. When Ethan looked up, he could see battlements carved out all around the hill with slits for cannons and other projectiles to be fired at oncoming enemies. There were also a few wide, tall battlement openings that were unprotected. Ethan wondered what those were there for.

Finally, Ms. Edgarton returned with their tour guide. He introduced himself and ushered them into a tunnel that would take them into the inner fort. He lectured them about the history and building of the fort. Some excitement returned to the voices of Ethan's fellow students as their voices bounced about the cave walls and into the inner fort. Perhaps they would enjoy this day more than they had anticipated. Ethan himself was excited. He was twelve years old, and finally, he was visiting a place he had wanted to for as long as he could remember.

"You see… the Calanor Stronghold was built just over five hundred years ago," the tour guide explained as they reached the end of the tunnel. The tunnel they had used to enter the fort ran along the edges of the hill. Ethan looked out of the battlement as they came to a stop. The fort itself had some cosmetic scars, but otherwise, it was well-preserved. As Ethan thought about how it would have appeared five hundred years ago, he felt his eyes turn a darker shade of his normal blue color. Regardless of what the guide was telling them, Ethan's eyes certainly did not believe that was the true age of the fort.

Ethan could see a large area of the Calanor Stronghold district when he looked out of the battlement. He could see even more of Imperium Aendor, off in the distance. They were only blocks from the outer wall of Imperium Aendor. Ethan could see a gate with a line of trucks and cars waiting to leave the city. He wanted to see the gate open and watch *somebody* actually leave the city. He had never done so before.

"Ethan, come along," said Ms. Edgarton. The rest of their group was now heading into the inner portion of the fort. He forced himself to look away from the gate before it opened and walked back into the cave through the hill which connected the fort to itself. Reinforcements could have moved quickly from one side of the fort to the other through these tunnels, back when the fort was still being used for its original purposes, not educational tourism. There were also tunnels for barracks, kitchens, and a great hall as well. The group ventured upward into the cavernous hill.

At the direction of their tour guide, Ethan's class stepped into an expansive inner chamber which dominated the rest of the tunnels.

When he looked up at the cave ceilings, it looked like a planetarium. Ethan could see the trail of the eagle, the raven's stars, the prowling dragon, and the swooping hawk portrayed as constellations on the domed ceiling. When Ethan looked closer, he began to see more than constellations. He began to see images of what he had only previously read in comic books about mythical legends.

He began to see Eedon Rath-ni depicted on the stone ceiling. While their guide continued to drone on, and his fellow students looked around at eye level, Ethan continued to look at the ceiling. Illuminations of ravens, eagles, dragons, and hawks gleamed at him from above. No one else in his class seemed to have noticed them, not even Rich. Ethan kept his discovery to himself. All the Eedon Rath-ni bore riders. When he looked at each of the Eedon Rath-ni individually, he understood them differently.

Ethan felt more magical when he looked at the ravens. When he looked at the eagles, he felt stronger and faster. When Ethan looked at the hawks, he could hear conversations that people were having from far away. Finally, when he looked at the dragons, a rage boiled inside of him, surging to be let loose. He didn't dare to look at the dragons for any longer than a moment. Naturally, Ethan decided it would be best to look at the ravens the longest.

Eventually, he found a raven on the ceiling which matched his most magically potent eye color—violet. He looked into its illumination, and suddenly, he heard a voice within his head. Ethan felt his eyes close. Her voice was sweet, soft, and serene. *I've found you. You're mine forevermore. We'll meet here one day,* the voice told him. When he opened his eyes, the illusion on the ceiling took full form in front of his eyes for just a moment. Although the raven was not really there, Ethan felt like he could see her right in front of him.

I am called Violet, and you will know of me now, forevermore, the voice finished.

After the illusion faded, he again had to run to catch up to the rest of the class. They had begun to ascend the stairs to the summit of the hill, and from there, they were going on to the top of the tower.

"So, you see, this fort was originally built to quell a rebellion that had broken out in this district some five hundred years ago. Since then, it has served as a retreat for the royal family. If you look out to the west, you can see the city's center, and within it, The Spire, the home of the House of Lance—the center of all government, business, and internal matters. It's the tallest building, but there is a close second," their tour guide explained as they reached the top of the tower. They had entered a round-shaped observatory, and everyone spread out.

Ethan looked out across Imperium Aendor, with the rest of his classmates, at the tallest building in the city: The Spire. It was a bright, yet windy day in fall. The Spire, a glass skyscraper, rose high into the sky, and it reflected the light of the sun in all directions. At night, its spire would glow red, using the light it had taken in throughout the day.

To the left of The Spire, a square-shaped tower rose over the rest of the city. It was only around a hundred and fifty feet shorter than The Spire, and it was the home of Tagros Aleium Lance, who was second in command of Iishrem, having somewhat recently married his sister, Reialya, to the Emperor Sax Drugren the 12th. Targos was the sword that the emperor could not always carry himself. He enforced with an iron fist, and the country's economy was all the stronger for it.

Emperor Sax Drugren the 12th and the Empress Regent had a single descendant—Prince Lance the 13th. He was not much older than Ethan, only 6 years or so. Sax Drugren was nearly two hundred and fifty-six, and he had held power for the last hundred and twenty-five years. There had been plenty of heirs before that, but the emperor had married them off and dispersed them around Iishrem to retain his influence. When Lance, his thirteenth child, was born, Sax had quickly realized he was the heir he had been waiting for. While Ethan knew normal humans on Rehem could live for a hundred years or more, he also knew Iishrem had had an Emperor or two who had lived for over three hundred years. Scientists long ago had discovered genes that greatly increased life expectancy in some, but it was a rare trait. Somehow throughout their reign, the House of Lance had benefited from many of its prevalent members having this rare trait. There were several separate lines of House Lance. House Aleium Lance was not graced with the same length of lives, though Tagros was in his late eighties and still looked surprisingly youthful.

After having processed all his thoughts, Ethan felt like he was going to ace his politics test next week. He smiled. The tour of the Calanor Stronghold concluded upon that note, and Ethan was ready to go home.

Back at home, Ethan eagerly wrote down his experiences from that day. He had felt so magical within the heart of the stronghold. He'd never felt as magical before in his entire life. He wrote down how his eyes had been dark blue when he had seen the illuminations. He wrote about the eagles, the hawks, and the dragons, and he sketched several images of each. He then drew a man turning into a lion. His blue eyes faded back to normal as he finished working in his journal. He had concluded by writing about and sketching Violet. He listened for her voice again but heard nothing.

That weekend, Ethan logged onto his computer and accessed Iishrem's internet, which was divided into sections specializing in specific purposes of use. Ethan went to the shopping section, and from there, he searched for lore stores close to his home. Ethan then narrowed his search results to lore shops that carried lore for the Eedon Rath-ni. Unsurprisingly, his search results only turned up with the comic store he already frequented. Maybe the store's owner would be able to connect him with more lore about the Dravens and the Eedon Rath-ni.

Ethan begged his parents to take him by before it closed. Reluctantly, Carth obliged, and they got there an hour or so later. Ethan already knew the shopkeeper by name.

"Hey, Roland," he said to the man behind the counter. "You have any comics about the Eedon Rath-ni and Dravens?"

A large, hairy man thrice his age stood up and looked down at Ethan behind the counter. "Sure do, follow me," he told him. Roland waddled all the way to the back with him in tow, where on a single, relatively thin bookcase there sat three different books. The first one he saw was, The Magic of Colored Eyes.

"When the Eedon Rath-ni were at their peak, everyone knew how their particular types of magics were linked to the colors of their Draven's eyes," he explained. Ethan nodded and took the last copy.

Above it, there were several copies of the same paperback book titled *Eagle Rider, Book 1: Legends of the Bald Crown*. Roland handed him a copy. The book looked like it was about three hundred pages or so long. Above that was another paperback of a similar length titled, *The Hawk who beat The Dragon*. All three books were by a Maria Lewis Knowles.

Ethan was a little disappointed. "Do you have any new books about ravens?" He felt his eyes yearn to turn violet, but he was nowhere near the Calanor Stronghold now. In fact, he was closer to The Spire.

"Sorry, kid. She doesn't really sell too much, but I hope that'll change one day," Roland told him while he looked over her photo that graced the back cover.

Carth was waiting for him upfront. He paid for his three new books and then took Ethan home. Ethan planned to use them as the basis for a paper and presentation he would have to give in two weeks for class. He had been assigned to present a real-life lore that he believed his class could benefit from in the present—one which he could apply to a job field when he was older. Ethan planned just to make an argument for the existence of Eedon Rath-ni, the potential of magic, and then he would give his evidence to support it.

He read each of the books over the next week and took notes in a notebook while he did. Ethan slowly formulated a theory around his powers. He wanted to make an argument, linking them to the Calanor Stronghold and what he had seen while there. He wanted to end his presentation with a demonstration of his magic, so he came up with the idea of having all three of the books open by themselves and flip through their contents, page by page, at the same time.

At the end of that week, when he had finished writing and rehearsing his presentation, Ethan began to practice his trick. He couldn't get his eyes to turn violet on command, and no other color he had tried would successfully yield his intended result. After a few more attempts, he decided to go to bed. Ethan wasn't too upset. He still had a few more days before the presentation to get it right.

By the day of the presentation, Ethan still had not been able to do his trick successfully. His presentation would proceed regardless, and he would still attempt his trick, even though he figured he would probably only embarrass himself.

He sat in the back of the class at his desk next to Rich. Ethan's presentation would be next. He felt nervous, but not because he hadn't gotten his trick to work yet. It was only normal jitters like he always had before speaking in front of the class.

"And so, class, that's why I believe the lore surrounding the history of Dargen, a sport played feverishly around the world, could be useful to a future career in sports broadcasting. For Dargen, in particular," said a boy named Vyden, who was Ethan's age. Vyden had a short black-haired cut and blue eyes. Ethan didn't get along well with Vyden; he constantly bullied Rich and him.

Modest applause echoed about the classroom at the end of Vyden's presentation. Even Ethan and Rich gave him a few claps, just to be nice. Vyden smiled while he packed up his presentation and walked back to his desk, which was almost as far away as he could sit from Ethan. Even so, Ethan met Vyden's gaze when he stood, and Vyden sat back down. Vyden blew a raspberry at him, and Ethan shuddered. He began to gather his supplies for his presentation, which included a three-sided poster board and his three books.

"So, class," Ms. Edgarton began, "next we have Ethan, who'll be telling us about the mythical Eedon Rath-ni, Dravens, magic, and why he thinks they were once real."

A few of his fellow classmates snickered while Ethan made his way up to the front of the class. He couldn't tell who had snickered, but he strongly suspected one of them would have been Vyden. Ethan wasn't particularly surprised or bothered. After all, much of what he was about to present on was generally regarded as mythical fantasy having never *really* existed. In general, the subject of Ethan's presentation would have been regarded as nothing but folklore and legend—from people who had nothing better to do with their lives at the last turn of an age. Consequentially, when the House of Lance had first taken power over all Iishrem, they had declared a new age over all Rehem.

When Ethan reached the front of the class, he unfolded his poster board and held up each of his three books for the class to see. "The Magic of Colored Eyes; Eagle Rider, Book 1: The Legend of the Bald Crown; and The Hawk who beat The Dragon," Ethan told his class, showing them each of his books, one at a time. When he was finished, Ethan laid each of them down on the table.

"At the end of the 3rd Age, stories and legends of the Eedon Rath-ni and Dravens held the interest of many people in Iishrem. However, I believe these stories were more than just legend. They were truth," Ethan told the class, beginning his presentation. More snickers abounded throughout the classroom.

"Class," said Ms. Edgarton in an exasperated tone of voice. At least his presentation was not the first one to have earned such snickers. She placed her hand on top of a black telephone, which sat on her desk. At the moment that she did so, all snickers and gossip ceased instantly. Ethan was free to continue.

Ethan continued his presentation by outlining why he believed people in Iishrem at the end of the 3rd age thought magic, Dravens, and the Eedon Rath-ni were fact and not just legend. Using the

internet, Ethan had been able to find four accounts of people having encountered an Eedon Rath-ni. More specifically, there was
an account for each kind of Eedon Rath-ni—even a dragon. Ethan
summarized each of the experiences.

After that portion of his presentation, Ethan moved onto where
he thought the Eedon Rath-ni had vanished to and what he had
thought the Dravens had left behind. "Class, I believe that the
Eedon Rath-ni fled both Iishrem and Allirehem at the end of the
3rd age to their homes within the Shrouded Sea—never to return,"
Ethan told the class. Like everyone else, Ethan knew that the
planet they lived on, Rehem, was round. The two continents of
Iishrem and Allirehem were connected by land, with the Eldeic
Ocean to the North, the Monetic Ocean to the south, and the
Allaeyic Ocean in the middle of Allirehem. Beyond that, on either
side, were the borders of the Shrouded Sea.

Ethan pointed to several pictures of the Shrouded Sea that
he had glued to his poster board. As far as anyone knew, the
Shrouded Sea covered the other half of the planet in thick gray
clouds. The gray clouds, which apparently never lessened, hid the
Shrouded Sea from pole to pole, and from Daemon Bay in Iishrem
to Aceor in Allirehem. Anyone in history who had sailed into the
Shrouded Sea from either side had never been heard from again.
Both Iishrem and Allirehem had sent multiple expeditions. Many
explorers had tried. Ethan even knew some of their names. There
had been far fewer since the scientific community had come out
with their explanation for the thick shroud several hundred years
ago. Everyone had bought into it, and anyone who challenged it
was balked at and labeled as crazy or some kind of fanatic. Ethan
half expected the same was about to be done to him.

"I believe anyone who sails onto the Shrouded Sea is killed by the Eedon Rath-ni. I've researched a little on Daemon Bay and Aceor. One of Daemon Bay's main attractions is a statue of an enormous dragon. The same goes for Aceor, but there it is the statue of a raven. People travel to those cities from all over the world, to go up in their towers and see what they can," Ethan told the class.

This time instead of snickering, multiple students within the class rolled their eyes or groaned. Ethan was okay with that. He only needed his friends to like him. Then Vyden looked up from his desk and said, "But no one ever sees anything, Ethan. None of this is real. Why are you wasting our time?"

Ethan wasn't going to engage with his bully directly. Instead, he looked to Ms. Edgarton. Before she could say anything, Vyden said, "It's strange that no one has ever been able to sail around the world. Do you also believe in magic and Dravens too?"

"Vyden," said Ms. Edgarton, "this is Ethan's presentation, not yours." Vyden went quiet.

Ethan was ready to wrap this all up. "Anyways, I'm about finished, but I have a trick to show you all first," he told the class.

"A card trick? How amazing!" Vyden shouted to the class.

Ethan was beginning to get angry with Vyden. He really wished that his school was closer to the Calanor Stronghold. Maybe Vyden wouldn't be such a nuisance then. He felt his eyes flare at Vyden, but he could tell that they remained their normal shade of blue.

"My eyes change color. Maybe a few of you have noticed," Ethan admitted.

"That doesn't make you magical, it just makes you strange." That insult came from a brown-haired girl who was one of Vyden's cronies. It was his crush—Kiera.

Ethan huffed. He was ready for all of this to be over. He turned to Ms. Edgarton, and she gave him a look that seemed to say she agreed with him. He wasn't offended.

"Okay, for my trick, I'm going to change the color of my eyes to violet and make these books flip through themselves on their own," Ethan told the class.

At that, Vyden and Kiera grew silent, and the rest of the class waited in anticipation. Ethan walked behind the table that he had set his presentation upon and took down his fold-out poster board.

"This should be good," said Vyden from the back of the room. Ethan ignored him and focused his eyes on the books. He tried to quiet his mind and find the magic within him. After about twenty seconds, he still felt nothing. Ethan forced himself to look at the books with even more intent. He focused his eyes on the purple raven that was on the cover of The Gaze of Ravens and began to feel something inside of him.

"Alright, Ethan, I think that's enough. Good job. Class, how about a round of applause for Ethan?" Ms. Edgarton said.

Ethan felt himself flush as the class gave him a sarcastically loud round of applause. Vyden and Kiera both stood and cheered very loudly with their hands held far in front of their faces in his direction to clap.

"Bravo!" they both cheered in unison. Several other students around them began to giggle at him.

No, Ethan thought. *Why can't I do this?*

Suddenly, Ethan did feel a small spark of magic flow through his veins—although he did not think he would be able to control it enough to be able to do his trick. Ethan felt like he was back inside the Calanor Stronghold. The purple raven on the cover of the book began to move, just like the raven he had seen on the ceiling.

When he listened, Ethan could faintly hear her voice. Ethan felt his eyes turn violet.

Oh, young Draven, you do not yet realize the power you possess. One day, you will. For now, though, I can only show you a little taste, Violet told him.

Violet, was all Ethan could manage to think back. *A little taste?*

"Ethan?" said Ms. Edgarton. He still felt red and embarrassed as he turned back to look at her. "Please take your seat."

Ethan reluctantly obliged. Dejectedly, he gathered the supplies for his presentation and returned to his desk. *Yes, a taste. That one there,* she said when he began to look at Vyden while he walked his way to his desk. Ethan put his stuff down and stood there next to his desk. *He seems to bother you a lot. Let's embarrass him, shall we?*

Ethan felt his eyes naturally focus on Vyden. Suddenly, all the laughter and jeers ceased at once, and Ethan heard a new sound and smelled a new smell. He looked at Vyden across the room, who had reddened and had risen to run for the exit of the classroom. He had pissed himself, and the wetness had run all down his pants. As the children began to realize, they all began to laugh at Vyden as he ran out of the room.

It'll take his popularity months to recover from that, Violet told him. *How did you like that?*

Ethan sat down and tried not to be noticed. *Can we make that happen each time he's mean to me?* he asked Violet.

Haha. No, you will have to wait many years for that opportunity. Now stay strong, love, and don't lose your faith in me until we can see each other with our own eyes. Her voice was gone from his mind after that. The rest of Ethan's day took far too long, and when he was finally alone in his room, about to go to bed, he began to cry. He felt like a freak because he could change the color of his eyes, and he believed he was going insane, hearing the voice of a mythical creature inside his head. He spent a good portion of that night crying, trying to convince himself that he was just a normal kid. Eventually, Ethan succeeded and fell asleep.

Chapter 2

The Song of the Phoenix (katie 1)

IMPERIUM AENDOR, IISHREM

FALL 1141 – SPRING 1146, FOURTH AGE

katie and her father rode in their family station wagon to a ballet studio she did not want to attend. He was going to honor his agreement to teach her to fight, but at his digression, he was going to make it take longer as well. "Before you can learn to fight, you must first learn to run. To evade. To tackle. Then, only once you've learned to tackle, will you need to learn to strike. Because you're so young, you've got time to master all of this. Hopefully, before it ever matters. But I do hope there won't be a war going once you turn eighteen," her father told her on the way to a gymnastics studio.

"But, Dad! Gymnastics is just dancing for taller, thicker, uglier girls," Katie complained.

"Well, ouch. I hope that's not why you think I'm enrolling you in it!" Carth explained, snapping back at her. She looked down at the floor of the van with a frown. "Hey, it was just some tough love," her dad explained. "Learn to let it make you stronger because the physical punishment of fighting is going to be much worse."

Carth turned their van into a parking lot and took a spot near the front of the studio. Katie grumbled, and she punched her father in the arm with a curled fist once they had come to a stop. When she hit him, Carth did not groan or grimace, but he did blink once. Then when Katie dropped her fist, he put his arm to his shoulder and said, "Oww."

Katie leaned back in her seat. "Do I really have to do this?" she asked.

Carth nodded. "Come on."

Her father opened his door and got out. She did the same, stepping down onto the asphalt parking lot. "Archie's gymnastic studio. Well, this looks interesting," Katie said, unable to hide the strife in her voice.

Carth looked down at her and grunted before pulling her inside by the arm. They were asked to check-in at the desk and then told to take a seat. Eventually, a tall, thin woman with wide hips and short black hair approached them.

Katie was told, "We'll start her in ballet and then see where she can go from there." This time Katie groaned out loud and stomped her feet. Carth gave her a swift swat around the back of the head.

"Ouch," she said, flinching backward. How had he caught her so off-guard? She should have been able to avoid that. "That really hurt."

She tried to look scared and hurt, but her father did not apologize. That was all the motivation she needed to make this portion of her training as brief as possible. However, she would make this first day hell for everyone else, especially her father. Twenty minutes later, Carth couldn't help but watch and groan while Katie made a fool of herself in her black leotard. Several times, Katie watched him put his head in his hands as she tripped, fell, cried, and argued with the instructor.

When they were finally finished, Carth took her straight home and sent her to sleep without dinner. Katie didn't mind. She knew that she had gotten the better of him that day. The next time Katie went in for ballet, she went in focused.

Once she was finished with ballet a year later, as a ten-year-old, Katie moved onto gymnastics. That was when Katie really learned the use of her arms for climbing and perseverance in a fight. Thanks to her time spent in ballet, Katie quickly found her legs on the balance beam with both jumps and somersaults. When she moved to the bars, she swiftly learned the use of precision, agility, dexterity, and arm strength. Much to her dismay, Katie quickly had to get used to wearing her bushy hair in a braided ponytail. But if it was better for her in a fight, Katie would learn to put up with the trouble.

Katie's next opportunity for a fight at school came a week later against two new opponents, both a grade up from her—a small, skinny boy with short brown hair, and a black-haired girl who had a frame similar to Katie's and also wore loose-fitting clothes. Early into the fight, it became clear to Katie that the boy was just trying to win the approval of the girl that he fought for. He didn't know how to fight, and it left Katie wondering why the girl with black hair wanted him to fight her. The small, skinny boy with brown hair ran in first for her, throwing punches that Katie was easily able to dodge.

When the boy stumbled forward after lunging for her and missing, Katie curled a fist and jammed it into his jaw from the side. He crumbled to the tiled floor and collapsed again when trying to get back up. That left the rest of the fight to Katie and the girl. She felt so confident of herself after flooring the small boy. Katie walked up to the girl in black slowly and moved in close for some jabs. She threw a few punches and hit her mark, but she found nothing but baggy clothing. Katie tried to grab her, but the girl huddled up and shoved her off. Katie was about to retreat when she found out that the girl in black knew how to tackle, and her guard had been down.

The girl in black tackled her to the ground in a rush. She felt her head hit the padded wall of the gym, but at least she knew what to do. Katie brought her arms up to cover her face and tried to sit up while flexing her elbows to cover the blows the girl directed towards her stomach. While she was down on the ground trying to protect herself, she could see nothing but darkness in front of her. Katie felt a punch hit her in the face, knocking her backward, just as teachers were finally arriving on the scene. It was an indoor recess. She should have known better when she saw the pair approaching—the main supervisor teacher was out on a smoke break, and the alternate was only a mere substitute teacher.

Katie began to hear a voice in her head, and she suddenly felt her eyes change color from brown to yellow. Suddenly, she felt stronger again. In her mind, Katie began to see a vision of her brother's bookshelf. There, in the middle of the top shelf, turned sideways, stood a copy of *Eagle Rider, Book One: Legend of the Bald Crown*. On the cover was an illustration of an enormous bald eagle.

Katie looked at the bald eagle on the cover. Suddenly, she could see it in front of her—full-sized. The eagle looked to have a wingspan of almost sixty feet, and from beak to the end of its tail feathers maybe three-quarters of that. When on the ground, the eagle stood a little over 16 feet tall with its neck erect. The eagle looked at her and bent down, wings outstretched as if to offer her a ride.

Katie opened her eyes to look back out at the scene in the school. Time seemed to have slowed down around her. She looked up and could see a pair of teachers finally restraining the girl who had been hitting her and pulling her away. Katie closed her eyes again for just a second, now fully noticing the fact that time had indeed slowed. *I'm so sorry, young Katie,* said the eagle's voice in her head. *You will not always have to take on every fight on your own.* After that, the voice was gone, and time picked up around her again.

Katie got up from against the wall, feeling strong and not badly hurt from the fight. She had lost for sure, but at least she wasn't crying.

Her father punished her for having gotten into the fight—even though she insisted that it wasn't her fault. It really hadn't been, but still, he delayed the beginning of her training in boxing for another six months. She made a promise to herself to run away from any future fights after that. At least then she couldn't get in trouble with her father.

Eventually, Katie progressed both in fighting ability and agility. According to her father, she showed a good understanding of striking, wrestling, and evasion. It was for that reason Carth entered her into some games and competitions at the Capitol Spire for the Emperor's birthday. Sax Drugren, the 12th Emperor of Iishrem, was turning two hundred and sixty that day, and she was turning fourteen. She would perform in gymnastics and ballet in the Friday games, and then on the Saturday games, Carth would allow her to engage in a wrestling match with a girl her size, and then a boxing match with a girl five pounds lighter and two inches shorter than her. "Are you sure you're ready for this? These are your first official matches. People will remember how you do—as will you," he told her.

"I'm ready," she said, looking up at him and smiling. "I wanted to fight a boy, though." She had a wide smirk plastered on her face. Katie really did feel as ready as she ever would.

"So be it," her father told her, and then he put their family station-wagon into park in a multi-story parking garage, just outside of the Capitol Approach. It was just the two of them for now. Marleigh and Ethan would be along later to watch. The area around the Capitol Spire was much more awe-inspiring than the rest of the city. No vehicles, except light emergency and military armor, could come within the circle-shaped perimeter of the district. Its area was 5 miles in diameter and had both the Capitol Spire and Aleium Tower rising into the sky in the center of it all.

Katie grabbed her athletic bag and followed her dad out of the car. Carth grabbed his wallet, phone, and keys and shoved them in his pockets, before grabbing her boxing gloves, which were tied together. She had everything else she needed in her bag. The two of them took the stairs down to the ground floor, and she savored the fresh spring air once she was outside of the garage that smelled obnoxiously like petrol. The sun partially blinded her when they opened the door to the beginning of the Capitol Approach.

All buildings throughout Imperium Aendor were limited to a maximum height of a hundred and sixty feet, but within the approach, there were a dozen or so buildings that reached five hundred feet into the sky or higher. The Capitol Spire itself had a maximum height of one thousand, one hundred and twenty-five feet, which was symbolic to the year in which it had been completed. That made Aleium Tower one thousand and seventy-five feet high in comparison. Seeing the Capitol Spire up-close and in-person was quite intimidating to Katie. She gulped as she looked up its side. The Capitol Spire consisted of a hundred stories. The spire itself looked like an architecturally designed phoenix. Its base was sturdy and rectangular with several different heights to it, resembling a fire at the top. This was before it narrowed into two towers which rose high into the sky.

The two square-shaped towers rose into the sky with a slight counterclockwise twist for the north tower and a clockwise twist for the south. The two towers were also connected to each other by three walkways, and none of them were any closer to the ground than halfway up. Beyond connecting the towers, the walkways also continued out on either side, heading towards the ground at a slight downward angle, almost as if they were wings.

At the top of the two towers, the spire became one building again and rose another twenty stories into the sky, with an antenna that rose another fifty feet above that. Katie believed that that was where the royal family lived most of the time. The spire occasionally gleamed during this partly cloudy spring day, which had had some intermittent sun showers.

"Well c'mon," her father said, and he took her hand. Katie didn't need help, and so she snapped it back a second later. They both had a good laugh about it afterward, though.

The rest of the Capitol Approach was quite a sight to behold. Since it was quite a large area, and there were no cars allowed. There were several monorail lines that ran on elevated tracks to different sections of the approach. To get to them, she and her father walked to a station, which was down the central brick-paved promenade.

Katie could see most of the rest of the Capitol Approach once they were up in the station. Most of the outer sections of the district were parks or green spaces, with shopping, entertainment, and dining lining the promenades which made their way towards the center. Once they were farther in, there were embassies and governmental bureaus with housing for diplomats, bureaucrats, and regional representatives. There was even a stadium that could seat eighty-five thousand people. Along the outer edge of the southwest of the circle, was a large military base and airfield. Katie could hear the engines of several warplanes and helicopters coming from that direction at that very moment.

They rode straight for the Capitol Spire. The promenades of the approach currently hosted seemingly every type of person from Iishrem that Katie could think of. There were thousands of people everywhere, with street performers busking, street vendors selling, and paparazzi stalking celebrities, politicians, and bureaucrats alike. After stopping at two other stations first, their train arrived at the station within the Capitol Spire. She excitedly held her breath when the train first entered the glass skyscraper through a section cut out of its face. She did not exhale until the train doors were open again.

When the pair exited the train, her father did not try to hold her hand again. She was thankful for that. Everything was calm within the spire, although it was very crowded. Despite it having been a windy and cloudy spring day outside, any heat kept in by the glass had been preserved well, and it was dispersed throughout the open atrium. People inside walked in a relaxed fashion. "C'mon, it's this way. And keep close," her father told her, leading the way. She quickly followed. She did not want to fall behind.

Carth led her down an elevated walkway with glass railings on each side, one facing the outside and the other the inside of the spire. Katie maneuvered her way over, wanting to look out over the edge at the floors below. Light gleamed up at her, but she could still see people clearly. When Katie paused to listen, she could hear voices excitedly murmuring. It sounded like someone of importance was coming. She stopped and watched the citizens below suddenly stop and begin to move back to provide a space for the figure or figures to walk through. This resulted in an orderly cleared corridor. Thankfully, Carth noticed that she had stopped before too long.

"Do you recognize any of those people down there, Katie?" he asked her.

Indeed, she did recognize some of them. Now walking through the cleared path was an entire congregation. Most of them were guards, but Katie could recognize who they were guarding. She recognized Tagros Aleium Lance first—an old man who still had quite a youthful stride but balding grey hair. He walked with a thick brown leather leger in hand. Behind him, was who Katie had hoped to see while she was here—the royal family. The important ones, at least.

Sax Drugren, the 12th Emperor of Iishrem, walked stride for stride with Empress Reialya, and several feet behind them was the heir, Lance, the 13th son of Sax Drugren the 12th—and the future 13th Emperor of Iishrem. She couldn't stop herself from taking a good look. She set her gaze first to Lance, who was closest to her in age, although he was almost 8 years older. She liked his golden-blond hair and firm but slender build. The Empress was a middle-aged woman, somewhere in her early forties, but she still looked like she was in her twenties with her perfect skin, blonde curly locks, and tall, strong figure. Sax Drugren looked like a drunken swine compared to her, with his greasy, thick blackish-gray hair and his jiggling beer gut. When Katie completed that thought, she felt a painful headache and her eyes glow red. They had never done that before, but then the aching stopped, and her eyes returned to normal when she took her eyes off the royal family.

Katie realized she had never answered her father. "Of course, I do. I watch the news," she told him.

"We ought to keep to our schedule. Let's go," he replied, and they set back off toward the spire arena, which contained a private five-thousand-seat performers' arena, with a full-sized court for sports, which could be converted for small-court Dargen or Palm Pass. Of course, it could also be configured for gymnastics and boxing—like it was being used for this day. Katie and her father were going to check-in for her events.

They found the check-in area by following a series of signs, leading them down a maze of corridors and hallways. Katie checked herself in with her father standing right behind her. Once that was done, they hugged and said goodbye, and Katie walked into the girls' locker room, which was patrolled by several stern-looking older women. Katie wanted a bay of lockers to herself for privacy, but after finding the room to be full of other female participants around her age in various stages of undress, she decided to just take the first empty locker she could find and just get it over with. By the time she was finished changing, all the other girls were ready, and it was time for them to head to the arena.

She and her fellow female participants were led by the stern women to the arena through another series of hallways, where they were seated in a specific section away from the general observers. Before performances could begin, the National Anthem of Iishrem needed to be played. Everyone in the arena stood and looked towards the painting of a black phoenix on a red background hanging on the wall. A marching band began to play the mostly musical anthem, but near the end, there were a few lyrics.

The Shadow reigns, the Shroud has won,
All Iishrem paid the price,
For order that we know today,
Was paid,
By flame in price.

The banner of the Shadow and Shroud,
Will reign forever high.
Remember,
Oh Remember,
The price for those who died

Raise your banners,
Raise them high,
Proclaim your feelings true.

For those who only feign belief,
Will surely meet the Shroud,

And just before their ending comes,
The terror it shall be,
They'll know the truth,
The earnest truth,
The shadow reigns
And will never die.

At the end of the anthem, there were several minutes of boisterous clapping and cheering from everyone. Truly, attendees
were recalcitrant to stop applauding and often watched those in

the obvious press boxes for their feigning interest. When everyone was seated again, Katie looked up to the emperor's box, where she could see the royal family and other important spectators. One of the women, in particular, in the box stood out to her. She stood near the railing, seemingly looking right at her. The women had black hair and forest green eyes. She winked at her and then walked away. Katie couldn't think much of it for the moment; she had to focus on her upcoming competitions.

Chapter 3

Sovereign (katie 2)

CAPITOL SPIRE, IMPERIUM AENDOR, IISHREM

SPRING, 1146, FOURTH AGE

*T*he next day, Katie returned to the Capitol Spire for the second day of games and competitions. Her journey there was much like the first day, but this time she and her family all went together. "Promise me you aren't going to get hurt," Marleigh expressed, walking into the Capitol Spire with her.

Katie sighed. "But that's what happens in fights—to both sides," she told her mom. "But I am going to win." At that moment, Katie braided her last few strands of hair, and then she tied it off with several bands at the bottom. She felt ready now—but she would feel even better when she was only in her shorts and top, with her gloves up. Inside that ring and on the mats, there would be just one other girl to beat. She smiled confidently and hopped up and down to shake herself out. When she was finished, it was time to say goodbye.

"Well, this is where you have to go to your seats," Katie told her parents.

Carth nodded and gave her a brisk hug, while Ethan wished her luck with nothing but a handshake. Her mother came up to her blubbering and threw her arms around her, pressing her face against her neck. *What's bringing this on? She knows I fight often,* Katie thought, perplexed over her mother's irrational fear. Katie wriggled herself free of her mother's grasp as quickly as possible and ran off into the locker room—at least, she did not have to share it with anyone she was fighting today.

She changed in silence and put on her hand tape as best as she could. She began to put on her gloves, but of course one of the locker room attendees had to help her finish. Once she was ready, Katie was ushered out into the seating section of the arena to await her turn to be called up to fight. Boxing would be first on that day.

The national anthem was played again, and while Katie stood, she once again noticed the older woman with black hair and green eyes looking down at her. Something about her face and cheeks looked familiar—but not her hair or eyes. Why was she looking down at her? She didn't know the woman. The woman also wasn't in the same seating box as she had been yesterday. All the same, she was all the way at the top—executive-suite-level seating. She had to be someone important, or at least privileged enough to know and see what others did not.

Katie sat again and tried to push the woman's presence out of her mind. For the most part, Katie succeeded, yet she couldn't help but take the odd glance once in a while. The woman moved around a lot, and Katie was not always able to find her, but she could always feel her eyes watching.

When it was Katie's turn to box, she was completely focused. Her father was not allowed to coach her through either event, so she could only rely on herself through the bout. When she first laid eyes on her opponent, Katie was not intimidated. That quickly changed once they were in the ring, dancing with each other and trying to land their punches. Katie was hit hard with an uppercut to her chin a moment later. It stung her, and the pain did not let up quickly.

She backed off. She would be safe for a moment, and then she could recover for a full attack. Her eyes closed for a moment, and then she looked up at the woman in the suite. Their eyes met.

Katie pressed the attack, channeling her inner mastery of time and fighting prowess. The more she pressed her attack, the stronger she could feel herself becoming. She was moving faster, punching faster, and her attacks now found unblocked areas on her opponent on a regular basis. The tide of the fight had turned in Katie's favor, but it wasn't over yet. Her opponent—who had intimidated her once with her power—now seemed like a desperate cobra trying to keep a larger badger at bay. Katie then found her moment.

Katie felt as if the eagle was in her presence again—like her fights at school—and felt her eyes turn yellow again. She opened them in the middle of the ring as her opponent stood before her. The girl with short brown hair punched, striking her in the stomach twice. Then she shouldered Katie around, trying to get in some more stomach shots, but Katie had purposely allowed all of this to transpire. She shoved her opponent backward and then punched her to the stomach once, and then she pounded her in the forehead as hard as she could. Her opponent quickly crumpled to the mat, and the referee called a halt to the match. There were some modest cheers from the stands. Then she felt the woman with black hair and green eyes watching, and Katie again looked up to find her doing just that.

She had moved to another box once again, but there she was, just watching. Now it was really starting to bother her, but there was nothing Katie could do about it. She couldn't run up into the box or shout at her—all she could do was tentatively return to her seat in the stands and wait for her next event. Once she had retaken her seat, she quickly lost track of the woman and tried to push it from her mind. For fifteen minutes, Katie was able to rest and focus on her wrestling match. Then a stranger sat down next to her and threw off her focus.

The stranger had snuck up on her, and Katie had not yet seen who it was, but when she turned to look, the stranger stopped her and spoke instead. "You know already who I am. Do not look up or over; remain perfectly calm. Settle yourself down and then speak slowly," said the woman.

"Who are you?" Katie asked, knowing the black-haired, green-eyed woman sat beside her.

"My name is Talia, but you know me by a quite different name—Maria Knowles. I wrote those books your brother seems to love so much," Talia explained.

"You say you're Maria, but where's your flowing blonde hair?" Katie asked, still quite perturbed.

"Maria Knowles is a pen name, but I always want you to know me as Talia. And that blonde-haired woman is just an actress I work through—so I can publish my material and keep my job within the spire. She's very good at her job, but one day the world will know me as Talia Knowles, and my husband's name will command the same fame. It won't be such positive fame, but that isn't important right now," Talia told her.

"What *is* important right now?" Katie asked.

"What's important right now is that you follow me out of here and don't ask another question."

"And if I refuse?" Katie replied, still holding back her trust.

"Well, I guess you won't get to meet your eagle then," Talia told her. "Now get up slowly and follow me."

Katie hadn't expected an answer like that, not at all. Her heart began to race, and she couldn't help but slowly get up and follow the woman. While she made her way up the stairs, Katie excitedly held her breath like she had on the train the day before. The two of them made their way up the stairs to the concourse, and then Talia led her down a corridor before taking a left. The two of them walked for a while, passing only a few general visitors, but there were far more men and women in business suits. She had even seen someone wearing the garb of an official representative of Sax.

I can feel you close to me, Katie, she heard in her head. She thought of the eagle of her dreams and visions—it was his voice. *I'm Sovereign. I can't wait to lay my eyes on you.*

Her excitement had peaked. Katie felt giddy while she walked behind Talia. It was not much longer before it was just the two of them walking down a dimly lit, quiet, empty hallway. "We're underground, aren't we?" Katie asked.

"Indeed we are, but that's not where we're going. It won't be long now, so just wait," Talia told her.

The two of them approached a tall brown door on the left and came to a stop. The hallway seemed to continue for a quite a way, and she would have no idea how to get out of there if Talia wanted to lose her. Katie also wondered if she was going to miss her wrestling match. *It doesn't matter now, one way or another. This will be much more consequential to the story of your life,* said Sovereign, reading her thoughts.

Talia held up a key card for the door, and the door unlocked a moment later, emitting a green blink from its sensor. Talia grabbed the handle and opened it. "Follow me." She then disappeared through the doorway.

Come in and see me, encouraged Sovereign.

Katie exhaled and tried to calm herself. She couldn't believe this was real—no one would ever believe her, except maybe her brother. Katie walked into a dark hallway where she couldn't see anything. Darkness consumed her vision, and she stumbled forward. She thought to call out to Talia but decided not to. This was all between her and Sovereign now. *Where are you?* Katie thought.

Forward. Just in front of you. Open your eyes. Katie opened her eyes, and this time she could see the hallway around her. It was a dimly lit, brown, circular chamber with windows looking into an open space inside the chamber. Katie walked up to the windows to look inside. The area inside was several times bigger than the arena within the spire. When she looked up, she could see the sky. It was a sunny day, just turning a little darker through the semi-transparent covering. At the very top, there was a large circular exit.

Then she saw him. Sovereign was perched on a tall pile of boulders that sat over a steep drop. He was just as big and majestic as she imagined. As soon as the bald eagle spotted her, he floated over as close as he could. When he landed, Katie could feel the floor she stood on shake just a little. Her heart began to pound excitedly, and she cautiously stepped all the way up to the window. She placed her hand to it while Sovereign rubbed his forehead on the same spot the other side.

Her eyes turned golden again, and Katie felt as clear and strong as she ever had in her life. *Talia tells me you're quite strong and imposing for a girl of your age. You certainly look so*, Sovereign told her.

Katie smiled, and she saw his vision narrow. He closed his eyes again and rubbed his forehead against the glass once more. Then he retreated a few feet. She still felt strong, even after he left her. *We seem to complement each other in that regard,* she told him. *Is this real?* She felt foolish asking, but she just had to.

As real as yourself, Sovereign answered, looking her in the eyes. When Katie met his gaze with her own, she felt as free and light as ever. She closed her eyes, and in her mind, she could see freedom. She had never been outside of Imperium Aendor in her life—she had only seen pictures and films of other places. Now she could see so many other places and lands, and she only had to think of each one to see it.

Katie thought of Beratile in Reyvula, with its tall, wide structures that formed the city itself, which sat atop an expansive plateau surrounded by steep, sharp mountains below. She thought of Malin Harr, with its gleaming skyscrapers built in accord with the forest of the area which rose half as tall. There was a deep canyon that ran through the center of the city, and there were many bridges that ran across it, but there were also subway tracks that ran down into it. At the bottom of the canyon sat a castle and complex of other buildings, which Katie did not know the purpose of.

We cannot dream of places that we have not been to—at least, not as vividly as this. You can see all this because of our connection, and because it's the way I came to see you from my home within the Shrouded Sea, Sovereign explained.

You live in the Shrouded Sea? Katie replied. She wasn't surprised—he had only confirmed her suspicions. Ethan would be so jealous if he knew for sure what she did now. Katie wasn't going to tell him. That was his own truth to learn, in his own time.

All my life, he confirmed. *I can't wait until the day we'll be together forever, and I can see more of your human world.*

Katie felt saddened at that. *Why can't we be together now? When will we be together?* she asked him.

You will have to continue being strong on your own for quite some time. But a war will soon begin, which will provide us the opportunity to be together, fight together, and bask within each other's strengths. It'll be glorious, Sovereign told her. Her visions ended at that.

Talia suddenly reappeared next to her, seemingly out of nowhere. Katie jumped, fearing someone had caught her somewhere she was obviously not supposed to be. "It's time to go," Talia told her, looking down at her. She was only a few inches taller than Katie, but Katie knew she was still growing.

You've got a wrestling match to win, haven't you? Sovereign asked.

How do you know what wrestling is? How did any of this even happen? Katie asked. She knew this wasn't a dream, but still, she had been expecting to wake up ever since the moment she had first laid eyes on him.

There are old secrets between the Eedon Rath-ni and men, and your friend Talia knows them. She's the only reason this first meeting could happen this way. I just had to see you with my own eyes. Although I always knew of you, Sovereign told her.

Katie wasn't ready for this to be over. "Come, before someone catches us," Talia told her, touching her on the shoulder.

"Just a second," Katie said. She needed one last look that she could remember until she no longer needed to. *Must we fight in the war to be together?* she asked.

The coming war is the only reason we will ever be able to be together. It is our purpose for existence, I promise, he told her.

I will wait to see you again soon then. Goodbye, Sovereign, she told him, and then she turned to go with Talia, back out the way they had arrived.

Goodbye, my rider, he replied anxiously.

Katie turned her back on him and followed Talia back to the arena. Sovereign's voice and his last words to her would stay with her from that moment on. *Goodbye, my rider,* rang in her mind throughout the rest of the day. At the end of her wrestling match—which she won—Katie believed she had only won because she had met her eagle.

The match had not gone well for her at first—much like the boxing match. Each time Katie found herself in a bad position or uncomfortable bind, she would think of Sovereign, and she would find the strength and persistence to persevere.

Chapter 4

Violet (Ethan 2)

CALANOR STRONGHOLD DISTRICT, IMPERIUM AENDOR, IISHREM

SUMMER, 1146, FOURTH AGE

Ethan wasn't particularly nervous about the day ahead, but he had still been particularly anxious about its arrival all the same. Anxious to get it over with. Several miles from his house, he set his eyes on the brick premier school sitting in front of him on a cloudy day at the beginning of summer and walked in. It was time for him to take his Provenance test.

He strolled into the high school and set his path for his typical homeroom. The rest of his classmates were there too—except for those who had accepted their alternative option and chosen not to participate. Capitalism, the House of Lance had branded such an endeavor. It was always something Ethan had thought of, but not something he wanted to trifle with just yet. He wanted to be a graphic artist and paint when he was out on his own, but he didn't feel like he was ready yet. He hoped he would score well on his Provenance test in sections that interested him, and therefore he'd be more likely to receive an offer for an occupation he could enjoy—at least, for a while.

The Provenance test would test his knowledge and passion for everything he had learned in life and from school so far. There would be multiple-choice questions for subjects such as history, math, science, and economics. There would be writing sessions for politics, biology, and extra open space to make a plea for something, in particular, he felt could pay off in the future if given enough time to develop. Artistic people like him who lacked the benefits of families or individuals who had successfully toiled in Capitalism most often tried to make a plea for their artistic abilities that way. Maybe if Ethan explained and portrayed his ideas well enough, he could get a one-year art sabbatical. Artistic sabbaticals weren't handed out often; Ethan just wanted to do as well as he could.

Ethan, of course, had certain expectations though. He loved his creativity and ability to draw, but the quality of content just wasn't good enough for him yet. So, he kept working on his skills. The presentation of his art was just as important as the intent or meaning. The purpose or context of his art was always what he had had the most trouble with. It was still an endeavor that he cherished though, so whether or not his content was any good or particularly artistic, Ethan brought what was in his head into physical form. He would always like his art, even if no one else did.

"Students," said his teacher, Mr. Fintchner, as he entered the classroom from the back.

Conversations between the students had been light, to begin with, so just more than half of them greeted the teacher, himself included. Mr. Fintchner walked past Ethan in his button-up plaid shirt and khaki pants. He walked to the front of the classroom, which had several long and wide windows looking out onto the city and dropped several manila folders down on the desk. Two test officials in black tuxedos walked into the room and up to his desk before he could open either one. One of the guards was a pale-faced man with light brown skin and black hair. The other was a woman in her mid-thirties with wavy orange hair.

The guards inspected the content of the folders—first one, then the other. Once they were satisfied, they allowed Mr. Fintchner to pass out the contents of each folder to the students, one by one, under their direct supervision. One folder contained an answer form, and the other held the Provenance test itself. Once that was done, the guards left the classroom and the test began. Ethan knew he was in for several hours of hard work.

He got to work on answering the first few sections and then hit quite a good stride when he got to the history and politics sections. The geography portion of the test was a breeze too. Once he finished with those portions, Ethan's progress began to slow again, and his mind began to wander as he lost interest in the next few subjects like math and biology. Ethan forced himself to slow down and take a break. It was important to him that he not stress himself out too much or try to finish too quickly.

No one seemed to notice him taking a break from his test, and he took it as a chance to survey the other classmates that he knew— he saw Kiera, and Rich was not too far away from her either. He was still close with Rich, but perhaps not as close as once before. They nodded at each other.

Kiera looked up at him and gave him a piercing glance of indifference. She had grown a lot since his presentation about the Eedon Rath-ni in class several years ago, as had he. After his presentation, Ethan was regularly laughed at, becoming the butt of several jokes for the weeks that followed. He hadn't been particularly popular, to begin with, so that was nothing new, but the ridicule was still hurtful. There were times he cried himself to sleep at night, and his magic never exactly left him. Mostly, now he just channeled it into his anger or into helping him get his chores done. His Maria Knowles books still sat on his bookshelf, but he hadn't opened them in a couple years.

A timer at the front of the classroom began to ring, signaling the end of the first testing session. There would be two more, and then Ethan would be free. He'd probably walk home; hopefully, it wouldn't be raining too hard. "Okay, students. You've got twenty minutes to yourselves to go to the bathroom and grab a snack. Just don't be late; we're starting the break now," said Mr. Fintchner from the front of the room. The two test officials from before re-entered the room and collected everyone's testing materials. They put the materials back into the folders, and once that was done, Ethan could leave with the rest of the students.

Ethan didn't have any plans, in particular, for his few minutes of freedom, but going to the restroom and getting a snack from the vending machines seemed like a good idea. The hallways of the school were pretty silent when Ethan and the rest of the students left the classroom. Breaks were staggered for all testing sessions. Ethan quietly walked himself to the bathroom and took care of his business before making his way to the vending machines down the hall.

He wasn't too sure what he was in the mood for when he got there, but it looked like Rich was trying to make the same decision. His friend was standing there in front of the snack machine with his arms crossed, his palm and fingers to his mouth. Rich hadn't noticed Ethan yet. It had honestly been a while since Ethan had talked to him, but he thought it would be nice. "Hey, buddy, what're you thinking about?" he asked him.

Rich turned to see him and grinned, having recognized his voice from behind. "Ethan," he said. They fist-bumped each other. "Well, what do you think? Chips, chocolate, or maybe steak strips?"

Ethan lightly laughed at Rich's last suggestion, although it certainly hadn't been meant as a joke. There really were dried steak strips sitting at the bottom of the snack machine. "You know anyone who orders those usually gets sick the next day," Ethan replied.

Before Rich could step up to make his selection, Kiera inserted herself in front of him and said, "Oh, were you going to use this?" she asked. "Too slow." She facetiously pouted at him for a second, before she inserted a credit card and made her decision.

Ethan saw Rich's face redden at Kiera's stunt. He opened his mouth to retort, but Ethan put his hand on his friend's shoulder before he could speak. "We're in no hurry," he told her. Ethan tightened his grip on Rich's shoulder as they each took a few steps back, which aligned their level of vision with that of Kiera's round butt in her tight jeans for just a few seconds while she finished making her decision. Rich looked at him and smiled, then nodded. Unfortunately, Kiera was still dating Vyden—as she had been on and off for several years now.

Kiera had selected a chocolate bar with peanuts and another one with caramel. Once both had been dispensed, she turned around with a smile and held out both, one in each hand. It surprised Ethan—he didn't exactly know what she meant by it at first.

Kiera laughed at him. "I got one for both of you to share since you're such close friends. You both could kiss in the middle if you ate it from both ends," she laughed sarcastically.

Ethan was a fan of her banter, but all he could manage at the time was to reach for the chocolate bar and say, "Thank you."

"Really, that's all you've got to say to that? Sheesh, don't fail too hard," she told him with a pat on his shoulder, and then she walked off.

Rich was still standing there next to the vending machine with his soda as she walked off. "That was strange," Rich told him. For just a moment, Ethan felt his eyes turn violet, and then he walked over to the cold walls to lean against them. Rich bought him a cola when they had finally been allowed to use the vending machine completing his snack without him having to pay for anything.

Ethan opened his soda and took a drink. "Now, I just need to figure out how to return the favor and then strike up a conversation."

Rich grinned. "Do you think she'd let me stick my chocolate bar up her cooter?" The two of them burst out laughing.

The two of them spent the last remaining minutes of their break just chatting, before they both decided to head back, making it just in time. They nodded to each other, before returning to their seats. The doors closed behind them, and the second session of the test began after their testing materials were returned to them by the Provenance test officials.

As Ethan got to work on his remaining sessions, he felt his eyes turn violet again. He was currently working his way through science and physics—two subjects he had never been particularly fond of. Suddenly, he began to feel himself hit a stride when answering the questions. It wasn't just that Ethan knew he was answering the questions correctly, but also figuring them out was a breeze. Over the next forty minutes, Ethan knocked out the rest of the test, except for the writing session on politics and the section where he could make a plea, personal case, or leave samples of his creative ability. He decided to leave those for the final session of the test.

While Ethan was hitting his stride, he could tell his eyes remained violet the whole time. It started to bother him a little, and it made him wonder why it was happening. The Calanor Stronghold was a few miles away, and his magic had been so irregular over the past few years. Ethan still made himself take breaks from the test, even while he was hitting his stride.

When he did, Ethan would usually look out the window at the cloudy day. He didn't notice anything in particular, but there was a single black bird on the horizon that looked small enough to be over the school's courtyard, which Ethan could see into five-hundred feet away from the third story. At first, it seemed like any other bird, and Ethan paid it relatively little attention. *You can see me, Ethan, I know it. We'll soon be together,* said a lush, sultry voice in his head.

It had been quite a while since Ethan had heard her voice. Violet's voice. The thought of it worried him, and he had more pressing matters to attend to. The timing was so inconvenient. He ignored her voice in his head and put his eyes back to his test. Ten minutes later, Ethan decided to take another break to look out the window. The single black bird was still the only thing that he noticed on the horizon. This time, the black bird looked bigger and much closer than before. It looked like no other bird that he had ever seen before. In fact, if he were being honest with himself, the bird looked quite a lot like the raven on the cover of his copy of *The Magic of Colored Eyes*—currently, sitting at home on his bookshelf.

You won't be able to ignore me by the end of the day, young Ethan. I'm sorry to tell you this, but that test you're taking might not matter much after today. If only you knew what was going to happen this day, Violet said.

Ethan was beginning to get annoyed now. He would respond to her. *I don't think you're real, and I've got work to do,* Ethan responded. He was convinced that the black bird he saw on the horizon could not really be a raven, and neither could it be Violet. It wouldn't be the first time that he had seen things that weren't really there. His eyes were still violet, after all. Violet didn't bother him for the rest of the test session, and a few minutes later, he was allowed a break again.

Ethan needed a breath of fresh air—and a small toke of Hurinst's plant. Hopefully, it would be all he needed to ignore Violet and finish off the last session of the test. This time, Ethan took himself straight out via the nearest exit. When Ethan got outside, the cool air and light rain of the day were quite refreshing. Thankfully, the first exit had been on the other side of the high school, which looked out towards the Calanor Stronghold and the walls of Imperium Aendor, not towards the Capitol Approach. After a brief search of the gray skies yielded no sign of a large black bird pretending to be a raven, Ethan allowed himself to relax. Then he took a short brown joint out of his pocket and lit it. He took a nice long draw, and then he inhaled it a few seconds later.

Ethan felt the relaxing effects hit his body, perhaps a bit more quickly than usual as he leaned back against the brick façade of the school and closed his eyes.

The same door that Ethan had come out of half a minute ago opened again. "Is that really what I smell?" asked a hypnotic female voice. It was Kiera. Ethan opened his eyes and smiled when he saw Kiera standing in front of him with a playful scowl on her face. "Sure smells like it's Hurinst's plant. Didn't peg you for one that smoked."

This time, Ethan was not so hesitant as to find something witty to say. "I know the trick of it you see. Acrabiniz and a little paper roller for the wand, and fire for the magic," he told her, then he offered her a hit.

Kiera pincered the joint out from between his fingers with the softest touch. For a second, her fingers touched his hand, and he felt that damn spark of magic again. He felt alive again and full of curiosity. She backed away slowly and leaned against the wall with him before taking a hit herself. "What kind of occupation do ya think you'll be offered?" she asked him, clenching her jaw when she finished. She had a father with quite a name to live up to.

"I don't know. Honestly. My parents always said I'd probably be best suited to a life of having a really clean room. I could have created some kind of revolutionary cleaning tool they told me." He looked over at her, and she looked confused.

Ethan cursed himself for ruining the good conversation by following up by saying something as stupid and nonsensical as that. *She didn't take it that badly. Give her a second,* Violet said in his head.

Not this again, not now, Ethan thought. *Can we at least save this until after the last test session?* he asked, attempting to reason with Violet.

She did not respond at first. Ethan still saw no sign of the black bird in the sky, with the school likely obstructing any potential vision. *I suppose there is enough time. I'll find you afterward. We'll meet soon, my rider. And soon you will know why I'm here,* Violet told him.

Finally, Ethan snapped back to the scene and happily found that Kiera was laughing at his joke. There was even a cough here and there in her laugh to go along with the dank smoke. "I didn't get it at first, but then I thought you must be joking," she told him.

Ethan pressed his luck. "I still don't get it," he said, shrugging his shoulders and looking over at her. Ethan watched Kiera look him over, before meeting his gaze with her dark brown eyes. Ethan could have sworn that they were green before. He brushed off the thoughts and returned the same gesture. Kiera had long brown hair and was relatively tall—only a few inches shorter than him. She had quite a nice curvy figure and wasn't too skinny either. "So, what do you think you'll get?"

Kiera showed her palms. "Maybe I'll be an extreme archeologist. Explore old castles, old mines, and the unmapped caverns and catacombs of Dak Soliem. I think that'd be fun," she told him. Kiera took another hit and then offered it back to him.

Ethan took the joint from her fingers and sucked a final puff, before putting it out and then tossing it away. He had a second one for after the test in the side pocket of his cargo shorts. "Thanks for the smoke and the laugh, Ethan," she told him. She blew him a playful kiss and made her way off without looking back. Ethan smiled, and then he jogged back in to finish the final session of his Provenance test.

Chapter 5

The day the World Remembered Magic (Ethan 3)

CALANOR STRONGHOLD DISTRICT, IMPERIUM AENDOR, IISHREM

SUMMER, 1146, FOURTH AGE

*T*he wind and rain had kicked up significantly by the time Ethan was finally free of his Provenance test. When he got outside, Ethan thought about hailing a cab, but then he decided his mood was somehow in sync with the current weather, so Ethan joined his spirit with the weather and took off towards his home as the city hummed with activity.

Kiera had not given him as much as a look before she walked out of the classroom door in front of him. Ethan knew he could talk to Kiera again later, but right now, he just wanted to clear everything else from his mind. For just a moment, Ethan *was* able to clear his mind and look around the city in front of him. Zoning there was mixed industry, business, and residential buildings in typical city blocks with green and open space around him.

The last of the distant voices from the high school continued to fade away until it became indifferent from the harmonic sounds of the city and the citizens around him. A car slouching through rain-soaked streets; a ringing bell sitting above a door waiting to chirp when opened. There were some light construction sounds in the area, but the city seemed peaceful to Ethan, and then he saw her again.

Violet, Ethan thought as he spotted her perched atop a long three-story brick factory that looked like it had been deserted for several years.

None other, she told him, her eyes meeting his directly for the first time.

For a moment, he thought of nothing. His mind was blank while he stood looking up at her.

He could see Violet close her black eyes for just a moment. When they opened again, they had turned violet. Ethan felt his eyes gleaming violet too. She stepped up to the very edge of the building she rested on and bared her full wingspan. From tip to tip, she had a wingspan of about fifty feet, and she was easily forty from beak to talon. When standing fully erect, the top of Violet's head reached almost thirteen feet off the ground.

Violet took flight and crossed over the threshold of the roof and into the air. At the moment she did, Ethan became fully aware of just what was happening. Violet was gliding down towards a ground full of cars, pedestrians, and bustle, in the middle of the afternoon—and yet not one pedestrian or motorist had taken any particular notice of her. *How is this?*

Now, Violet was only a dozen feet from flying right into him. Was she going grab him and carry him off somewhere? Ethan felt his heart pause for just a moment, and he began to bend.

Don't be afraid, my rider. All will be explained soon, she told him. Then Violet suddenly shrank her size to become little larger than a barn owl. The raven landed on his shoulder and gripped him tightly with her talons, stinging him. Ethan was not quite ready for it. He struggled with her at first—her chaotic movements—as if he were trying to bat away a bee. *Settle down, you blasted Draven*, she told him. Violet flexed her wings while on his shoulder to balance herself out, and then she bit him on the earlobe. That searing pain finally caught Ethan's attention, and he calmed down enough to check his ear lobe for signs of bleeding. There were none, and Violet did not bite him again.

Several people had noticed Ethan acting strangely, but now that Ethan had stopped freaking out, they stopped looking at him and resumed their lives as if nothing was amiss. They certainly didn't seem to notice the mythical bird perched on his shoulder. *They can't see me, or they choose not to. Not yet, at least. Soon, they shall see again, but for now, I am hidden from them. In my larger form I would still knock everything over, so this is easier for me.*

Ethan still refused to believe this was happening, so he walked into an alley off the street, where he could get some space to be alone. *This isn't some vision from something I smoked earlier?*

Violet's eyes turned dark-blue, and then Ethan felt something begin to ruffle and furl around in his pocket. The object began to snake its way out and then into the air. It was his second yet-to-be-smoked joint he had planned to have on his walk home! The joint levitated there in front of him, and then it dropped straight into a pool of rain at his feet. *Your petty nonsense with this damn plant will melt your mind, and you'll need your wits about you for what I'm about to show you*, Violet told him. She took flight from his shoulder and ascended several dozen feet into the air above him, while remaining in her smaller form. For just a moment, Ethan thought he heard his name being called from far away, but he wasn't able to catch where it was coming from.

Ethan soon found himself unable to look away from her while she flew slowly in front of him through the air. Violet led him several blocks away from the high school and his home, towards the northeast of Imperium Aendor. *Where are you leading me?* Ethan asked, his legs beginning to tire.

You will soon see, she told him. *You didn't always have so many questions when you used to let me in more easily.*

She was chiding him for his lack of continued faith in what he had always thought he was: magic. Ethan cursed himself, but the revelation didn't stop him from trying to let himself off the hook. *You were never actually there. It was always just me in front of the world, flailing to find you. Now you're here, and I look even more like a fool. When will the world see you?*

Violet looked down at him from the sky, still with those violet eyes. *Are you quite finished?* Her words were like a swift slap to the face, and she squinted her right eye to the side. Apparently, there were much bigger issues than his petty discontent with the situation. *You're only sixteen; you aren't that old yet. You should have kept your faith longer, but, regardless, at least you can see me clearly now.*

Well, where were you for all this time? Ethan asked. Again, Ethan thought he heard his name called—this time by a familiar female's voice that wasn't Violet's. When he looked around again, Ethan still couldn't tell where it had come from.

The raven resumed her flight towards their destination, which was still unbeknownst to him. *Stuck within the Shrouded Sea, never to leave or see the other half of the world. At least, not until the right circumstances came along, which you're about to see. Keep up; there isn't much more time,* she explained.

There was no pushing this out of his mind now, and it was honestly quite a relief now that Ethan knew he *hadn't* in fact been *crazy* to believe in magic and the Eedon Rath-ni all this time. Ethan continued to follow Violet, block by block, until he began to recognize his surroundings. While they made their way there, streams of pedestrians seemed to naturally give Ethan a wide berth, allowing him to walk through without issue. He also never seemed to have to wait for very long at the crossing intersections either. In fact, he hadn't yet come to a complete stop.

By the time Ethan began to recognize the portion of the city they were in, he had been following Violet at an easy jog for probably twenty minutes. He was starting to get a little winded. *How much farther?* Ethan asked.

Not far, Violet told him while she looked back at him from above. *You've heard from me there before. By now you should be able to guess where we're going.*

Ethan had had a strong feeling of suspicion for a while now. *The Calanor Stronghold,* he thought.

Right again, Violet told him levelly.

What is it that I need to see? he asked her.

It's a surprise, she told him. *No more questions. Just follow,* she finished as she flew on. The two of them were only a few blocks from the Calanor Stronghold. The roads and buildings around him were beginning to clear up, so he could see it in front of him, rising a few hundred feet into the air. By the time they reached the parking lots surrounding the ancient fort, Ethan's legs were aching. He saw that the parking lots were completely empty, and the main entrance was closed off. His surroundings were almost completely silent, and there was no one else around but Ethan and Violet. They made their way up to the main gate.

Okay, we're almost there. Get inside, and then I'll meet you all the way at the top on the roof of the observatory, Violet told him.

Um... okay. And how exactly am I supposed to get inside? Ethan asked her. Suddenly, Ethan saw Violet's eyes turn orange and then felt his own mirror hers and lock onto the front gate. He concentrated for a moment, and then the gate mechanisms came to life around him. The gate began to rise and locked into place about twelve feet off the ground. The result still didn't particularly appease Ethan, and this time, he couldn't keep himself from complaining. *How about you turn huge again and come down here and give me a ride up?* he asked spitefully.

Someone would see you, she told him. *Questions would be asked by men you do not want to meet.*

Ethan huffed in exasperation and jogged into the Calanor Stronghold. He had always had a strong sense of direction, and it enabled him to jog through the tunnels and into the fort itself, then up through the planetarium, finally taking the short climb up the ladder, which put him on the roof of the fort itself.

Rain was falling, and the wind had picked up again when Ethan stepped out onto the roof. It was made of stone, like the rest of the fort, and had seemingly been left alone, for the most part. There was a railing for those who were allowed up here for work or for tourism, along with several sets of mounted binoculars for gazing out toward the horizon. Once Ethan had caught his breath, he looked out across the stone roof and could see Violet once again at her full size. Seeing her up close was something else entirely.

Can all the Eedon Rath-ni change sizes like you? Ethan asked.

Only we ravens can change size. You know about hawks, dragons, and eagles already I understand, Violet told him. She had turned around to do so, and she finished her thought by pointing a wing at him and gesturing for him to come over to the edge with her.

Ethan tried to relax, so he could walk over to the edge without feeling like he might tumble over it. Slowly, Ethan approached the railing and gently leaned upon it. As he looked over the edge of the fort, Ethan felt more magical than he ever had before. Even though the weather was abysmal, he felt perfectly at peace, and he could see for miles. *You can feel it in you can't you, Ethan? We're two parts of one whole, you see. You a magical Draven, and I a raven of the Eedon Rath-ni; we were made for each other. And this world must remember what people like us can do. For the truth of our power has slumbered for a thousand years too long. It is time for the world to remember again, and now you will see.*

"Ethan, is that a raven? Don't make eye contact!" Kiera's voice exclaimed from behind him. It must have been Kiera calling his name before. Ethan looked back at her and called her over to his side.

"Kiera, it's okay, I promise. She's friendly," Ethan told her. *She's a friend,* Ethan thought to Violet in his head. *How come she can see you now? Can everyone see you now?*

Ethan, Violet scolded him in an annoyed tone. *You're about to miss the great big reveal!*

Ethan turned away from Kiera and looked out across the city towards the Capitol Approach, where what he saw left him both terrified and awestruck. First, Ethan heard a screech pierce the sky and city around him from far away—by the Capitol Spire. It was the screech of an eagle—a golden eagle. Ethan saw the bird swooping towards the ground from high above. For just a moment, the comfort of Kiera's arm around his shoulder and head close to his heart pulled his eyes away from the Capitol Approach. Her touch gave him a modicum of solace on the inside, and then it was gone in an instant when he heard a monotonous growl, again from the direction of the Capitol.

Again, Ethan turned his vision toward the spire. Kiera left him to go and use one of the sets of mounted binoculars. A menacing green dragon rose into the air to meet the eagle at a lumbering rate. More sounds came onto the scene of the fight, and a loud alarm began to toll over the city as the screams of the Eedon Rath-ni locked in a duel and shocked pedestrians witnessing the spectacle sounded around them. The scene resonated in a cacophony of pain, which would keep Ethan's gaze locked on the fight and nowhere else.

He jogged over to Kiera, took her hand, and watched the green dragon lumber up into the air to meet the eagle. Ethan noticed the eagle was much more agile than he had originally expected; the dragon also seemed to be much less enthusiastic about the fight now. *The dragon is Karthon, and the eagle is Anacarin,* Violet explained.

Anacarin, the eagle, began to circle around Karthon at quite the rate, pecking at the dragon's skin with her beak and ripping at its chest with her talons, repeatedly. In the meantime, Karthon flailed upwardly in a reeling fashion, trying to grab the eagle or burn it with fire but had little success.

He began to think about his copies of Maria Knowles' books, which were still sitting in his room at home. *Eagle Rider book 1: Legend of the Bald Crown,* in particular. The fight he was watching looked just like the cover. Just then Ethan heard Karthon growl and roar, while Anacarin squeezed his large chest with one set of her talons, before ripping it open a second later, spilling out the dragon's blood and guts. Grasping the dragon's monstrous black heart in its talon, the eagle began to recoil and retreat. The life of the dragon did not leave its falling corpse particularly quickly; he began to spew fire in every direction. *Can you see it, Ethan?* Violet asked him. *The dragon is done for, and here comes the emperor out of the tower. I just know it.*

Crackling gunfire rang out over the sounds of the duel, and Ethan quickly saw several windows up upon the Capitol Spire begin to shatter and break from inside. *Okay, you really need to see this as well as you possibly can, Ethan. Look through my eyes. This is but a taste of the capabilities we'll have when we're trained and together all of the time.*

While Ethan watched through the eyes of Violet, he could see everything in greater detail—as if he were only a few dozen feet away. That was when Ethan could see the emperor of Iishrem, Sax Drugren the 12th, pushed up to the edge of the open window by a man who was shrouded in shadow beyond the veil. Sax Drugren put his hands up and said something. He did not look like he was bargaining for his life, but there was weight to his words, and they had quite an effect on the man who received them. A moment later, Sax Drugren the 12th was shoved out of the tower and cast into the open air from the tallest story of the Capitol Spire. Ethan watched the emperor flail while falling, tumbling repeatedly.

Sax Drugren the 12th Emperor of Iishrem plunged into the smoke and fire of his own dragon's dying breath, as it had already hit the ground, and then disappeared out of all sight into the gaping cavity where the dragon's heart had once been, which was a bloody, burning, smoldering mess. Then from far off, in the direction of the Capitol Approach, Ethan could hear a cacophony of screams. Kiera turned to him now and lingered closely. As she gently leaned against his shoulder, Ethan felt the warmness of her heart on his, and he listened to them share a heartbeat together. It was a spark.

"What is happening?" she asked him.

Ethan was at a complete loss for words. When nothing came to mind, he decided silence was better and leaned in closer to Kiera. He did have thoughts though. *Why is this happening? How can this be real?*

Stop doubting yourself, Ethan. You're meant for more than just a normal life, Violet told him. Ethan felt cursed for what he had just watched transpire. Sirens were ringing menacingly all over the city, and Ethan could finally hear both helicopters and warplanes firing up. He gave the eagle, which now had a rider on its back, the man who had pushed the emperor out of the window, one last look. They were already headed off toward the horizon. *Your government and society have lied to you for your whole life, Ethan, and one day they will come for you. You must not let them find you until we can escape together. His name was Christian, and you can thank him and Maria Knowles for having had the opportunity to meet me. None of this would have never happened any other way,* Violet told him. Ethan closed his eyes, and for just a moment, there was silence and peace, but then it popped like a bubble.

You're going, aren't you? Ethan said sadly. *You didn't come so we could be together yet, you just came to prove your existence. What're you doing with me?*

This war will be unavoidable to you, Ethan. You have to fight, or you will die, and you must fight for the right side, Violet finished, and then she gave Ethan one last look before her eyes turned back to black. Ethan's returned to blue. *I must go now, Ethan. Keep yourself safe and await my return. Our time will come in this war,* Violet told him, and then she flew off toward the horizon.

For seemingly the longest time after Violet was gone from sight, Ethan and Kiera just stood on the roof, wondering what to do next.

When Ethan felt it was time to go, he gently stepped back from her then just took her hand. "What do we do now?" she asked him while looking around at the aftermath.

Ethan wanted to kiss her right then and there. He leaned in close to her and looked into her eyes and waited. Kiera edged just a little bit closer meeting his eyes, and then Ethan felt himself close his eyes and lean in the rest of the way for the kiss. She kissed him back, after a moment. A few seconds later, Ethan smiled and confidently said, "Let's get back to our homes, and then we'll just go from there."

The two of them climbed back down through the tower and exited via the main gate a few minutes later. They exchanged very few words, only glances and an occasional touch. When they eventually descended the hill and reached the parking lots, Ethan found himself wanting to hail that cab now, but he was unable to do so with the chaos of the day's events. It took the two of them another forty-five minutes to make the short walk from the Calanor Stronghold back to Kiera's townhome, which was only another mile from Ethan's house. Ethan wondered if his legs were going to fall off by the end of the night.

"I never should have made fun of you with Vyden that day in class long ago, or all those other times," Kiera told him.

Ethan wanted her to stop. "You never needed to say sorry," he told her with a smile. She gave him a kiss on the cheek and ran inside.

Chapter 6

A Viewing of a Bombing (katie 3)

A week and a half after the world had its perception of reality shaken to its core, Katie found herself waiting in a long line behind thousands of her fellow Iishremites. She and her family had been invited to a closed-casket wake for Sax Drugren, the 12th Emperor of Iishrem. For a moment, Katie felt her hair—which was pulled back and braided into a thick ponytail—blow to the side. Normally, Katie only had to wear her hair like that during her fights, and she certainly hoped she wouldn't experience any fighting today.

Her mother turned around to check on her from in front of her in the line. She nodded, and they said nothing. Ethan stood behind their father, and that completed their ordering while they waited. The line slowly moved forward, and then it came to a stop yet again. Katie groaned out loud, which made her head hurt, earning her another glance from her mother. The four of them were still not within sight of where they were going. With everything else that had gone on in the last few days, and the blistering heat of the day, it was all starting to frustrate Katie. It bothered her even more that she couldn't complain about it without giving herself a headache.

While Katie had nothing else better to do, she thought about everything else that had happened and what she had been through over the past week and a half. The successful assassination of Sax Drugren the 12th had been executed by a man now known to all Iishrem as Christian Knowles. There wasn't much else to know about the man himself— that the House of Lance was willing to share with the public, at least. There were pictures of him all over the place, on every street corner. Yet, there were even more images and videos of the assassination and duel between opposing Eedon Rath-ni circulating the most significant Iishrem news websites.

It was anyone's best guess how exactly he had done what he had, but on another note, Katie knew orders for Maria Knowles past books were flying in. She had also announced an upcoming new book entitled A Court of Fire and Embers, which she said was inspired by the older histories of the House of Lance throughout the 2nd and 3rd centuries of the Fourth Age. After the successful assassination of Sax Drugren, a plethora of varying events shook through Imperium Aendor and rippled across Iishrem as a whole.

By the next morning, martial law had been declared through-out every corner of Imperium Aendor, and other similar policies had been enacted throughout the other major cities and populated regions within Iishrem. However, such a declaration had been largely ineffective at stemming the tide of civil unrest—which had by now included riots, protesting, looting, and a rash of other politically motivated assassination attempts, with a few even prov-ing to be successful.

Currently, standing far back in a line that seemed too lethargic to move in any direction, Katie had an opportunity to purvey some of the damage. For the first few days, the military, government, and police presence throughout Imperium Aendor was sluggish and disorganized. So far today, Katie had seen several burnt-out or looted businesses. This was the religious section of Imperium Aendor. With several damaged businesses and a modest amount of debris still waiting to be cleaned up, the district had seen its portion of civil unrest, but Katie had seen many districts in worse condition on her way there that morning. The line began to move forward again. When Katie and her family finally rounded a street corner, it was a relief to her that she could finally see the Cathedral of Imperium Aendor.

The cityscape of Imperium Aendor perforated outwards around the cathedral so that it's base and structure could be seen by all who approached. As far as the cathedral itself, only its base was largely visible from the surface. It stood in the center of the district surrounded by tall buildings on all sides which jockeyed for position so its occupants could look down. The National Cathedral of Imperium Aendor—or Nat-ree Veil-as—was no ordinary cathedral, originally constructed for all Iishrem, at the order of Eifren Venuli, the 2nd Emperor of Iishrem. Instead of its 5 spires rising into the air, they descended into a dome-shaped pit in which the cathedral stood. It was also supported by several thick beams across the open sections of the pit it stood in the center of.

Several lines of mourners were approaching Nat-ree Veil-as from various directions, and hers moved forward yet again. She noticed a formal clothing shop to her side. For a moment, she turned and admired herself in a dark window of the closed shop. She wore a mid-cut black dress with a downward slant and short shoulder sleeves. She stared at herself for a moment and then playfully smiled at her reflection. She thought she looked posh, refined, and like she could kick some ass if given the opportunity. The dress even accentuated her features to shapes and sizes she liked even more than she had before, and she had always been confident.

"Katie!" her mother snapped at her, catching her in her moment of self-attraction. That was embarrassing. The line had begun to move again, and she was getting left behind. Katie stumbled forward, still mastering learning to walk in heels. She wondered how Ethan would do with them.

Finally, the pace of Katie's day seemed to speed up around her. While the line began to move forward at a walking rate, the bells of the cathedral began to toll, which caused the ground to shake. One viewing must have just finished letting out, and Katie knew it would be their turn next.

She began to hear sounds that made her uncomfortable. Sounds which she had become all too familiar with over the last week and a half. Helicopters were chopping through the sky, and troops on the ground held everyone in line while they uncomfortably milled about. To Katie's delight, she could no longer smell the putrid smell of rotting flesh that the dragon had exhumed over Imperium Aendor for several days after the assassination.

Yet Katie now found herself rapidly approaching the entrance to Nat-ree Veil-as. "Keep it moving, citizens. Keep up," said a portly army commander wearing a beret and sporting a thick brown handlebar mustache. "Don't fall behind your family or other group members."

Their party followed a line up to the railing of the pit, where Katie was afforded the chance to look down upon the inverted cathedral. Its exterior was brownstone with dozens of red gemstones sitting on its exterior like pores on her face. Katie looked down into the pit, which was well-lit by the light of the sun that broke over it on a hot summer's day. She could also make out the lights that kept it lit throughout the night. Its five inverted spires descended into the reinforced earthen pit in elongated cones to varying depths. The four corner spires descended two hundred and fifty feet, but the one in the center descended to a staggering four hundred and fifty feet and had a tunnel which connected it to the base itself, underneath which Katie had heard were the archives. Its exterior had many cut-out crags and carved depictions of past emperors, patron saints of the church, or well-known angels and demons. Her father turned around to face each of them while he moved forward toward the cathedral. "We've both meant to bring you each here at some point, and here we are. I just wish it weren't under these circumstances," Carth told them.

"It's really quite beautiful inside," Marleigh admitted. "I mean, it should be, I guess. My words aren't going to do it justice is what I am trying to say."

For a moment, Katie listened for Sovereign in her mind, but there was nothing there. When they were only a block away from the cathedral entrance, Katie began to excitedly study her surroundings for the first time. Nat-ree Veil-as was enterable at the center of a circle, which had four crossing access bridges with brick-paved roads. Of course, the road had been closed and was lined with police and dozens of government agents.

Around the circle, there were shops, cafes, and other religious offices that the cathedral used. Above those were apartments, where Katie knew many of the pontiffs and priests resided. There were also ludicrously baroque fountains all over the circle. The last thing Katie noticed before going inside the cathedral was the Boar.

The Boar was a specially modified armored van for the emperor and his family to ride around in from place to place throughout Imperium Aendor. Members of the royal family were here now, and Katie was going to see them, again.

Step by step, Katie and her family began to walk across a bridge, which crossed over the molded, reinforced, earthen pit and connected the entrance to the cathedral to the rest of the city. The four pathways descended gradually about one-fifth of the entire structure into the dome itself, where the church of the cathedral resided. When they crossed over the threshold of open air and the pit, Katie could feel the air grow stale. She looked down into the pit and noticed the way it was structured out of the ground. There were visible beams like stone and mortar made roots that descended into the earth in a warped fashion. When they approached the doors, the four of them had to pass through a security checkpoint first. Once that was done, Katie's world grew darker and cooler as she entered the cathedral for the first time. Her surroundings became quieter, and voices reverberated off the walls. Meanwhile, the sounds of warplanes and helicopters, which had been so loud just before, dampened almost to silence.

The inside of the cathedral was beautiful. The floors were ornately painted, as well as the thick columns 25 feet in circumference which descended into the spires and supported the entire structure. It was grandly lit with many chandeliers and candles, and there were many stained-glass windows on the outer walls. Katie and her family followed their line to the path that cut through the center of the nave and approached the altar, with many wooden pews on either side. Beyond that, for just a second, Katie felt her eyes turn yellow, and she felt stronger. Katie began to hear conversations shared between people from farther away, above the ones closer to herself.

"Oh my, that's Tagros and Lance the 13th. They're right there," said Marleigh. She didn't seem to believe that they were really seeing both the future emperor and the second most powerful man in the house of Lance at a viewing for the previous one. Carth just shook his head. He was not quite as star-struck as his wife.

Katie followed her mother's gaze while they continued to stand in line. The casket of Sax Drugren sat in the center of the altar, at the front of the head of the altar. When approaching the altar, the inside of the cathedral became a little brighter as those who were on its railing could look down into the central spire. It looked as intricately carved as the rest of the cathedral was elegant. Tagros and Lance the 13th were both standing together to the left of the casket. Two guards stood on either side, and Katie honestly thought they looked more intimidating than either Lance or Tagros. For a moment, Katie watched the two of them talk amongst themselves, while several citizens said their goodbyes to the twelfth emperor before bowing or curtsying and moving on with their day.

"Where do we think he is?" Lance asked Tagros.

Tagros held an electronic tablet in his hands while he manipulated it with his fingers. He didn't seem to be paying much attention to the viewing itself—or any citizens who may have wanted to speak. Katie figured that most people probably would rather talk to Lance instead—if any of them were going to be so bold as to talk to either one. "We have some good leads, but the worst of the damage is done. We'll find him and bring him to justice, but we might have bigger problems than just Christian Knowles," Tagros replied.

Lance's eyebrows narrowed at that; Katie could tell he was quite angry. "Problems like what?" asked Lance.

"There haven't been any condolences sent over from any of the leaders of the four United Nations of Allirehem. There might be something to that. They could be holding something back, or even worse, they could be trying to cover something up," said Tagros.

"Well, what would they be hiding?" asked Lance.

"I'm not sure yet," admitted Tagros.

"Katie, what're you doing? Keep up," her father said from the front. She felt herself flush and took a quick pace so she could catch up with the rest of her family.

"What is it you think you're doing?" Ethan asked her when she was close enough to hear.

"Listening," she told him. Katie didn't need to explain herself to him. "Turn around; magic pants." Ethan flushed his eyes and turned away from her. The two of them had been quite testy with each other since the assassination.

The line began to move again, and Katie stepped even closer to hopefully having this whole ordeal behind her, though somehow, she sensed that everything was just beginning. While she continued to move forward, she tried to keep her mind distracted at the thought of being so close to two of the most powerful men in Iishrem. Of course, that was when her parents began explaining the proper etiquette and protocol for being in the presence of two such individuals.

"It's very important that you act properly when you're around Tagros and Lance, kids," Carth began, sounding meek.

"Make sure your posture is good and relaxed. It's important to be calm; they're human beings just like us," Marleigh told them.

"So, you mean to tell me they aren't just Eedon Rath-ni in disguise?" Ethan asked.

Katie let herself laugh sarcastically loudly enough that Ethan would hear her, but quietly enough that it wouldn't draw any attention to them. Neither one of her parents laughed, and both grimaced at each other before scowling at their children. "Don't make any more jokes," Carth told them.

"We probably didn't need that explained to us," Katie told her father.

"Just be respectful and keep quiet," said Carth, seeming resigned.

"Don't look at them in the eyes, and then take a quick bow, Ethan. Katie, you curtsy," Marleigh told them. "Also, don't touch the casket. Just look at it and then look down and say a prayer. It's easy."

"How much more wrong could it go?" Katie asked. Carth and Marleigh looked at each other tentatively again, but there was no chance to answer her right then because they were so close.

By then, the four of them had reached the altar. Katie guessed that they were now only about fifty people back from the casket. When Katie turned to her left to continue following the line, she saw a projector playing the news at the back of the choir wing. She turned away from the news but then continued to listen just in case. Instead of hearing the TV, Katie began to hear the conversation Tagros and Lance shared again.

"Phoenix ashes. Here comes the newest statements from the other heirs," Lance told his uncle with contempt.

"Iel-shland?" Tagros asked, looking up from his tablet again.

"I've told him where I'd like him to remain, yet he insists on coming out to visit me? Do you think he means to challenge me?" Lance asked Tagros.

"My lord, such a thing hasn't happened in Iishrem in over seven hundred years. The House of Lance does not fight wars haphazardly against itself, but there are always rifts and rivalries," Tagros told Lance.

"This would happen now though. My father *would* just spitefully spurn the rest of his children and then get assassinated by someone he had trained and entrusted to protect him. His sloppy, dirty politics brought him down when time wouldn't else do the job itself. Killing Christian's parents was the last straw," Lance explained.

"You mustn't burden yourself as if you were responsible. Stick with me, my future emperor, and we'll see the House of Lance and Iishrem come through this stronger than ever. This is why your father brought the Aleium branch back into the forefront with a marriage. I can give you truth and stability. Now we only need the patience and time to find it," Tagros admitted.

"I suppose it would be foolish to do something rash and let the situation get any worse. It's just—" Lance paused. For just a moment, Katie saw his eyes glow yellow like hers did. Yellow like her eyes currently were.

"What is it?" Tagros asked. Katie looked away quickly and tried to look normal. Out of nowhere, her head began to ring. Her heart raced, and she thought of Sovereign once more. Again, Katie didn't hear anything from him in her mind.

"I sense other Dravens here. They're close, and they know they are too," Katie heard Lance say.

Goosebumps began creeping up her back, and she felt like there was someone behind her, *watching*. Katie looked up at her father in front of her and then behind to Ethan and her mother. Each of them seemed to be perfectly fine. "There may be several. But do you want to make a huge scene just so you can find them now?" Tagros responded.

Lance took a moment to think about such an option, and then he decided against it. "I suppose not. How much longer do we have to be here? Can't we just have several of your lackey's here to manage this?" Lance asked his uncle.

"Just through this last viewing, Nephew. Then we're finished."

"I trust you," Lance admitted. Katie intentionally stopped listening after that, and the ringing in her head seemed to alleviate itself. Katie and her family were only five people from the casket. She could hear the news playing in the background, but she did not care to watch or listen. When it was Katie's turn to approach the casket, she didn't quite know what to do so, she just stood there and looked at it for several seconds.

From behind, her mother tugged on her dress sleeve and then folded her hands and put her head down, like she was praying. Katie felt herself huff—quietly exasperated—but she refused her urge to show any disrespect. *Okay, fine*, she thought. Katie folded her hands, put her head down, and then closed her eyes. Darkness covered her vision, and for a second, no thoughts filled her mind. Then she saw him.

Katie could see Sovereign and the surroundings of where he was in her mind. He was perched on a thick, strong branch, halfway up a tree. His perch was high in the air, near the bottom of a steep mountain range which extended far beyond him on his right, and on his left, Katie could see cliffs with beaches below. *Sovereign*, Katie thought in her mind. Suddenly, Sovereign looked straight at her and did not say a thing. *Where are you?*

I'm sorry, my rider, but that isn't for you to know just yet. Don't worry; you're about to find out. You may not hear from me for a while but keep yourself safe. We'll be together one day, Sovereign told her.

The two of them shared one last look, and then Katie felt herself being pulled back to the scene at hand. Katie opened her eyes and saw a multitude of different reactions to what was now being played over the Iishrem National Broadcast System. Before she could watch or listen to it in any great detail, Marleigh was grabbing her by the arms and shaking her to attention while she stood in front of her, just beyond the casket. "Katie, come with me!" Marleigh yelled with all the stern authority of a mother.

Katie did not resist. The two of them weaved their way through other citizens and government officials who were watching the broadcast system to an empty pew, where they could be together with Carth and Ethan. Once all of them were *safe*, Katie could refocus on the broadcast.

The broadcast had gone from one of Sax Drugren's many sons droning on about strength and unity, to Christian standing on the precipice of some megalithic superstructure which Katie had never seen before. His eagle was several steps higher behind him, and it had its wings unfurled around him with an intimidating gaze. Ethan's reaction to the broadcast told a different story—he seemed to know exactly what he was looking at. "He's in Nahirehem, and that's the derelict Council of Nations and Dravens behind him," Ethan explained.

"I had hoped that no one thought me dead when I murdered Sax Drugren the 12th last week. Then I figured maybe I should introduce myself to each of you more formally," Christian said on the broadcast. "I'm Christian Knowles, and it's time for the world to know me better." He paused for a moment, and Katie took it as a chance to look around and study Christian's surroundings more. Tagros and Lance were already nowhere to be seen, and Katie saw far fewer government agents in the cathedral now than there had been moments before.

"Last week, *I* murdered your emperor to show Iishrem and the world the truth. It's time for the world to know of magic and the Eedon Rath-ni again. Since the beginning of this age, the House of Lance has sought to repress the knowledge of magic throughout the world and keep the Eedon Rath-ni contained to their homes in the Shrouded Sea, where none would ever know of them. Citizens of Iishrem, your government has lied to you all your lives, and when this is over, I'm sure they'll lie about me as well. For now, know this. There will be Dravens among you, and your Eedon Rath-ni will soon come to find you when the time is right. If that happens, you must not be afraid to fight, for a war is coming that will determine the fate of Rehem and those who live on it," said Christian before taking a moment to pause.

"You will all have to find something to fight for. Fight for your family, fight for your lives, fight for your freedom, or fight for glory and riches. The House of Lance murdered my parents, executing them for some imagined crimes. If you think you might be a Draven and they find you, what *could* they do to you? What side will you stand on? What will you fight for?" Christian continued.

"To anyone who may think they're a Draven, come forward and fight with me. I can promise you a safe place to master your unique skills and abilities, so that you may survive this war that has been over a thousand years in the making. To the House of Lance, I say, come and find me. I'll be somewhere on the other side of the world. Oh, but the rest of Allirehem will stand in your way." Christian finished there, and the House of Lance regained control over their National Broadcast System so they could cover what was happening in Nahirehem.

A large fleet of naval battlecruisers and destroyers were sailing into the harbor of Nahirehem. Citizens of the vibrant, beautiful old-world city which seemed to rise right out of the sea in stone and glass, and stood before sharp mountains and tall trees, were in a full-scale effort to find shelter. Hundreds of thousands of citizens were trying to find their ways underground any way they could, but there were too many of them, and all the people were too late. Katie could see the most people were clamoring to be let into the Council. It looked full to the brim of people. Then the fleet of ships began to fire upon the city, and at the Council of Nations and Dravens in particular. The bombing of Nahirehem did not end quickly.

Chapter 7

The Girl who Could not Seem to Fall (Bailey 1)

Bailey knew the feeling of falling quite well by the time she was twelve years old. It was normally a wonderful feeling—when she planned it. When Bailey didn't plan it, however, the feeling of falling—or in this case stumbling—was very different. It was a good test of her reflexes when she hit a bump in the trail while riding through the forest on her dirt bike. Bailey first knew she had slid into the bump, by the sound her dirt bike made.

The feeling of unintended falling snapped her out of her cruising and back to attention. Quickly, her vision seemed to improve its focus, so she could see each aspect of the trail much better. Goosebumps and that rush of sudden adrenaline from falling kicked in all at once, and her reactions came effortlessly while Bailey fought to stabilize her balance on the dirt bike.

When the back tire of her bike slipped into the rut, Bailey felt every inch of air between her hands on the handlebars and the bottom lip of the front tire while it was in the air. Rather than letting the bike come back down to the trail naturally, Bailey pulled back on the handlebars and jumped the bike out of the rut and over a branch sitting in the path. A few seconds later, Bailey landed back on the trail and slowed down so that she could catch her breath. She was on her way to a park where she could see the edges of the Shrouded Sea, and she was almost there.

The dirt bike quieted down as Bailey decreased in speed and came around the final bend in the trail. The trail ended and opened to a park at the top of the world, on the cusp of the Shrouded Sea. Bailey motored her way over to the double-wide bike-rack and locked her dirt bike to it.

The world was more peaceful after she'd shut it down. She smiled and looked around before grabbing her backpack and heading over towards the cliffs. The park was completely hers this early in the morning. There were several cars parked in the lot and another bike at the rack, but the gazebo, charcoal grills, and benches were all still empty—so everyone else was off hiking? Bailey pulled back the last of her bangs—which she kept in two thick strands—and tucked them into the rest of her dirty blonde hair, which she pulled back into a sinewy pony-tail that ended just below the nape of her neck.

She leaned against the wooden fence that kept visitors from falling and took a long breath of fresh air. She closed her eyes and listened for a moment. The wind swept through her hair and loose fall clothing, and the waves crashed on the rocks below at the bottom of the cliffs. When Bailey opened her eyes, she studied the Shrouded Sea for the first time in months. Seemingly, nothing had changed.

Bailey looked out over the northern edges of the Eldic Ocean and saw nothing but roiling tides and a few small ships passing here and there. When she looked as far as she could see, Bailey saw the very beginning of the Shrouded Sea. Thick and intimidating clouds covered every inch of the northward horizon, and they rose from sea level to varying heights. Bailey wondered if the clouds covered the entire Shrouded Sea or if there were areas where they were less dense, but she expected never to find out.

Bailey had to admit, though, that her chances of seeing the other side of the world one day had gone from non-existent to unlikely over the last few weeks. When Bailey had first learned of the news from Iishrem and the return of the Eedon Rath-ni, she hadn't been totally surprised—unlike Iishrem. She thought about the images of the Eedon Rath-ni—and their riders now publicly known as Dravens—that she had seen. While the Iishrem government had done a solid job of scouring their own websites for all of the images and videos of the assassination that they could take down, they had had much less success doing the same with the Allirehem and other regional interwebs around the world.

There was still several feet of open space before the cliffs after the fence, and she wanted to have her feet hanging over the edge, so she bent herself between the bottom and top rail of the simple wooden fence and slid the rest of her thin body through it, before sitting down at the edge of the cliff—once she was sure it would not erode under her weight. Then she paused and thought. She had seen her fair share of images and videos of the assassination since it happened in mid-summer. A man of shrouded background named Christian Knowles was now the center of the world's attention, and everyone knew of his eagle, Anacarin. When Bailey had initially first learned of it, she had been working a part-time job.

She had to grow up quickly, once her mother passed away after her 'apparent' climbing accident. Bailey was perfectly aware of the intended purpose of her hometown of Seems by the time she heard the news from Iishrem. A secluded, well-off, politically protected, and neutral city-state between Iishrem and Allirehem at the top of the world, Seems was quite an attractive getaway spot for those who could afford it, and it catered to many diverse tastes. At the very moment Bailey found out, she had been helping manage the check-in desk at one of the most expensive resorts in town.

A rich petrol baron, who claimed to be from Dar'hi Rehem, was checking in with an obvious trophy wife—perhaps one of several based on the customs of Dar'hi Rehem—and two sons. "We ought to be safe here, my dear," he had told his wife with plump curves who seemingly staggered to stand in place, with her legs close together and her hands holding her small purse in front of her breasts. "Are you boys excited to go snowboarding?"

One of the sons had scowled and looked up at his apparent father. "Is it anything like dune surfing?" he had asked.

"Somewhat," the petrol baron had replied.

"What if I wanted to see one of the Eedon Rath-ni? A dragon would make me feel so rich," the mistress pouted.

"Mhmm, well you should have found another baron to cozy up to. I don't want to be around any Eedon Rath-ni that could chomp me to bits," he had replied.

"The Eedon Rath-ni are back?!" Bailey remembered she had exclaimed.

Once she had finally gotten the affluent family from Dar'hi Rehem to their suite on the third floor, Bailey had run straight back to the lobby, grabbed several local and regional newspapers, and then jogged over to her favorite café to sit down and take it all in over some tea. In the wake of the assassination, all of the resorts in town were entirely booked for months, packed with affluent capitalists from all over the world, all looking to stay as far away from the coming war as they could while enjoying their time as they did so. Bailey put the memory out her mind and returned her vision to the crashing waves below the shrouded clouds far north of her.

The reason Bailey hadn't been surprised when the Eedon Rath-ni returned, was because Bailey didn't have to keep her faith in the stories of their legends for very long—the existence of the Eedon Rath-ni and the Dravens had quickly become a reality for her. Other people she knew had been less willing to believe at first, but none of them could argue with the video evidence for very long. She hoped to see one soon and even hoped she herself would be a Draven one day.

You will *be a Draven one day*, said a voice in her head. *We'll make our mark on this world when it is our time.*

Bailey felt herself smile on the inside when she heard that voice in her head for the first time. It was the first time she could distinctly remember hearing his voice in her mind, but it still sounded quite familiar. It was like a voice from a dream she could only remember half of. By then the sound of *his* voice was all she had left of it, but she knew his name too—Hector.

I can see you, Hector told her. Bailey did not want to believe that she was a Draven until she could see and ride her Eedon Rath-ni for the first time. Hector, if he were real, could sense her thoughts. *I'm sorry that you won't believe in me until you can see me, but if you look at the skies now, you might just catch a glimpse.*

Bailey looked high into the sky, to the top of the clouds that she could see. It looked just the same as it had been before, but then she saw him between flying between two thin clouds on the edge of the Shrouded Sea. For just a moment, Bailey could see a flash of brown feathers with a white underbelly checkered with brown spots. She could see a large yellow beak, and a head of brown feathers all in the shape of a hawk. Bailey lost sight of him quickly and did not hear anything more from Hector.

When the sun was a little higher in the sky, Bailey knew it was time for her to head home. One more time, she closed her eyes and let the fresh salt air fill her lungs. She smiled when she opened her eyes again, and then she gathered her belongings. After that, she returned to the bike rack to unlock her dirt bike. She sat on the bike and kicked it into gear with her foot before feeling it quake between her legs. Bailey revved the engine twice before she let it go and felt the bike surge forward. She leaned in closer to the handlebars and smiled as she felt the wind blow through her hair.

Before Bailey had gotten her dirt bike for her 10th birthday, visiting the Shrouded Sea lookout had required her father to drive her. Her visits to the lookout had become much more regular after her 10th birthday, especially since it was only thirty minutes away on her bike. For just a second, Bailey looked down directly at her front tire, and she watched it quickly move dirt out of the way. She knew it would continue to move forward at different angles over varying terrain if Bailey kept her balance. It was a nice gift from her father, but it didn't make up for the fact that he was constantly absent with work.

Her father always apologized about it when he *was* around, but somehow it just didn't even out. Mildra, her grandmother on her father's side, was around often, and they had a close relationship, but that didn't mean she particularly liked her. It all made her even more reliant on her friends—of which she had several. Clancy was in the area today, but she had no idea what he would be doing or if he would even be home.

When Bailey was about two miles from her house, she jumped her dirt bike off the forest trail she had been following home and onto the road which would take her to her driveway. The road was empty, and there was no one else around. Bailey and her father lived in a cabin far outside of town. Suddenly, her engine began to sputter, and the bike began to slow down. *Blast,* she thought. Occasionally, Bailey had to walk the last mile or two. It wasn't so bad. The gas tank on her dirt bike usually stored just enough fuel to make it to the lookout and back, but Bailey guessed that she hadn't quite filled it up today.

She came to a stop, stepped off her dirt bike, and walked it over to the other side of the road. The road in front of her was straight in both directions, providing long lines of sight. Not too far in front of her, she could already see the parting in the line of trees where she knew her driveway was. Then she saw a man with short brown hair come out of the woods in front of her, not too far from where her driveway began, followed by two enormous eagles in the air above him. One of them was a brown eagle, the other golden.

The eagles kept their eyes on the path in front of the man and did not seem to notice her. The man walked at a casual pace, and Bailey could see he carried a hexagon-shaped cylindrical black-clad suitcase at his side, which contained something she could not see. Before Bailey could process what she was seeing—or pullout her binoculars for a better look—the man crossed the road and began to walk down her driveway out of sight. However, Bailey could still see the eagles for a while because they flew above the tree-line.

Bailey got a better look at the eagles with her binoculars several seconds later. She recognized the golden eagle as Anacarin, Christian's eagle. *And that man must have been Christian,* Bailey thought. She quickly got a very bad feeling about what might be about to happen. From behind her, Bailey began to hear several heavy vehicles moving down the road. She turned to see them coming around a bend, about a mile away where the road curved out of sight. She saw two Humvees with machinegun turrets and a transport van normally used to carry around twenty troops rolling down the road.

As soon as her mind put the pieces together of Christian and his eagle going down her driveway and the heavy vehicles and troops from Iishrem hot on their heels, Bailey dived down the short hill that led off the side of the road and pulled her dirt bike along with her into the forest, hoping they had not seen her. For a second, she returned her eyes to where she had seen the eagles. She had just enough time to see Anacarin dive below the tree-line, where she knew her wide driveway was. The other eagle remained in the air and Bailey noticed that it had a square, shiny, silver suitcase attached to a strap and held in place behind her neck. After that, as she heard the heavy vehicles rumbling closer and closer to her position, she watched Anacarin ascend back into the air above the trees with Christian on her back. Then they took off towards her house.

Bailey burrowed deeper into the trees and crouched behind some thick bushes until she saw the military vehicles from Iishrem pass her position without stopping and turn onto the long drive-way to her home. Only once they had disappeared was Bailey sure they hadn't noticed her standing on the side of the road for just a second while they approached.

Bailey needed to get home, *now*! She grabbed her dirt bike and wheeled it next to a tree close to the edge of her driveway that she knew she could find later, and then she took off for home. Bailey ran much faster without her dirt bike holding her back, but her home was still a mile down the long driveway. Bailey wondered if her father was home—she honestly wasn't sure one way or the other.

Bailey kept running through the forest and eventually shifted over towards her driveway. She stopped behind some thick bushes to catch her breath for a moment and listened. At this point, Bailey knew she still had four or five minutes of good running to reach her house.

She wasn't hyperventilating, but she was panting heavily. Her driveway was gravel, so while she had been running, Bailey had been able to hear the military vehicles from Iishrem traveling down the driveway beyond her. She noticed the absence of tumbling gravel quickly and assumed that the vehicles had stopped in front of her house.

Bailey had her cell phone on her. She grabbed it from her backpack and auto-dialed her home phone. Somehow, her call got through, and even more surprisingly, her father picked up a second later.

"Bailey? Are you safe?" he asked, seeming tentative and nervous.

"Dad, where are you? I don't know how to explain this, but Christian is coming with two eagles, and I just saw two Iishrem Humvees and a troop transport coming down our driveway. What's h-happening?" she stammered while she tried to explain and ask many things at once.

"I know," her father told her. "He's already here. He's going to protect us, and he'll explain everything afterward. Bailey, stay hidden until the fight is finished and then the three of us will talk."

The line cut off there, and then gunfire rang out from the direction of her home. She was definitely not going to stay hidden all the way out there; she needed to see this. She took off, finding the shortest path home, and running faster than she ever had before.

The gunfire was relatively light over the next few minutes, while she panted and ran. By the time she reached her home, out of breath and wheezing, the gunfire was reaching an apex. Bailey found some good cover to hide behind, and then she hunkered down to watch the fight. At first, Christian and his eagles were nowhere to be seen. The soldiers from Iishrem had already peppered her log cabin home full of bullets, and all the windows on the front of the house were now broken.

Her home's driveway came to an end in front of the cabin in a round turning circle with a diameter of perhaps a hundred and twenty feet There were a few trees and several mulched gardens in the middle of the turnaround, but other than that, it was clear of everything but grass. All around, her father's property was then clear of trees and bushes for another twenty-five feet. Bailey could see everything pretty clearly. If the driveway turnaround was a clock and the beginning of the turnaround was 12, then her home was at 6, and she was hiding out at 3.

The two Humvees had driven into the middle of the turnaround to cover both sides of the front of the house, while the troop transport sat at the edge of the driveway entrance. Bailey saw that the troops had already filed out of the van. They had split into three groups. She saw six or seven troops in cover around the turnaround and the front of her house. Bailey figured that meant that the other two groups of soldiers must have gone to search the sides of her house and the backyard. After that, everything began.

The first thing she heard was the screech of an eagle, swiftly followed by another one. The first screech made her cover her ears, and the second one forced her out of her cover, deeper into the forest, and she reflexively closed her eyes to lessen her disorientation. By the time Bailey had returned to her cover to watch the fight, the sound and rate of gunfire had returned to a climax. The clangor of the brawl rang in her ears and concussed her even further.

By the time she had regained her vision, several soldiers were already lying dead in the middle of the turnaround. Then she looked up and saw the two huge eagles swooping down from above each of the Humvees. Both turret gunners were screaming and firing rapidly in circles as the eagles descended. Bailey watched the eagles deftly descend in a spiral pattern while they outmaneuvered the turret fire by staying just ahead of its firing path. There were several other soldiers still in the circle, while the other two groups had not yet returned. They fired at the eagles—and even scored a few hits—but the caliber of bullets that they were using just seemed like a pinprick to the eagles.

Simultaneously, when both eagles were just 12 to 16 feet above the Humvees, they finished their dive and unfurled their talons. Anacarin pulled the turret gunner right out of Humvee by his head with her beak, ripping it from his corpse in a misty spray of blood and bones. Then she grabbed the rest of his body with her talons and tossed him like a rag doll towards two other soldiers who were approaching from cover. The turret gunner flew right into both, batting the approaching soldiers back into trees at the edge of the forest. Bailey assumed that the force of the impacts from that exchange knocked out the two soldiers but did not kill them. For a second, Bailey watched their bodies lie in front of the trees they had hit, and they did not get back up. After that, Anacarin grabbed the Humvee with her talons and rose back into the air with it. Bailey watched Anacarin drop it directly onto several troops returning to the front of her house from the far side, blood shooting from underneath as it landed.

The other eagle landed directly on top of the turret, crushing the gunners head against the Humvee with one set of her talons. The brown eagle grabbed the Humvee with its talons, spun around in the air, and launched it towards three more approaching soldiers. The Humvee hit the three of them dead-on and rolled over several times before landing upwards on the edge of the round-about. It still looked operable to Bailey.

Both eagles then landed in the center of the turnaround. The remaining soldiers rapidly tried to encircle them, and Bailey was honestly surprised they weren't retreating. The ten soldiers prepared to fire upon the eagles, but that was when Christian reappeared. He came out of the front of her house and quickly gunned down three soldiers at the top of the turnaround with three consecutive bursts from a burst-action rifle, which struck each of their targets in the head.

The last seven soldiers attempted to fall back to the trees for cover, but Christian continued to fire his weapon from behind a pillar that supported the patio awing in front of her cabin and took out two more. Then before any of the soldiers could make it to the trees, the eagles took off in two separate directions pursuing the fleeing groups of two and three soldiers. Anacarin took out the larger group of three soldiers by curling in her wings and performing an alerion roll back onto the ground, which collected and crushed two of the three soldiers. Then she sprang back up and seized the last fleeing soldier with one set of talons, before ripping him in half with the other, tossing the remainder of the body not too far from the front patio. The other eagle took out its two fleeing troops by landing on them from an angle, impaling them each three times with its razor-filed talons. It then also tossed one of those soldiers over towards the front patio of their house, where the body landed next to the one that Anacarin had hewn in half.

When the fight was finally over, Christian and the two eagles regrouped in the driveway by the front door. Her father also came out of the front of the house, looking more than a little befuddled and distressed. Christian patted him on the shoulder and put his arm around Clancy's back when he was close enough. Christian then said something to her father that Bailey could not hear.

"Bailey!" her father screamed in fear. "Come out!"

Bailey felt like she had no choice. Her hair was entirely frayed and messy by then. She ignored it, stood up, and dusted herself off before she walked out of the trees toward her home. When she approached the eagles, their eyes narrowed at her, but they showed no aggression. Christian stepped up to Anacarin and patted her gently before pressing his forehead to her beak. Then she took off and flew over towards the woods, where Bailey believed there were two unconscious but surviving Iishrem soldiers.

"Where is she going?" Bailey asked.

"To wake the last two soldiers. We need them alive; they'll help us close up some loops and keep you safe," Christian told her.

Bailey watched Anacarin land at the feet of the two knocked-out soldiers and gently collect them into one set of her talons. She rose back into the air and brought the two of them over, close to their group, then laid them out in front of their feet. Their faces and clothes were battered, beaten, and wetted with blood, but Bailey had no doubt each was still alive. She had no idea what Christian was doing or how this would help them close some loops and keep her safe. Everything she had just seen was so over her head.

Christian looked back at the two of them and gestured for Clancy to take her and step back a few feet, which he did. Christian stepped up to the two unconscious soldiers and then stripped them of all their weapons. Once that was done, he had Anacarin secure them in place with her talons, in case any of them woke too early, and then he stepped up to the other eagle and grabbed the shiny silver suitcase off the strap around its neck.

"Bailey, this is Raejen, my eagle," Clancy said.

"Hello," she said, putting up her hand to wave to the eagle. Raejen squawked at her, intimidatingly, and Bailey shied away. "What happens now?"

"You'll see," Christian told the both of them. He gathered the two of them closer together, and then he opened the suitcase for them. What Bailey saw inside was quite disturbing. She saw a skin mask in the shape, size, and look of her own face and her father's, but they were not quite either of them, yet. It had a nose shaped like hers and a messy mop of dirty blonde hair at its top as well.

Underneath the skin faces and around them were black shadows that pooled like water, mixed in with murky, wispy gray shroud thicker than fog. "Just a little closer," Christian told the two of them. The two of them squeezed in closer to each other and the suitcase, and then Bailey noticed for the first time that the faces did not yet have any eyes. "Smile."

Bailey looked up at the top lip of the suitcase and saw that it had some kind of camera, which then snapped a picture of the two of them. Once that happened, Christian pulled the suitcase back towards him as it came to life and its mechanisms began to print eyes for each of the masks—the eyes of herself and her father.

The two soldiers that the eagle had singled out laid close to the end of the patio. Christian walked over to them and gestured for them to follow. When the three of them stood in front of the two dead soldiers, Bailey then also saw that an outfit of hers was sitting outside on the patio, along with another her father would wear. Christian stripped the two soldiers out of their uniforms, then redressed the one who had been ripped in half with her clothes, and the other with that of her father's. Bailey somehow couldn't look away, but the entire exchange made her feel so numb.

That's when Christian walked over to them with the open suitcase, which had just finished printing their eyes. "Gently, with two hands, take your face and put it over the soldier's," he told the two of them.

Bailey grimaced, but her hands did as she was commanded, and she did not flinch when she laid her face over top the face of the soldier who had been ripped in half. Her father placed his face perfectly over top of the other soldier as well. Once they had each withdrawn their hands from placing the masks on the dead soldiers, the underside of the thick skin masks began to bubble for just a few seconds, fusing the mask onto the original face seamlessly.

Next, Christian grabbed the cylindrical suitcase she had first seen him carrying while he was walking. He opened it, and inside Bailey saw a long, majestic red feather. "It's a phoenix feather," he told the two of them, while he held it in his hands not too far away from them. He walked back over to Anacarin who had the two still unconscious soldiers pinned under her two sets of talons. "Even just a few of its barbs can indoctrinate the minds of men for years—when exposed to them directly. They'll believe everything I tell them, without even a second thought."

Christian split the feather into two, top and bottom, and Bailey watched the edges of his irises crack red in a circle around the pupil. Christian grabbed a silver Relnás lighter out of his pocket. "Okay, the two of you will have to watch from inside. Remain hidden, and do not come back out until I call for you." Again, Bailey did as she was told and walked herself into the lobby of her home, and her father followed closely behind. She heard Clancy close the door behind her, and then she looked down to the ground to take extra care not to step on any of the shards of broken glass or cracked wood.

"Why is he here?" she asked her father, looking up at him. "How did he just kill all those men, and what is he doing now with the survivors?"

"I don't know, but we can't do anything but trust him until this entire ordeal is resolved. Trust me," he implored her. She sighed and trusted them just enough to take a left into her living room, where she could watch Christian's actions through the window. The soldiers would not be able to see her or her father, because the windows were darkly tinted. Christian nodded to Anacarin who woke up each of the soldiers by softly squawking in their ears.

When the soldiers woke, they looked up and saw Christian standing in front of them and then began to flail violently, trying to escape the clutches of Anacarin. She held them down firmly in place and did not shift an inch.

"I'll kill you!" screamed one of the soldiers.

"You'll burn in Hedeth'rehem for what you did to Sax!" yelled the other.

Christian shushed them repeatedly, and Bailey watched as he crouched next to the first soldier, and then he lit the barbs of the feather with his lighter. The barbs of the feather burned, but they were not consumed by the flame. To Bailey, it looked like the portioned feather glowed an even brighter red. Then Christian pressed the burning feather into the eyes of the first soldier and held it there for several seconds until it disintegrated into them completely. While being burned, the soldier had felt the pain and showed it greatly. Once the feather vanished through, the soldier quickly calmed down. Christian repeated the process once more with the other soldier.

When that was done, Anacarin released the soldiers from her grasp. They got up and looked generally unharmed, and their eyes were intact, if not just a little red. Their minds were blank and faces emotionless. They looked at Christian and did not recognize him. As they looked at him, Bailey could see Christian clapping his hands together, congratulating them on a mission well done. He stepped behind the two soldiers and put his arms around them, then prodded them towards the dead soldiers with her and her father's faces on them.

"As your commanding officer, I could not be more impressed. There just remains one final thing to complete," Christian told them as he removed a machete sheathed on the leg of the soldier. He then handed the machete back to the soldier. "Proof."

The soldier took the machete and bent down next to the imposter body of her father. While one soldier began to hack off the head, the others turned to Christian and asked some questions. "What happened to all of the other men?" asked one.

"How did we survive?" asked the other.

Bailey saw Christian smile as the soldier with the machete finished hacking off the head of her imposter father and then moved to her imposter's body. She watched the soldier hack off that head too with a sadistic sense of intrigue.

"Well, Seems special forces showed up as you were attacking the father and daughter and routed your forces. Then they took off to raise the alarm and gather reinforcements for a further investigation. They must have taken you for dead in your unconscious state. I guess Seems doesn't want us too close to their sovereign territory with the approaching war between Iishrem and Allirehem. They'll be back in a few hours, but you completed your mission, and now you've got the chance to escape back to Taerit safely, where you'll surely receive a hero's welcome for a job well done," Christian told them.

Bailey could not believe what she was seeing, but the soldiers really didn't have any concerns about anything they were being told, and soon enough, Christian had ushered them back into the remaining Humvee with their proof in hand. Bailey watched one soldier put her and her father's head into a suitcase and then get into the Humvee through one of the side doors, stepping into the turret. After that Christian sent them on their way, telling them he was going to covertly stay behind to gather intel. Again, Bailey was in perplexed awe to see the soldiers believe everything Christian told them and then drive away, back up the driveway and out of sight, as Christian waved them off.

Once that was done, Christian joined them inside and they had a talk in the living room. "That should all take care of any loose ends, for a while at least," Christian told them. "It was a bold move for Iishrem to try and pull off a personal attack like this, but I suspect they thought they could get away with it because Seems is just a city-state, without much of a standing army, and it was done outside of the official borders. But it was an accomplished mission, with proof, survivors, and when Seems learns of this, it'll be all over their presses in the morning. Everything will match up; I'll meet with the administration of Seems personally."

"What a mess," Clancy said of the condition of his house.

"My people will pay for it, and it'll be repaired in a few weeks. In the meantime, does Bailey have another place she can stay?" Christian asked. Bailey felt a lump form in her throat.

"My mother, Mildra, isn't too far away," Clancy admitted to Christian, and the conversation went on from there. Christian explained that the both of them were Dravens, but it was her father's turn to be trained right now. Her time would come too, one-day.

"I need your father to come with me to my academy, where I can train him to fight in the coming war," Christian told her. "You both have a very important role as Dravens living outside of Iishrem, but I can't train you yet, because your hawk isn't ready yet to leave his home within the Shrouded Sea."

"I have a hawk?" Bailey asked quickly. She was not particularly surprised though, remembering Hector's voice and seeming to see half of him earlier in the day.

"Oh, yes," Christian told her. "Until then, I would have you live with your grandmother on the other side of town, is it?"

Clancy nodded, and after that, there wasn't much more to discuss. Soon enough, her father had packed for a long journey, and she had packed to spend a month at her grandmother's. Christian promised her she would receive the rest of her valued belongings in due time, and she accepted his word after her father pressured her to. She was exhausted, mentally frayed, and had seen so much that she just wanted her day to be over. Clancy drove her across town to her grandmother's while Christian flew over on Anacarin, and Raejen followed behind them. "I'm sorry that I have to go. Ever since the war began a few weeks ago, my dreams have been filled with visions of Raejen, and now she's found me. You have a hawk too, have you heard anything from him?" her father asked. He sounded like he was just making excuses, but he wasn't going to change his mind. She could already tell.

"I don't want you to go, Dad," she pleaded with him, ignoring his question in the car. He began to cry as they pulled into her grandmother's driveway.

When they arrived at the front door, her grandmother greeted them with a wave—clearly, quite shocked to see the most infamous terrorist in the world landing in her yard with two eagles. "I love you, Bailey. I'll be back to visit as much as possible," he told her.

Bailey huffed exasperatedly while she looked away from him out the window. "I'm sure you will," was all she could manage.

"There's one more thing before I go," he told her before the two of them got out of the car.

"What's that?" she asked. She looked over at him.

"I've signed you up for a regional paintball league with kids your age. I think it'll be good for you since I'll be gone so often," he told her.

That sounded good to her. Then the two of them got out of her father's car and hugged briefly before they walked into her grandmother's house with her belongings. Once Bailey had gotten comfortable in her room, and her father and Christian had explained everything to Mildra, they left after some more tense goodbyes. Once they were gone, Bailey took herself off to her room close the door. She tried not to cry too hard.

Chapter 8
Ethan's Confession (katie 4)

IMPERIUM AENDOR, DUSK, IISHREM

FALL, 1150, FOURTH AGE

"I'm just telling you is all," said the short boy named Fordo with long locks of brown hair, who sat in front of her, "Women kiss women naturally much better than any man could ever kiss another man. They just have to—it's the way they're brought up before they go to college."

As Katie sat on the couch in her dirty university three-room suite and surveyed dozens of empty beer cans strewn about and a handful of empty liquor bottles, Katie knew she had just been told for the last that women to be better at kissing women than men were at kissing men, they just were. What a galling argument, if ever a one made from a freshman desperate to see some action while drunk in college. Katie felt her eyes flare yellow, while she sat on her couch in the living room of her university 3-room dorm suite she shared with 2 other roommates. It came complete with 2 bathrooms, a kitchen, small study, and small deck overlooking the local district within Imperium Aendor. Her parents lived about twenty miles across town from her, which normally took a little longer than forty-five minutes to travel by subway.

Katie could think of several remarks to make to the statement she had just heard uttered, but of course, before she could say anything, a taller male student named Drage added, "My sister graduated to university a few years before me, and one night before she went, she hosted a party with a dozen of her girlfriends and 8 or 9 jocks from one of the fraternities on campus," he paused, leaning back in the rocking chair while he looked up.

"I can't remember which one," he failed to remember, in reference to the fraternities permitted by the University of Rhylls Grelsby, "but of course, while I was trying just to get an in with one of her friends, she couldn't help herself from making out with at least 3 of the jocks, in plain sight of everyone, and two at once! Then, just as I had finally persuaded one of her friends named Shwewn to come back to my room with me, I caught her making out with one final douche up against my bedroom door! Actually, it was a little hilarious. Getting caught by her little brother killed his mood, and he took off, then she yelled at me and ran crying into her room. That just left me and Shwewn, and our attraction to each other, which had risen greatly, of course, through the confrontation. We took it out on each other in my room for twenty minutes afterward, and she took it all." His smile a smirk while he looked up at the ceiling and remembered fondly.

Katie liked his story upon its completion, and perhaps she liked him even more, as she looked him over from top to bottom. Tall, slender, and green eyes on high cheekbone he was.

Laughter came from Glance in response to Drage's story and snickers from Gestwen and Estien. Katie saw the eyes of her brown-skinned friend Gestwen from Gazsamine darting to look at

Estien while she held her hand close to her mouth. Estien squinted her eyes, holding them together with her thumbs. Katie admired her light olive skin as she knew Estien was from Kafari.

"That sounds like a wonderful time," said Glance. Katie looked Glance over. He was a little shorter than Drage, with medium black skin and brown eyes. The two of them shared a bit of a history together, but they weren't together or anything. They were both just on their perspective wrestling teams at the university. They had humped after practice on one or two occasions. Katie also knew that Glance had a range of inclinations. She liked him that way.

"Yeah." Katie drunkenly leaned forward, finally having a chance to interject. "Just the part about seeing your sister making out with four different guys on the same night."

Drage sat in a desk chair across the room. He leaned back and groaned with his hands behind his head. "Oh, she excels at that—even got caught by our parents with her first boyfriend, at least once," Drage admitted.

"I can't imagine catching my brother in the act of something like that!" Katie laughed, balking at the embarrassment of an awkward situation such as that.

Somebody groaned from around the room, but Katie knew who it had been before she heard his shoes hit the linoleum floor a moment later. "Yes, but what does that have to do with the argument?" Fordo asked annoyed.

Glance laughed and shook his head at Fordo's efforts to return to the argument, instead of just letting it drop. Estien and Gestwen simply laughed loudly to each other, again, and Katie began to zone out just a bit. There was something she felt standing over her back, like there was something she was supposed to be doing but had forgotten about.

"Oh, well," sputtered Drage, perhaps still basking in the memory of his past hook-up. Drage smirked sitting up, leaning off the desk chair. Katie mused that he had just wanted to distract them from Fordo's dumb argument. He was just making himself look desperate. "Well the next day I after the party, I heard that she and 3 or 4 of her closest friends practiced, well you know, on each other. So, they could be better experienced for when it came to college, she said kissing girls in front of other guys is more enticing than just being attractive."

"Well, there it is," said Fordo trying to look confident. "Seems like your sister proved my point exactly." So, there it came to it. Katie had heard stories about Fordo's past experience too, more like the lack of any. He really had no idea how much he ruined his chances with Estien by inserting these dumb arguments during their free time. He was a true virgin freshman.

"Yeah, now all we need is an in-person demonstration," said Drage in jest, seeing if there was any interest in such an exchange taking place. It seemed like it could, by the way she saw Estien and Gestwen look at each other at that moment in time.

Katie stood up off the couch and turned off the TV. Drage pouted about that claiming, "I was watching that. They were showing the highlights of last night's Exodus attempt by Ashlin Nensor. She was a range Draven trainee at the CDA, who had recently become a little popular to those who paid attention, thanks to her skills record. She was a range Draven several years older than herself, with high cheekbones. Ashlin was well known for the intricate detail of her disguises, which often included changing the color of her hair.

"It's big news," said Glance. "You already know she passed."

"But I wanted to see what she had to do for the variant stage," Drage complained. While Katie walked into the middle of the living room and surveyed the six occupants, she knew that an Exodus attempt was the required exam before any Draven trained at the Iishrem CDA could graduate. The exam came in three stages and were quite popular events to see in person, in Malin Harr, or watch on TV. They were also one of the few events that anyone could gamble on in Iishrem.

While she stood in the middle of the living room, at that moment she thought about Sovereign. When would he come for her? Was he coming for her? Was he still alive? And what was the thing she had known about before that she was forgetting about now. Something loomed close, but until it came for her, Katie pushed that all out of her mind.

"I'd see a demonstration of such," Katie said, "But only if we can see an equal demonstration from the other gender, as well." She looked at Gestwen and Estien while they looked at each other. Glance laughed again, and that drew her attention away from them to him across the room. Drage came across the room, from where he had been sitting on a recliner and stood next to her, and gently held her left elbow with his fingers like a pincer.

Katie was in a good mood, and she like Drage, so she didn't mind. Katie didn't mind trying new things. It seemed like the only one who did was Fordo. Drage kissed her on the cheek, while he looked at Glance who was out of her vision behind her. Katie instead had her eyes on Gestwen and Estien who were edging their open mouths inches closer to her.

"Is this what you wanted to see?" Katie asked Fordo who now was uncomfortably locked out of the cluster the rest of the room's occupants had formed in the last few seconds.

"It is," he said, "But I kind of wanted to get involved myself too."

Everyone broke apart for just a second when he said that. "Well this is all you get," Katie told him.

"Yeah," said Drage.

"You have to be the judge of who kisses better Fordo," Gestwen said slurring her speech haphazardly, "Girls on girls, or guys on guys." Everything resumed then. Katie smiled at that and closed her eyes, as she felt Glance's big arms slide around her back and lightly cup her breasts in both hands, which had become even more bodacious since she left premiere school. Her nipples stiffened on his caress.

"Gods be damned" Fordo swore, and he took a seat on the couch, but he couldn't help but watch the action.

Katie opened her eyes and then saw several interactions taking place. Estien and Gestwen had their lips locked, smacking back and forth while they held each other in a tight embrace. Their exchange intensified as Fordo watched from a few feet away, jealously. She saw Estien push down a corner on Gestwen's blouse a second later, exposing a bell-shaped breast, with a small pointy nipple. That was before Katie felt her back jostled from behind just a bit. She turned to see Glance and Drage kissing each other too. Katie looked down for just a second and saw the head of Drage's emboldened member poking out the top of his jeans while Glance had put a hand down his jeans to grab it.

Katie lost track of exactly what had happened to Fordo for just a moment and felt hot. She puckered her lips and joined Drage and Glance in their kissing. Then she wondered just how far this whole exchange would go if they had the time and space. *Ah, college,* she thought while she traded spit and tongues with her two male friends. She wanted to kiss the girls too, just one time. Katie left Drage and Glance, giving each of them one last look, then walked over to Gestwen and Estien. Katie closed her eyes and kissed her two female friends in a triangle fashion, like she had done with Drage and Glance.

Then there came a knocking on door to their suite. The knocking came loud and incessant, for several seconds. It killed the encounter almost instantly, as everyone began to break away from each other quite flustered, and Fordo announced, "I'll get it." Perhaps he was relieved to have a reason to break up what he had started. Just before he could open the door, it began to sway open itself, revealing Katie's brother Ethan standing behind it.

Ethan was dressed professionally for an occasion, with his hands behind his back and a small grin on his face. The sight of him made everyone instantly break apart and disperse. Katie watched his grin turn to an awkward smirk. His eyes were orange, and finally, Katie remembered what she had felt hanging over her shoulder for the past twenty minutes. Ethan had an art show this evening, and she was supposed to go.

"Hey, I'm Ethan," her brother said to Fordo, who was standing in front of the door wondering how it had opened without any effort from him. "Nice to meet you."

"Did that door fall out of the lock hinge, again?" asked Estien. There was a brief round of hasty introductions after that, between Ethan and her friends. Then all of them left the two of them alone, as quickly as possible, perhaps embarrassed at being caught in what just happened.

"Ethan," Katie said loudly, uncaring about the situation in her drunken state. He walked up to her. "I forgot about the art show," she told him, trying to a little bashful while she looked just down at him.

"It's not a show, just a canvas reveal, okay? There's time. Sorry, I seem to have caught you at a bad one. Looks like you only need about ten minutes to clean up," he told her tensely.

Katie wanted to understand what he was going through, but instead, she laughed loudly at that as if she couldn't, or wouldn't cooperate, but she quickly set about getting ready to go. She told him to have a seat while he cleaned up, and she was ready to leave in the timespan he gave her, although she had to rush. There was no one left to say goodbye to when Katie stepped up to the door to the hallway, which was just next to their small kitchen, so the two of them just went ahead and left.

They would walk the apparently short distance between her university dorm and the art studio they were headed to. Some of Ethan's friends and their parents would meet them there, as well as a small audience to see the unveiling. Not much was said between them while Ethan led her away from campus and into a ritzier section of Imperium Aendor, at large. In the mid-evening, the sky was an orange overcast, with a light breeze and intermittent drizzles. Along the way, Katie noticed a wide overpass that went over a road that ran beneath it. Painted on the walls of the tunnel were several graffiti murals. At that point, Ethan picked up the pace.

"Hey, hold on a second," Katie said from behind him. She slowed down, pretending to stumble a bit in her semi-inebriated state, "You're going to lose me."

Ethan groaned as he stopped to let her catch up. Katie thought she knew why Ethan wanted to pick up the pace there. He *had* gotten a government-sponsored art sabbatical apparently from having done so well on his Provenience Test. "What is it?" he asked her when she caught up.

Katie stopped and her eyes drifted over towards the murals. Graffiti, or the art of the streets, was encouraged throughout Imperium Aendor, where it was prudent, and if it was deemed *actual art.* "It's nothing really," she began to tell him. "It's just that I always would have pegged you for one to take to graffiti as the delivery of your art." A few of the murals were proudly lit up, and had several admirers milling about underneath them.

Ethan bristled and laughed at that. "I thought about it, for the longest time while I waited for my sabbatical to start. You have a larger canvas to express yourself with graffiti murals, sure, but it's a closed circle. Sure, there are a few famous examples many people know of, and they have a handful of stout critics, but at street level, many of them ever get the exposure they deserve. No, if you ever want your art to ascend into any of the tower galleries, you have to start in the two-story houses."

He had answered her question, and she nodded for him to start walking again. He pointed out a brick art gallery three blocks away and said that was the one he was headed for. He continued his explanation without her asking him, but she listened. "This gallery wasn't my first choice, and at the brusque length of time they gave me to get settled and create something, this gallery will have to do.

Katie had a question. "Don't you fear your stepping into something you aren't ready for? Do you believe in what you have prepared?"

Ethan huffed while they crossed the street. "The thing is, Sister, this may go poorly anyways. Who can tell when critics are inclined to give their approval of a work? But the vision and talent are there, in form, if not always perfect," then he smiled at her. "The thing about critics and art is, if your work threatens them, if they take personal offense to it, they'll judge it poorly regardless of its quality or latent potential. They'll unleash on you, and spill all of their *secrets* to how it could have been better, and how everything you did was a failure."

Now was Katie's turn to bristle at a statement he made, as they approached the gallery just one block away. "Ethan, that sounds awful, truly. Why would you put yourself in that position? Do you think you'll even want to paint again if it goes that poorly?"

She feared for him just a bit now. "My dreams are laid much deeper than any stinging critique or commentary I could receive tonight sister. And like I said, if it does so, those who hold their opinions in such high esteem will tell me all their secrets," Ethan told her.

"But your name could be ruined. People remember," she told him.

He turned to her annoyed. "I don't have time for everything," he told her. "Some artists never have their work observed by anyone. Some only achieve renown posthumously. Sometimes you need a baseline. I could always change my name or move. The art lives on, and I think you'd find that most people don't really care and normally forget anyways. Now that's enough, let's get this over with." Ethan held the gallery door open for her, and they entered one after another.

Ethan took them inside and led them over to a section on the left, where Katie saw several other works. His work would be in a section with other new pieces from artists like them, and when Katie stepped up to read the offered information about each, she saw that most of them had been revealed for the first time just recently. His work to be unveiled was covered by a tarp, but Katie could see his signature uncovered by the tarp in the bottom right-hand corner.

A collection of various people had gathered to attend Ethan's showcasing. Katie quickly spotted her parents, Carth and Marleigh, standing next to each other away from the rest of the attendees by the windows. She waved, and they came over to greet the two of them. "Glad to see you both made it here—and not too late," Carth said.

"We were afraid we'd have to unveil the art ourselves," her mom told them. The four of them shared a laugh at that. "Well, you have something to show us." Then Marleigh shooed Ethan away to go do his thing. Ethan smiled and took his leave, then slowly worked his way to the tarp-covered canvas.

While he did, Katie took a further look through the attendees. She first saw Kiera standing not far from the side of the canvas near to the dark windows. They waved to each other. She also spotted Rich hanging out in a corner with a small group of friends. Katie judged there to be about forty people who had mostly separated into several small groups, however, she also observed several outliers meandering around from group to group, by themselves. When she looked at the attendees who lingered by themselves, they were all different, looked different – but she knew, they were all the same type of person: a critic.

Katie narrowed her eyes at a few of them. She didn't know of any of them by name, but he had surely found a few, by her judging. There was one who lurked in the back, whom she worried about. He had a messy mop of short light blond hair and dimples. He dressed casually enough, but everything he wore was expensive *brand* named apparel. Denim jeans, with a black sports jacket, low sitting glasses, and a tiny notepad, holding a red pen. His lips looked to pout necessarily, while he pursed his lips, and his eyes ran blood-shot red all the way around. Her head pounded when she looked at his eyes, and for several seconds she couldn't look away. Her vision even blurred at the edges. A migraine, no less, perhaps much more.

"Everyone, everyone," Ethan began, holding his hands in the air. He walked himself over to the left of the hidden canvas. "It's a Saturday night, and unfortunately we're at a dry galley, so I wouldn't want to waste any more of your time than necessary." Although, the fact that they were at a dry gallery after hours hadn't stopped Ethan from bringing a marron flask, which he pulled out of his coat pocket and took a sip from. She could see it was a brown liquid—that whiskey he had talked about more than likely. He capped his flask back up and stuffed it back into his coat pocket, taking extra care to make sure to leave some space between that and a fat, dark brown cigar, which was still in the wrapper. While he took a drink from his flask, several of his friends cheered him by raising their generic light beers in their hands. Several of the critics drank wine, but not the one that Katie was watching. He had coffee.

At his request, the several small packs of guests began to curiously meander into a thick arc, centered around his hidden piece. Katie had seen about five people she thought were critics. Four of them were men, only one of whom was black, and one white woman with blonde hair in a bun. Two of them hovered in the front row, one at each corner on the back row, and the man she had observed most of all lingered over toward the back wall of the section they were in where he leaned against the wall.

There was some quiet classical music playing throughout the galley, which Katie picked up on at that very moment. Her brother began to talk again. "It's been over four years now since our nation was attacked. On one day, eagle and dragon spared with each other in the open air, our emperor was assassinated by a notorious terrorist, and all Rehem remembered its magic, as well as why the other half of our world is covered in Shroud. Yes, we all learned much that day. Some of us saw more than others. Without further ado," he said grandly. "I give you 'Raven's Night'."

Ethan gently pulled the tarp off the canvas from one top corner to the other and let it rest on the wood floor of the gallery a few seconds later. He got a mixture of varying reactions from his audience, while he walked to the outside of the arc and stood somewhere near the middle of it, smiling as *he* admired his work. It was a large canvas. On the right, the solid outline of half a raven in perspective held one wing out across the rest of the canvas, stretching to the end, and growing ever thinner as it did. A cloudy grey sky sat above and below the raven's feather, with a detailed painting of a streaking eagle above it, like it was the sun in the sky.

The cityscape of Imperium Aendor sat mostly beneath the raven's feather, punctuated by The Spire, which had its red eyes watching the scene near its peak. Its radio tower met with the tip of the raven. Further below the outstretched wing was another detailed painting of Karthon rising to meet the eagle in the sky, above the city. Lastly, there were several naked corpses rising into the air, as if they were ascending into Rendeth-threium—the belief in a heaven shared by the predominant religion of the Allirehem Resistance.

Just as the reactions began, Katie drunkenly laughed, "Psst, some of them are naked."

A few glanced at her, but most didn't notice her comment. The rest of the smaller buildings of the city spread across the right of the canvas also had significant detail compared to the violet raven itself. Katie thought the painting showed a lot of passion and promise—after her inner laughs from her joke wore off.

The reactions Ethan got were various. Most of his friends clapped lightly, and a few even cheered "Ethan," while they raised their generic light beers again, taking swigs of them while they did. Her brother seemed quite happy with that at first, if not perhaps just a little reserved. Katie was going to go easy on him, but honestly, she thought the varying levels of detail clashed. Of course, before she could do that, the critics milled their way to the front of the arc, and the one in back even decided to move closer as well.

They all stayed quiet until the black male with a short grey afro, wearing a brown jacket, glasses sitting low on his nose, spoke first. "The perspective is all off," he said.

The blonde-haired woman with sharp eyes, "Seems like it could be much more patriotic as well. More to the reason of having the raven and eagle presiding over the scene. They were the ones attacking."

Another one just took notes, and the fourth with red hair quietly put his white wine down on the drink table and walked off. Ethan quickly noticed, and his expression was sullen. His friends would be supportive, mostly, some more than others. However, those he didn't know and deigned to impress were not reacting the way Ethan would have wished. While the last one worked his way up to the front, she felt sorry for her brother. Katie watched him let his eyes down, and he let his posture slack.

"It's just off. Contrasting tones, varying levels of detail, needlessly naked corpses rising into the sky goes against our state religion. Some promise on the vision, yes and the structure, perhaps not so much anti-patriotic but just trying to show the scope of Christian's god-condemn-him-to-hell victory, but it just doesn't seem like you've got it yet. Mhmm, sabbaticals are going to thin in the future for others because of pieces like this," said the critic, and then he shot Ethan a look.

Katie had been watching her brother, while the critic had been speaking. For a second while his posture slacked, she could see his eyes begin to wet and his fingers fidget like he was holding something in. Then she saw his eyes gleam violet like she had before when he had used his magic on her. Or at least she believed was possible. His back stiffened. He was going to say something.

"Well, thank you for coming, and thank you for looking," he told the critic with blonde hair. Then the black critic and the woman began to walk off, as the other two had several moments ago. Katie saw at that moment for the first time that the critic with blonde hair walked with a limp in his left leg and used a long thin cane to help him. He was leading the critics out of the gallery, and then one step before he was able to put the cane down, it snapped.

The critic stumbled, swayed to the left, and tripped over a low-hanging marquee rope. Then, before catching himself upon the side of the wall, he punctured another painting in several places to stop himself from falling. His colleagues quickly rushed to his aid and helped him stand upright again. When he was standing straight again, supported by the black-skinned male, the woman took a jaunt outside to hail a cab. One pulled up just a few seconds later, then idled.

The blonde-haired critic looked at Ethan and said, "I'll tell you one thing, young Ethan. It's different, yes. It gets attention. But you're infatuated with yourself, and you still have much to learn."

As Katie watched from her spot in the back, still a little drunk, she turned out to be in the way of the critics' escape. "Out of the way, little missy," said the critic whose cane had snapped.

"Geez, sorry. Careful not to tumble over again on your own opinion," she told him as she pushed off, out of their way.

Finally, the last of them left the gallery. She looked at her brother, whose eyes were wide open and looked changed. Kiera stood in front of him with her fingers interlocked with his. She pushed his hands up into the air and gently, slowly made them shimmer in motion like a dancing flame. Katie began to walk closer, but something told her to only get so close, he needed his space.

She heard what Kiera said to him, while their parents were also quick on their heels to console him.

"You made something great," she told him. "You gave life to inanimate molecules of lifeless paint. You gave them meaning. Meaning that impacted someone's life in this world."

Ethan told her, "I'm going to be okay," he strained through stifled tears. The criticisms had affected him. Then he put his arms around Keira's waist and pulled her close. Carth and Marleigh stood behind him with their hands on his shoulders.

"A chance you let walk by is one you never catch up to again, and a regret you won't live down," Carth told him.

"I love it, Ethan," Marleigh told him. "We're proud of you."

Ethan thanked her too. Over the next handful of minutes, the rest of Ethan's friends left the gallery, most of them said nice things about the painting. It helped him cheer up a little. Their eyes met several times, though, like he wanted to tell her something.

"Well, we'll see you at home next time, Son. Keep your head up," Carth told him and then he put his arm around Marleigh's back and they followed the rest of the crowd out, leaving just the three of them.

"There was something he wanted to tell you," Kiera told her. "It's just for you. Before we can tell you, though, you've got to swear not to tell anyone else."

Katie held up her right hand and swore. "Let's take this outside," Ethan suggested, and the three of them strolled out of the gallery and stepped into an alleyway that ran behind the gallery.

After checking there was no one around, Ethan spoke. "Mom and Dad don't, but the truth is, this piece was more personal to me than it came out as I intended. I'm a Draven," he admitted, "And the painting I prepared was what I felt I saw that day. The day I met my raven and watched the assassination from afar."

His reveal to her was shocking, and her headache and dry eyes returned all at once. She could feel herself watching her brother with her red eyes, and she felt like someone was watching her, behind her back, with their hands pressed down against her shoulders. "And you thought to tell me this now?" she asked.

His eyes looked from side to side. "Look, it's a lot to come to grips with, and I'm an artist. I don't really want to fight in a war, maybe I'd fly. But I'll never know when she'll be coming back for me." Kiera was at his side. "I just thought you should know. You've always seemed to have. Neither one of us live with our parents anymore, perhaps we need not trouble them with this."

Her eyes darted around, and for a moment she thought that she should be forthcoming with him about her meeting with Sovereign all those years ago, but then her head prevailed and hammered her in the forehead, forcing her to bat her eyes and her vision to distort. By the time her head pains left her, and she could focus, they were both quite concerned.

"Are you okay, Katie?" he asked her. He helped her steady herself, holding her arms around her elbows, and Kiera assisted with a hand at the side of her left arm.

She shrugged them off firmly a second later. "I'm fine," she told them. "Thanks for letting me know. If you ever just suddenly disappear one day like the rest of them, I'll know what happened to you. And yes, perhaps it's better if you keep this all to yourself from now on and don't bother Mom and Dad about it. They've got enough on their plates," Katie finished, and she knew she had nothing else to add.

Ethan sighed and agreed to her terms, then the three of them walked to the nearest sidewalk along one of the roads of Imperium Aendor. Ethan and Kiera went to the right after saying goodbye, and Katie went to the left to go find her friends.

Chapter 9
The Tiger of Maish (Brian 1)

MAISH, GALLIEM, ALLIREHEM

SUMMER, 1153, FOURTH AGE

For a moment, Brian pressed his hand on the door to his storage unit. He could feel the sun on his face, shining through the space between a few overpasses which passed directly over him. He could feel the sweat on his brow; the day was an absolute scorcher. Finally, Brian unlocked his storage unit with his key and pulled it up.

Once the door was fully open, he smelt stale petrol. Brian smiled as he laid his eyes on his one true possession in this life—his Burcgetti chopper. He could go anywhere he needed to on it; it had been with him for so long it was a part of him.

With a huff, walked inside to the back. He reached over to a box at the back of the unit, which contained a portrait of himself and his parents a few months before the last time he had seen them. He picked it up lightly in his hands and smiled at it. A single tear ran down the length of his face as he put the portrait back in the box.

Years had passed since the riots in Raegic which sparked his career in Sen Rhêt Hill, but his patience and effectiveness had eventually bought him his freedom to operate at his own prerogative, far away in a place no one had ever heard of him. Brian now had spiked crimson hair and pale white skin. His jeans were tattered, and today he was wearing a faded T-shirt. He had a scruffy five o'clock shadow and lanky figure. Outside of his storage unit, Brian could hear the city, and its smells seemed to seep into the unit to assail his senses. Maish was bustling today. He took one final look at his chopper, grasped one of its handlebars, and then grabbed a deck of cards and a black plastic box crate. Brian left his storage unit and locked it behind him. With his crate in hand and cards in his pocket, Brian joined the crowd of people on the busy streets headed for one of his regular locations.

Along the way, he stopped in front of a display window to an electronics shop. The window was filled with all the newest TVs, and each of them was playing the latest edition of Galliem's national news. On screen, an older woman was reporting the latest news about the war with Iishrem. She had long brown hair, bags under her eyes, and a significant nervous twitch. The dialogue of the news anchors was captioned at the bottom of the screen, and Brian was a quick reader.

And in other news, the Iishrem Army has now reached the city of Ferrum. The city is under siege, and there are not enough Allirehem resistance troops to hold back the onslaught of the Iishrem Army. Fighting is expected to intensify, and it's estimated at this rate that the Allirehem Resistance will concede the city within the week. If that happens, Iishrem could reach Maish as early as mid-summer.

Brian knew by now that spring was dead, and summer had begun. Several strangers muttered various reactions to the news as they passed by. "I'm headed for Maravinya in a week. Not my problem," muttered one man in a business suit.

Another spoke a little more optimistically, "They'll never make it here by summer. Fall at the earliest."

With a frown on his face, Brian left the store window and rejoined the stream of people. He had been living in Maish for several years now, and he had really hoped that he had finally found a new home, since he had done so much to achieve it before. He had a nice loft on the city's edge which could use some work but got by on a source of income that was just enough to cover his expenses, and even a girlfriend—Macie. He occasionally took small, simple jobs on the side still. Living costs were extremely low in Maish, and there had been recent social welfare reform. He wanted to make things work here, but it didn't seem as if it would be that easy. If Ferrum fell, the nation of Galliem would be the next that Iishrem would seek to conquer. To make matters worse, Maish would certainly be the first city to be besieged. Worst of all, Allirehem's one weapon against Iishrem was seemingly largely absent from the war—the Dravens and their Eedon Rath-ni. Iishrem had Dravens fighting for them too, but there were less *supposedly*.

Dravens were these legendary soldiers with unique powers who were supposed to be nearly unbeatable. Brian had yet to see one single Draven fighting for Allirehem in person, and he knew the war would soon get much worse— especially now that The Long Road had finally been completed. The Long Road traversed the expansive distance between the two continental superpowers— Iishrem and Allirehem—wriggling across a vast desert, through a dense forest, and between a range of razor-sharp mountains. With the road completed, Iishrem could now send a full-scale invasion force into Allirehem, instead of just smaller attacks. Brian believed that Allirehem didn't have the population or resources to contend in a war with Iishrem, and their only legitimate hope in the war seemed to believe they had better things to do at the moment.

Finally, Brian reached the location where he would work for the day. People passed by as he cleared off a little space on the sidewalk and laid down his crate. He took a deep breath and then held up his hands, chanting, "Step right up, step right up and test your luck. Simply pick your card out of three after I mix them up and win $20. $5 to play once, $12 to play three times." Several people looked back at Brian with disinterest.

"This game is so easy, even a Draven could win!" he yelled, and that got a few sarcastic laughs from the people passing by. Brian continued chanting until he finally had his first customer of the day—a little boy with short brown hair. His mother, who was directly behind him, sponsored his entrance fee. Brian took the boy's bill and put it in his pocket, then he pulled out his deck of cards and revealed forty different cards.

"Choose any card," said Brian.

The boy reached over and pulled out the seven of dragons. "I choose this one," he said.

Brian took the card from the kid's hand, laying it down in the center of the crate. Next, Brian took out two more cards—a nine of hawks, and the green eagle card. He laid the two cards on either side of the child's, and then he turned all three of them over.

"All you have to do is choose your card once I've finished mixing them up," Brian explained. The kid nodded, and Brian feverishly jumbled the order and position of the three cards over the next dozen seconds. He finished the game with the black seven of dragons back in the center of the crate.

Brian looked up at the kid. "Choose," he said.

The child thought for a moment and decided to choose the card on the left. "Ah, sorry, kid. Better luck next time," Brian said as he turned up the nine of hawks. He also turned over the seven of dragons in the center. Brian had sleight of hand, he always had. He used it to his advantage, making the players believe their card finished in one position, but he had swapped it with another. Sometimes customers would guess correctly, that kept more of them playing, with the war on their minds.

The day dragged on until the sun began to set, and the streets began to clear. People were headed home. After one more game, which Brian won, he decided he was finished for the day. He figured that he wouldn't get many more customers anyway. It had been a profitable day for him. Brian had just put his cards in his pocket and crate under his shoulder when a stranger caught him by the shoulder and knocked him into the wall of the building to the side of him.

"Excuse me," said the dark-skinned man. Brian was a handful of inches taller than the man, so the force of the check that the stranger delivered caught him off-guard. The stranger had a husky build and was wearing pitch-black sunglasses. He took off his sunglasses and hung them over the neck of his shirt before he asked, "Surely you must have time for one more player today?"

The man stepped back, to play off bumping Brian into the wall. He was wearing jeans and an overcoat. Brian peeled himself off the wall, staggering to regain his balance. "Well, I actually have somewhere to be soon," he began, but the man looked unsatisfied. While he put his sunglasses back on, he began to curl his other fist. "But since you're so eager, I guess I could make time."

He laid the crate back down on the ground and pulled the deck of cards out of his pocket. Again, Brian revealed all forty cards. The man handed him ♣5 and chose the black dragon card. "That's my lucky card," Brian exclaimed, laying the card in the center of the box.

"Not today it isn't," said the man smirking.

Brian picked out the eight of eagles and the purple raven card. He laid the cards on either side of the black dragon, and the game began. Brian jumbled the cards again for the last time as furiously as he could. He mixed them so fast even he began to lose track of where the black dragon card was sitting on top of the crate.

"Choose your card," Brian said, looking at the man when he had finished mixing the cards.

Without a moment's hesitation, the man flipped over the card on the right revealing the black dragon. "Dravens absence!" yelled Brian.

The both of them stood up together. A small crowd had gathered to watch the outcome of their game. Some watchers were shocked, and there were others who were celebrating the stranger's victory. "I believe you owe me ♣20," he said smiling.

Brian reached down into his pocket and pulled out the money. Suddenly, the man forcefully pushed Brian back into the brick wall again. Brian groaned trying to escape, but the man held him up against the wall with his elbow under his chin. "Careful not to choke on your cards. Wouldn't want to overplay your hand trying to tame something you were never going to control anyways," the man told him.

"What're you talking about? Just let me pay you," yelled Brian. The crowd was watching with shocked expressions. With a sudden burst of strength, Brian threw his hands against the man's chest and pushed him away. The stranger stumbled back and knocked over a bystander or two before he came to a halt. The man collected himself and bolted back in towards Brian. He blocked two meager punches from Brian and landed a swift kick to the chest, which knocked Brian back into an alley. The man followed, and Brian hit him with a meager punch to the stomach, which did little to impede his assault.

The man stumbled back and taunted Brian. "I'm not interested in your money. I'm here to find a tiger in a man. I'm here to find someone who can show me something."

Brian threw two more punches at the man, both of which were promptly blocked. The man pushed him up against a dumpster.

"Go find a Draven!" yelled Brian.

"I've found one already," he said, smiling. The man backed off, collecting himself just long enough to deliver a kick to Brian's chest, which knocked him back into the dumpster. He fell to his hands and knees and then looked up. A kick was coming for his face. Brian narrowly avoided it, but then the stranger stomped on his hand, sending him writhing in pain.

Brian started convulsing. Then the man kicked him again, and suddenly, the pain he felt began to feel like a numbing drug, coursing through his veins. It was something he wanted more of. A craving even. The man stepped back and smiled down at him. *You will be so powerful one day,* came her voice in his head.

"Show me who you really are, Brian," said the man as he retreated out into the street. Brian's vision changed from usual color to shaded overtones of yellow, like a tiger's. He saw himself rising from the ground. His skin was now being replaced by striped orange and black fur. His arms and feet transformed into paws, and he grew a long tail. The convulsions stopped; the transformation was complete. Brian had transformed into a tiger.

Clumsily, with paws that weren't his, he turned around to face the road. The smart people in the crowd had retreated to a safe distance, and others stood in place, watching in dumbstruck awe. The stranger was now standing in the center of the street. Brian wanted nothing more than to maul him. He stumbled out of the alley and lunged at the stranger. He simply turned himself sideways as Brian flew past him, and cars had to swerve around them.

Then the man retreated to the other end of the block. When Brian found him again, he let out a deafening roar, setting off a couple of the parked car's alarms. By now the whole section of the road between them had emptied except for himself and the stranger. People were cautiously watching from a safe distance.

The man was still smiling. Why was he still smiling? Brian watched the stranger look into his eyes and nod. It was almost as if he was saying, *come get some*, without any hint of fear at all.

Brian decided he had had enough of the man, and he charged forward. The man did nothing. As Brian reached the other end of the block, he leaned back against his hind legs and pounced. His front paws were out, his claws unleashed as he glided through the air towards the man. He was ready to crush him between his two paws, like a cat trapping a mouse.

The man took off his sunglasses. For a moment, his eyes turned green and flashed as he met his gaze. Once more, the stranger smiled. Suddenly, out of the tiger came Brian. Brian was lifted, over the man, and landed in the cleared intersection on his back, before rolling over a couple of times and coming to a stop.

The man stood over Brian smiling almost sadistically, and Brian began to feel himself slip out of consciousness. The last thing he could remember was something the man said. "I'm Mason Black, and I thought you might like to know you're a Draven. It's about time you showed up."

Chapter 10

Recruitment (katie 5)

K atie stood near the end of a long line composed of her fellow students graduating that night from the University of Rhylls Grelby. It was a large college by student population, but Katie was graduating near the top of her class, within the top 25 actually, so she would be one of the first to walk across the stage and receive her temporary diploma. Her real one would, of course, be mailed to her several weeks later. She did see many familiar faces around her because Katie was not graduating with the rest of her major, Sports Medicine, but that didn't much matter to her now. She'd have to stand around for a shorter time, and there would be less walking with her seat so close to the stage. The line of students approaching the stage they would walk across stepped forward again. Katie felt her nerves pick up, as she was just three students away from her turn now. She would not trip while wearing her heels.

For just a moment she saw Glance, their elected class president. She fondly remembered their friendship and occasional humping from throughout their college careers, but things hadn't ended very well when he had decided to quit wrestling and get into student politics. Katie wished him the best of luck. She couldn't tell if he had noticed him looking at her, but Glance paid her no mind, seemingly only pre-occupied with gazing at the large banner depicting Lance the 13th, hanging from the rafters in the small arena that the University had on its campus, where the graduation ceremony was being held.

"Graduating within the top 25 of her class," a voice on a loudspeaker began, as Katie's vision snapped back into place. She cursed herself for being inattentive and took two steps forward so she could put her hand on the railing that was anchored to the four steps which would take her up to the stage. "Katie Campbell is awarded the BS of Sports Medicine. She'll soon be taking a position at a local sports rehab practice, and her continued boxing career, at her digression, continues to be one of the worthiest to note, throughout all of Imperium Aendor."

Katie walked up the stairs and began to make her way across the stairs as soon as she heard her name called. As the voice on the loudspeaker reverberated around the arena from one of the press boxes somewhere, Mrs. Gayle Heatherway stood beamingly waiting for her. She was black and had short curly black hair, had a short round figure.

Katie shook her hand and accepted the fake diploma. "Congratulations Katie," Heatherway told her.

"Thank you," Katie managed, and gave her a solemn look. After that, she focused entirely on walking in her heels back to her seat. She was just able to avoid tripping or falling off the stage, but she did feel her ankle start to buckle once or twice.

Some forty minutes later, when Katie was back at her seat and all the students had walked across the stage, the speeches began. Mrs. Heatherway would go first.

"Students, you've reached your future. It's right here in front of you. If you can take it, the future is yours," she said. There was a light round of applause. "I remember how some in this class responded when our city and our country was attacked by the notorious terrorist—God condemn him to hell—Christian Knowles." There was silence. "There were those in this class who stood up and asked how they could help. Food drives, cleanup efforts, outreach, construction efforts, I couldn't be prouder. That is why we accepted each one of you into the prestigious university in the first place. I don't need to say anything else for this class. They can each speak for themselves. But while that would take too long, here's class president Glance Clayborn."

Katie felt her throat stiffen as Glance walked up to the podium and pulled the mic up to his level. He began talking, but Katie didn't listen much. She still had not had a talk with her brother about their heritage, even though he had been honest with her. She feared bringing it up in any way may make it fester, and they would experience a breakdown in their relationship. But she *needed* to say something. The two of them needed to trust each other, Katie thought at least. *Better to say something while you can, before it's too late*, said Sovereign's voice in her mind.

Sovereign, Katie thought. *It's been so long. Is this happening now? Are you out there?*

You shall see by the end of the night, Sovereign told her.

If only that didn't sound as ominous as shit, she replied, looking up at her brother where she saw him sitting with Kiera and her family, in the stands. Ethan's eyes glowed violet at her, and then he looked away. Kiera held his hand, wearing a black dress and sporting a jazzy haircut. Maybe Kiera could help facilitate a talk between the two of them as she had helped Ethan through his confession near to two years ago, but Katie didn't really want to tell anyone else she was a Draven. After the assassination, Tagros issued an imperative order to all Iishrem citizens suspecting themselves of being Dravens to come forward and work out a deal or role in the war with them. Since then, several conspiratorial stories had begun to circumvent the more esoteric websites, which attempted to hide their articles from the government for independence from oversight.

Katie had read several stories of negative encounters with Dravens of all ages who did not want to come forward and make themselves known. The government had taken a stance of outing those suspected of Dravenry—if they could prove it. Four arts of Dravenry had been officially recognized by the House of Lance. Magic, like her brother; strength, like herself; and then there were those with unique skillsets in espionage or range and those who could turn into great beasts of various sizes and animals. Apparently, it was the essence of their personality that determined which animal form they took. The size of their transformation could also vary both on intention and training.

Of the negative encounters that the articles claimed, apparently the House of Lance had begun to abduct a handful of unwilling potential Dravens. Even more troubling were the reports of the squad which was used to pull these abductions off. This was giving her a migraine just thinking about it all. The article even alleged that family members had been killed or imprisoned to obtain obedience. It all made Katie very tense, but she didn't know what to do. She hadn't seen Sovereign since the few weeks before the assassination. She wondered how the government could possibly know of her abilities. Katie hadn't told anyone, and no one else knew—except her and Talia.

Katie hadn't heard from Talia again, but she had scoured each of her new books for messages that might seem like they would be to her from Sovereign. It resulted in Katie feeling like she was crazy. Again, she was forced to accept the tense reality of not knowing what was going to happen when Christian's war came for her— or how it would work out for herself and her family. Katie had resigned herself to the fact that it would one day happen, but she wasn't going to bring it on intentionally.

Glance was beginning to wrap up his speech. "...And so, my fellow classmates, as we go forward into the future—be it to the war, to the state, or to the economy—know that you can do your part. And, hey, you could be a hero too. Anything's possible," he finished. Glance capped off his speech by brushing back his brown hair before stepping away from the podium to retake his seat. The rest of the ceremony seemed to pass by rather quickly after that.

When they were dismissed, some twenty minutes later, Katie met her family in the concourse, and Ethan was the first to greet her. "Good job in not tripping, Sister," Ethan told her jestingly.

"Are you sure you didn't need to use magic when you got yours?" Katie responded, raising her eyebrows. Ethan flushed and looked around when Katie said that, appearing uncomfortable.

"We're so proud of you," said Marleigh.

"In earnest," said Carth, clasping her elbow for just a moment.

Okay, maybe now I should have a talk with him, she thought, but this wasn't the time or the place. Maybe Sovereign was lying, maybe he wasn't real at all. Just a voice in her mind, and a memory she had made up of him to make herself feel better, about herself. He had made a mistake by confessing his truth, the way that he did.

He shouldn't have waited years to tell her, he should have told her as soon as she knew.

She should have too. She remembered her first meeting with Sovereign.

She wanted to end tonight on a good note with him, and so she leaned in close. "Why don't we have a talk soon, now that we've both graduated?" she asked.

Ethan stepped back and looked at her. "Okay, sure. Soon," he said supportively. Their party broke up and dispersed after that. Katie went out to drink with some friends.

Later that night, when Katie was drunk and had finally finished dancing at the clubs, she hailed a taxi and tried to relax. She had already moved out of her college dorm a week and a half ago. So, for a few weeks, while she looked for an apartment to move into that she could afford with her new salary, she was back with her parents. The taxi ride was too brief for her to sleep at all, so when the taxi pulled up next to her home, she paid her fare and walked inside, after unlocking the door with her keys.

Katie was grateful. It was going to feel good to lie down and wonder about her future—as if it were really right there in front of her. When she came in, it was already quiet, and only a few lights were on in the house. Katie nearly instantly felt like something was seriously off with her house. Her parents were still supposed to be waiting up for her, or at least asleep on the couch, but they were nowhere to be seen. They had probably just gone to bed.

She wanted to hold her cat, Cali, and feel him purr. It was therapeutic for her, and if she were lucky, Cali would sit on her stomach for a few minutes. If Cali wanted Katie to find her when home, the cat would usually go to the kitchen, so Katie headed that way. When she reached the kitchen, Katie discovered that a tall, muscular, bald man with scarlet eyes was sitting in a wooden chair, holding Cali. "I thought we might be able to have a little chat between the two of us—and your brother. if he's around? If not, I'm sure he'll be joining us later," he told her. The man was wearing dark jeans and a combat polo. Katie could see two silenced pistols holstered at his sides. *Is that a wand as well?* She asked herself, seeing a stick-shaped object that looked like one, attached to his belt. Strangely enough, Katie was not nervous as she sat down across from him, at the kitchen nook table.

"Who are you? What're you doing here?" she asked. The bald man held his fingers up to his mouth and shushed her. "Let my cat go!"

Cali remained comfortably sitting in the man's lap. He even purred, for just a moment. Katie recoiled, pushing herself back from the table. "Cali, come here," she said, reaching out her hand towards the cat. The cat jumped out of the man's lap but did not run over to her. Cali disappeared skittering off, somewhere upstairs. Katie was not pleased. Who was this man? Should she have screamed to wake up her parents? Call the emergency services? All the while, she did her best to look calm.

"Where are my parents?" she asked.

The man smiled and leaned back, then he pulled a Relnás lighter out of his pocket. He flicked it open and struck it, then he put it out with one look from his scarlet eyes. The flame did not flicker as it died; it simply vanished in an instant. "Sleeping," said the man. "I did not think we needed to wake them yet." He leaned back in his chair and waited for her.

"Who are you? What do you want?" Katie asked again.

"That's not for you to know yet." He smirked while he shook his head at her. "You can wait patiently—I'll even let you go upstairs to be with your cat—or we can do this the hard way," the man told her. "We're still waiting for your brother anyway."

"I'm going to call someone and have you arrested," Katie told the man.

"No. No, you aren't." The bald man leaned forward and laid a fold-out badge on the table. He was a Master Recruiter from the Center for Draven Abilities in Malin Harr. "Allovein Camnair is the name, and you've been officially sanctioned until I can proceed with my questioning. And your parents. Oh, and your cat. Feel free to remain under house arrest while we wait for your brother."

Katie was through with this rubbish. "I don't have to listen to you," she told the man. She kicked the table forward with her heels and broke one of the table legs. Her heels shuttered from the kick, and she recoiled backward several feet. Katie realized she had forced Allovein to spill coffee down his jacket sleeves. Slowly, he wiped them off and looked down at the broken table.

He loosened his jacket a bit and spoke quietly into the open side of it. Then he looked back to Katie, smirked, and said, "The hard way then."

The front door burst open and several soldiers came strutting in. As soon as they did, Katie saw her father's bedroom light turn on. "Katie, get down!" Carth screamed from inside his room.

"Oh, what is this?" Allovein rolled his eyes. He rose and walked over to the bedroom doorway where her father was waiting to greet him with the family shotgun. Carth pointed it directly at Allovein's chest, holding it with a firm grip. "Soldiers, hold for a moment. I'll give you one shot. Don't miss." Allovein looked at Katie's father with scarlet eyes. Marleigh cowered behind him with a crowbar. Her father took Allovein's bait and fired.

A fraction of a second later, a golden flash of bright light blinded Katie. When she reopened her eyes, Allovein was unhurt and locked in combat with her father over the shotgun. Suddenly, Katie felt herself stumble as she was grabbed. The three soldiers in body armor were trying to tackle her and force her to the ground in the living room. She dived forward into a roll and took off down the hallway, trying to make it up the stairs. She had a thick club upstairs—if she could just make it to her room.

When Katie looked down the hall, she could see her father still locked in combat over possession of his shotgun with Allovein, and she felt her shoulder being grabbed at by one of the guards behind her. Her father fired the shotgun's second shell, just as she had passed its firing path. The soldier trying to grab her grunted from behind. He had been hit. The force of the shot propelled him into the closed front door and then down to the wooden floor, where his blood began to pool.

As she made it to the top of the stairs, Katie saw a flash of Cali's fur dart into the dark guest bedroom's doorway. Katie never reached her bedroom. One of the soldiers caught her by the shoulder as she hopped off the last step and turned her around. He had his gun slung around his back—so, they were not trying to kill her. He lunged forwards at her, and Katie stepped clear to the side. He stumbled a few feet down the hall while the second soldier stepped up to throw a few punches. Katie was able to sidestep another punch and catch the man's arm as he tried to recoil. That was all she needed, but she didn't have the space, time, or experience to win.

Katie drove the man to the ground, holding onto his arm, and then she jumped on top of him. She had just enough time to dislocate his arm out of his joint, and then jump on top of him. After that, two of the other soldiers pushed her off the screaming one and restrained her. Katie felt her face hit the wooden floor of her hallway, and then they took her back downstairs. This time, when she walked into the living room, Allovein was already waiting for her, with her parents both handcuffed at the dining room table. Allovein gestured for her to sit down, and Katie complied.

"Ethan should be here soon, I'm told," Allovein informed everyone else. "My raven, Scarlet, is seeing to it personally."

Chapter 11
Scarlet (Ethan 4)

IMPERIUM AENDOR, IISHREM

SUMMER, 1153, FOURTH AGE

his parents, he, and Kiera were watching Katie's graduation from halfway up the first bowl of seats near center court, it was nearly over now. He turned away from looking toward Katie and looked to Kiera who sat on his right. Kiera was wearing a tight black dress, which made him appreciate her curves even more than usual. His parents sat on his left, rather silently—except for the occasional sniffle from Carth or some light sobbing from Marleigh. Kiera smiled at him and said nothing, while Ethan looked back at her and lightly ran his hand through her wavy, brown hair. He watched her close her brown eyes and lean forward just a bit. Ethan closed his eyes, turned his head slightly to the left, and moved in with his lips.

Their lips met in the middle, and as soon as they did, Ethan felt himself inhale deeply. Their lips moved lightly together in unison for several seconds. Ethan felt like magic when they stopped kissing.

Ethan turned away from her and held his hand for her to grab. She took it and he looked back to the stage, but that didn't mean he was going to listen to whoever droned on next. It probably wasn't too different than what he had gone through several years before. Instead, he thought about Violet.

Ethan listened for Violet for a moment.

The war carries on, and it will define you tonight. Everything you know will have changed drastically by the morning, her voice told him. Ethan felt himself roll his eyes.

What does that even mean? he thought, huffing in frustration.

If I tell you what's going to happen, then it'll only happen differently, Violet told him.

Are you still out there? How can you expect me to take this all on without you? he thought.

I'm sorry, but this can all only happen in one way. Be patient; you'll soon see. We will survive this and be together soon, she told him. He wished that she would just stop being so cryptic all the damn time.

What about everyone else I love?

She said nothing else after that. He wished she would just join up with him now or never do it. He wanted to live a normal life, not sit around constantly waiting for one night when it all might change. Ethan had a feeling that something terrible was going to happen, and there was nothing he could do to stop it. For the rest of the graduation, he tried to keep thoughts and voice like that out of his mind.

"And so, future Iishremites, remember this as you're about to go forward and onto the rest of your lives. No matter what future occupation you've been offered or chosen to select, if you play your role properly with passion and respect, our country and society can progress to a state we cannot even begin to imagine. Who knows what magics and truths you could discover if you put your mind to it? Imagine what you could make, what you could add, what you could give to Iishrem and the House of Lance—if only you put your best foot forward. Try not to forget that. I never have."

The ceremony was unmistakably wrapping everything up; Ethan was glad for that. "Graduates, it's now official. Go forward and make the future that you see as your own. It's all your opportunity now. Congratulations, graduates of the class of 1153. You've done it," finished Mrs. Gayle Heatherway. As soon as she stepped away from the podium, Katie's class president, Glance Clayborn, rose from his chair on stage and threw his confetti into the air. The rest of the graduating class quickly followed suit. Ethan spotted Katie again, and he watched her throw her confetti into the air, producing a colorful, vibrant cloud.

After that, the four of them collected their belongings and walked down to the concourse area to find Katie.

When he saw his sister, she chided him about his magic and hinted to wanting to talk about something important with him this weekend. While Ethan was curious as to what exactly she would tell him, he didn't want to think about it too much. All he wanted for the rest of the night was Kiera.

After a round of goodbyes between the five of them, Ethan and Kiera headed for the subway in one direction, and his parents, with Katie, did the same in another. The two of them said little while they made their way through the station terminal with several dozen people around. They boarded a train together, and after two stops, they had to squeeze tightly together. The shifts in the train's speed while they both held onto a ceiling loop between some seats near the middle of the car caused them to make gentle contact with each other as if they were dancing.

The car was dim and quiet except for several crying children. Ethan wondered only about Kiera. She looked at him with her dark-brown eyes, never looking away. When Ethan and Kiera were finally free of the underground and walking beneath the stars, Kiera finally spoke.

"Are you thinking about Violet?" she asked him.

"Who else?" he resigned. They had talked of her several times since the assassination.

"I know you don't want to come out about it, but maybe at least while Violet isn't with you, perhaps you could continue to live a normal life without any weight or dread on your shoulders," Kiera told him.

Ethan exhaled. "Honestly, I think it's all out of my hands. It's all coming to a head, and we just need to find out how," he told her. He was confident no one had overheard him. Imperium Aendor was buzzed around them, with typical 11 pm weekend activity.

"Maybe we should spend it like it could be our last night together," Kiera suggested.

That struck Ethan to the core. "Are you unhappy? Did I do something wrong? I'll fix it," Ethan told her, afraid he was losing her.

Kiera laughed, punched him in the arm, and said, "No, that's not what I meant. I meant what're we doing with each other if it *is* our last night together?" she asked him. She looked up at him slyly with a smirk and leaned in close. She then pushed him away playfully.

"Oh," Ethan said, pretending to stumble back a few steps, trying to make up for his embarrassment at having taken her so seriously.

"Look, we both know the Eedon Rath-ni are back, and the world is full of magic. But while that's not here in front of us, for one more night, let's act like we're normal fucking people, Ethan," Kiera told him.

Ethan understood her hints. "Like we're normal *fucking* people, Kiera," he said seductively.

They had arrived at his apartment building and were about to take a side entrance shortcut together. Kiera gave him a smile and then stole his door keycard out of his hands and made a dash inside the building, catching him off guard. She got the door closed before he could catch up to her, which left him locked out. Ethan smacked his hand upon the glass door and playfully yelled back at her, "Damn you, Kiera!"

Kiera shrugged her shoulders and pretended to pout, saying, "I'm going straight up to your room. Let's see how much of a mess I can make by the time you catch up." She then winked and ran off down the hallway towards the elevators. Ethan would have to jog around to the front desk and show identification to get his reserve key. He took it at a jaunt, thinking about nothing else.

She's really quite great, Ethan. There's time enough for one more time, Violet told him. Violet—his Eedon Rath-ni, his raven—was not going to stop him from this.

Can you not right now? Ethan asked her, but Violet did not respond. Ethan walked in through the front door of his apartment building, which was located about three miles from his parent's house, southwest of the Calanor Stronghold. He walked up to the desk and asked a guard he did not recognize for his key. The security guard checked his ID and then grabbed his key, giving them both back. Ethan was off, making a mad dash for the closest elevator. He lived on the fourteenth floor of a twenty-three-story apartment building. When Ethan finally got into his modest apartment, all the lights were off.

"Kiera?" Ethan asked happily, before turning on a few lights. He had walked into the entryway, which led into a small hallway.

His kitchen and small dining room were to his left down the hall, with the bedroom to his right beyond the wall and his living room to the right. The bathroom was attached to the master bedroom and the living room at the top of it. Also, to his left, there was a small office where he kept his paintings.

"Come find me and play, Ethan," Kiera said flirtingly. He heard a door open somewhere, but he was not sure which one. Ethan loosened the top few buttons of his button-down shirt and kicked off his dress shoes. He walked around to his room, which had a line of windows directly behind his bed. He found the room dimly lit and the windows with the shades up so that the stars and city could be looked out upon. Kiera was laying on his bed in intricately laced black lingerie.

"Ethan," she said sitting up on his bed while he stood in the doorway. "Why are you still clothed? You're not tired, are you?" She leaned forward towards him, arching her back and leaning forward on her knees.

Ethan felt his throat stiffen. He approached the end of his bed, and Kiera grabbed his tie and pulled him close. "I demand you sacrifice at least three pieces of clothing. Otherwise, it's not fair for me," she told him.

Ethan smiled on the inside as he reveled in what was about to happen. He stepped into the room and put on some alternative rock. "Typical!" Kiera said, chastising his selection of music. She leaned back on her hips, holding herself up with her arms. Ethan walked around to one side, unbuttoning his shirt, and then he tossed it off across the room. He grabbed Kiera by the hips and stepped in for a long kiss. Kiera met his lips with hers and kissed up at him furiously. She unbuckled and loosened his pants but did not quite pull them down.

Ethan backed away from her for a second, and she leaned back down. He took another walk around the bed and dropped his pants, leaving his tight grey boxer briefs up. This time he stepped up to the bed and leaned over. Kiera smiled and got on her hands and knees, approaching him on the bed like a cat. Then when she got close enough, she stood back up on top of the bed and began to step off, which forced Ethan back a few steps and put him off balance. Ethan heard Kiera laugh, and then he watched her arms push him across the room and up against the wall where they passionately kissed. He closed his eyes, and darkness was his world.

When he felt her hands stroking his groin, Ethan opened his eyes again. When Kiera recognized that his eyes were open, she took a few steps back and removed her top. Ethan truly admired her substantial round breasts, and he felt that tinge of magic he knew so well. His eyes were violet again, he knew.

Kiera sat down on the bed, then asked "Can you feel your magic? I see you're hiding a staff in your pants."

Ethan knew what she wanted. She moved him to the side of the bed, then playfully pushed him over and removed his last piece of clothing. Ethan smiled when he felt himself naturally snap back from her reveal. He leaned up and looked down at her while she slyly worked her way up his legs, kissing him with her mouth and running her tongue lightly up his legs. She grabbed his thick member with her hand and smiled. She put him in her mouth, loving his tip before she worked her way down to his bottom. Her kisses were long, wet, and the relief gave him the best feeling he had felt in his life. When Ethan was grinning from ear to ear, it was his turn to return the favor.

Kiera laid her back on the bed, and then Ethan knelt before putting his lips between her legs. He kissed her over and over, and then he used several fingers to spread her lips apart just a little further or play with certain areas of hers that stimulated her even further.

Several minutes later, they studied the moon and night sky together. Kiera kneeled with her knees at the head of his bed with one hand on the windows that overlooked the city. Their combined breath fogged up two circles on the windows, while he took her from behind, but also leaned in close to kiss her on the cheek, or whisper in her ears. He loved Kiera—he knew it for the first time that night. Ethan interlaced his left-hand fingers with Kiera's left hand, which she held on the window. Ethan looked out at the sky, with her. All he could feel were hearts, all he could see were stars, all he could hear was love. Ethan thought to himself, *All magic to its source.*

When they had finished, Ethan continued to lie next to Kiera in the bed. She had her head on his chest. It was just past midnight. Suddenly there came a tapping from behind him. Ethan rose, turned around, and saw an unfamiliar raven in its smaller form had landed on the ledge outside side of his window. The raven looked him in the eyes, with dark black eyes of her own. Ethan felt transfixed like the small raven could see right into his very soul. *Violet?* he thought in confusion.

My name is Scarlet, the raven thought to him from outside. *You've lingered in the shadows for far too long now, young Draven. Ha-ha! Hee ha, he-he. Nevermore! The war comes for you tonight, but first, it is time for you to meet my master,* she told him. Suddenly, Scarlet's eyes turned a thick, dark scarlet red, and Ethan fell unconscious under her spell.

When Ethan finally came to, he found himself back in his parent's living room, handcuffed at the dining room table with the rest of his family. His parents and Katie each wore an outfit that Ethan had seen them wearing many times before. Someone had redressed Ethan in the clothes and shoes he had been wearing earlier in the night. A bald man from a dream that Ethan could recall but not properly remember sat across from the three of them sipping tea. "Good; you're awake. We can begin then," the bald man said.

Ethan felt disoriented. "How did I get here? Where's Kiera?" he asked frantically.

"Kiera's gone to you, Ethan. She's not yours to know of anymore. Scarlet, my raven, put you under her spell, and then several of my men collected you and the girl. Kiera will be seen to—as will you," the man said.

"No!" Ethan screamed in anguish. For the sake of being polite, the man introduced himself to Ethan as Allovein Camnair, the master of magic dravens and ravens at the Center for Draven Abilities. The four of them had been officially sanctioned for questioning.

"I want to contest this; you have no right here!" Carth spat, trying to get to his feet, only to have his knees hit the bottom of the table, forcing him back down.

Marleigh sat feebly next to him, crying. Her eyes were wet with tears. Ethan wanted to reach out to comfort her, but he had no way to do so. No way to put his arms around her back and tell her he was sorry. There was something he *could do* though. He still felt magical. He looked over at his mother with violet eyes, just strong enough to steady her and calm her spirit.

"I don't know love. What do you want?" she asked Allovein.

"Your children. Tell me please, by now surely you must know your children are not normal. They've both got certain abilities—

you do know that, don't you? Your son watched the assassination candidly from afar with his raven and... um, *future* girlfriend, Kiera McNeill, at the deserted Calanor Stronghold, when it was supposed to be locked—and don't tell me you think your daughter is normal either. A girl of her size with her raw athletic prowess; we've seen the way her eyes can change color like her brother's," Allovein said, looking at the both of them. There was a pause in the conversation.

"In what way do you want them?" Carth asked the man.

Allovein bore Carth a cantankerous glare with his scarlet eyes before calling his raven to him from across the living room where it *had* been roosting atop a bust of Empress Nair'eia Flen'tel the 5th—one of Iishrem's two previous empresses. Scarlet landed on Allovein's shoulder and then rose before rearing back and bearing its wings at the rest of them. *Be drawn from the shadows, young Dravens!* spoke the raven. All occupants of the room heard the raven Scarlet speak in their minds.

"Need you more proof of my intent?" Allovein asked his parents. "I mean to take your children to the Center for Draven Abilities in Malin Harr, where we can *call* their Eedon Rath-ni to them. I mean to have them trained to master their magic and strength and then send them out to the war to play their part."

"Out to the other side of the world where they would meet nothing less than the same that Allirehem has to offer but pitted against them? And I tell you, Christian with his Dravens and the Allirehem Resistance Armies worry me in a war. Not to mention our navy is relatively green—except for the Cromellas. How would we know we'd ever even see them again?" asked Carth.

"How do you know you will ever see them again after tonight anyway?" Allovein asked Carth.

Ethan felt terror grip his heart and twist. "Dad, what's he talking about?" Ethan asked as he rose, all the while trying to wriggle out of his handcuffs, but to no avail.

"The two of you should have come forward long ago, Ethan and Katie. You've let your parent's down," Allovein told them.

Allovein was instantly disputed by both his parents: "No, no, no, you didn't. We've always been proud of you both, Ethan and Katie."

"Mhmm, well... yes. While you may think that, Carth and Marleigh Campbell, but the state does not agree with you. You killed one of my men, you gave me a real bad bruiser, and the two of you knowingly stayed in the shadows for years. There are to be consequences, but they'll be over soon," Allovein told them as he began to stand.

"We're sorry about your man," Marleigh explained. "We were only trying to defend ourselves." Again, Ethan tried to stifle his tears while he reached out with some of his magic to comfort her.

Ethan could also see Katie and Carth leaning on each other with their shoulders, while he said something to her. Then his father said something to him. "I love you, Ethan. I love you, my wife. I want you all to know that," Carth told them.

"I love you both," said Marleigh.

Allovein breathed in heavily through his nose in exasperation, while he pressed his eyes closed with his thumb and first finger. Then he said, "No, no. There is too much love here. Okay, here's what's going to happen, pals. I'm taking your children back to Malin Harr with me, where we'll indoctrinate them and then call their birds to them, so they can be our weapons until they're spent. The two of you will be executed as treasonous citizens—for harboring unregistered Dravens and failing to come forward about it," Allovein said as he got up from the table.

"No! Stop this!" Ethan said. He leaned forward and lunged across the table toward his mom to try and defend her one last time, but he only succeeded in hitting the bottom of the table, and he landed back on the ground, only able to look up at his mom or dad. He looked up to see Scarlet rising into the air and coming to a rest atop the chandelier. The lights flickered, brightened, and then dimmed. Then the lights of the chandelier turned scarlet. Once again, the raven stretched her wings and then bore her gaze deep into his mother and father. For several moments, Ethan watched in horror as Scarlet seemed to draw all the color out of their eyes until they were entirely white. In the process, Scarlet's eyes glowed even brighter than they had before, and his parents made nothing but small little mumbles or grunts. When his parents were all quiet, Scarlet closed her eyes, and finally, Carth and Marleigh let their faces fall straight onto the table. They were dead.

Katie had a mortified scowl on her face with her mouth agape. She cried and moped, unable to move her arms around. Ethan screamed loudly in anger and rage. "Fine, here you go!"

Allovein rose from the table with orange eyes. Suddenly, Ethan felt his handcuffs loosen before they fell off altogether. Ethan dove for his mother, only to find he was too late.

Allovein walked out of the dining room and to the front door where he spoke to his man. "Give them five minutes alone with their parents, and then they can have ten minutes to pack one suitcase each. Keep it tight, and call me when they're on their way," Allovein told him.

"Yes, Sir!" exclaimed the soldier.

Christian's war had finally come for Ethan and his family.

Chapter 12
dinner with Macie (Brian 2)

Three weeks had passed since Brian's incident—where he had turned into a tiger. He remembered what had happened. He remembered the fight, he remembered the man—Mason—he remembered what he had become, and most of all, he remembered what Mason had said. *You're a Draven. And it's about time you showed up.* Perhaps those words were what scared him the most.

Just then, the sound of gunfire pulled him out of his trance.

His heart began to race, looking for its source—had Iishrem made it there already? There it was again, but it was much too quiet to be an actual threat. That was when he realized it had been coming from the television the whole time—the news was talking about the war with Iishrem. The reporter was an older man with grey hair and glasses. Allen Carver was his name, and he had been the lead anchor of the Galliem Evening News for twenty years. People revered him.

Even before Brian heard his voice, he knew in his heart what was being reported. "Ferrum has fallen," Allen reported as if he were speaking at a funeral. His face left the screen, and clips of the fighting began to play on the screen. "The last of the Alliance Forces pulled out last night." The clips showed only death and the destruction of a once-pristine city. "In the days to come, many refugees may come to Maish. Those who weren't lucky were either killed or now live in an occupied city. My fellow residents of Galliem, as the refugees come pouring into our country, I urge everyone to be as good an ally as possible. It is with great sadness that I report that Galliem will undoubtedly be the next country on Iishrem's warpath. Here with a report on how to prepare your-selves is our chief foreign analyst."

Suddenly his phone began to buzz. It was Macie. *See you in an hour for dinner,* the message read. He had almost forgotten! Brian sprung off his couch and ran into his bathroom. He stripped off his clothes and threw himself into the shower. Fifteen minutes later, he had showered and shaved. He spiked up his red hair at the front and pulled on a pair of tan dress pants. He grabbed a red button-down shirt and matching tie out of his closet and threw them on too.

A moment later—after grabbing his wallet, keys, and phone— Brian whirled out of his flat, locked the door, and headed for his storage unit. It was a cool, brisk night, and the streets were oddly quiet for a Saturday evening. Brian made it to his storage unit quickly. Along the way, he had counted seven large moving trucks, each parked outside of various high-end apartment buildings. The rich looked frightened as they packed their belongings into vans that were headed for anywhere but here.

The poor were not so lucky. Brian also passed three gun shops during his short trip. He couldn't remember any of them having been there before the war began. Two of the shops were closed because they were already sold out of guns and ammunition. The third one had a line of people that stretched around the block. With thirty minutes left till dinner, Brian reached his storage unit. The door rattled upward as he opened it.

Brian looked forward to the short ride to the restaurant. He pushed his keys into his chopper's ignition, turned the engine over, and his favorite possession in life roared to life. A moment later, Brian closed his storage unit and rolled out into the city, headed for Chapelagio's.

Tonight was special—it was his one-year anniversary with Macie. He hoped that if they could make it through tonight, even the war might not be enough to break them apart.

When he got there, Brian parked his chopper across the street in a quiet garage and made his way down to the restaurant. Chapelagio's was a small four-story brick building with a giant sign of a portly black chef on it.

"Name, sir?" asked the host when he entered the lobby.

"Bringsly, Brian Bringsly. I have a reservation for two at eight-thirty," Brian told him. The man looked down at his papers, using a single finger to go through the names. The lobby had a peaceful look to it, and Brian welcomed that amongst all this talk of war. Once in the dining area, the tables were placed on top of a red carpet, which was surrounded by wood-finished floors. On the upper floors, there was extra dining space, a bar and cafe, and some slot machines. Even with all the space, reservations were usually required at least two weeks in advance.

"I see your date isn't here yet, sir. Would you like to wait in the lobby?" he asked after finding the reservation.

"No, thank you. She'll be here soon; I am a bit early," Brian explained as he looked down to check his phone for messages. There were none.

The host smiled and grabbed two leather-bound menus. "Right this way," he said, ushering Brian into the dining room. He took him up the stairs and over to a table for two located against the railing which overlooked the first story and staircases of the venue. Brian loved the view. "Your waitress will be with you shortly," he said with a smile before he took his leave.

While he waited for a waitress, Brian looked around at the other patrons. The second floor was mostly for couples. A couple of tables down, one couple was smooching across their table. Across the stairway, another one was arguing and trying their best to be quiet about it. There was only one person at the bar. He was turned around, but he had a large figure and seemed to barely fit on the barstool. He was hunched over and had a tall frosty draught. Something about him seemed familiar.

"Where's your date?" asked a young waitress with blonde hair and a thin figure.

"She's on her way," Brian said confidently. *Where are you, Macie?* he wondered, looking down at his phone.

"I'm sure she'll be here soon," said the waitress, and she smiled. "I'm Mya, and I'll be your waitress for the night. Can I start you off with a bottle of wine?"

"Yes, please. Can you find me a good red? Just not one on the top shelf," said Brian.

For a moment Mya looked confused, but then she smiled and said, "Fair enough." She turned around and walked into the kitchen.

From behind him, a familiar voice said, "Tonight must be a special night for you two." Instantly, he knew who it was, but he didn't want to believe it. The man at the bar put down enough cash to cover his bar tab and walked over to Brian's table. It was Mason. He had onyx eyes.

In an instant, Brian felt tense. As discretely as possible, he tried to get out of his seat. He backed up, but the chair would barely move an inch against the carpet. "Easy there, Brian. I'm not here to fight with you again. It took you three weeks to get this reservation, didn't it? You don't want to have wasted your time do you; I just want to talk."

"Why should I believe that?" asked Brian.

"Is he your date?" asked Mya returning from her expedition to the wine cellar a few seconds later.

"Oh no, Ma'am. I might wish so, but I'm just an old friend of his. What's that you've got there?" asked Mason.

"One of our best red wines—Flornt de Ill," she said, reading the label.

"Hmm, a good choice, Brian. You'll make Macie incredibly happy tonight," said Mason. Brian growled quietly. The waitress put the bottle down into a small bucket, which was on the center edge of the table. She placed two wine glasses on the table, pulled the cork out, and poured a little of the wine into one of the glasses for Brian. Nervously, Brian swished it around the glass and then in his mouth. It had a sweet taste and was not too dry.

"Very good, thank you. Macie will be here soon," said Brian, and Mya left the table.

"Why are you here?" asked Brian when Mya had gone.

"I know you don't like me, and I don't blame you, but I need you to listen to what I have to say. It could just save your life." Brian did nothing but nod. "Do you know who I am?"

"You're Mason Black. You ride a green dragon, you turn into a bear, and you teach at Christian's Academy. But where are your students? All I see is Iishrem about to invade Galliem," said Brian.

"So, you know who I am, and you know about the academy. Do you know where it is?"

Brian did not answer.

"It's the best-kept secret, and it has to be."

Mason was about to continue. "Why? So you can hide your precious students there?" Brian interrupted.

Mason's smile faded away. "You know, you really shouldn't insult your own kind."

"I don't know what you're talking about," Brian responded quickly.

"You do. Don't you wonder how you got back to your apartment after you turned into a tiger? Don't you wonder why you weren't arrested?" asked Mason. "I took you back there. I told the authorities you were not to be trifled with. They were happy to oblige after they saw what you did. What you could offer to the war—given the proper time to develop. You didn't disappoint me, Brian. You set off car alarms and caused three accidents. That's some impressive stuff right there."

Brian slammed his fists down on the table, rattling the wine glasses. The chatter of the restaurant stopped for a moment.

"You know what you are, Brian. Embrace it. I can tell you why you always fight, I can tell you why you turn into a tiger, and I can tell you why you dream of dragons. You're a Draven."

"Why are you here?" Brian asked again.

"Let me ask you a question first. How many Dravens do you think have graduated from the academy in the seven years it's been open?" Mason asked.

"A thousand," Brian guessed. "But it's probably far higher."

"Wrong. In seven years, we've only graduated five hundred or so Dravens—Christian Knowles and I included. Now I'm not at liberty to say what all of them are doing, but you can be sure they're all doing something to help us win this war. You know Iishrem has Dravens amongst them too—I've run into a few myself. They're as good as we are. We've got more in training, and a new class is coming in at the end of summer. I am inviting you to be part of that new class," he said, staring directly at Brian.

"Why would I want to do that?" Brian asked.

"Here's what I'm offering you, Brian. If you come to the academy, you'll be far away from the war, and we will teach you to master your unique skills. With those skills, you can protect yourself—and the ones you love. There you will find other people like yourself. We'll train you from fall to spring for three years. During the summers, you'll be given an assignment to complete before you can return to the academy. Once you graduate, you'll be fighting the war in whatever way we see fit. When the war is over, you'll be handsomely rewarded."

Brian thought about it.

"While you ponder it, let me ask you a question. What will you do in a couple of weeks when Iishrem arrives? Hide and hope to survive like you're some child incapable of defending yourself? Or will you do as you've always done and fight? I'm not asking you to stop fighting. I'm asking you to fight *for* something," said Mason.

"I have a girlfriend, an apartment, a chopper, and a life here. Maybe I don't want to leave?" Brian explained.

"When Iishrem makes it here, they will hunt you down and kill you," Mason told him plainly.

"How will they know I'm a Draven?" Brian asked before Mason could continue.

"That's something to explain when you've come to the academy. For now, all I can tell you is they have exceptionally good intelligence. As far as your life: sell your apartment, pack up your stuff, take your chopper, and bring Macie. She's welcome to stay in Meinghelia City while you train. You can go on acting as if the war isn't happening all you want, but it won't do you any good when it comes for you. You want to protect her, don't you? I am offering a way for you to do so."

Brian groaned, finally folding to his argument. "Okay, what do I need to do?"

"You've been officially invited to the academy. But you must find your dragon before you can be trained. The academy is in the nation of Maravinya—in Meinghelia City. You won't find its real location on any map today, but your dragon, Alyisay, already knows the way. Do you understand?" asked Mason. He poured himself a sip of wine and drank it down, savoring every drop.

"But how will I find my dragon?" Brian asked.

Mason smiled. "Brian, when the time comes—"

I will find you, said her voice in his head as Mason finished speaking.

Alyisay? he thought, but he heard nothing else.

"Brian, I wish you luck. The new term begins on the first day of fall. Be there, and you may have finally found a permanent home."

With a smile, Mason got up, put on his sunglasses, and walked down the staircase and out of sight. Brian slowly exhaled. He picked up his menu and tried to think about what he'd order, but all he could think about was what Mason had said. A minute or two later, Macie finally arrived.

"Macie," Brian said with his gaze meeting hers. She was wearing a forest green dress with a necklace and black heels. He got up and kissed her on the cheek. She had a moderately plump body and wide lips, and Brian really liked her a lot.

He pulled her chair out for her and walked back over to his own. "Sorry about my boss making me work late. They're preparing to close down the shop before—" she began.

"Let's not talk about that," said Brian. "How have you been?"

"Good," she answered. She looked down at her leg and grabbed something.

"I got something for us—for later tonight," she said, handing him a gift bag under the table. The bag had a blue on brown polka dot bra with matching thong in it.

"I can't wait to see you in it," he said, gently placing his hand on top of hers on the table. He poured her some wine, and after tasting it, she quickly decided that she wanted some more.

Mya then returned. "The lovely lady has finally arrived, I see. I was afraid I was going to have to be his date."

Macie giggled quietly and ordered before Brian did likewise. The two of them talked about life, family, and politics. Brian made sure they didn't talk about the war or his incident. He still wasn't sure how much she knew about his situation. He could deal with it another time. They laughed and drank and smiled and ate.

When they were almost done, he ordered another bottle of the same wine—after Macie had drunk most of the first. The bottle came out with the check. Brian paid and left a generous tip, then they both sipped on the second bottle together until it was time to leave.

Upon getting outside, Macie grabbed his tie and pulled him down to her height for a long kiss. It was warm and soft and left him smiling widely. "I know we've only been dating a year, but I don't care. I don't care what happens in a few weeks when the war gets here; I'll be with you—for better or worse." She didn't have enough money to leave the country.

"I may have a solution to that," he said before he could think.

"What?" she asked.

"We'll talk about it later. Come on, let's go back to my place," he said. Macie grabbed her bag and followed him to his Burcgetti. While they rode back to his apartment, Macie grasped his pecks lightly with her hands, and he smiled. He could feel her body gently cooing to the rumbling of his motorcycle. He dropped her off at his apartment, handing her the keys. "Make yourself at home. I'll be there in fifteen minutes." He rode his chopper to his unit and jogged back to his apartment, making it there in less than ten.

When he got there, the lights were dim, and he found her lying on his bed with nothing on but the lingerie from earlier. He could feel his throat stiffen as he spoke. "You look beautiful," he said.

"I hoped you would like them," she admitted. She sat up, staring into his eyes.

"I think they would look better on my floor," he told her while he met her gaze.

Macie smiled and took off her top, revealing her breasts which gelatinously matched her body type in a quivering, quaking motion. By the tie, Macie pulled him in and kissed him again. After that, Macie took his hand and pulled it in, underneath her thong. Brian smiled when he felt a finger slip inside of her. Then he joined her on the bed and began to take off his clothes.

Chapter 13
The Whistles of the Wind (Bailey 2)

SEEMS, MIDDLE REHEM

SUMMER, 1153, FOURTH AGE

ailey stopped running for a moment and crouched behind inflatable cover while she caught her breath. It was a sunny, hot summer's day, and she was currently a few minutes into her second game of a paintball tournament near the outskirts of Seems. Her team had lost their first game, and if they lost again, her team would be out of the tournament. She *wanted* to play for longer today—this tournament was important to her. If her team won, they'd soon enough move onto a more regional qualifying tournament with teams from several other nearby communities—ones that were several hours away by car. Bailey *needed* her team to win this tournament, but she would have to start with this round first.

Bailey forced herself to catch her breath, and somehow, that only seemed to exasperate her hyperventilation. They would hear her—the other team—and she only had herself and three other teammates left. Several seconds later, when she had gained enough control over her breathing, Bailey took a moment to lean out of her cover and look around at her surroundings. First, she looked behind her to see her teammates that were still in the game.

Bailey first saw her friend Amanda—a tall, skinny blonde-haired girl. Amanda had her back to an upward inflatable cone of cover, which was just wide enough for her to stand behind. However, Amanda did have to squeeze in her shoulders while she did. Her cover there wouldn't last long. Feeling bold, Bailey leaned up out of her cover to search for Ben and Corso. She was now lying down behind a plastic corrugated pipe, which she could jump into for cover if she needed. She'd be able to get off some good shots at the opposing team, but she'd be more exposed and locked in place while she did so. Her shots would really have to *count* there.

Bailey began to hear the wind whistling around her as several paintballs narrowly zipped past her head. Once they were gone, she took it as her chance to jump into the pipe. "Cover me!" she yelled to the rest of her team before she popped up and fired several shots at one of the opposing players who she had caught out of cover. Her first three paintballs missed, looking to be on target the whole time until they seemed to blow away right before hitting her target. Bailey adjusted her lead and fired three more shots, striking the boy twice in the chest. He had fired back at her while out in the open but to no avail. The boy Bailey hit held up his hands, stood up, and jogged his way off the course.

Bailey sprang up and dove into the middle of the pipe, feeling her boots hit leaves and dirt below her. Ben was in front of her, shouldered behind a small, square wooden fort. Instead of going into it, Ben chose to back around it to the far side, where Bailey lost track of him again. Ben was a full head and shoulders taller than her, with a thick mop of messy brown hair, which he often left unkempt. He had the body of a thick but fast Dargen player. She heard him yell and watched him fire several shots from his position towards an opposing player who had popped out from behind similar cover to fire at him. Ben was successful in the engagement. The round was beginning to even out—it was down to four on six. This was an eight on eight tournament, with two available subs.

Corso was also farther in front of her on the course, but he was to her right while Ben was on her left. Bailey remained in the relative center of the paintball course, and Amanda was at the back, using *her* sniper rifle—Bailey had loaned it to her for this round. It was good for her to get some experience playing other roles in these games. She had traded it for her burst-fire paintball rifle.

Corso had somehow found a way to perfect being both clumsy and dexterous while playing paintball. He was often her team's good luck charm. Even though her team was outnumbered by two, the four of them had great control over two-thirds of the course, which had allowed them to cluster the remaining six opposing players into a tight area, without enough cover for them all. The opposing team needed to spread out or they would lose. Bailey knew that a surge from the other team was coming.

Bailey enjoyed having Corso on her team. He wasn't a great shot, but he was a reliable player who knew how to play his role well. He was currently in the middle of a dried-out river embankment, crouched down with just enough cover for himself, close to a cluster of three enemy players. Bailey and her team had worked out some rudimentary hand signals in their time together. Corso gestured to her that he was going to give himself up to chase the rest of them out. Bailey smiled and liked his thinking before she softly called out to Ben and Amanda and gave them the same information through their hand gestures. Once the three of them were in place, Corso made his self-sacrificing move.

He got to his feet and held his rapid-fire paintball rifle at his hip. He ran up to the back of the opposing team's controlled area and leaned his back against some cover before jumping in to force them out. Meanwhile, Bailey, Ben, and Amanda peppered the other team's area repeatedly, with some light return fire back. When Corso was ready, he gave Bailey one last look and then ran into their area from the back, screaming. A fury of whizzing paintballs and grunts ensued.

"Bailey, crouch!" Amanda yelled from behind her. Two of the opposing players were leaving cover to make a charge forward. Bailey had just enough time to fall into her cover, narrowly avoiding several shots. She turned back to see Amanda taking aim at those two players, now from behind a paneled wooden fence—which provided much better cover for her than the inflatable cone had.

Bailey could not afford to watch Amanda any longer. Not if she wanted to stay in the game. She turned back to face the other team's players. Two balls hit one of them in the chest. Those shots must have come from Amanda. Bailey yelled and pointed her gun at the other player. They both fired at one another, but Bailey's shots did not miss. She got up and aimed her gun down its sights while she upped the pressure on the other team's remaining players.

Corso had already exited the course by the time she spotted him again, but he had been successful in knocking out another player. Now it was three on three, and the tide had unmistakably turned in their favor. However, Bailey knew the round had not yet been won. She and Ben needed to keep the pressure on the three remaining members of the opposition if her team was going to complete the comeback. Amanda might not be of much help while she was so far away, and timing along with pace were keys to winning paintball matches. Bailey had known that for almost as long as she had been playing.

Bailey got behind some tall cover, caught her breath, and looked for signs of Ben. She leaned back up out of her cover and found he was right where she thought he'd be. The three of them had their opponents enclosed within a relatively open square, halfway deep in the center of enemy territory. If Bailey and Ben didn't finish the round now, the tide could turn against them again. Their team had a plan of attack for this very situation.

"Hawk Swoop. Give me hawk swoop!" Bailey yelled the formations codename at the top of her lungs.

There was a small crowd watching their game, behind some fenced nets outside of the course. They cheered and seemed to watch more closely as Bailey's team began their attack. *Hawk Swoop* called for two players to pinch the edges of the enemy formation into a triangle from two sides, while a final teammate ran straight towards it down the center. The three of them would then proceed to pepper the team with fire once taking cover.

There was one more aspect of this play, which was personal to Bailey—the morality of her digression. She had a role to play here, and she could vary how she played it depending on her mood. She was at her best in paintball when she could choose how to react with intent. How many times did she really need to shoot an opposing team's player to knock them out of the game? The rule was one to the chest, but sometimes Bailey added an extra two or three just for good measure, or maybe just a second one to the ass just as the player stepped off course.

Bailey had several racks of firecrackers for distractions in one pocket and a lighter in the other. She pulled them out and lit them, then she tossed them over a fort and into the enemy formation.

They went off a second later with a snap, crackle, and pop, and Bailey and Ben charged in. She came around the corner with her gun drawn and quickly fired several bursts at the three players who were out in the open, behind several stacks of sandbags. Bailey quickly took out her man, and then she pressured up on the remaining two players who were giving Ben more trouble. Bailey had a chance to get behind them. Diving around some cover and then climbing over a fort quickly brought her into position for a clean shot.

What Bailey didn't expect though was to be shot in the shoulder by Amanda. It stung her back and made her put her gun up. She missed. One of their players had her dead to rights, but suddenly, in a splash of yellow paintballs, Amanda finally hit her original target.

"Aw, fuck!" the tall, bulky male screamed in exasperation.

A few seconds later, Ben finally finished off his opponent, and the round was over. As soon as it was, the rest of her team ran back out onto the course and all hugged it out. Bailey pushed herself straight into the middle and had her friends Ben and Corso on either side of her. Amanda, Skovick, and Staylie made up her clique.

Their win in that round set them up to continue their advance through the loser's bracket. When it came to their next game, Bailey continued to hit her stride, but she felt like there was always something right behind her. Someone watching her from the crowd. Someone whistling to the wind under their breath, and each time her shots then seemed to miss.

Bailey looked around for anyone who looked suspicious, and she found one face among the others which she deemed out of place. The man had a dirt-tooth grin and a wide-brimmed hat. Bailey noted the looks of that man, so she would not forget later. Mildra was not her ride—she was probably off at the casinos several hours away in the mountains. Ben had driven. The six of them had pooled their resources for a van—except for Lachien and Salem who always had their own ride and reservations. Bailey's team got knocked out in the semi-finals, much to her chagrin. "Don't worry about it, guys," she told them an hour or so later, once they were back in the van. They had just finished eating and were heading to a private lake house for after-game activities.

Ben looked down at his feet and then ran his hand through his thick hair and said, "Yeah, screw them though."

Corso looked up at her. "Did you see my play in that one round?" he asked her.

"You did great," she said jokingly, and then she pretended to take aim at him with an imaginary rifle. He matched her jesting taunt with an over-embellished screech and flinch of his own. They both laughed moments later, looking into each other's eyes. She playfully patted him on the elbow, and he slowly pretended to punch her in the side. Bailey let him hit her with his fist just lightly in the side, and then she loosed her mouth agape at him. "Corso!"

He looked over at her and reddened before edging closer to her. Bailey shuddered and turned away, "Oh. Not right now then," he said a moment later. The rest of the van giggled at Corso's gesture, having seen what he'd attempted. Bailey gave him an eye, maybe she'd make it up to him, later.

Bailey turned herself away from him and looked out the window at the endless forests which bordered the feet of the sharp, snowcapped mountains. She knew if they drove far enough north, she would see the Shrouded Sea again, but that was not their destination now.

"Go left here," she told them about twenty minutes later. They were about twenty miles across town from Mildra's home. They turned down a dirt road which led to a hidden lake within the forest. The piece of property which her father owned came complete with a lake house and pier. The lake was several miles in diameter in a meandering oblong circle, and there were several other properties around, but no one would see them if they didn't wish to be seen.

The tires of the van hit gravel, and the vehicle rattled to life, waking up the rest of the team from their stupor. The van smelled like dirt, grass, paint, and sweat between the lot of them. There was nowhere to shower at the paintball park, and they had gone straight from there to a Duskinian fast food restaurant for burgers. Ben drove them down the half-mile driveway and pulled up to the lake house, which was situated at the end of a roundabout.

They quickly unloaded the van and settled into their rooms. Bailey took herself right up to her room, which she knew had a mini-fridge, and her suitcase was already there. She grabbed a light summer beer out of the fridge and popped it open to take a swig. She grabbed her Bluetooth speaker and a skimpy two-piece bathing suit—one with a forest camo pattern with sniper rifles spotted across it.

She took both downstairs and into the living room, where everyone else was going to reconvene. Amanda, Skovick, and Staylie were already waiting downstairs; Ben and Corso had yet to return down. "Bailey, we're heading down to the lake," Staylie said, holding a beach ball and a bathing suit. She was still wearing her dirty clothes from the paintball game. Staylie had nice brown skin, black hair, brown eyes, and a sporty build.

"I'll join you in a few minutes," she told them, sitting down on a leather couch and turning the TV onto news of the war. She really would—in a few. The news was covering a story about forty thousand Iishrem troops landing in the northern Haishian hinterlands for a surprise invasion last night. Their orders were to cause chaos and burn shit down. Their soldiers sounded like *savages* to her. What they would do for a war to expose a truth—which only their continent had entirely lost faith in at the end of the last age. Such truths that Iishrem was rediscovering now had never quite been so unknown to Allirehem and the rest of the world.

"Bailey, you coming?" asked Ben, carrying a similar load to the others before, with Corso in tow. They were all going to go skinny dipping. The boys seemed more desperate to try it than the girls of course, but then Bailey spied Staylie stripping down on the pier before anyone else. She rolled her eyes. It was always her first.

By the time she had returned her eyes to the TV, a story that would have caught her eye had already passed its due reporting *Iiasmaeic troops spotted in Seems*. "A few minutes," she told them and took another swig of her beer.

A few minutes later, Bailey walked out of the backdoor and onto the wooden patio, which led out onto a pier into the lake. Bailey stepped out in her dirty clothes into the hot summer's day. She carried her stuff down to the end of the pier where Ben and Corso were standing buck-naked.

"It's alright you know, but don't you both think you're standing right next to each other in full sight of everyone else for just a bit too long?" she asked with half of a laugh. Corso and Ben nearly jumped out of their skin. Apparently, she had caught them. Bailey put her stuff down and then turned towards the lake, to see Corso turning towards her. He quickly looked down at her and then began to laugh as Ben pushed him into the lake. Bailey looked Corso over, while he haphazardly tumbled his way into the water, ass and all. She was not unimpressed with what he had to work with.

Ben remained on the top of the pier with her, stepping away from the edges so that no one would jump up and pull him in. He began to walk towards Bailey without hiding himself at all. They both kept their eyes directly on each other's, and then Bailey began to back up and undress. She wasn't too playful about, she was sweaty, and honestly, she smelled like grass and dirt. She bent down and kicked off her boots, took off her sweatpants, and then stripped herself of her shin guards and knee guards. She looked back up at Ben and walked towards him, standing upright and with excellent posture. She pressed her fingers to his chest, just above his pecks, and suddenly, he began to move backward.

Bailey took off her hoodie and tossed it back across the pier. She took off her shirt and tossed it away too, leaving only her underwear. Before she pulled that off, she pressured Ben to the edge of the pier and looked him in the eyes. She kissed him lightly on the lips and then pushed him into the water with as much force as she could muster. Ben came up out of the water, sputtering for breath a moment later. She had taken a look at Ben's endowment the same as Corso's, and she was more impressed with his, but that wasn't always what had interested her in the past.

She jumped in after Ben—once she had removed her underwear—and then swam after Corso. "Bailey," he said happily. She splashed him in the eyes and then surprised him with a kiss before he could open them again. When comparing both of them, Bailey would rather experiment with Corso.

If she wanted anything though, she'd rather go to Ben. She hadn't been with either of them yet. *Perhaps tonight?* Bailey thought.

She swam away from both and got some space to herself, which was exactly what she needed at the moment. She began to listen to the world and all its sounds of silence, peace, and happiness that were all around her. Now, before the war would begin. A war that Bailey knew she would not outrun forever.

For a moment, there was peace. Her naked friends bounced around in the water with their beach balls and swimming noodles, discreetly looking at each other when the others weren't watching. A few minutes later, she finished up, one of the first to put her actual bathing suit or shorts on.

They continued to splash around or toss beach balls to each other or lay out and tan for another hour or so, before Skovick, Ben, and Corso got out and dried off. They wanted to get the grill running. Amanda and Staylie got out as well and headed up to their room to dry off and shower. That left Bailey out in the water by herself. She closed her eyes and listened to the wind.

The leaves, branches, trees, and wind rustled together in peaceful tranquility, which made Bailey wish she could stay at the lake with her friends forever. No more investigating tourists in town or looming threats of a war—or her having an Eedon Rath-ni and being a Draven. For several moments, she had her peace. Her friends were in the background, beginning to drink on the patio, and they faded into the background. Then there came a lurching sound that grumbled from the driveway. Bailey felt her eyes snap open, and she looked into the forest, where she saw two troop transports for ten soldiers each grinding down her driveway, while they were escorted by a machine gun Humvee at its head and rear.

Then Bailey began to listen even closer. She listened to the wind and then looked into the sky where she could see the man with pale white skin and long black hair from the paintball game. He flew in a circle around the property on top of a black eagle. Bailey swore under her breath, and exasperatedly swam her way back to shore.

This was the last thing that she needed to have happen today, but it was okay; Bailey had prepared for such an eventuality. No one had had to tell her to practice with real guns occasionally, when her father had signed her up for paintball and left her to essentially her own, in the middle of her childhood. She would at least go down fighting with her friends; for her friends. Bailey got out of the water and pulled on her after swimming outfit as quickly as she could. Once Bailey got dressed, she jogged back into the lake house, passing through the cabana pool, horseshoe patio, and BBQ deck first. When she reached the back of the cabin, the rest of her friends were drinking and dancing around in their swimwear. The boys had begun to panfry split-open hot dogs with craft council-lieean cheese on duskin-iean toast.

"There are soldiers coming! Soldiers from Iishrem!" Bailey tried to yell over her very own Bluetooth speaker. A few of her friends seemed to see her mouth moving as if she were talking, but they were all just like, "Bailey, what?"

Bailey had to stifle her frustration with her friends. Why had she bought such a loudspeaker? She spotted it there, close to Amanda sitting next to the coffee machine in the kitchen. Bailey asked herself, how could she get all their attention at once?

Bailey remembered she had one more set of her firecrackers! She pulled out one set from her pocket and lit them with a Relnàs lighter.

Snap! Snap! Pap! popped the firecracker in the living room a few seconds later. The music and laughter in the room quickly ceased. "Quiet!" she screamed at her friends. They quickly took notice and fell silent. They stopped short of realizing the severity and danger of the situation, though. "As you may know, my father is the Regal Draven Commander of the Allirehem Resistance, and the Deck

Lieutenant of the ARF Clancy Triten," she informed them, far from the first time.

"Yeah, what of it?" asked Ben.

Corso seemed to shrink within his skin.

"We have to defend ourselves, and four of us here have trained with guns before. My father and I keep four such guns here: a shotgun, a sniper rifle, a pistol, and a bolt-action carbine," she told them.

"You're not telling me what I think you are, are you?" asked Amanda, who came running into the kitchen with a frayed expression.

"What? I don't get it!" Ben exclaimed, taking his time to comprehend what was happening.

"Well, I'm his daughter, and there is this whole *wary war boom de doom gloom* thingy going on right now. You know... Dravens and Eedon Rath-ni and shit." She paused, then turned to look out a big window that looked out over the front of the house and the roundabout. Again, like seven years previous, Bailey found it filled with Iishrem soldiers. When she saw the turret gunners in the Humvees turn toward her, Bailey ran. She had just reached the top of the stairs by the time the first window in the cabin broke via gunfire. Glass shattered, and guns racketed to life in a hail of gunfire from high caliber rifles.

Bailey needed to reach the weapons locker and get the guns to her friends, but she wondered if it would have been better for them to come to her. *Not today*, she thought.

Bailey felt her anger grow as she finally reached her father's weapon's locker. She dialed in the combination and pulled it open. She took the bolt-action carbine and thirty rounds of ammo. Bailey's friends would have to come to her while she held the

Iishrem soldiers at bay. Their team had a formation name for such a play as well. "Retreat to me!" she yelled at the top of her lungs. Bailey took cover at the top of the stairs in the wide-open entryway, holding her father's bolt-action carbine towards the ground.

She held her breath and steadied herself as she struggled to load the rifle as quickly as she knew she could. She would have to fight to survive, and although she was more than willing to do so, Bailey cursed her father and linage for bringing her into this war at such a young age. Christian had taken her only remaining parent from her when she needed him most. Her father had let her down by accepting it all and leaving her, but she cursed the House of Lance for their role, as well. "Arggh!" she yelled. Bailey shouldered the rifle that was almost as long as she was tall into position and aimed down its sights.

She was not particularly good with this gun; its recoil always bucked her armpits after she fired. But this time she held it firm and fired while she tried to cover her friends retreat up the stairs. Bailey fired again and again at the advancing men. She could see them taking cover behind army vehicles at the roundabout. Her shots seemed to be on target, and then they would just barely miss. She spat down the stairs, in anger. Then at the back of the army formation, she saw the man from before with his pale white skin and long, flowing jet-black hair. A thunderstorm began to rumble in the distance, but first, it began to rain outside. He stood next to a big, black eagle and met her gaze. The enemy Draven glared at her with yellow eyes and challenged her to fire. Once again, Bailey could not find her mark when firing at him, but that didn't stop her from imploding the heads of one of his cronies with her rounds which were smelted off the line to do such a thing to normal men foolish enough not to wear helmets against the threats of a nineteen-year-old girl over two hundred and fifty yards away. He must have been running up to inform his commander of something important. Some of the carnage landed below the commander's chin, and it looked like the blood had ruined his freshly lit cigar.

When the enemy Draven commander noticed what Bailey had accomplished, he glowered at her with his dark-green eyes. He grabbed his automatic assault rifle off his back to return fire at her. Before he could, her father, Clancy, and his eagle landed in the center of the roundabout in a swirl of wind and screeching. Now, Bailey and her friends had a fighting chance.

Chapter 14

A Clash of Eagles (Bailey 3)

SEEMS, MIDDLE REHEM

SUMMER, 1153, FOURTH AGE

"Hold your fire! Hold your fire!" yelled the Draven commander, holding up his hand in a fist to the rest of his comrades. "Don't be so overactive. Maybe we ought to have a talk after all. Clear the air. You know who I am?" asked the enemy Draven. He strode forward, in front of his eagle and said, "I know who you are." The Draven commander discarded his cigar and pulled a long cigarette from a tin within his coat pocket. He lit it before taking a draw and exhaling a moment later.

Bailey caught her breath and patted each one of her friends on the shoulder as they came up the stairs for safer positions. Bailey wanted Staylie and Skovick to hide in the bathroom. She gave Ben the shotgun—its recoil would, hopefully, affect his accuracy the least. She gave Amanda the bolt-action carbine and Corso the K-9 pistol. She then took the sniper rifle for herself. She ran her hand up and down its shaft for a moment, coming to respect its potential damage to herself and her enemies.

Before she leaned back out of her cover to watch the unfolding confrontation, Bailey ordered her friends into defensive positions. There were two halves to the second story of the lake house, which were connected via a balcony that crossed through the wide-open entryway that they were in now. The second story had a staircase for access on either side, with one of them facing the front door and the other the back. They would need to cover both staircases and keep a watchful eye on soldiers outside *and* their unarmed friends in the bathroom.

"Amanda, head into the bedroom facing the roundabout and see if you can take a few shots. Keep yourself safe, and don't get killed!" Bailey told her. "Corso, you go with her."

"Roger," they both said in unison before they both ducked down and sprinted down the corridor across the entryway.

"Alright, Ben, cover the front door and the hallway. Most of all, keep Skovick and Staylie safe. Your weapon has the shortest range anyway," she told him. Then she grabbed the sniper rifle and strapped it around her back. Ben caught her by the arm for a second.

"W-whhhere are *you* going?" he asked her. He let go when she looked back at him with a scowl.

She showed him the sniper rifle and scowled. "To a bedroom for a better shot." She headed for one with a window that looked out over the roundabout. There was a writing desk in the corner with a typewriter and a globe of the world on it. She jogged over to it and pushed it over to the window, so she could balance the barrel of her rifle on it while she took shots. Finally, when she had opened the window and knocked out the screen, she continued watching the showdown.

The enemy Draven commander had ordered his troops to encircle her father. At his command, his men aimed their rifles towards Clancy who was standing next to his eagle. The two Draven and Eedon Rath-ni pairs were separated by about forty feet. The troop transport vans had been parked out of the way where the driveway re-entered the forest, and the armored Humvees had taken strategic positions with good lines of sight.

Bailey had a clean shot at both of their gunners, but she did not dare to take a shot or even move the barrel of her gun or they may start firing. The enemy Draven commander noticed her reemergence into the confrontation as soon as she knocked out the window screen.

"You've been training her for this day, Clancy." Her father said nothing. "I'm Zeren Wikes," said the Draven with the black eagle as he turned towards her and looked her in the eyes. He took another drag from his cigarette while they spoke in Gallaeic. "I've got a bit of a history with your father, you see. It's a little personal, actually, but it's nothing against you, Bailey."

"She trains herself; I'm quite proud of her actually," her father said. How did he know her name?

Zeren's eyes were as cold as stone. "I'll kill her myself, in front of you, before I kill you last," Zeren told her father.

Bailey took a shot right at Zeren's head for that remark and missed wildly. Zeren turned right to her window and smirked at her with orange eyes. "She's got spunk, I'll give her that. Leave her be—as long as you can—but defend yourselves if she shoots at you first. Kill her friends!" Zeren told his men.

The troops began to disperse while her father and Zeren continued to have a staredown. Clancy drew his burst-action assault rifle, aimed it at Zeren, and fired several bursts at his chest. Each time a bullet from her father's gun hit Zeren, a bright, golden flash sparked from where he had been hit. The bullets fell to the ground crumpled up, and Zeren looked completely unharmed when her father stopped firing.

Then all the troops pointed their guns at her father and began to fire. Zeren and his eagle simply watched while he smoked. Raejen leapt a few feet into the air and then covered her father with her wings. The first few shots which hit her father resulted in similar golden flashes and sparks.

When Raejen landed in front of Clancy to protect him, not only the soldiers but the turret gunners in the Humvees began to fire upon the defensive eagle. This continued for several seconds. All the while, her father and his eagle continued to stay right there, seemingly absorbing it all. Magical energy, which looked like golden sparks, began to emanate from all over Raejen.

However, Bailey noticed that the bullets which hit Raejen were doing something different to her than what they had done to Zeren. When bullets hit Raejen, instead of crumpling and falling to the ground, the bullets stopped exactly where they would have hit her father and did one thing: they turned themselves back around toward where they had been fired from. A few seconds later, the smirk that had been on Zeren's face turned to a fearful scowl. "Stop! Stop! Stop!" he yelled, but it was too late.

For just a moment, all the gunfire ceased, then Bailey was blinded for several seconds by a luminous golden flash. While she had her eyes closed, all she could hear were the screams and grunts of dying men. Bailey reopened her eyes to see twelve of the troops Zeren had brought with him now dead or bleeding out on the ground. The armored Humvees lay silent and smoking, having been peppered by the unwelcome return of their own spent ammunition. Her father, Clancy, re-emerged from behind his eagle a few seconds later, looking like he had barely broken sweat.

"Perhaps you should have brought more men," Clancy said with a smile.

"You fools!" Zeren said furiously. "No matter. We can just have ourselves an old-fashioned duel of Dravens." He pulled out a silver rapier from behind his back and held it in front of his eyes for a moment before he beckoned her father forward. Her father took a moment to gather himself, and then a new sound entered the fray for the first time—it was quite concussive and disorienting. Bailey's head rang, and her vision swayed. She made her way out of the bedroom and back into the hallway toward her friends. The disorientation made her walk like she'd just pounded several beers.

When she looked back out one last time, she saw that the eagles were locked in another duel of their own. The eagles had spread out around the roundabout while they stalked and squawked at each other. Her father had drawn a cutlass from his back; he and Zeren were sparing in an epic sword fight. Her father turned to look at her and gave her a nod while he temporarily parried Zeren. It shocked her how quickly he had found and met her gaze.

The remaining eight soldiers began to sprint together toward the front door. Raejen quickly leapt into the air and snatched two of them with her talons, ripping them in half a second later. Bailey especially enjoyed the sight of their spinal columns, all covered in blood and marrow. Once Raejen had dropped the remains of her latest kills, she turned around towards the other eagle and began to circle it again.

The eagles clashed with weapons of their own and a set of their claws encased in metal bodies. Each eagle wielded a unique weapon called a gare-e-jien they grasped within one set of their talons, while they used their other set for grappling or clawing. The metal object they wielded resembled a combination of a three-pronged sword and had the forming of a shield between each prong. It looked to Bailey like the eagles could stab with the ends of it, cut with its sides, and block with its depth.

The thunderous shock of an explosion blowing open the front door downstairs pulled Bailey away from the duel of her father and the eagles and back to protecting her friends. The soldiers were coming inside! Bailey grabbed the sniper rifle and lugged it into the hall, raising it just as three soldiers entered in a triangle formation. She looked around to see the positions of her friends. Ben had taken up a defensive position behind a wall that faced the front door on the first floor. "Bailey," she heard called from the bathroom. It was Skovick. He tossed her several sets of firecrackers.

Bailey could not have been more grateful for his quick thinking. The firecrackers landed right at her feet, and she gently leaned the sniper rifle on its side against the wall. She picked up three sets of the firecrackers and drew her Relnás out of her pocket. She lit all three sets and then tossed each of them at one of the soldiers. While the hallway *popped* repeatedly over the next few seconds, Bailey spotted Amanda crouched with the carbine behind a tall, thick oak chest in the middle of the balcony.

More gunfire rang out from behind her, and Bailey felt the wooden railings that ran along the balcony begin to splinter. Three more guards had burst in through the back door. When she turned to look, Bailey heard the unmistakable gat of a shotgun followed by the sputtering of assault rifles.

Bailey looked to Amanda. "Move!" Amanda yelled to her and popped out of her cover to take two shots at another one of the disoriented soldiers. Amanda downed her man with a solid shoulder shot. Another one lay dead, pooling from a shotgun blast. Ben needed to retreat from his position on the first floor. He did that by shooting the final soldier at the front of the house in the legs, and then he knocked him over with a shoulder charge before surging up the stairs. In front of her, Corso fired several shots with his pistol, finishing off the soldier Ben had knocked down. Bailey grabbed her final remaining firecrackers and lit them. She tossed them over the other side of the corridor. Bailey then dived across to the other half of the upstairs and was greeted by Corso. Ben caught up to them, just as the firecrackers went off.

"You two okay?" Bailey asked.

"Mhmm." Corso nodded. Ben simply brushed his hair back.

The sound of a painful shriek rang out over the clangor of the confrontation, once again disorientating everyone who was unprepared. Bailey turned to look down into the kitchen, and she saw the three soldiers just beginning to regain their senses. Bailey turned around and saw the black eagle out the window of one of the rooms at the back of the house. He was headed straight for the living room. Bailey saw the eagle tuck its wings in as tightly as it could around itself before bursting into the expansive cabin with high ceilings through a large window. Bailey looked and saw the same yellow glow from before ripple all around Zeren. The debris the collision created did not get in his way, and his magic had no problem cratering its way through not only the window but also several significant sections of the walls.

In a jerking motion, Zeren twisted his hand forward at her, and a tiny double-barreled pistol popped out at the end of a track he had strung around his arm. Zeren fired at her, and pain stung at her shoulder, followed by the warm feeling of blood. The house shuttered again under the force of the black eagle as it exited the house through another hole that its shields blew out themselves. The shock drove Bailey to the ground.

Bailey fought to pick herself up as quickly as she could. She would be fine; it was just a graze. She watched her father follow Zeren through the now-gaping wound in his lake house on his own eagle. Clancy fired his burst action rifle at the three remaining soldiers, downing each of them. Then the pair fled back outside to open air, and after Zeren once again.

Once they were gone, the world finally began to quieten down again. The silence was soon broken by the trembling words of Amanda as she lay with her back against the chest, bleeding from her stomach. "Bailey, help?"

Bailey turned and looked to her blonde-haired friend. Amanda began to cough up blood, sitting there in her bikini bottoms and a light summer hoodie—both now covered with blood. Bailey quickly got to her feet and ran over to her friend. "Ben!" she screamed.

"Coming," he said from behind her. Bailey put her arms around Amanda and tried to comfort her while she waited for Ben.

"Here, hold your hands like this." Bailey paused, showing Ben how to hold his hands on top of each other, palm over palm with the fingers interlaced. "And apply pressure right here. Staylie, Skovick, bring gauze, bandages, and sterilizer."

A few seconds later, each of her friends had come together and huddled around Amanda. Bailey looked to Corso and saw that he was still carrying his pistol. *Good, he can be their guard*, Bailey thought. She grabbed the bolt-action carbine off the floorboards where Amanda had dropped it. It was full, and she knew she still had several clips of ammo in her pockets from earlier. "Corso, stay here and guard them. Look after her," she told him.

"Where are you going?" Corso asked.

Bailey was furious. "To help my father finish this fight!"

She lugged the carbine down the stairs and through the busted front door. Out in the front yard, the scene was quiet, and her father was standing next to his eagle Raejen, wiping down his sword. There was no dead eagle or screaming Zeren being beaten up by her father. He simply stood there next to his eagle, looking at the sky as Zeren and his eagle flew off toward the horizon. She ran out to the roundabout where her father stood in the center.

"Arghhhhhhhhhhh!" she screamed at her father into the quiet summer evening as darkness fell. She fell to her knees halfway to her father and fired one shot, high in the sky, and then dropped the carbine.

"Bailey!" he exclaimed, turning around and running toward her. Bailey shuddered and turned away from him as her father reached her. He threw his arms around her, towering over her. "Are you okay? You're shot," he said.

Bailey wasn't the one who was bleeding out in the lake house. "It's a flesh wound," she said, kneeling there and shaking her head. She was so angry with him. Bailey felt herself redden, and she turned to her father and yelled, "Amanda has been shot in the stomach! My friend who was simply just enjoying a summer vacation—before you and some of your friends just showed up out of nowhere.

"I'm sorry, Bailey, I didn't plan on this," he told her, sweating with angst.

"That's exactly what I thought you'd say. Come on, let's save my friend," Bailey pleaded.

"Of course. We'll fly her to a hospital in town," he told her. He backed away from her, then ran into the lake house. Bailey stayed on her knees and began to cry. Raejen nuzzled the tip of her beak against her shoulder a moment later while they waited for her father to return with her friend. Amanda had fallen unconscious but was alive when her father returned with her in his arms. Ben, Corso, and the rest of her friends trailed her father, asking questions of Amanda's health.

"Look, look. There's nothing else we can do for her until we get her to a hospital alright?" he told her friends. "Which one of you drove here?"

Ben raised his hand. "Alright. Well, the lot of you run off to the van and head to Seems General Hospital. We'll see you there," Clancy explained, waving them away. Ben and Corso waited for a second. She shook her head, looking back at them. Bailey already knew how she was getting to the hospital.

Her father carried Amanda towards Raejen, who was grasping her gare-e-jien in her talons. He laid Amanda into the shield portion, where she fit cozily in between two of the sword prongs. "Raejen won't drop her," her father explained. Raejen lowered her back and knelt so she and her father could get onto her back. It would not be the first time that she had ridden her father's eagle. "I promise."

"She can't die," she told her father.

"I'm not going to let her die, I swear," he told her. "We have to go; come on."

Bailey wanted to tell him that she didn't believe him. She wanted to tell him that once again he had ruined her life. She almost thought about grabbing Amanda and taking her chances on her own with the rest of her friends, but she decided there was no time for any of that. She climbed on Raejen and sat down in front of her father.

When they took off, she took extra care to keep an eye on Amanda, but Raejen did not have any trouble flying the three of them into town. Bailey felt quite cold while she rode on Raejen. They flew together in silence until a few minutes later her father pulled out his phone and made a call to the hospital. Seems, the city itself, came into view a few minutes later.

The city sat several miles inland on relatively flat ground before the city divulged up the mountains into its casino, nightlife, and entertainment district. Above all of that were the resorts and ski slopes. With early evening now having set in, Bailey looked up the intimidatingly tall mountains. There was still summer snow, around sixteen thousand feet up. The city was much more picturesque when lit up in the winter. Seems General was the tallest building near the center of the city itself. Its campus rose eight stories in the air and had several different smaller buildings and helipads on its grounds. True to his words, there was a group of doctors and nurses waiting to meet them upon landing.

Raejen landed, and they loaded Amanda onto a stretcher. The group of nurses, both male and female, strapped her onto the stretcher and were supervised by the two doctors who were taking notes. Bailey assumed that once that was done, the two of them would land to go in with them to see to her friend. She leaned over onto the side of Raejen and had almost hopped off when her father caught the neck of her shirt.

Clancy pulled her back onto Raejen and they took off into the air. As they did, Clancy told the doctors, "Her friends will be here in the next thirty minutes. Do you have the bandage and anti-infection supplies I asked for?" The head doctor nodded and had one of his nurses toss her father a first-aid kit, which he handed to Bailey. "Sit still while I patch you up," he told her. As he did so, the two of them began to rise back up into the air on Raejen.

As Bailey felt her father clean and bandage her stomach wound, she watched the doctors wait for an elevator with Amanda. That was when it really dawned on her that Seems was no longer her home, and she wouldn't get to say goodbye to her friends. Christian's war had ruined her life, and it had been her father's fault. Bailey fought for a second to escape his grasp, shouldering him in the gut and trying to roll away, but he ate each punch effortlessly and caught her arm each time.

"Bailey, Bailey, listen to me. We cannot stay here, or you'll put all of your friends and this entire hospital in even more danger," he told her.

Bailey threw another elbow back at his face, which he caught. By then the two of them had flown half a mile from the hospital—east toward the Eldic Ocean. "What do you mean?" she asked.

"You know I wasn't able to kill Zeren. He'll get more men and come back for us. He would tear through that hospital to get you—which could include killing more of your friends. But if we go, we can outfly him, and then he won't bother," he told her.

"What about Mildra? What about all my stuff?" she asked him.

"Honestly, I doubt my mother will even notice we're gone. Saw her at one of the casinos this morning—up ꩜20,000. Bailey, if you don't fight me on this, I'll make it worth your while. Iishrem is going to keep coming for you; we must get you somewhere safe. It's time for you to train as a Draven," he told her. "Have you heard from your hawk at all? What did you say his name was?"

Bailey listened to her mind and her heart for a moment and heard nothing but the crashing waves below and Raejen's ruffling feathers. Then she thought of him, *Hector*, and she felt warm again atop Raejen. "Hector," she told her father. "Should I have heard from him by now?"

She turned around to see her father's expression and found him to be looking concerned. "Have you seen any signs of him in person? Heard his voice in your mind?" he asked her.

Bailey knew that she *had* several times. She remembered growing up, climbing the trees in the forest as high as she could. She remembered the times she had learned to live in the forest, and the times she had learned to hunt, stalk, and then attack her prey. He had always been in her mind, and sometimes she thought she could see him just beyond the tops of the trees or in the next clearing within the forest, but he had never actually been there for her. And she hadn't heard his voice in her head for years. "No, not recently," she admitted.

Clancy looked disheartened. "Well, we'll have to deal with that. There could be several reasons for it; we'll get it sorted out in the morning," he told her. Clancy flew the two of them an hour outside of Seems, and they landed at a roadside motel, farther down the northern Gallaeic coast. The two of them would stay there for the night, and Raejen would find somewhere in the wilderness to sleep.

Clancy put his arms around her shoulders and turned her around towards him. He pulled her close to him for a hug. "I'm sorry," he told her. "I just need this one night, and then I'll make everything better for you. I promise. I'll find a way for you to keep some of the life you had in Seems. Just give me tonight."

It was far from a good ending to her emotionally compromising day, but she had to admit that it was looking up just a little bit—at least, from the gunfight earlier. This would do for one night, and then Bailey would sort the rest of her life out in a world she had not yet gotten to see. For once, *she* would be the tourist in the foreign cities and countries, and not just the girl seeing affluent misers and their families to their hotel suites. Bailey would be the one the locals deigned to impress. "Well, that's a start," Bailey told him. Then the two of them walked into the motel lobby together.

Chapter 15
Rebellion (katie 6)

Imperium Aendor, Dusk, Iishrem

Summer, 1153, Fourth Age

When Allovein had left their home, and they were *alone*—on the inside of their house at least—neither she nor Ethan made a move at first. For perhaps a minute, Katie did not want to look to her side and see who sat next to her, looking at her with his last glance in this world. For that moment she watched Ethan weep over Marleigh, who had her face down on the table with her left arm to her side and right hand near the edge of the table. The edges of Marleigh's fingers just touched the bottom edges of her father's arm.

Ethan began to sputter while he sobbed. Katie looked up at him while she still sat in her chair, watching him wipe away his tears for both of their lost parents. Suddenly, everything began to fall into place for Katie, and then her levy broke.

Katie looked to her left and saw Carth's dead eyes staring up at her. At the moment that Carth had met the raven's gaze, he had been looking over at her to say something. He had never had the time to finish what he was going to say or give any final look toward his son. "Daddy," was all she could manage when she saw his face and petrified body. Katie began to cry, and she put her arms around his shoulders, then she pressed her cheek to the space between his shoulder and neck.

For another minute, Katie could do nothing but cry. She wept over her father, Carth had been looking out to her and reaching for her when he had died. Perhaps if Carth had a few more seconds, he would have looked to Ethan next and to then his wife. Katie would never get to bury her parents, but what she was about to do felt right to her.

Katie gently held her father's face and turned it to look toward Marleigh. When Ethan saw what she had done, still sobbing over Marleigh, he motioned to do the same thing. Ethan stepped back from Marleigh, who had been looking out across the table attempting to reason with Allovein when she had died. Ethan seemed to sense what she was thinking. "She wasn't looking at him when she died," Ethan told Katie, pointing out a recent family portrait hanging off the wall on the other side of the dining room. "Seems like that was the only way she could think to be looking at all of us before he killed her."

Ethan gently turned her face and redirected it so that she was looking across the table to Carth. Katie stepped back from the two of them for a moment and saw that her parents were now looking at each other. Then she saw that Marleigh had been reaching for Carth's hand, just before both had met their doom. Katie took her father's left hand and placed it gently on top of Marleigh's right.

Ethan gently brushed Marleigh's hair out of her eyes, and then the two of them looked at each other for the first time since Allovein had left the house. Both understood there was one more thing they needed to do for their parents before Katie wanted to swap places with Ethan. Ethan would probably want to swap places with her too. The two of them said nothing while they looked at each other, and then Katie took the initiative to close her father's eyes with her hand. Ethan did the same with Marleigh a second later.

Katie traded places with her brother, by deftly maneuvering around him in the narrow dining room while he took a more direct route to Carth. Katie had only just had a moment to gently hug her mother's back when the front door opened, and four soldiers strolled into the living room. As soon as they did, Katie felt herself instantly snap to attention—almost like she had no choice in the matter. She walked toward them and stood at attention for them in the living room—as if their commanding officer hadn't just murdered her parents in front of her. Katie did not want them to hurt her.

The group of four soldiers was made up of three male soldiers and one female, and each of them had a very sturdy, stocky build. The woman in the formation—a tall, sturdy built black woman—stepped forward. She looked up at Katie as though she was egging her on to take a shot. Katie wondered if she would be able to take her, one on one, but then she decided to push those thoughts out of her mind when she looked at the three male soldiers. Katie was sure that there were several more guards outside overseeing their continued capture. There was no way for Katie to fight her way out of this. It would only cost her more harm to herself.

Katie was unwilling to be the one to initiate physical punishment upon herself, but that didn't mean Ethan felt the same way. He was still milling about in the kitchen, crying over their parents. "Young Draven," said the female commander. "They aren't your parents anymore, and you have your own place to be now. Your own role to play."

Ethan withdrew from the table and walked over towards the commander who stood in the middle of the living room. Katie knew the look she saw in her brother's eyes. She had seen it many times before. Katie had been on the receiving end of that more than once having grown up with Ethan. He was fancying a fight. When they were only steps apart, Katie looked back over to the commander. The commander cracked her neck. She already knew what was about to happen.

Katie wondered if she should help her brother. She wondered if she should stop him. The moment for her to do anything passed too quickly for her to decide. Ethan was a poor hand-to-hand fighter— or at least not nearly as good as herself—but when they fought, he usually had his magic on his side to even the fight. His eyes were their regular shade of blue when he approached the commander.

The fight with the commander that followed was brief, and it looked quite painful for Ethan. He charged right for the commander—who stood a few feet into the living room—when he was just a few feet from her. Katie simply tried to keep herself out of the way, retreating to the other side of the living room. The commander took Ethan on by herself, with one more soldier looming around for help. The other two soldiers looked after Katie. Ethan curled his fists and threw punches at the commander's face, but he missed both times. The commander simply ducked under each one and then pushed Ethan to the ground with an amount of force that surprised even Katie. The commander jumped on top of her brother and wrestled him into submission over the next few seconds. The scuffle made a huge mess of the living room.

Once Ethan was physically under control, the commander backed away and then stood at the front of the living room. "You want another round?" she asked Ethan.

Ethan looked to his side with a broke lip and said nothing.

"Good," said the commander. She stood in the front of the living room with the three soldiers behind her again. "Now that we're finished with the fun stuff, we can get onto everything else. I'm Commander Hillery. Behind me is Captain Dessen, Private Jenson, and Private Lee. You both are mine for the rest of the night. Tomorrow you'll be loaded onto a military plane and flown to the Center for Draven Abilities in Malin Harr. Now, this is no longer your home, and those cadavers are no longer your parents. However, if you should care to know, they'll be buried in an unmarked grave somewhere outside of Imperium Aendor—once the House of Lance is finished with them, at least."

"Can we at least have the location of the grave?" Katie asked, feeling like it was an honest and fair question. Private Lee rewarded her for that by punching her in the stomach with the butt of his rifle. She lost her breath and crumpled to the ground. It was a much more powerful punch than she had expected.

"Oh, this is going to be a long night," said Commander Hillery in annoyance. "Now, if the two of you are finished with fighting and your questions, we have one more thing to do before we go." Commander Hillery paused, and a new soldier came in through the front door carrying two red weekend suitcases. The soldier handed them to Commander Hillery, who handed one each to Katie and Ethan.

Katie held the empty suitcase with her hand. She would not be able to fit much inside it. "The two of you have five minutes to go up to your rooms and pick out a handful of personal items you'd like to bring with you. Clothes, pictures, books, etcetera, are all okay. Nothing harmful. It'll be all you get to remember your past lives by," she told them. "Now get to it."

Captain Dessen walked up to her brother and paused for a second, before grabbing him by the arm. Ethan looked like he wanted to fight again. Captain Dessen was taller than her brother, older than her brother, and thicker than her brother. He prodded Ethan to the beginning of the staircase. When Ethan reached the first step of the stairs, he grunted and tried to turn around. When that happened, Captain Dessen grabbed him by the back of the pants and the neck of his shirt and threw him up the stairs.

Ethan skidded up the stairs and came to a stop at the landing where the staircase turned left for the final two steps. He glared at the captain as he walked up the stairs after him, and then he ran off to his room. "Well, c'mon," said Private Jensen when he stepped in front of Katie.

Katie did not want to fight anymore. While she held the suitcase with one hand, she held up her other arm to feign her submission. Private Jensen stood to the side, and Katie walked up to the beginning of the staircase. He followed her up the stairs, and they creaked under their combined weight. Before Katie could open her bedroom door, Private Jensen put his arm between herself and the door. He said nothing to her but looked her over from top to bottom before opening the door for her. Katie reviled him for that gesture. She would have to be smart about how she got him back for that.

Katie stepped into her dark bedroom and unsurprisingly found it empty. Private Jensen did not come into the room with her and closed the door behind her. Katie appreciated the extra space he had given her while she had it. For a moment, Katie listened to her quiet room and looked for any sign of Cali. Katie couldn't tell if her cat had escaped, been killed, or been taken somewhere. She didn't know, and she didn't expect to ever find out. Katie looked out through her bedroom window into the dark night sky and saw nothing but the resting city. Then, something large glimmered in her vision for just a second on the roof of a residential building across the street.

Katie saw golden eyes, and then she heard his voice. *I can't sense your Cali anywhere in the area,* Sovereign told her.

Sovereign, she thought, looking out at him across the street. Katie wasn't sure how to feel with the night she had had. Sovereign was perched on top of a three-story apartment building. She could not see him particularly well at night, but she could see his outline. She could make out some white feathers on his crown and brown feathers on his body.

I'm sorry that it all had to happen this way, Sovereign told Katie in her mind.

So, you weren't lying? You knew what was going to happen, she told him, but she accepted that what had transpired was her fault, for her not having taken it seriously. *What is happening?*

Why we're breaking you out, of course. I'll not let you live your life as a powerful pawn of Iishrem—or myself as a slave of the Phoenix. It's time for us to finally be together. It's time for us to journey to Maravinya, where we'll make our way to Meinghelia City and train at Christian's academy. It's open to any Draven who promises to fight for him. We'll be free there. Safe there, Sovereign told her.

Katie huffed and put her suitcase down on the bed. She walked over to the window, put her hand on it, and looked out through the window at Sovereign. It was just like the last time she had seen him in person. Katie had not left the Capitol Approach with him that day. What was going to make this time different?

How are we going to get to Meinghelia City, Sovereign? How are we even going to escape Imperium Aendor? I can't even get myself out of this house, she told him. Katie felt herself start to cry again, and she wiped a few small tears out of her eyes.

I will show you how, Sovereign told her, sounding confident and strong. Suddenly, the roof of the residential building across the street illuminated itself around him. She saw another pair of golden eyes—a human pair of golden eyes. Katie could see Sovereign much better once the roof had illuminated itself around him. Now, next to Sovereign stood Christian Knowles, who was looking directly at her. Christian smiled at her while he stood between her eagle, Sovereign, and his eagle, Anacarin. *Christian came here for us and your brother, Katie. He wants us to fight for him. He wants to get us to get away from the House of Lance safely, and then once we're safe in Maravinya, he says it'll be our decision whether we want to remain on the run or train with him at the academy.*

That sounds much better than being a pawn for the House of Lance the rest of my life, Katie thought. The thought of the House of Lance burned in her mind for a moment. They had destroyed her life and killed her parents, but she could take it back and make them pay.

There's just one thing to this deal, Sovereign told her.

What's that? Katie asked, looking back at him.

Private Jensen knocked on her door from the hallway outside. Katie felt her heart begin to pound, and her eyes turned golden. *We can't rescue you from inside the house. But if you can incapacitate the guards inside and step outside, we'll have the rest taken care of by then. And we'll have a clear path out of the city*, Sovereign told her.

Katie closed her eyes and let the hanging silence of her bedroom wash over her. When she felt her eyes turn golden, she felt alive, rejuvenated, and full of emotion and passion again. Katie was not going to be a slave for a government that had just killed her parents and taken her home from her. She was going to fight harder and faster than she ever had before. She expected to fight alongside her brother for the first time tonight.

"It's time to go, young Draven!" yelled Private Jensen from the other side of her bedroom door. This time he did not wait to knock before opening the door, and Katie was ready for him when he did.

When he opened her bedroom door, he quickly understood the look she gave him, but he was not fast enough. Katie held her empty suitcase with her left hand and swung the bottom of it right for his head and shoulders. Katie hit the private into the door frame with her suitcase, then ditched it before she pressed her hands to his chest and drove him across the hallway, into the wall.

The walls shuddered and cracked in several places as the two of them began to grapple for position with each other. Private Jensen did not attempt to grab his pistol or assault rifle but went for his stun baton instead. While he fought off a punch from her with one hand, Jensen grabbed his stun baton from his belt and tried to strike Katie with the end of it. Katie knew she had been going slow and easy on him so that she could get him into some more open space, and she caught the strike Jensen had thrown at her in mid-air with a smile.

Jensen clicked the stun baton's charge button, and Katie waited for herself to get shocked. Instead, it was Jensen's body which began to contort from the shock of the baton—even though Katie was holding it by the shaft, and Jensen by the grip. That's when Katie got her first look at Ethan, who was beginning to fight back in front of his doorway down the hall as well—this time, with much more success. She could see his eyes glowing violet with a little extra red while he clashed with Captain Dessen and Private Lee. Katie took the chance that she had in front of her to defeat Jensen.

She slugged him right in the jaw with one of her hardest blows, then pushed him down the stairs.

"This is Commander Hillery," the commander spoke into her walkie-talkie as she jogged up the stairs to assist her soldiers. She never made it to the top. Instead, Private Jensen collected her in his tumble down the stairs, and the two of them landed in a heap at the bottom. Private Jensen landed underneath Commander Hillery, with his stun baton both still active and still within his grasp. The two of them were shocked repeatedly as they tried to get up and away from the other. Neither one was able to move far very quickly.

"Katie, help," she heard from down the hall. Katie looked away from the first floor to Ethan's doorway. He was beginning to struggle, fighting both Lee and Dessen at once, but now Katie knew that they had turned the tide and gained the momentum.

"I'm coming," she told him. Ethan took a punch to the nose from an angry Captain Dessen and was knocked back into his darkly lit room. Katie sprinted down the hallway and quickly engaged with Captain Dessen, who had been waiting for her in front of Ethan's doorway.

Captain Dessen put up his fists and took a guarded stance as Private Lee followed her brother back into his room. By then, Katie was feeling stronger and faster than ever. She felt her normally green eyes glowing a brighter gold than they ever had before. When Katie approached Captain Dessen, he looked warily at her glowing eyes for just a second. That was all the time that she needed. Katie kicked him in the back of the legs with the boots they had given her to wear after she had been handcuffed earlier in the night.

Captain Dessen stumbled forward toward her just a little from the force of her kick. He threw a punch at her face, and Katie stepped to her side, out of its way. When Captain Dessen missed, it put him off balance. Katie pressed her shoulder to his chest and cornered him against the stairway railing and a console table in the hallway outside of her brother's room.

Katie knew she had not beaten Captain Dessen yet; they both glowered at each other. Again, they began to grapple for position, using their arms, hands, legs, and their own body weight against each other. Katie felt like her entire career of training and fighting would be defined by this one moment, but she was ready. Every ounce of her body fought for her, using all her skill, training, and might. After a brief pause in the grappling between the two of them, Katie again pushed Captain Dessen into the hallway console table as hard as she could.

The console table was forced toward the stairs, where it was met and temporarily repelled by the stairway railing—but not without the railing taking several punctures, cracks, and splinters. Katie quickly observed the damage to the stairway railing. It looked like it would break with a similar amount of force.

Captain Dessen looked like he had had enough of this confrontation with Katie as he leaned on the console table. He stood in front of Katie, ready to keep fighting, but then Katie heard her brother say something from behind her. "Katie, get out of the doorway!" he screamed.

Katie felt her instincts take over, trusting her brother for one of the only times in her life. She dove down the hallway and landed on her stomach. Katie rolled herself over and turned around to see Captain Dessen still standing in the doorway with an angry expression, directed towards her. Katie suddenly noticed that

Ethan's room was quiet, free of any confrontational sounds. Then she heard something heavy and thick quickly being pushed across his wooden floor.

As Captain Dessen was about to reignite their fight, he was hit in his side by Ethan's dresser as it was seemingly self-propelled into him. The dresser pinned Captain Dessen against the hallway console table, which rocked repeatedly off its feet into the stairway railing. Ethan walked out of his bedroom door and seemed to be channeling his magic with his hands by holding them out in front of him in a pushing motion.

Katie watched Ethan focus just a little harder, and then she heard the stairway railing break. The console table, dresser, and a screaming Captain Dessen shook their home repeatedly as they all tumbled downstairs before coming to a stop on top of Hillery and Jensen. With the fight over, Ethan and Katie turned to look at each other. Without a word between them, Ethan and Katie met in the middle and hugged.

Katie knew the two of them didn't have much longer than a few seconds for a hug, but the one they shared still felt warm and calming. "I heard from a friend that you're a Draven like me," he told her.

"I heard from a friend that Christian Knowles is waiting outside of the house to take us and our Eedon Rath-ni to Maravinya. Should we go see?" Katie asked him.

Ethan smiled and nodded to her. The two of them broke from their hug and walked down the stairs, maneuvering their way around furniture and bleeding soldiers. Katie wasn't sure if each of them were alive or dead, and she didn't stop to check. The two of them walked right past them and up to the front door. Katie opened the door for Ethan and let him out first. She was right behind him.

Ethan and Katie found two more incapacitated Iishrem soldiers lying on the sidewalk just in front of their house. A large white van was idling in front of their driveway, and Katie could see a female soldier with her face on the wheel. A small area of the neighborhood around their two-story duplex had been cordoned off by some wooden barriers. In the middle of that stood Christian and Talia Knowles. Christian was flanked by two eagles and Talia by two ravens. Katie quickly let her thrilled eyes recognize Anacarin, and then she saw Sovereign next to her. His eyes narrowed upon his sight of her, and Katie suddenly felt overjoyed. Without looking anywhere else, Katie rushed past Christian and Anacarin and right up to Sovereign. She came to a stop right in front of him, beaming. Sovereign blinked his eyes and then lowered his head by a foot or two.

My rider, Sovereign said to her.

My Eedon Rath-ni, Katie thought back to him. She put her arms around his neck and pressed herself to his wings. A few seconds later, Sovereign folded his wings around her. For just a moment her world was night, strength, herself, and the warmth of her eagle. *I have found you.*

Now we can be together. Now we can bare our strength to this world, Sovereign told her. Katie opened her eyes and stepped back from Sovereign. For the first time in her life, her Eedon Rath-ni stared back at her with golden eyes. With Sovereign, at last, Katie felt as strong and complete as she ever had.

Chapter 16

Escaping Imperium Aendor (Ethan 5)

IMPERIUM AENDOR, IISHREM

SUMMER, 1153, FOURTH AGE

Ethan understood the look he saw in Captain Dessen's eyes, only seconds before the captain grabbed his arm with his hand and squeezed. He prodded him towards the stairs. It was a strict no-nonsense type of look—like it wouldn't take much from Ethan to get him to respond with physical violence. He had already grabbed Ethan's arm and put a firm squeeze on it. Ethan didn't want to fight again—at least, not at this exact time or specific location within the house. He took a moment to search for any of his magic that may still be within him and found himself feeling utterly normal. When Ethan thought about it, his eyes had last been violet earlier in the night, when he was having his romp with Kiera.

Ethan couldn't stop himself from thinking about Kiera—and the fact he'd probably never see her again. Losing her burned within him like a fire. When he thought about the fact that he had also lost both of his parents and had been essentially enslaved by the House of Lance, it was like someone had poured grease onto a fire.

By the time that Ethan reached the beginning of the staircase with Captain Dessen just behind prodding him onward, he'd had enough. Ethan would not allow himself to be *handled* in such a way as this. Especially within his own home. After he felt one more prod in the back, Ethan put both of his arms out and grasped the beginnings of the stairway railings with his hands. He needed to push back, but he didn't need to start a full-fledged fight.

Pushing back turned out to be a painful decision for Ethan, but he was fine with that. He believed the confrontation might take his mind off his parents and Kiera. Before Ethan started up the stairs, he pushed back against Dessen with his back and then tried to slide around him for better positioning. Ethan thought if he could pin Dessen to the wall, he might be able to get a few good shots in before getting tackled again. These people had already made his night hell. If he could, he would return the favor.

Ethan wasn't able to get around Captain Dessen or pin him to a wall; Dessen had been expecting something from him. Almost as soon as Ethan tried to resist going up the stairs, he felt the captain grip his clothes and body by the scruff of his neck, and small of his back. Then Dessen propelled him up the stairs like he was tossing a sack of potatoes. The force carried Ethan all the way up to the stairway landing, where he skidded to a stop by hitting the wall.

When Ethan had recovered a second later, he turned to look down the stairs and scowled at Captain Dessen, who rushed up the stairs after him. Ethan jumped up the final two stairs, and then took a right down the hallway to his room. Ethan pushed his door open and walked into his dark bedroom, slamming it shut behind him. Captain Dessen strangely did not fight to keep his bedroom door open. Ethan closed his eyes and let the darkness of his old bedroom wash over him. He had moved out long ago, so he wasn't sure what he was supposed to take with him.

All his newest possessions and favorite clothes were at his apartment, along with all of his art and his computer. Everything that had been his or a part of his home, felt so foreign to him now. His life had changed so much and so severely over the last few hours, Ethan could hardly keep up with it all—much less properly process the highs and lows of his emotional rollercoaster. Ethan tried to keep that all out of his mind, so he could move forward with the night.

A hydrographic violet book cover caught his eye, sitting on his bookshelf by his window across the room. Ethan already knew exactly what had caught his eye, even before he made his way over to the bookcase. It was his copy of *The Magic of Colored Eyes*, by Maria Knowles. Ethan grabbed the thin, well-worn paperback book and held it in his hands.

"Three minutes," Captain Dessen told him from outside his door.

"Yes, sir," Ethan responded begrudgingly.

When Ethan held the book, he was surprised that it made him feel calmer. He ran his fingers over the matte text on the front cover, and then he put his hand over the raven, except for its violet eyes. Ethan felt his eyes turn violet and the return of his magic into his mind and body. Ethan opened his violet eyes and then walked to his bedroom window, where he looked out across the nighttime horizon of Imperium Aendor.

Then, for only the second time in his life, violet eyes looked back at him from across the city. Ethan saw Violet on top of a three-story warehouse building, which stood at the corner of the next block over and back from his bedroom window. *My rider,* Ethan heard in his mind.

Ethan grinned at that remark and felt happy for just a moment, as if the rest of the night had not taken place. *How can you call me that?* he asked her. *I've never ridden you. I've only been able to touch you once.*

But you were able to hold me while we watched the world remember our magic. Now it's time for the world to see that magic, she told him. Ethan had a good feeling; he believed he knew what was about to happen, but he needed to hear Violet say it first. *There's someone here to help us do that, Ethan.*

Suddenly, the rooftop around Violet illuminated itself. Ethan saw everything on top of the warehouse much better—like he had all those years ago when he had watched Sax Drugren the 12th fall from the Capitol Spire. A woman with long blonde hair stepped forward out of the shadows. Ethan recognized her as Maria Knowles.

Suddenly, Maria's eyes began to glow a deep, dark shade of forest green, and then her facial features and expressions began to change in front of him. She seemed to shrink a couple of inches before his eyes. Her hair turned black and shortened itself and styled itself differently. Then Maria revealed a long oak staff with a dark green gemstone at the top, entangled within some thick twigs that had grown around it. *This is Talia Zenpher. Well, Talia Knowles actually,* Violet corrected herself in his mind. *She's married to Christian you see—has been for many years now. She created her pen name for her books when she met him—not only for her own protection and secrecy but also to anger the House of Lance doubly. When they find out that one of the most popular authors in Iishrem is actually secretly married to the world's most notorious terrorist, and they had failed to make the connection between their 'shared' last names all along, well...* Violet explained to him.

"One minute!" Captain Dessen yelled to him after pounding on his door with his fist several times.

"Ooooooookay," Ethan said in a mocking tone. He had questions about everything Violet had just told him about Talia—or Maria, he guessed. *How did she manage to pull all of that off?* he asked her.

Well, she's magically trained and much better than you I might add. Her father taught her how to hide in plain sight and develop different personas. Until now, she's been a spy deep within the Iishrem government. It's time, tonight, for her to reveal herself to the world, just like you. It's time for us to travel to Christian's academy, Ethan. She's here with Christian tonight. They have a plan to get us to Maravinya safely. Once there, we can decide for ourselves whether to run or train at the academy and fight in the war.

Violet paused there for a moment, and another raven came into the light next to Talia. *But they can't help us if we won't first fight for ourselves. Ethan, you must escape from your home on your own, but I can help you—as can your sister. In your old home, with our magic and your sister's strength, it may actually be a fight in your favor. You must save yourself from your old home. Christian and Talia can only help you once you make it outside,* she told him.

He was ready to fight; Ethan was ready to reveal his magic to the world! The world would finally see *his* magic. Captain Dessen did not give any final warning before kicking open his bedroom door, holding a pair of handcuffs with Private Lee close in tow.

"Did you pick out what you want to bring with you?" asked the captain. Both he and Private Lee looked angry and hurried. They were going to take him by force, but in their haste, they had underestimated him. Not to mention, Ethan had been taking it easy on them earlier in the night by not using his magic.

Ethan had a better answer than his question. "I don't need anything, because I'm not leaving with you," Ethan told him while he readied himself for a brawl.

Captain Dessen did not look surprised by Ethan's response, but Private Lee looked significantly more dumbstruck. "You're coming back with us. Kicking and screaming if need be. I'd be happy to make that happen," said the private.

"Settle down, Private Lee. Don't escalate the situation," Captain Dessen said. He opened one handcuff and then let the other one drop. Ethan saw an opportunity in front of him. If he could get Private Lee to charge in first, it might give him an advantage. This *was* his bedroom. He knew from experience that it was difficult to get around in his room during a fight, without tripping, running into furniture, being knocked into furniture.

Ethan felt his eyes turn a red shade of violet. He had never felt them do that when he had fought with his sister. *You've never really needed to use your magic for fighting against your sister like you do these men now. You've also never had me at your side for a fight against your sister. It's obvious the color of your most potent magic is violet, but it will tilt towards other colors based on what purpose you're using your magic for. Your sister's eyes turn golden to give her strength and speed. Now yours have turned red for power,* Violet explained.

"You will not see me kicking and screaming," he told Private Lee. "I'm going to laugh when you all find out just what I have up my sleeve."

That verbal joust was just what Ethan needed to get Private Lee to charge in at him first. "That was the wrong thing to say, wizard," the private told him.

Private Lee charged in, overconfidently and with extra intensity because Ethan had shamed his pride. Private Lee's hubris left him vulnerable. The captain had been standing in front of Ethan between his wall and his bed, which was in the middle of the room. To get to Ethan first, Private Lee had to shoulder his way past the captain. Such a move prevented them from tackling Ethan together.

Ethan felt his magical instincts take over—like whenever he was around the Calanor Stronghold or fighting his sister. He looked Private Lee in the eyes, and suddenly, the private didn't seem quite so sure of where exactly Ethan was. Ethan was able to easily duck under a punch from Lee and stand back up before the private continued running straight for the window. Ethan looked at the window and focused. The glass shattered and blew back in Lee's face, bloodying him significantly.

Ethan took a punch to the jaw from Captain Dessen. His teeth rattled and jaw clenched, while he felt himself begin to fall from the punch, but he was not out of the fight. Private Lee was just getting to his feet after being hit in the face with the glass. It was a grievous wound. Ethan still felt magical as Lee crumpled to the floor. The first thing Ethan did was look Captain Dessen in the eyes. Then he rolled underneath him as he attempted to pin him to the ground. Ethan rolled forward with enough force to knock the captain off his feet.

Ethan needed space if he was going to keep himself in this fight. He backed out into the hallway, where he saw Katie struggling in an engagement with Private Jensen, and Commander Hillery was running up the stairs. Private Jensen pulled out a stun baton to help him in his fight against Katie.

I told you your eyes had turned red for power for a reason, Ethan, Violet said in his mind while he looked at the stun baton. Then

Ethan began to focus on it. He smiled again a second later when the stun baton began to shock Private Jensen instead of his sister. After that, Captain Dessen ducked under his arm to get in front of him while Private Lee shakily waited to re-engage him from behind.

Ethan asked his sister then for something he never had before, "Katie, help?"

"I'm coming," Ethan heard her say. Ethan gave Captain Dessen a look before the captain turned to Katie, who was approaching.

Ethan left Captain Dessen behind him and focused everything he had left on Lee who was then standing in front of him. Ethan had honestly had quite enough of the private by then. *Want to show him a real trick?* Violet asked him.

What do you mean by a real trick? Ethan asked her.

Trust me, she told him. *Close your eyes.*

Ethan didn't believe her at first, and he hesitated and took a punch to the gut because of it. Once again, he stood between the end of his bed and his bedroom wall. It was a forceful punch, but Ethan felt strong and magical again quickly afterward. *What?* he asked Violet.

Trust me! she screamed in his head.

Ethan closed his eyes waiting for another punch—this time, to his face. It never came. When Ethan reopened his eyes, he found that Private Lee had run himself out of his bedroom window. *How did that happen?* Ethan asked. He could think of nothing else.

When you closed your eyes, you tricked Private Lee into thinking that you were standing in front of the window. And, well, in his haste, he ran right through it and fell to the ground, Violet told him while she beamed in his head. He couldn't spare a run over to the window to look for her or Private Lee. Ethan needed to help his sister, but he honestly didn't think he would fare well in a bout against Captain

Dessen. All he would do was get in the way of his sister while she fought him. Katie had always been *stronger* than him. *You will not always need your strength. One day you must learn to rely on your magic.*

So, show me, Ethan told her.

You can only show yourself, Violet replied. Ethan quickly looked at his bedroom dresser, which stood directly in front of his doorway. At once Ethan knew what he needed to do, but Katie stood in front of the captain in the doorway.

"Katie, get out of the doorway!" he yelled without looking to see if she had listened to him. Katie would *have* to trust him. Ethan focused his magic on the dresser and naturally pushed his hands out towards it, like he was going to pick it up from one side.

The dresser began to lift itself. Then Ethan moved his hands like he was somehow picking up the dresser from underneath. Ethan focused while he watched the dresser drag itself across the floor. Then once the dresser was in front of him, Ethan stood behind the dresser and pushed his arms forward, and the dresser accelerated. It propelled itself end over end and then threw itself into Captain Dessen and the console table in the hallway, where they all hung for a moment.

Ethan focused on his magic within. Finally, the stairway railing cracked under the load, which sent the console table, his bedroom dresser, and Captain Dessen falling to the floor. They all landed in a heap around Commander Hillery and Private Jensen.

Both Ethan and Katie knew the truth of it now. They were each Dravens, their parents were dead, and the only path forward was to step outside together and face their destiny. They came together for a brief hug, had a few words Ethan didn't particularly care to remember, and then walked downstairs and out the door together, each of them allowing themselves one look back at their kitchen, and parents. Ethan swore to himself he would make this right, one day. Ethan felt his eyes revert to his standard blue once he got outside. *It's so good to see you again, Ethan,* Violet admitted in his head.

Ethan stopped himself on the first step down to the sidewalk and looked out to where he saw Violet waiting for him. Christian, Talia, their Eedon Rath-ni, and his sister's eagle were all right there too, but Ethan rushed past all of them straight to Violet. The raven nodded to him when he stood in front of her and did not seem at all intimidated. Ethan took one step closer and put his hand forward to place it on Violet's dark, long beak. Violet did not resist.

Ethan felt his eyes close as he contacted Violet's beak. In his mind, he saw his parents and Kiera all standing happily in front of him. Ethan wanted to cry again. *We will make them proud, Ethan,* Violet told him.

Together, he told her.

Ethan opened his eyes and turned away from Violet to look at everyone else. The eight of them had formed a relative two-level circle within the area cordoned off around their house. Ethan, Katie, Christian, and Talia stood in the first circle; Violet, Anacarin, Talia's raven, and Katie's eagle encircled them.

"Ethan Campbell," Talia said, looking at him from across the circle.

"Katie Campbell," Christian said, looking across at Katie. "As the founder of The Academy for Allirehem Resistance Dravens, I'd like to welcome both of you to our recruiting program. You've both just passed. Congratulations."

Ethan smiled. "What happens now?" Katie asked from beside him.

"Well, we get the hell out of here, of course. I am, after all, the most notorious terrorist in the world. There isn't time for anything else," Christian finished without any hint of insincerity.

We really do have to go now, Violet told him.

Ethan wasn't going to contest leaving immediately. Katie nodded to him, and then she nodded to Christian as well. "Okay, follow me," Christian told them. "Talia, ready the birds."

"Of course," she told them. Talia put her arms up and began to usher the four Eedon Rath-ni into better positions for take-off. Christian took them over to the van and opened it up in the back. He stepped inside into the holding area, which Ethan was sure he'd be sitting in right now if Violet and Christian hadn't shown up. Christian pulled up the bench of seats by its lip, which revealed a compartment underneath. The compartment was filled with jackets, jumpsuits, and boots.

Christian turned to look back at both and handed them each a jacket and a pair of boots.

"I've already got a pair," Katie told Christian, lifting a foot to show him the boots she had been given earlier in the night. "But that jacket looks good about now."

Ethan loosened the button-down shirt that he had worn to Katie's graduation before putting his jacket on. He took off his shoes and put on his boots, figuring he wouldn't need that particular pair of casual shoes again. When that was done, Christian walked the two of them up toward the Eedon Rath-ni. At first, Ethan walked right up to Violet's side and looked at her excitedly. Katie did the same with her eagle.

"Oh, no, no, no. Neither of you is ready to fly yet, and we might have some company on our way out of town," Christian told them.

"Ethan, you're with me. Talia, take Katie with you on Embar. Sovereign and Violet will follow closely behind you."

So, his name is Sovereign, Ethan thought while he looked over at Katie's eagle. Christian stood next to his eagle, Anacarin. When Ethan walked over, Christian patted her on the side, and Anacarin knelt and unfurled her feathers to let Ethan onto her back. Ethan hesitated before he stepped onto Anacarin, feeling his heart seize up a bit. "Don't worry; she isn't going to hurt you," Christian reassured him from behind.

"Hey!" Ethan exclaimed when Christian picked him up underneath his shoulders and put him down on top of Anacarin.

"Quiet," Christian told him as he sat down behind him. "Lean down and stay close to her body."

Ethan didn't say anything and just tried to calm himself as his heart began to flutter. He had never flown before.

Get ready for a thrilling ride then. But it'll never compare to our first ride together, Violet told him.

When will that be? Ethan asked. Christian and Talia had had their Eedon Rath-ni fitted with special saddles. Ethan and Katie would ride in front with their boots in stirrups, while a spacious leather square saddle after that covered the backs of their Eedon Rath-ni. Christian and Talia would be able to sit on these squares and keep their grip with the strength of their inner thighs and years of flying experience. However, there were also boot clamps to step into if they needed to fire their gun standing up and grips to cling to at the end if they ever lost their balance.

She didn't answer him. Ethan watched Christian nudge Anacarin into gear by lightly bucking her sides with his boots. Anacarin let loose a non-concussive squawk and took off first.

"Ohhhh shit!" said Ethan as he began to surge into the air on the back of Anacarin. Anacarin took several lunges forward down the block, before putting out her wings and flapping them upwards. They gradually began to rise.

"Lean back," Christian told him. Anacarin tilted upwards and began to pick up both altitude and speed. Ethan leaned back against Christian's stomach while he tried to keep himself from screaming. He managed, for the most part, to make only nervous grunts and expressions as the ground and buildings of his neighborhood began to shrink around him. They had not taken a dive yet; Ethan expected he would scream more then.

Ethan turned around to look back at Katie and Talia while they rode together on Embar. Katie smiled at him, and he waved at her. He was beginning to enjoy flying. "Form up!" Christian yelled.

Christian had Talia line up behind them and to their right at an even altitude. Sovereign took a position behind Embar to his left, several feet above him, and Violet followed behind Embar to his left, but at a marginally lower altitude. For a second, Ethan turned to look around the city while it rested in the face of an approaching morning. Ethan looked to the Capitol Approach, where he saw the brightest activity at night. Aleium Tower and the Capitol Spire stood tall together, looking out over the rest of the city.

Instead of the Capitol Spire glowing entirely red at night, this night it just had red eyes near the top. Ethan felt like that building was somehow watching him, even now as he was leaving the city on Anacarin. His head began to hurt when he thought about Anacarin and looked at the Capitol Spire. He remembered how awestruck he had been when he had watched Anacarin engage in a brief duel with Karthon. Riding on top of her was something else entirely.

Ethan turned back for one last look at the Calanor Stronghold as their formation approached the nearest gate of Imperium Aendor. He remembered how much that building had influenced him and his magic. Now he was leaving. The stronghold would continue to rest in the shadows of the two tallest skyscrapers in Imperium Aendor. Then they began to dive.

Ethan did scream then—as did Katie. "Quiet please," Christian told him from behind. Ethan forced himself to stop while they dived at a steep rate towards the closest gate. He felt Christian begin to move around on Anacarin. He was doing something, but he couldn't turn his head far enough to see what.

"What're you doing?" Ethan asked.

"A little parting gift for Iishrem," Christian told him. Finally, they began to level out of their dive. Christian stood up on Anacarin while they approached the closest gate, only flying perhaps two stories above the top of it. Ethan looked at the soldiers guarding the gate. None of them had noticed their approaching sortie yet.

Ethan turned back and looked up to see Christian had drawn his assault rifle and had it aimed towards the gate. He looked back to see Talia standing up as well, with a different assault rifle in her hands. Her eyes were glowing dark green like her raven's eyes, and for the first time since taking off, Ethan was afraid of what was going to happen next.

I'm sorry, Ethan; this is war, Violet told him in his head.

Ethan's ears began to ring when Christian began to fire. He closed his eyes and covered his ears, then he felt his body try to shrink itself while Christian fired a powerful gun from behind. Talia began to fire as well. Ethan watched as several soldiers fell dead, and then the rest began to scramble around the gate. Ethan looked down and saw that Anacarin was carrying something with one of her talons. A bomb.

When their formation was only a few dozen feet from the gate, they pulled up again and began to gain altitude. As they did so, Anacarin dropped her bomb. Ethan watched it fall towards the ground, headed directly for the military gate station. There were a few dozen soldiers running around down there. An alarm was buzzing, and there had even been some light return fire, although it had been no trouble for them.

"Look away," Christian told him, and Ethan did as he was told. He turned away just as the bomb went off. A moment later, Ethan felt the heat of fire, heard the sound of a thunderous blast followed by the screams of dying men and women, and turned around to see the world flash orange, yellow, and red all around. Then, for the first time in his life, Ethan left the borders of Imperium Aendor. He would finally see the rest of the world, and the rest of the world would finally see his magic.

Chapter 17

The Alligator (Brian 3)

MAISH, GALLIEM, ALLIREHEM

SUMMER, 1153, FOURTH AGE

I t was a bright day when Brian opened the door to what had been one of the most popular cafes in Maish. Today, it was deserted, but Brian took a table near the back anyway. He only wanted Macie to hear what he was about to tell her. The wood paneling of the café creaked under his feet, and he spied the owner of the café who must have had nowhere else to go. Brian sat down with his back against the wall.

He could hear a radio in the front of the café. "You want anything?" asked the café owner.

Did he want something? Was the café not open? He looked down behind the counter and saw her crouched against the corner of a walk looking up at him, with her legs very much closed indeed. He laughed on the inside, "Uh, yeah, how about a black coffee, a café latte, and two brownies?"

"You got cash?" asked the owner.

Brian rolled his eyes at the irony of the café owner asking *him* that. "Have you not seen me out there with my game before?" he asked her, frankly. He put down a bill large enough for the food and coffee, but not much more than that, considering how dangerous she apparently thought it was to currently be outside of an emergency shelter in the city of Maish. "I'm gonna have a seat in the back. Maybe I'll tip if you hurry enough. A little extra for your invasion survival fund."

He strode away from the counter and did just what he said he was going to do. He had a seat in the back and began to shake a couple of sugar packets.

Brian heard the café owner begin to rattle around in the kitchen putting his order together. He could also hear her muttering under her breath, to herself about paying good money for better protection than this. Brian smiled knowing he was still owed a favor or two by three or maybe five mafia racketeers in the city, and his connections were still good internationally. There was a radio next to his table, so he reached over, turned up the volume, and listened. Ferrum had fallen, and a week later, Iishrem had launched its attack on the official border of Galliem. The Allirehem Resistance had been fighting the Iishrem Army there—little more than a hundred miles to the west. There had been little progress in either direction to that point. Brian cursed the location of Maish. Maish was close to the border—so close to the Straten mountains that Iishrem had to funnel its forces through.

His phone began to buzz. *Be there in 5 mins, hun,* read a message from Macie.

Five minutes later, she opened the door to the cafe. At the moment she walked in, the owner of the café was working her hardest. Apparently, she needed multiple machines running at once to make their order. It was so loud that Macie didn't hear him when he called her over. He sighed when she began to look around for him, and he had to stand up and wave to get her attention.

"Can you make any less noise while preparing the simplest of orders," Brian tried to yell above the din of the coffee machines. The coffee-making process quieted down just a little, and Brian must have spoken loudly enough for Macie to hear. She smiled at him and waved, then joined him at the table.

"You haven't gotten drinks yet?" she asked, sitting down across from him.

"That's what she's working on," Brian began. Then he leaned in and said under his voice, "I don't think she really wants to be here. Like she might leave at any moment if she hears something over the news. So, I figured that the usual would do."

"Oh, the usual is fine," she told him.

"Order's ready," came the owner's voice from the front of the café. Brian turned down the radio and walked to the counter to retrieve their order. She had left it for him there on a tray.

"Uh, thanks," he told her. She was nowhere to be seen. Brian pulled a handful of wadded up bills out of his pocket and tossed them across the counter, then he grabbed the tray and walked back over to the table.

"I still don't see how you can drink black coffee, it's just so... raw," Macie told him when he sat down across from her.

"But why?" he asked slyly. "It's so delicious." He put the cup up to his lips and took just a sip of the hot coffee. I needed to cool. Then another small sip.

Macie smiled and pulled him in for a kiss by the collar of his shirt. When their lips parted, their eyes met. The bliss helped reassure Brian of what he was about to say. When Macie finally took a bite of her brownie, Brian felt ready to say what he had always wanted to.

"Macie," he began. She looked up at him from her drink. "How long have we been dating?"

It didn't take her long at all to respond. "A year now. I mean, a year and a few weeks if you want to be specific," she told him.

His nerves returned. "There's something I have to tell you, and something I have to ask you. Will you hear what I have to say?"

"Okay." Macie put down her drink and said, "Go."

The words caught in the back of his throat as he said, "I've found out that I'm a Draven you see—and not just any Draven, but a Beast Draven. My Eedon Rath-ni is a dragon. She'll come for me soon. She's been in my head for years now, driving me down this path from East Rehem to here with you now."

"What do you mean?" Macie asked. The smile on her face had faded, replaced by a look of sheer concern.

To escape the crimes he had committed, Brian had spent time with local mafia syndicates across East Rehem. His ticket out of the syndicate he served, and his ticket with papers across the Monetic Ocean, came with pulling off one last job. He would not disclose the essences of the last mission with her, but he admitted his career of roles withing several syndicates.

Once he had gotten across the ocean, there hadn't much between then and when he had met Mason, just a few weeks ago. Brian told her how he was the Draven that all the newspapers had sighted a couple of weeks ago. Macie's expression was relatively neutral to that admission. Then he finished his story with how the infamous Mason Black had confronted him on the night of their special dinner and invited him to come to the Draven Training Academy for the fall term.

"Well?" Brian asked when he had finished.

Macie seemed to be at a loss for words. "You're sure?"

He nodded. She went quiet and returned to her latte and brownie instead. Brian felt himself relax again, and he leaned back against the chair. He was almost comfortable. Finally, Macie said, "Well, I guess that would explain why you often growl like a tiger when we have sex," she said, giggling.

"I'd never noticed," he lied. "You don't seem as surprised as I thought you would be."

Macie giggled to herself. She took a minute to consider all the evidence. "Well, I always knew there was something *off* about you. Nothing in a bad way, just something all the same. This explains it." She took a sip of her coffee and looked up at him. "What did you want to ask me?"

"What?" asked Brian.

"You said you had to tell me something and ask me something," she explained.

"Oh, right," he said. "Well, after thinking about it, I've decided I will go to the academy, in Maravinya. I'd like you to come with me."

"You're serious?" He nodded again. "And what would I do, just pack up and leave?"

"Well, yes. To put it bluntly," he explained. Macie said nothing. "You know what could happen any moment now. Are you sure you really want to be around for it?" he asked.

That shocked her. "What about my apartment and my belongings?" she asked. Brian had packed his last night. He wondered how long it would take her to do the same.

"Macie, this city is already dying. The only people who stay are those who have nowhere to go. I am giving you a place to go. Please, I don't want to see you killed," he pleaded. He took her hand. When he did, she looked away. *Why are you so loyal to this city?* he thought. His heart was low, and he was sure she would say no.

She didn't say anything. "Macie."

"I'm thinking!" she said.

A moment later, she turned around and smiled. "Where will I live? When will we leave?" His heart leapt back up.

"We'll go to Maravinya, and from there, we'll travel to Meinghelia City. I'll be just a few miles away. We'll leave as soon as possible," he said happily. She had said yes!

"How will we get there?" she asked.

He had thought of that as well. "I got two seats on a train to Kardadin," and his chopper would ride in as storage care. Kardadin was a vacation city on the coast of the Allaeyic Ocean. "From there, we'll charter a ship across the ocean to Draxion City. Somewhere along the way my dragon will find me, but it shouldn't be a problem," he lied. He didn't trust a dragon he had never met before around her. *I could send her on ahead of me,* he supposed. She would be safe enough on her own once they had made it across the Allaeyic Ocean. She would be safe in Maravinya for the time until he could find Alyisay. "Once that is done, I'll pick you up, and we'll fly on to Meinghelia City. You'll be safe."

"Your dragon you say?" she asked.

"Yes. I've seen her in my dreams. Her name is Alyisay," he explained.

"What color is she?" asked Macie.

"Orange for sure," he told her. Brian felt his eyes turn tiger-yellow for a moment.

"Okay I'm in," Macie decided.

"Great!" Brian pulled her in for a passionate kiss. *Things are going to be okay*, he told himself as they parted from each other. "Well, let's not waste time. I'll help you pack."

"Okay," she said, smiling. The two of them got up from their table and began to leave the café. That's when an alarm began to sound, just like a fire alarm. Brian covered his ears; the alarm was surprisingly loud and coming from outside. Then the radio in the café began to sound the same siren. Its volume turned up automatically, and a message came in over it.

"Citizens of Maish, this is the emergency broadcast system. This is not a test," said a man's voice on the radio. There was a pause.

"Fighting continues on the border of Galliem between Resistance Forces and the Iishrem. However, we've spotted a deployment of Iishrem troops headed to our city from the Southeast. They are only an hour out."

At that moment, the café owner frantically ran back out into the café. "Have fun making it to your shelter, card man. I put a little extra ground in your coffee if you know what I mean. Should help you bowel out of the city just in time. No such punishment for the latte lady. I mean, she's cute. I like her—a nice set of tits, and those cheeks; it's Rosa, by the way," the woman with tanned brown skin and brown hair informed him, and then dashed out the door.

Brian watched her dash out of the café and disappear into the hordes of scurrying civilian foot traffic outside, quite ticked off. He tried to spit out whatever he had recently drunk and tossed away the nearly full coffee. Maybe he'd had an ounce, and it'd tasted fine. Maybe she was just messing with him. But either way, he couldn't worry about it now. He pressed forward with his plan of escape and tried to ignore a little gesticulation going on down in his bowels.

"Please do not try to leave the city. Instead, go to your designated underground bunkers and wait there for further instructions. Resistance forces are on the way." The transmission ended.

He took Macie by the hand and said, "We need to leave now. We can catch the 4 o'clock train for Kardadin."

"But my belongings," Macie began.

She was right; Brian had to think about things. Was there enough time for everything? "You're right," he told her. "But if Iishrem takes this city, we'll never be allowed to leave. We could get killed. Your belongings can be repurchased, but your life can not."

"But they said not to leave the city," she explained. "Resistance troops are on the way."

"Macie, trust me. If we ever want to get out of the city and do this, the only time is now. The radio said Iishrem is coming at us from the Southeast. The station is twenty minutes away on the north side of town. The engineer is a friend of mine, and believe me, the train will leave on time." The time was 2:50 pm.

"Okay. Can we stop at my apartment for something?" she asked.

"What do you need?" Brian asked.

"Just a few keepsakes and essentials. It'll only take a few minutes," she said. Brian couldn't take long to decide; he knew what he was losing. Time.

"Okay, let's go," he said. Brian took her hand and led the way outside to panic. The streets were a mess. People were screaming and running everywhere. Cars could barely move. The treads of tanks and growls of Humvees could be heard in the distance, and first responders had their vehicles with their sirens on doing their best to direct people to safety. Brian could see his Burcgetti right down the street, and they took off for it. When the two of them got there, Brian handed her his spare helmet, put his on, and jammed his keys into the ignition. Brian rolled his Burcgetti into gear as soon as he felt her hands around his waist. He didn't hold anything back when he took off into the city. They had had to go. Then he cursed himself for thinking about that and clenched his cheeks together a little tighter.

Maish's city streets were packed with what was left of the city's population. Brian could see families dragging their belongings in suitcases to the closest underground bunkers, many of which were converted subway stations. Drivers were ditching their cars, not even bothering to take them into a garage or park them off to the side. On his chopper, it took Brian forty-five minutes to traverse the usually twenty-five-minute trip from the cafe to his storage unit, weaving in and out of cars. By the time he reached it, Brian was very frustrated, but he still thought everything would be fine once they got away.

When Brian reached his unit, he grabbed his backpack which contained his computer and important papers and a suitcase of clothes. He then stuffed his family portrait in. His Burcgetti seemed to have just enough space for everything. As he finished closing the storage compartment, he had to back up slowly and strain his ass again. Maybe the café manager really was that much of a bitch for just a little flamboyancy on his end. No matter, if first came to worst, it would be far from the first time.

When Brian was finished stifling himself, he locked his unit shut and returned to the frayed city. Another twenty minutes later, they made it to Macie's apartment building. Macie jumped off the bike before Brian could bring it to a complete stop. She didn't fall. "Be quick," Brian urged her.

Macie nodded in response before she disappeared into the stream of people coming out of her building. Another announcement came over the public address system in the city. "Citizens, the Iishrem troops are three miles away from the southeast border. Get to your bunkers now; do not try to leave the city." That seemed to make everyone even more frantic—if that was even possible. People were getting knocked over by other people. The police directing traffic had lost control, and accidents were happening all over the place. The message continued, "Citizens watch out. In the north" —the transmission cut out for a second—"corner of the city there is a dra"—there was more static—"igator fighting for—" The transmission cut out again and did not come back.

Brian wondered what he had missed within the static. What had been at the end of the dra? It could have been a Draven or dragon—or even worse, both. He and Macie were in the northern part of the city, but the train station was on the northwest side—normally only twenty minutes away, but in this chaos, it would likely be closer to forty.

Brian took a moment to sit back down on his chopper while it idled to brood. He knew that it was now or never. If they didn't leave the city now, they might not ever have another chance. Brian decided to accept the gamble.

Several minutes later, Macie still had not returned. It had been too long; what was taking her so long? What was so important to her? That's when Brian heard a loud hiss and then a thunderous roar over the panic. Brian had never heard a similar hiss before, but he had certainly heard a similar roar before in his dreams. He knew it wasn't Alyisay's, and his heart began to pace. One small positive, his feeling of incontinence had abated, temporarily.

Still, Macie was nowhere to be found. The streets were slowly beginning to clear. Perhaps people would make it to their bunkers. Maybe it would be better for him to just stay there. He could hear the echoes of helicopters in the distance, the rolling of tanks, gun-fire, and then an explosion. The explosion was louder than all of them. It came from behind him. Brian turned around to see one of the tallest buildings in the city get hit with a powerful artillery shell. Chunks of the building began to fall away when it was hit again a moment later.

Brian could feel the earth shake as the rubble hit the ground. The screams he could hear from blocks away, they sounded ter-rifying. Finally, Macie returned with a small suitcase in hand, a backpack on her back, and she wore a necklace he had never seen before. Out of interest, Brian asked, "Macie, what's that necklace?"

"It's a family heirloom. Supposedly, we've had it for over three hundred years," she explained while she got on to the chopper behind him. The necklace was tattered and beaten, but somehow it still held beauty. It was a silver chain and crescent moon with a small dragon held in the middle by the two ends of the moon. Without another word, Brian turned his Burcgetti back on, and they sped back out into the streets.

Two blocks later, Brian had them turn a corner, entering onto one of the city's main corridors. By now it was sparsely populated by pedestrians, but Brian could see tanks and resistance troops were moving onto the scene. "Get off the streets; it is not safe here," the police urged. After that, there it was again; Brian heard a screeching hiss and a deafening roar. Both even louder this time.

A few blocks ahead, the resistance had set up a roadblock. When he saw it, Brian took his foot off the pedal for just a moment, slowing his progression. "You on the chopper, stop right there! There are enemy troops in the area. Turn around and proceed to your designated shelter!" said a commander on a loudspeaker. At least they weren't threatening to shoot him. Brian looked back at

Macie before continuing and saw her nod at him. They would take their chances.

Brian turned his eyes back to the roadblock and revved his engines, speeding back up. Macie screamed behind him at that moment, it was one familiar to him, from their bed life. The roadblock which was still two and a half blocks away was composed of two tanks and two standard army Humvees armed with mounted machine guns. "Really though, there's an enemy dra—" the commander began again on the loudspeaker. Brian drowned his voice out with the thunder of his motorcycle and rode right through the space between two Humvees in the roadblock and continued. He paid the price for his antics with a return of his thoughts to the potential laxative he had consumed a drop of. It was getting a little more difficult to hold back the dam.

At least the roads were relatively clear after they made it through. After a few minutes, Brian could see the train station come into view. They would make it there just in time! There was a train at the station, which still looked prepped to leave. A few other people seemed to have had the same idea as him, though. Brian was going to escape the city with Macie. He sped up, and now they were only three blocks away from the station. Brian could see the ramp where he would ride his chopper onto a train car, which would tow it for him while the two of them stayed in the sleeper compartments. That's when Brian heard the loud hiss again. This time as if it was right in his ear. Suddenly, the earth quaked, and both he and Macie were into the air, off his chopper.

Brian flew off and rolled into the tires of a parked car. He groaned as he hit the tires with a thud. His back ached, his vision blurred, and his hearing became distorted. He struggled to his feet. In the distance, a small building began to collapse, section by section, into a pile of rubble. It was as if it was being rooted out from the inside. A cloud of dust swirled out of the building, only a few stories tall. When the dust cleared a moment later, something began to move amongst the rubble. Brian couldn't see what it was, but it was of mammoth size. The first nugget sized piece of shit squeezed itself out of the back of his ass just then. He groaned and shuddered.

Without having to be told, Brian knew he could not stay in the middle of the road. Brian went to look for Macie; she *had* to be fine. He found Macie lying unconscious but alive next to a car across the street. He pulled her up and slung her across his shoulder. In his pain, he struggled with her weight. That's when he saw his Burcgetti. It was wedged under an overturned car. He would never get it out of there by himself! Another sizable piece of shit fell into the bottom of his boxers, then rolled up against the side of his leg.

"Fuck!" he swore, crumpling over to the side for a few seconds. "Help me!" There was no one around. Brian looked out over the three blocks to the train station. The train was still there; he knew that he had to try. They limped on as fast as he could get them there. Progress seemed to be nonexistent. Suddenly, the world grew dark as a shadow threw itself over him. Brian felt warm air against his back, and he heard the hiss again. He stopped there and shuddered. For a moment, Brian closed his eyes. While they were closed, he could feel a loud *whoosh* of air whip around his back. Meanwhile, the ground trembled. Then Brian opened his eyes again.

There was an enormous green alligator in front of him. Brian had a good opportunity to look the beast over, and it looked like it was about eight times the size of a city bus. It had all the appropriate armor and claws which would enable it to rip through small buildings and roll over tanks. Its horrifying green eyes looked straight into his, and Brian felt himself start to collapse. He could do nothing but stop. He gently guided Macie to the ground with him. *Help me*, Brian thought. *Help me turn into a tiger and fight this monster. I want my chopper. I want this woman in my arms*, he briefly thought in his mind about Alyisay. Where was she?

I'm busy, Brian. Sorry, he heard her whisper ever so faintly.

That is not meant to be, said a new voice in his head. It was a man's voice this time. It was the man inside the alligator. *I am Calion Gordon. Do you fear me, young Draven?*

Brian thought nothing. He looked up at the alligator with his yellow eyes and growled. Then he rose off the ground with Macie, picking her up in his arms. Brian would at least get on the train. The alligator knocked Macie up and out of his arms with a claw, and then he impaled her stomach with it, twisting her body across the pavement several times like it was the end of an eraser.

Brian collapsed to his knees as the gator retracted his claw. He lost all control over his bowels at that moment. He could feel his face contort from the shit he took, at the same time his body ached as much as his heart wanted to cry. Oddly enough, it didn't smell much worse, over the other general smell of burning buildings, asphalt, and flesh. Brian didn't understand. He crawled over to Macie with his head down and pressed his fingers to her neck to feel for a pulse and found none. Brian began to sob, and it wasn't quiet. He put his head into his hands while he lay in the street and screamed.

The earth began to tremble again. Calion was moving in front of him. His tail brushed into Brian's back as Calion shrunk his alligator form in half. *Ahhh, I see that face you're making*, the alligator's eyes narrowed at him. *You met Rosa? I'm the one who cajoled her into doing that for me. I'm an anti-insurgency specialist, you see. All I had to do was threaten to take her daughter back to Iishrem. So young she is, but she's got hella spunk, and she'll ride a dragon like you, one day. I'm the reason your girlfriend is dead, and the reason you shit your pants.*

Brian felt his body and mind writhing in agitation. "And my bike," Brian sputtered out loud. He was more of a fighter than this, he could have at least spat in the face of Calion.

Ahh yes, just such, Brian. But you don't have to die or be harmed any further, if you kneel before me, and come with me, Calion told him.

Shut up, ass. Fuck you. You killed my girlfriend, Brian told him. *A laxative, really, are you a juvenile or something?*

Well, you were mean to her, Calion told him. *She did as I told her to, but I can hardly blame her.*

How do you know I was mean to her? Brian asked.

Calion thought for a moment. *Well, that isn't important. Let's just say that I was able to, overhear.*

Fuck you, scum. Why don't you go to Illias where they eat your kind? Brian informed him.

Scum, ay. That makes my advice on how to treat people in the service industry invalid? And you never exactly answered my query! Calion finished.

Brian bared his teeth. *As if I would ever join you,* he told him. He had been on his knees, but the pile of shit that had accrued in his pants and boxers really began to get to him in places. He fell over a little bit, onto the road.

Off in the distance, he saw a huge brown bear. It was bigger and taller than the alligator but not nearly as long. *Mason,* Brian thought.

Pity, pity, Brian, Calion told him. *You could have been great for us.*

Brian knew now was his time to move, as Calion turned around to face Mason. With all his remaining coordination, he dragged himself and Macie's body to safety, after first avoiding being swatted by Calion's giant tail. Mason charged while Calion crouched down, and Brian reached the sidewalk with Macie's body, just as the duel began.

A moment later, Brian watched Mason lunge at Calion. When they landed on top of each other a block and a half away from him, Brian stumbled to the ground. His ass was really in his own shit, now. When he recovered, he watched the bear and the alligator circle each other, then the alligator jumped. Calion swung his front leg out at Mason while he tried to chomp at his neck, and Mason had to stand on his hind legs to avoid the attacks. When he could come back down, Mason attacked his opponent's head more accurately with his claws. Mason ripped into Calion's neck, until Calion whipped Mason off his feet with his tail, the exchange briefly separating the two of them.

They engaged again in the middle of the road. The alligator pushed itself up onto its hindlegs a little way, and Mason met the alligator in the middle with their claws and paws clashing against each other before the alligator crouched back down to try and get underneath of the bear to chop at his legs. Mason didn't fall for this. He jumped onto the alligator and began to maul his armored back. Brian watched the alligator's eyes grow frustrated and then he saw the alligator tuck its legs and roll Mason off into the broad side of a brick building.

That's when an explosion hit the alligator in the face. Resistance forces had arrived! Two tanks began to engage Calion while Mason got up and began to ward him off. Before the tanks could do much damage, a thunderous roar echoed in the sky. Brian looked up and saw a monstrous black dragon circling above. A moment later, he tracked two balls of fire shot down towards the tanks. They set the two tanks ablaze, but more were beginning to arrive on the scene. An entire deployment of troops, Humvees, and tanks was coming; escape was Calion's only option.

A wall of fire erupted between the two great beasts—so high that Brian could not see over it, and Mason had to back away. A moment later, the black dragon landed behind the fire. "We'll continue this later, Mason!" Calion yelled from the other side. On the back of his dragon, he took off out of sight. A moment later, the wall of fire faded away entirely, and Calion could no longer be seen.

Cautiously, Brian walked over to Macie and gently kissed her goodbye, holding her in his arms one last time. With Calion gone, the city almost started to sound normal again. The scout unit had been dispersed, and Calion dealt with without too much damage. The tread of tanks and growl of Humvees sounded much louder now than the city. "There was nothing you could do, Brian," said a voice from behind him. It was Mason. He began to sniff at the air. Brian stood up, finally, and shifted his legs around in each of his pant legs trying to shake some of the loose chunks out of the bottom. He'd have to visit a restroom as soon as he got onto the train. Gracefully, Mason said nothing. It must have been completely normal, to him.

With tears still in his eyes, Brian stood and faced him. "Why?"

"Brian, you will have a hard life. But you can change that. You can make things better," said Mason.

"How?" Brian asked.

"Get on that train and find out," Mason urged.

"I have nothing to fight for," Brian told him. Not his Burcgetti nor Macie.

"You will find a reason to carry on," said Mason as he put on his sunglasses. Brian had nowhere else to go, so he slowly walked to the station.

Chapter 18
The Flight (Bailey 4)

A dream played for her. She had not left Seems, and she was older too. Her father was not around in her dream, so he hadn't just ruined her social life or taken her away from her childhood home. Bailey was still just a girl who liked to enjoy herself outdoors—when she wasn't running around her hometown gathering information on affluent visitors from out of town that she could use to her advantage. Her information had often paid off for her in big ways—especially when she sold it to the right person. Sometimes it was even the person whom the information was about. That was when Bailey scored her biggest pay-days. Now she wasn't sure if any of that work she had done really mattered anymore.

A couple of hours later, Bailey woke from her dream; Clancy opened the motel door just after she opened her eyes to the dark room, and light flooded into the room from the sunny mid-morning summer's day. Bailey rose out of bed, wiping her eyes, knowing she couldn't sleep any longer.

Her father sat down at a round table. "Breakfast ended an hour ago, but I grabbed you a biscuit with gravy, a banana, and some grape juice," her father told her, taking each item out of a brown lunch bag, one by one. "How did you sleep?"

Bailey rose up, out of the sheets just a bit in the bloody silk undershirt she had put on after swimming, and she had taken off her shorts before getting into bed, but when she looked below her sheets, Bailey still had her skimpy bikini bottom on. "You got out early to get me a few outfits?" she asked him, looking him over in his soldier regalia, she wanted boots like his.

"Yeah, that's what I did. There are a couple outfits in a bag on the other side of the bed and some other clothes too. Pick out what you like and then put it on or pop it in the suitcase at the end of the bed. The rest will go to some resistance recovery efforts in more war-torn parts of the world," he told her. "Also, lemme see those bandages of yours?"

"I can tend to them myself," she informed him, as she tucked herself into the sheets of her bed and rolled off the side of it, pulling the sheet along with her. She grabbed the suitcase her father had indicated and took off into the bathroom. Bailey would put her father's sense of youth fashion to the test. What she found was unsurprisingly very modest. It would do for a few days through. Bailey took her time showering, and then she picked over what her father had purchased for her. When Bailey was finished dressing— wearing jean capris and a long-sleeved light grey T-shirt—she walked back out into the room and sat down at the table, across from her father.

"So, where do we go from here?" she asked, hoping he would have a good answer for her. There was a lot she had just *left behind.*

"How would you like to see Illias for a week before we make our way to Meinghelia City? Once you're there, you'll have the rest of the summer to yourself. Your first semester at the academy starts on the first day of fall," Clancy told her.

Bailey felt her interest pique when he mentioned Illias. For years, she had dreamed of walking its parks and promenades. She had heard stories of their cafes in the days and their nightclubs in the evening. The shopping districts and city architecture were world-renowned—not to mention the city had an enormous harbor, rivaled only by Minon Cromella, and an over-water market, which held all the flavors, tastes, and fashions of the world. Of course, the city was renowned for its brothel's as well, and illicit trades of a certain kind. Her knowledge of the situation wasn't perfect.

In Illias there was also a more politically motivated darker side of trade, politics, and business, all of which was negotiated offshore in waters infested with pirates and sharks among men. Such a contrast between culture and politics created an interesting cityscape filled with gangs, over-worked policemen, political activists, and private security forces hired by the rich. Some citizens were able to hire much more than their own private security force—if they had the money to do so.

"That sounds like a good deal, but there's something I want to finish discussing first," she told him.

Clancy blinked and then looked from side to side. She suspected he knew what was coming. "Yes, yes, you want to discuss the home, possessions, and relationships that you just left behind. I figured as much. I can get you *some* of your favorite possessions. You've got to be reasonable, but I'll do my best to help you get through this," he told her. It began to dawn upon Bailey, he was showering with her with gifts and the breakfast. What was he hiding?

"Dad," she began. She stood up from the table and told him, "You know what's most important to me is my safety, mobility, information, and friends, most of all. Friends. It's the carbine, my dirt bike, phone, and home I want. But You know something that's happened. Tell me it isn't" Bailey told him testily, drawing him out on his bullshit. She didn't fancy long conversations.

"Bailey," he began. Clancy stood up from his seat, like she had, and opened up the space between his arms in a circle, just partially.

All at once, Bailey felt her reasonably good mood of pensive optimism, rip into shreds of terror, agony, and anger. "No," she began before she seized up, and her eyes began to water. "She isn't?"

"I'm sorry, Bailey, but Amanda was pronounced dead before they could get her to the operating room," he admitted at last. The silence seemed to last for almost a minute. "Are you sure you don't want me to look at those bandages for you?" He softly tried to lift up her shirt around her stomach just an inch or two.

"Get away from me!" Bailey told him, blocking his fatherly advances with her arms, and then pushing him out of the way to run outside. Bailey pulled the bedroom door open and dashed out into the open to find Raejen waiting for them in the middle of the parking lot. It was bright as day, and the second-most wanted Eedon Rath-ni in the Allirehem war effort was waiting directly outside of her motel door. This time, her emotions overpowered her control into an exasperated huff that sounded like a lot of Zs and Vs blended together, while her fingers on both hands curled.

"We are an hour, an *HOUR* south of Seems, and you have her meet us right outside? Where could the snipers *not* be hiding?" she asked him. "Your very presence around me creates risk. How are you going to secure *my* safety, by being this out in the open about exactly who you are?"

That truth cut him deep, and she knew it. Clancy said nothing, and then he tossed her a pistol with a scope and walked off. Clancy returned five minutes later, with his assault rifle strapped around his back. "Don't you have any faith in my own reconnaissance skills? How do you know I don't have an advanced guard of my own Dravens? I am their Regal Commander after all. I had one of them deliver your clothes. That pistol, and some extra ammunition. It's a big wide war, Daughter, and you ought to consider yourself lucky about how long it took to come to you. At least it didn't take everything from you. Most of your friends are safe."

His truths cut to her too. He was right. She couldn't escape her fate forever. Her existence as a Draven was incontrovertible. The two of them took off within a few minutes and flew directly for the coast. They set flight as if they were riding atop a ship with an endless expanse of water around them. It was almost freeing.

Once Bailey got over the initial thrill of flying, she found herself utterly bored, and she longed for the technological amenities she had left behind at her home. Until Bailey met her own Eedon Rath-ni, the fact that she hadn't heard much of anything from Hector by now was beginning to make her uncomfortable. The two of them flew on together in near silence for hours.

With the sunset behind them, Bailey and Clancy began to make their way into the Bay of Illias. When they were about an hour out, Bailey noticed the first ship that was approaching it. There wasn't anything special or grand about the boat. It looked to Bailey like a personal vessel on its way back to port, but soon enough, personal boats were far from the only type of ships that she could see.

When they were about thirty minutes out, Bailey could see the harbor and beginnings of the edges of the city itself. She was about to start cataloging all of the different types of boats she saw heading into port, but then Clancy caught her attention.

"There. Look west," he told her. Bailey looked to her left and quickly saw what Clancy had been referring to. "Raileem-Green Shipyards. The largest shipyard in the world, east of Minon Cromella. But they're behind schedule. Why could that be?" She could see five separate building sites, each with a launch canal of their own. Three of the stations looked to be working on a trio of frigate class battlecruisers, one housed a skinny aircraft carrier, and another contained a halfway-completed submarine.

Bailey knew the answer he was looking for from her experience with tourists from Haisha. "The shipyards owners—Raileem Malgeic and Abel Green," she told her father.

"Right you are, Bailey. Allirehem's most influential pirate commodore, and Haisha's wealthiest buyer, with enormous support from the populace. They build our ships sure, but they also build their own, and they keep them on the side for their own protection. A fleet for just the two of them you see. The Fool's Fleet," he told her.

"What about the ships they do build? Are they good?" she asked.

"Well, we'll see if they were good enough to survive a journey through the Shrouded Sea. There's a surprise coming for Iishrem. In two weeks, the naval side of the war will look entirely different. So, it's not all bad. The Haishians keep things interesting you see," Clancy revealed.

That was actually shocking news for Bailey. She had not yet heard that the Allirehem fleet had successfully passed through the Shrouded Sea. She hadn't even known there had been an attempt. *Is that where Christian is?* she wondered.

"That's never happened before!" she exclaimed. Bailey knew of at least a dozen expeditions into the Shrouded Sea since the end of the 3rd age. They had each ended either in mystery or disaster. No expedition had ever completed a journey to the other side. "How do they plan to pull that off without being destroyed, one by one?"

"Sorry, Bailey, I can't tell you that yet. It's going to work, though. You'll see," he told her.

The two of them flew own, farther into the bay. Illias began to approach them at an increasing rate as a portion of the city reached out into the bay to greet them. The Bay of Illias had an obtuse diameter of about twenty miles, without any particularly round edges. The city of Illias seemed to center itself at the central northern edge of the bay. The first portion of the city that Bailey could see with any great detail was the over-water market.

The market spread out into the bay in a maze of spindling, meandering, piers made of wooden planks or concrete and steel. Trading canoes maneuvered their way through its bridges and waterways with ease, while yachts filled with cheers of revelry and drinking pulled into port. When ships made port, near the center of the harbor, there were several canals available that flew farther inland.

Once they flew beyond the borders of the market, Illias itself looked quite different. Once out of the water, the city's only natural barriers that prevented its further growth was a quick rise of steep mountains and a lush rainforest that Haisha refused to dig too far into because of how costly the land was to repurpose. The city's only thoroughfare northward was a handful of tunnels that cut through the mountains and two highways that followed the river out of the city. Illias didn't have much of a skyline except for a few skyscrapers spread out across the city—and these weren't grouped together in any particular fashion. However, Bailey knew exactly where the city's power stood as soon as she saw it.

The Raileth'eon rose above the rest of the city, baring the sky-scrapers, on a rectangularly plateaued hill three hundred and fifty feet high. Haisha's seat of central government power governed and resided there. Bailey could see the houses of the Four Masters and the Chambers of the House and Senate. The buildings on the hill—made of marble stone pillars and columns—looked older than the rest of the city.

Before the two of them began to approach the Raileth'eon, Raejen crabbed her flight to the northwest, toward the section of the city the two of them would be staying in. They descended into a portion free of any skyscrapers. A portion of the river flew through the city there, interlaced with bridges, cutting off a chunk of it. "We'll be staying in District Lampshire; I was sure you'd like that," he told her.

Bailey pulled her hair back and smiled up at him before she said, "Looks like a good area to me. Can't wait to see how big the pillows are so I can scream and cry into them over Amanda."

He looked down and frowned "I'm sorry," he told her again, barely helping her mood. "How can I make you feel better?"

She had a good answer. "How about a resistance credit card for my own personal use?" she asked facetiously. Clancy merely shrugged and grabbed a thick wallet out of a satchel that was still attached to Raejen. He opened it and grabbed a wad of several resistance credit cards before selecting one. She felt unethical tak-ing it, but she wasn't going to turn it down.

Before she was able to take it, Clancy said, "But look. Really try an optimistic attitude. Amanda would have wanted you to see the world clearly, not mope over her and miss important details."

"Fair enough," she told him, and then she took his credit card, planning on misappropriating a massive amount of taxpayer funds. Raejen alighted onto a brownstone hotel, several blocks from the river promenades, which contained the shopping, cafes, and night clubs. It was a good area. Bailey smiled as she stepped off Raejen. It felt calming to walk about on top of the building and look over the city in every direction on this cool, overcast night. She couldn't wait to get out into the city.

Bailey was going to enjoy herself at his expense while she was in Illias, but she would allow him to dictate how they spent the first night. "What would you like to do first, Dad?" she asked him.

"How about dinner?" he replied as they collected their bags from Raejen.

Bailey grabbed her weekend suitcase, planning to add to her new wardrobe so she could fit in with the locals of the city like a chameleon within a few days. She also planned to find a place she could begin to learn Haishian. If she was lucky, perhaps there might be a cute boy who could speak some broken Gallaeic. If she was even luckier, she would hear from Hector and learn more of his position—or whatever else he had been up to. She was beginning to wonder about him.

Clancy gave Raejen a hug and dispatched her, which resulted in her flying out of sight into the jungles that bordered the mountains. "She'll have a good chance to hunt some rare game there—feral foxes as large as hounds and flying crabs with pincers that can crack skulls. Life changes drastically once you move into the jungle hinterlands—until it ends in baron lands and favela slum guerilla terrorism," her father added.

"That could change one day if only someone could unite the hinterland tribes," Bailey told him.

"How do you know so much about Allirehem politics?" Clancy asked her.

She shrugged her shoulders and rolled her eyes halfway over. "I'll be speaking their language within three days, you wait and see," she told him while she pulled out two long, braided bangs. He led her inside the hotel via a door on the roof, and they walked down the first flight of stairs before taking a side door through to the top floor; they headed down to the end of the hall, where they turned left.

Clancy pulled out a key card with a pattern of holes that he pressed into the card slot and opened the door inwards a moment later. "Compliments of the Allirehem Resistance," he told her. Clancy let himself in first because of his large suitcase and the thin hallways, but he held the door open for her to pass through behind him.

Bailey walked into a spacious two-room suite with a full kitchen, laundry, master bedroom with bath, a guest bedroom, and a home office attached to that—which upon further investigation by Bailey had one of the most advanced desktop computers she had ever seen. It had no less than six monitors and two electronic console tables as well. Battles could be won from rooms like this, and wars could be managed.

The suite also had a living room with a large TV, an expansive deck that had a small grill, and chairs for smoking. "There really is every amenity of home right here," Bailey turned to him and said. She resolved herself to taking her suitcase to the guest bedroom. Clancy offered her the master bedroom, but she refused his offer. "I really think I would feel strange. Perhaps next time."

Clancy flushed in front of her before saying, "Oh, um... yeah, sure."

Bailey turned away and walked into her room. She stripped naked and took a long, hot shower. By the time she emerged dressed for the night and ready for dinner, Clancy had already cracked a beer and grabbed some chips and dips. He didn't look particularly embarrassed when she pointed it out to him, and she wasn't particularly upset with him. She was hungry though.

The two of them walked out of the room and down the hall to call an elevator, which they took to the lobby, from where Bailey and Clancy left the hotel. Knowing he had been in Illias before, Bailey let Clancy lead the way to the restaurant he had chosen. It was one of the most renowned Haishian seafood houses in the Lampshire District, which had close access to night clubs and shopping as well. "Once we've eaten, you're free to go off and do as you like. Just please pick up if I call you, and be back midnight, alright?" Clancy asked her. He handed her a basic burner phone, which she turned on and put into her pocket.

"I'll do that. And you'll get me what I asked for? Including reliable contact with Ben and Corso?" she asked him.

"All in good time," he told her.

Bailey nodded and let her father check them into the restaurant. He even informed the staff that it was her nineteenth birthday, even though it was not. That had come and gone several weeks ago, but she appreciated his effort.

"Dad!" she exclaimed while she flushed in confused excitement. Bailey didn't want anyone to make a big deal of her birthday, but the staff ended up singing to her anyway.

After the dinner, Bailey did not stay out for long, but she did tour the river walk. The river walk was a great area until one went too far east, and then it turned into shady politics, business, and lucrative trade. It was there that she listened in her mind and thought, *Hector, are you out there?*

Bailey looked out over the river and waited.

Bailey, his voice came through faintly.

She felt her heart race and spent the last hour of her night searching for Hector and his location. She eventually had to turn herself away. Perhaps she was tired and delusional. It had been a long day.

When Bailey crawled into bed that night in the guest bedroom of her father's suite in Haisha, she hoped it would not be much longer before she heard from and laid eyes on Hector. She needed to know where he was and why she couldn't find him after losing everything else in her life. She needed him. Bailey got no further response and drifted off to sleep.

Chapter 19

The Shadow of a Colossus (Brian 4)

KARDADIN, GALLIEM, ALLIREHEM

SUMMER, 1153, FOURTH AGE

*T*he train station was nearly empty, and no one spoke. Somehow, the world had grown cold during what was previously a bright and sunny day. At least, that's how it felt to Brian. When he tried to think about everything that had just happened, he found only shock and grief. Brian felt like he wanted to collapse upon the station platform and just lie there and die. His legs would have none of that though. They carried him onto the train without any input from his wounded mind and fractured psyche.

Brian figured he had shaken about half of the shit out of his pants on the walk over from where Macie laid dead. Instead of feeling her loss, he just bore down his vision and got onto the train as quickly as he could. Clouds of dust and smoke plumed into the sky, and the sounds of distant explosions and gunfire had still not ceased. He thought of his chopper wedged underneath an overturned car. At that thought, Brian struck his fist against a window on one of the train cars and held it there in rage. After that, of course, he thought of Macie and how he had just had to leave her body in an alleyway. All of it just angered him greatly, but first, he needed to get onto the train and then find an empty bathroom to clean himself up. By the time he had done both, it was all he could do just to find his seat and fall asleep. Thankfully, no one had the seat next to him, and while he had done a decent enough job of cleaning himself up, some of the smell persisted, and his pants were dirty. Finally, after another ten minutes, their train departed the station and left. They were slated to travel all through the night and arrive in Kardadin during the mid-morning the next day.

Once the train left the city and entered into the Galliem countryside, sleep took him quickly, but Brian didn't dream—he was too angry to dream. When he woke, it was already morning. A blue sky looked him in the face as the train rapidly approached Kardadin. Kardadin was an immense city with small-town communities and resort towns resting on the beaches of the Allaeyic Ocean. However, no homes or hotels actually sat on the beachfront. There were cliffs all around the edges of the city that touched the coast, the lowest cliff still being some two hundred feet up. The beaches could be accessed via stairs or elevators, but the tide came in at night and brought the level of the cliffs above sea level down to around a hundred feet. Anyone on the beaches after that would be swept out to sea. Tall hotel buildings went up and down the shoreline, and there was a boardwalk at the pinnacle of the beaches filled with shops, bars, attractions, and restaurants. The rest of the city had a popular high-income district and night-life scene. Finally, the train finished pulling into the station.

A soft voice broke the quietness of the train. "Thank you for choosing Galliem Express for your trip to Kardadin."

The doors opened, and the few other passengers began to exit. Brian leaned back in his chair and exhaled. He slowly made his way off the train.

When Brian stepped onto the platform, the first thing he noticed was the mood of most people in the area. They all seemed like they had nothing in the world to worry about, and around half of them looked drunk. Kardadin was well over two thousand miles from Maish, with nothing but towns and cities in between. Perhaps if the resistance could do its job, Iishrem would never make it here. If there was a safe place to be in Galliem it was Kardadin. Brian moved into the city and headed for the boardwalk.

After another thirty minutes of bus rides and walking, Brian reached one of the most popular roads in the city. It was situated within an extremely popular tourist destination, and the people there seemed happier than ever. By the time Brian had taken just a few steps onto the road, he had already seen two young girls clinging to a tall male friend for help walking. Some men seemed to be acting more boisterous than usual as well. Brian passed one bar where several men were playing a drinking game, trying to impress a few women behind them, and then there was another where a fight had broken out. Noticing the mood of everyone else, and the debauchery taking place as well, it was just enough to lighten his spirits just a bit.

Brian walked down the boardwalk for a few more blocks and decided to stop in at a little pub called Ambley's, taking a seat at the patio bar by himself. Ambley's was not remarkably busy. Brian felt for his wallet, grabbed it from his pocket, and opened it. *Four hundred Allies*, he thought. His phone and wallet were all that had made it with him all the way here. He didn't think about how long he could live off that little money.

"Maybe some Rehemic tequila to mark the official start of the war in Galliem?" asked his bartender. Her name was Amber, according to her nametag.

"Why not?" he agreed, and she poured him two shots, then one for herself. Before they drank together, Amber shot a look across the bar at one of the runners. "Ralph, I told you to get this drain cleaned out back here. I can smell it over the low tide."

A greasy man several years younger than Brian scowled back at Amber. "It's clean look down, and it's high tide," Ralph informed her, and then he took off.

When the two of them were alone at the bar, relatively, Brian asked what they would toast to.

"To Galliem. To survival. To the resistance," Amber told him.

"Here, here," he told her loudly, and then he drank his shot with her in unison. He was in no mind to argue for now, long as she would let him drink for the rest of the day in peace. He ordered a lager, and once he had that, Brian slunk his way to a booth in the corner of the room, and then made sure to visit the bathroom a few moments later, where he purchased a bottle of cheap-ass cologne.

When he returned to his table, Brian simply continued to drink. But quite annoyingly, Amber took her time in getting him more drinks throughout the day, and his mood sullied as the night grew dark. "Another two shots of the same whiskey, and the same beer again." She hesitantly complied once he had put down enough As to cover his tab.

She returned with his drinks. "What's the matter, mister? You're here, almost paradise. The safest place in the country to be from Iishrem—far, far away."

"Don't you think maybe it's where I just came from that's the problem? What I may have lost," Brian replied to her.

"Are you a refugee?" Amber asked him

"That's not your concern," he told her at his booth, curtly. "Just bring me more drinks let me be."

Amber shrugged her shoulders. "So long as you've got the funds," she told him. Brian held back on a balking expression he made until she had fully turned around and was out of sight. Brian continued to drink on well into the evening. Many people shuffled in and out of the pub. Then night came, and it lifted his spirits just a little. He smoked a cigar to lighten his mood, yet he just couldn't get over losing Macie and his Burcgetti just hours ago, so he drank until he was agitated and could barely stand or walk. When Amber told him they were closing, he wanted to keep drinking. He refused to leave. At first, she went along with his protests, like it was just playful banter. He was the last one in the bar.

"C'mon, it's time to go. You got a hotel to go to?" she asked him. Brian shook himself awake. He had been at the pub all day and spent most of his money. The bouncer to the pub joined the two of them at the counter on Brian's side.

The tall, husky man bore a striking resemblance to Mason. The bouncer asked him to leave, but Brian still did not want to go. He wanted one last shot, so he asked for one. "No," Amber replied. "You've had enough."

"You've only been serving me water for the last thirty minutes. I'm sober now," he told her in slurred speech. The bouncer put his hand on his shoulder. When he did, Brian saw red and slapped it off.

The bouncer frowned and recoiled away from Brian by just a foot or two. "Amber, this guy smells like shit, looks like it too. And you were trying to say I hadn't cleaned out the drain, it looks like you haven't taken out the trash," the bouncer with greasy hair said.

"Fuck your trash," Brian sputtered and surged over the counter to grab a nearby bottle of tequila. The bouncer tried to grab him, but he drunkenly stumbled away and gave himself just enough space to get it open and take a big swig, before the bouncer could approach him again. Mason had been the one to bring all of the bad news that he was a Draven down on him. Brian was never going to that academy. When the bouncer tried to grab at him, Brian shattered the tequila bottle on the counter, leaving only shards remaining, then he shoved the broken bottle at the bouncer, Amber shuddered.

The fight was short-lived. The bouncer easily avoided the clumsy jabs he threw at him with the bottle. After one, in particular, he swayed away to his side and kicked the bottle out of his hand. The bouncer then grabbed him by the collar of his shirt and slammed his face into a nearby table. Brian's head rung, and he tasted blood in his mouth. He struggled to his feet and threw one more measly punch at the bouncer who caught it in the palm of his hand.

Slowly he twisted his arm back, sending a surge of pain up through his spine, compounding the pain he already felt in his head. The bouncer looked down at him, breathing heavily with his fist in the air. He let him go, and covered in his own blood, in dirty jeans, smelling of his own shit, passed out on the floor of the bar.

Brian dreamt. It was a simple dream. He was on a beach. To his left, there were tall cliffs, and to his right was the ocean. Behind him was nothing but endless miles of the same beach. In front of him, however, was an orange dragon more fearsome than any he had seen before. *Alyisay*, Brian knew.

Brian struggled to his feet. His body ached. When he stood, the dragon got on all fours and roared at him. The wind blew through his hair and knocked him down to the ground. Fire came later, but he felt no heat when it blanketed over him.

Alyisay stood there with her eyes of red and black. Her back had fewer spikes than other dragons that Brian had seen pictures of. Her wingspan stretched from the cliffs to the edge of the beach—about sixty feet —and with its tail, the dragon looked to be about as long. Brian was confounded.

Alyisay? he asked.

I can feel you closer now. I'll find you soon, and then you'll be mine, he heard in his head. It was her voice, strong and smooth. She said nothing more and sent another wave of fire showering over him. When Brian woke up the next morning, he was behind bars.

Chapter 20
The Valkyrie (Ethan 6)

MONETIC OCEAN, IISHREM

SUMMER, 1153, FOURTH AGE

hen Christian dropped the bomb that he had brought for one of the gates of Imperium Aendor, Ethan began to wonder if he was actually better off with the most notorious terrorist in the world than a lifetime of warrior servitude for Iishrem. "Are you mad?" Ethan screamed backward at the man who had just rescued him. He was unable to turn his head far enough around to see him while they rode into the night on Anacarin.

Ethan flinched a second later when he felt Christian's hot breath in his ear, "What kind of question is that to ask a man like me?" Christian asked.

"You better get used to his bombastic nature," Talia told him from sitting on Embar, while she smiled affectionately at her husband.

Ethan looked across the night sky to see his sister and Talia riding through the night to their left, a dozen feet behind them. Katie had her hair pulled into one big, bushy ponytail that was tied at the top and bottom. She looked like she didn't exactly know how to feel about flying. Their formation had changed to a diamond, with Violet to their right a dozen feet behind Embar, and Sovereign bringing up the rear directly behind Anacarin.

Far back in the distance, Ethan could hear screams, sirens, and the sound of an alarm beckoning the local military activity to its location. By the end of the day, all of Iishrem would know of Christian Knowles' return to Imperium Aendor—along with his subsequent abduction of two CDA recruits with their Eedon Rath-ni *and* bombing of one of the city's gates. Ethan began to think back to the first day he had seen Christian all those years ago, and for the first time, he thought about the rest after the assassination, and not everything that led up to it or watching the assassination itself.

Ethan remembered the rest of that day after leaving Kiera at her house vividly. He had gone right home to be with his parents and Katie. Katie was already there, but his parents arrived shortly after he did. Then they watched the state media coverage of the assassination on the family TV. After thirty minutes of media coverage telling them nothing that they didn't already know, Ethan and his family went up to their rooftop patio. He remembered the dozens of squadrons of warplanes he had seen fly over Imperium Aendor throughout the rest of that night. The sound of helicopters did not cease before morning, and it was the first time in his life that Ethan saw the Capitol Spire glow any color other than red.

Ethan waited for the familiar sound of helicopters and warplanes to make their entrance into the fray of the night.

"Mmm, love. Sounds like some company wants to join us," Christian told Talia a few seconds later. "Why don't go ahead and ruin their night a little further."

"Embar and I know just the thing," Talia told him. Ethan turned around to look back at Imperium Aendor. Most of the city seemed to still be asleep, but the area around the gate Christian had destroyed had woken up. Ethan listened to the sound of warplane engines flying through the sky, and he spotted three squadrons flying in the direction of the gate. There were already three attack helicopters hovering over the gate, with two more on the way, which may have been media helicopters. It wouldn't be long before they found them.

I think you'll want to watch this, Violet told Ethan in his mind.

What's happening now? Ethan asked her.

You will see, she told him but said nothing else.

"Are you actually going to get us out of Iishrem safely?" Katie asked Christian, looking quite annoyed by his antics at the gate.

"Quiet, both of you, or we'll throw you off and leave you on your own," Talia told them sternly. Her eyes began to glow a thick gray, and Ethan turned himself away a few seconds later; he found her eyes too strange to look at like that. "Now just let me work, and we'll be safe in an hour or two. This has been a long day for us as well."

Ethan, trust me; trust them, Violet told him.

I trust you, he admitted, although Ethan was unsure if he did truly *trust* her. Ethan looked away from Talia's eyes and began to watch his surroundings instead.

"The sun will be up in a few hours. By then, we'll be long gone, safe and—if we're lucky—asleep," Christian told them. "You'll see." But he could hear the warplanes and helicopters getting closer.

Katie didn't look like she had any other questions, and Ethan was content enough to let Christian and Talia show them what they could do together to get them out of Iishrem. Ethan's heart still raced, but he actually felt pretty calm. At least, compared to the rest of his night. When Ethan's surroundings around him began to change, he felt calmer than he had at any other point in the night.

Talia grabbed her staff, which had been at her side, and then she began to wave it around in the air in slow, haphazard circles. The gemstone at the top of the staff changed from forest green to gray, like Talia's eyes, and then wispy gray clouds began to vent from the top and sides of the staff. Ethan watched Talia while she mumbled something that he could not hear, and then she continued to wave her staff.

The gray clouds began to rapidly multiply and expand, rising into the air around them. Ethan watched them rise high into the sky, and then he saw the clouds of the night sky mimic the movements of Talia's staff. Soon enough, the clouds above them created tendrils, which began swirling down to meet them. Ethan felt the wind around them begin to grow cold and then saw two large, wispy clouds sitting in their flight path.

When Ethan and Christian approached one of the cloud tendrils that was stretching out to meet them, the cloud tendril hollowed itself like a tunnel for them. Just before they entered it, Ethan could see Katie and Talia approaching the other cloud tunnel, with Sovereign close behind.

I'm right here behind you Ethan. We're going to be fine; they're taking us to an airship. The night is almost over, Violet told him. He could tell she was behind him, inside of the cloud tunnel.

When Violet told him that his night was almost over, Ethan did not believe her. He closed his eyes and let the wind wash over him, kissing every inch of his exposed skin. He held his eyes closed and forced himself to straighten his posture and point his face out towards their destination. The wind currents around him swept and swirled into one stream, which flowed right through him. Ethan felt the wind hit his heart like the truth he knew it was.

He began to think about all of his experiences with magic before this night. Of course, he wondered if there was anything he could have done to make this night happen differently. Somehow, he was sure that the events of this night had been his destiny since the moment he had first discovered his magic. Then Ethan felt inside of himself for her connection with him and found her. He had found Violet. At least he now had her, and he still had his sister.

I'll always be here for you, Ethan. We'll bravely make our way through this new reality together, Violet told him.

Ethan felt his eyes turn violet once again, and he reopened his eyes. He looked around to see that their formation had left the two cloud tunnels and reformed itself in the middle of a vast, hollow cloud. Ethan looked around in every direction and could see nothing but clouds. He looked closer at the clouds themselves, only to find that they appeared like no other clouds he had seen before.

"These are no ordinary clouds. They are the same shroud you would find ever guarding the borders of the Shrouded Sea," Christian told him, somehow sensing exactly what Ethan would have asked had he been given the chance.

Ethan was beginning to feel emotionally fatigued from the events of the night. He felt as if he could fall right over onto the back of Anacarin's neck, asleep like a baby, but Ethan had a question instead. "Where are we?" he asked, barely stifling a yawn.

"We are where we've always been, Ethan Campbell. We were just waiting for our ride," Talia Knowles told him with a smile. Her eyes were no longer glowing gray. "And here it comes."

As soon as Talia finished speaking, something far larger than any of their Eedon Rath-ni began to make its way through the shroud in front of them. A huge, cylindrical brown airship began to poke its way into the hollow cloud and approached them at a slowing speed. The enormous brown zeppelin stood in stark contrast to the hollow cloud. "That's the *Valkyrie*; you'll love it," Christian told him.

Ethan wanted to get this all moving along, but he felt powerless beyond complaining. "I'm sure I'll love the beds you have onboard," he told Christian, who sneered at him before he bucked Anacarin into gear again. They flew towards the airship at a rate where they would meet somewhere in the middle of the cloud. Ethan took a good look at the front of the airship and found it to be relatively unremarkable. The *Valkyrie* had gun turrets at each of the four corners of the front of the ship, and there were two more in the center. He could also see a brightly lit bridge and several dark figures.

When their formation was only several dozen feet from the front of the airship, the *Valkyrie* blew its horn, which made Ethan shudder awake again. After the horn sounded, their formation continued to approach the center of the airship, which by now had fully entered the open space within the hollow cloud. After that, Ethan heard a vaguely familiar screech—one he had heard on the news and in media. It was the screech of a hawk.

From behind, Ethan felt Christian snap to attention as soon as he heard the screech. Ethan turned around to see Christian putting on a pair of white and black gloves. "I would tell you who's coming and what's about to happen, but it would be over by then. You'll just have to trust me again," Christian explained.

Ethan thought he could hear Christian turning his head from side to side several times by the way it ruffled the neck of his thick jacket, while he searched the inner expanse of the hollow cloud.

Ethan turned to look at Talia, who also seemed to know that *something* was about to happen. She was smiling, looking giddy, and had her eyes on her husband.

"Hallway between nine and three, love," Talia said, after putting the end of her staff to her mouth first. Ethan heard her quite clearly, over the din of the ship.

"I see him. Dive, Anacarin!" Christian said loudly.

Their formation dove down to the bottom of the ship a second later, which resulted in Ethan experiencing a brief moment of free-falling. For that brief moment, Ethan felt like his heart was going to jump right out of his mouth; he was glad that didn't happen when they stopped their descent, as their formation reached the bottom of the airship. "Who is coming?" he asked.

"Only a friend; calm down," Christian told him. Ethan felt Christian stand up and turn around on Anacarin's back. This was something he needed to see.

Ethan pulled one of his legs from around the end of Anacarin's neck and put his knee down lightly on her back so he could watch. Ethan saw Christian looking back the way they had come, and he quickly saw what he was looking at. A single rider on top of a red-tailed hawk approached them. Ethan could not see the rider particularly well, because they were lying down along the back of their hawk, with a long black sniper rifle pointed in their direction. Ethan looked at the sniper rifle that the rider held, and he saw quivering red eye next to the rifle's scope. A second later, a lens flare from the scope on the rifle temporarily blinded Ethan. He heard the gun fire thunderously.

A second after that, Ethan heard Christian snatch something fast and round with a sharp end, then he groaned in a small amount of pain. When Ethan reopened his eyes a moment later, he could see that Christian had caught a long, thin, sniper bullet with his hand. Ethan looked at Christian's eyes and was unsurprised to find them golden, but then they changed to dark brown a second later. Christian's eye color was nearly the same shade of brown as the *Valkyrie*.

The rider who had fired at them stowed away his sniper rifle and sat back upon his Eedon Rath-ni to catch up to their formation, while they continued their flight along the bottom of the ship. Christian held the bullet in his hands and smiled, then he tossed it across to the rider who caught it when he joined their formation a few seconds later. "Naliais!" Christian exclaimed. "So good to see you again." Ethan now saw that Naliais had a short, moderately thick figure, and he wore combat pants and a hooded trench coat.

"You're five minutes behind. I've been monitoring Iishrem's radio chatter since you blasted your way out of Imperium Aendor," Naliais began. Their formation had reformed itself into a for-ward-pointing arrow, with Naliais now leading the way. Ethan watched Naliais look over to Talia. "Hi, Talia!"

"Naliais," Talia said to him with a smile. "You'll be in for a big hug, once we get on the ship. So nice to finally meet you in person."

"Mhmm. Well, allow me to be the first to congratulate you on your new position with the academy. We're all so glad to finally have you join us," he told her.

"Thanks, Naliais. It'll be nice to finally be close to those who matter to me the most."

"So, who are the new recruits?" he asked.

"Why, where are our manners, love?" Christian asked Talia with a jesting look. "This young *Draven* is Ethan Campbell."

"And this rugged, strong, and witty young lady is his sister, Katie," Talia said to Naliais.

"Ethan, Katie, this is Naliais. He's the best range Draven we have in the war," Christian told him.

Naliais grinned at that, and the red-tailed hawk squawked at the lot of them. "Oh, Christian, you really are too kind. It's only possible for me to let you down now with compliments like that," Naliais told his superior commanding officer.

Ethan watched Naliais take off on his hawk towards the rear portion of the ship, where two brown panel doors were beginning to split open. "That's our way in," Talia told Ethan and Katie. She kicked Embar into motion and propelled them through the air to the opposite side of the ship, and from there, they headed into the open docking area within the *Valkyrie*. Along the way, Ethan saw many more manual and automatic gun turrets, and when he looked closely enough at the actual material of the zeppelin, it began to look ethereal. It looked like a viscous material—likely one which could hold its form while also venting shroud-like clouds to mask its location.

The inside of the ship was dimly lit but well-lit enough to see at least an outline of the expansiveness of the inner deck of the *Valkyrie*. Their five-bird formation alighted into a landing area that looked like it could easily support a mass take-off or landing of up to twenty similarly sized Eedon Rath-ni. A ten-man team of soldiers was waiting to greet them, with the obvious leader of those men standing at the center. Naliais was already almost halfway across the deck by the time Ethan was able to hop off Anacarin.

This was Ethan's first real opportunity to marvel at the inner architecture of the zeppelin. He walked toward the commander who was waiting to greet them without watching or listening to the encounter. Ethan looked to the front of the ship where he saw two resting dragons, both hanging upside down with their wings folded in by their back talons, which gripped the same beam that was directly beneath what appeared to be the bridge Ethan had seen. Along the sides of the airship, Ethan could see apartments and living quarters that lined the port and starboard of the ship. Ethan observed several more Eedon Rath-ni of each type, and his mouth simply fell agape.

Katie nudged him in the arm with her elbow.

"Accelron, these two are quite tired. Take them to their living quarters," Christian told a tall, thin black Draven. Ethan looked back to their formation, which by then had largely dispersed.

I'll always be in your mind when you want, Ethan. You'll find me roosting in the shadows of the other ravens while it pours outside, Violet told him. He sensed her take off behind him, and then he saw her fly in front of him towards the starboard middle of the ship.

"We'll see you both in the morning," Talia said with a smile and cheery attitude, and then she and Christian walked away with the remaining group of soldiers, disappearing out of sight a few seconds later. It looked to Ethan as if the ship was just beginning to wake up, and the two of them would finally be going to sleep.

"Right," said Katie.

"So, you two are the recruits from Iishrem. The ones we came all this way for?" posed Accelron, stepping up in front of the pair. Accelron had dark black skin, a curly brown afro, and he was taller and slimmer than Ethan, but not as tall as Katie.

"I... um..." Ethan felt himself start. He looked to Katie, who was as speechless and dumbfounded as he was.

"You speak our language? How kind," she replied without flinching at him.

Accelron smiled and smirked. "Ha, I'm kidding. You two are far from the only reason we made this trip. Come, let's get you to bed," he told them in Iiasmaeic, beckoning them to follow.

Accelron took them across the ship. He pointed out a few key places for them to keep track of—like the mess hall and sectional viewports—while they made their way to their living quarters. "Since you are foreign captives of the good variety, you'll each have your own small room with a toilet, sink, shower, bunk, and desk. It sounds spacious, but it isn't really. The two of you are tall and relatively thin." He stopped himself and turned around. "Well, maybe not so much for you, Katie, but you'll fit."

"Gee thanks," Katie told him, reddening.

They made their way over to the port side of the ship and began to ascend one of the catwalks. "Ahh, here we are," Accelron told them. He stopped their ascent up a staircase and had them exit at the next landing before taking a left down the hallway to the outer edge of the ship. "401 and 402," Accelron told them, handing each of them a room key attached to a plastic keycard. "Feel free to walk about the ship or visit the library. Return to your rooms during lockdowns. Dinner is at six."

Ethan turned away from the unfamiliar Draven, ready to open his door with the turn of his key. First, though, Katie had a question. "Is there anything you think we ought to get into in the meantime while we make our way towards Maravinya?" she asked.

Accelron laughed and said, "Yeah, actually. Varly will be around from tomorrow morning, each morning at 8, to teach you Gallaeic and Maravinyian. I'd make sure to rest up. You'll be in for some tongue twisters soon enough." He gracefully took his leave with one look to each of them. "If you need anything, you have a phone in your room. My number is 415. Call me first. Don't call the bridge and disturb Christian. You're important, but he'll seek you out when he wants to see you," Accelron told them, and then he walked off.

Once he was gone, there was no final hug for the night between the two of them. Ethan simply said, "Good night, Katie."

Katie looked at him intently, and then she turned around and opened her door. As he pushed the door to her dark room, she said, "Good morning, Brother."

Ethan opened his door and walked into his living quarters. He flipped on a light switch and found that his accommodations really were quite small, but he was still grateful to have them entirely to himself. He stripped out of his clothes down to his boxers, figuring they would probably give him new clothes in the morning. There was a small circular window in front of his pillow that he could look out of. There wasn't much space to roll around on the bed, but the mattress was comfortable, and Ethan could turn over easily to look out over the horizon.

Ethan did not think of much when he took one short look out at the burgeoning sunrise, which was beginning to envelop Iishrem as it woke below him. He was asleep before his head hit the pillow.

Chapter 21
Two dragons Over Minon Cromella (katie 7)

MINON CROMELLA, FALCLAINE ISLANDS, IISHREM

SUMMER, 1153, FOURTH AGE

er whole life, Katie had never spoken another language beyond modern Iiasmaeic. She had scarcely even heard a foreign language. Modern Iiasmaeic was the only official language throughout Iishrem, and the House of Lance had outlawed the speaking of other languages long ago—shortly after the flooding of Reyvula, in fact. Although now, of course, students were allowed to learn other languages used throughout Allirehem and the rest of the world, for obvious reasons. Thanks to the actions of Christian Knowles, Katie now knew much more about the earlier centuries in the Fourth Age than she had previously.

Towards the ending of the 3rd Age, the House of Lance, led by Lance the 1st, fought a war of attrition for over thirty years against the people and countries of Iishrem. They did this to capture, hold, and indoctrinate them with the power of the phoenix. Their conquest had begun with the two weakest states on the continent of Iishrem at the time: Fuet and Rhollian. Over thirty years later, the war all but came to a close when the final remaining Dravens who fought against the House of Lance and their allies lost a final battle for the capital and finally ceded control of Imperium Aendor— which at that time was known as Calanoria. The years of the war ravaged nearly all of Iishrem and left many regional populations decimated.

The Dravens who fought against the House of Lance and survived that battle all fled to the edges of Allirehem. Here they built Christian's academy, which he would only open well over a thousand years later. Except for Draxion who stayed behind to watch over the Council of Nations and Dravens, Acentrina of the Stars was the only other to remain in Iishrem. She took her allies to her homeland of Reyvula, which had largely been left untouched by the rest of the war. Academics postured that the House of Lance left their conquest of Reyvula for last because of its dense forests, sharp and plentiful mountains, and because the country had a tremendously sparse population outside of its two most populated cities: Rune and Beratile. There were even a few more daring scholars who claimed that Lance the 1st considered the indoctrination of Reyvula as optional because he not only respected Acentrina of the Stars, but he also *feared* her.

For the first half of her life, Katie never heard of the name Acentrina of the Stars, and she had believed that Lance the 1st had died of old age in the year 206FA. Then Christian assassinated Sax Drugren the 12th, and suddenly many facts that Katie had never questioned before came to light. Now, it was the opinion of the majority of scholars, historians, and even a handful of family members within the House of Lance, that Lance the 1st and Acentrina of the Stars had died together in the flooding of Reyvula after a duel of epic proportions forced both of them, and their Eedon Rath-ni, to drown—as did approximately a hundred thousand others at the time.

The House of Lance nearly broke after the sudden death of Lance the 1st, due to his overzealous and foolish actions in his more demented final years. However, Eifren Venuli came quickly into his reign as the 2nd Emperor of Iishrem. He quickly cemented Reyvula as an official piece of his empire after draining the waters that his uncle had released, welcoming in the decimated and scared remaining population of the country. The actions of Eifren Venuli officially ended the War of the Great Purge of Iishrem—over two hundred years after Lance the 1st had abandoned his conquest of Reyvula to rule the rest of Iishrem instead.

By now, ten descendant emperors and two empresses had ruled almost entirely without challenge for nearly seven hundred years. Over those years, the House of Lance and its representatives had plenty of time to finish installing their cultural hegemony over the rest of Iishrem. They forced all of Iishrem to learn to speak a single language *officially*, with only a few regional dialects in cities such as Mos Marron allowed.

When Varly knocked on Katie's door for the first time a day after coming aboard the *Valkyrie* with her brother, Katie didn't recognize a single word Varly said for nearly five minutes. That was until she stopped attempting to immerse Katie in what she assumed to be Gallaeic and began bombarding Ethan who had just opened his door hearing the commotion with similar tactics but in a different language that sounded like Maravinyian. The entire ordeal made Katie wish that Talia would just teach her and Ethan Gallaeic. It made her even more thankful that Christian and Talia had been willing to speak to them in Iiasmaeic before when they rescued them.

Finally, after about another couple of minutes of bombarding Ethan, Varly stopped, caught her breath, and finally said something in Iiasmaeic. She spoke it well but with a heavy accent that blurred several of her consonants. Varly was an older woman, around sixty, with a pointed nose and curly brown hair that was graying at the top. She had naturally yellow eyes, "You ttttwo didddd about as well asssss I expected you tooooo. Don't worry. You'llllllll become more fluent in Gallaeic and Maravinyian as the days move on, but there will be work and struggles ahead. Come with me," she told them.

Katie looked at Ethan, who looked like he wanted to groan loudly, but he refrained. This was their life now. They *had* to learn these languages and customs in order to fit in at the academy; Katie expected that competency in Haishian and Rehemic would be added to their workload as soon as they showed fluency in Gallaeic and Maravinyian. Varly took them away from their rooms and farther into the center of the airship, where they studied and worked on their immersion for three three-hour sessions a day.

For her first three full days aboard the *Valkyrie*, Katie kept herself mainly to her cramped living quarters, outside of eating and her language studies. It was a good opportunity for her to mourn the loss of her parents, her old friends, and her life in general. It had taken her two days of petitioning Christian through Accelron, for her to get access to the family photos that she had stored on her main social profile—through the official Iishrem social media platform known as Iishia. Of course, by then her profile had been *erased*—more than likely by some denizen within the platform's administrative team. Such a discovery at first had been devastating for her, but a day later, thanks to one of Christian's skilled Iishrem internet hackers, Katie had printed a fairly comprehensive photo album for herself, with an extra copy for Ethan. Such small things, and the few hours a day that she had to herself, kept her sane and allowed her to begin processing her grief. This when she wasn't sleeping, eating, or drowning in her immersion of new languages.

By the fourth full day of her journey, the *Valkyrie* had propelled itself far enough southwest for Katie to see a vast endless ocean for the first time in her life. The Monetic Ocean. Their course had taken them across Dusk, over the southeastern sliver of Lake Rholl, and into Gazsamine before crossing into Kafari. Once they made it to Kafari, it wasn't much farther before they began to fly above the ocean, by first flying out over the Kafarian Gulf.

When Katie had first looked out over the vast ocean from her thin bunk, it had been a sight for her to behold. It didn't make any sense to her, but she almost marveled more at the sight of endless water in all directions than being inside an enormous airship with nearly thirty Eedon Rath-ni and their Dravens aboard. When the airship finally reached the open waters of the Monetic Ocean, Katie felt much safer. They hadn't gone through any troubles on their journey southwest, and there were no midnight attacks or pursuing Iishrem-allied Dravens that she knew of. For all Katie knew, Christian had picked up her and her brother, only after he had directed the *Valkyrie* to fly within a hundred miles of the heart of Iishrem.

Katie couldn't fathom how he had done that, so effortlessly and with no hiccups that she knew about. Then once they were out over the open waters of the Monetic Ocean, the *Valkyrie* began to descend out of the stratosphere and back into the troposphere. Here Katie could begin to see greater detail in the vast, endless ocean. She began to see glints and flashes of metal and steel as they descended. Then those glints began to take shape. The *Valkyrie* had linked up with a fleet of numerous battlecruisers, destroyers, and one small aircraft carrier, which were followed and surrounded by other essential ships within a fleet: transport vessels, scout boats, and gun yachts. Katie was sure that there must have been several submarines escorting the fleet from underneath them as well, although she had not seen any yet.

It did not confuse Katie that Christian had brought a fleet along with him into Iishrem when he had rescued her. Katie thought back to what Accelron had told her. Ethan and she were important to the resistance cause, but they were far from the only reason that Christian had come back to Iishrem. What confused her was the direction the fleet of ships was sailing. The ships were sailing east as if they had come through the Shrouded Sea, but Katie knew no journey through the Shrouded Sea had ever been successfully completed before.

On the tenth full day of her journey, Katie was woken for the first time by the sound of a full-scale ship alarm. She pulled herself out of her bed and stepped out of her room. Ethan was already waiting for her in the hallway outside. "Do you know what this is all about?" she asked him.

Ethan nodded with a gaunt look in his eyes. "I've got an idea, but I don't know for sure. I figure for the last five days now we've been making our way east towards neutral and Allirehem waters. That means there's one major city and place of power left along our route back to Allirehem that's still standing, at least. Minon Cromella. It's Journey Week, and Christian *must* have brought this fleet here for something," Ethan told her.

As soon as Ethan mentioned Journey Week, all the pieces of the puzzle began to fall into place for her. Of course, that still didn't mean she knew how Christian had put it all together. Journey

Week was a weeklong holiday celebrated only by the citizens of the Falclaine Islands—and especially by the city of Minon Cromella. It was meant to commemorate the weeklong sea voyage that Minon Cromella had made into the Monetic Ocean to discover the Falclaine Islands, found his city, and claim it as a piece of Iishrem near the beginning of the 2nd age. The first day of the celebrations were normally calm and sober. Respectful. By now, however, it was the fourth day of the celebration. The city would probably be half-drunk by now—even some of the sailors, soldiers, and pilots who guarded its citizens. It seemed to Katie that after today, the celebration of Journey Week for Minon Cromella would take on a whole new meaning. One of death and destruction.

Then Katie saw Christian and Talia waiting for them, leaning on the railing of the corridor outside of their rooms, and she opened her eyes wide in surprise. Although she didn't feel very surprised to see Christian and Talia standing there, it didn't take Ethan long to wonder what she was staring at.

"What's happening?" she asked Christian. Streams of soldiers that were bustling into position or to their stations all around them.

"You'll soon see," Talia told the two of them while she smiled up at her husband.

"Come with us. The two of you are going to have one of the best views possible of the assault," Christian told them.

He gestured for them to follow him, and Katie felt like she had no other choice. Christian and Talia led them down the corridor towards the middle of the ship, where most of the available walkways across the center of the ship to the other sides were located. Katie was jostled several times by unfamiliar soldiers that she bumped into, and she instinctively ducked down several times when several Eedon Rath-ni flew too close to her.

Sovereign, where are you? she wondered. She searched for her connection to him within her mind, and for his actual location within the airship. While she followed Christian, Katie looked all around the open space and spotted Sovereign next to Violet. They were exactly where she had seen the two sleeping dragons before when she had first come aboard.

I'm here; I see you, he told her. Her connection with him almost seemed to naturally pull her gaze to where he was, although there wasn't *that* much open space in the *Valkyrie.*

What's happening? she asked, wondering if he would really know any better; did she really needed to keep asking?

Well, I can see every other Eedon Rath-ni and their riders amassing at the back of the ship where we entered. It's quite an impressive force, along with the fleet of human ships below, Sovereign told her. He seemed to feel some remorse that neither of them would be taking part in the upcoming assault.

Don't worry, Sovereign. Soon we'll be trained and able to fight. Right now, we'd only get in the way, Katie thought to him.

That was all she could say to him right now. She had to focus on keeping close to Christian and Talia as they made their way across the center of the ship. When Christian had led them to the center, there was a staircase that would take them to the top of the ship where the bridge was. This was the location of the living quarters for the most important crew members and Dravens aboard.

"Up we go," said Christian, nodding for them to take the lead. By then the ship was not quite as bustling as it had been. Most of the soldiers had made their way to their stations. The four of them quickly began to climb the stairs to the top of the ship. She could see the bridge at the top. It was surrounded by the widest corridors and had the most connections available to other portions of the ship. It had many square windows that looked out into the open area of the ship, and unsurprisingly, it looked to be the most spacious compartment within the ship.

When the four reached the top, next to the bridge, Christian turned left and led them down a corridor towards another compartment within the ship. This one looked nearly as spacious as the bridge. It was Christian and Talia's living quarters.

"In you both go," said Talia.

The ship alarm had been turned down by then, and now it was just an annoying background noise. Talia twisted the large spinning doorknob to the room and pushed it open. She waited for Katie and Ethan to walk in. Accelron was waiting for them when they got inside. Not only Accelron but Anacarin and Embar as well. Christian and Talia's spacious living quarters had enough space for everything they needed. There was a king-sized bed and full bathroom, along with a workbench—where an assault rifle had been deconstructed. Next to that were several weapons lockers, which were opened and contained an entire arsenal of various pistols, shotguns, and rifles. There was even an RPG.

On the other side of the room, there was a state-of-the-art console desk and computer monitor, with several other monitors in various strategic places along the walls. When Katie stepped into the room, she had to hold her hand in front of her eyes for a moment. She could see the sun brightly through an open hatch— one large enough for their two Eedon Rath-ni to enter and leave from. Katie felt the wind blow through her long, curly hair—which she had kept unfurled since coming aboard.

When Katie looked through the open hatch, there was quite a scene to behold. The Monetic Ocean crashed beneath them, and in front of them, on the horizon, was the island city of Minon

Cromella. The city of brick and glass skyscrapers rose out of the ocean on a nub-shaped island. It had a bay at its southern central edge which housed the city's harbor. The top of the island plateaued because of significant mountaintop removal, and here it housed the city's airport and airbase, as well as its spire. The city itself sprawled out across the island in several tiered levels, but Katie could also see entrances into the island itself.

Katie had seen pictures on the internet of the labyrinth of corridors, subways, and government facilities that were inside the island itself. She could see their viewports, gleaming in the morning sun. Then she looked below to the waters much closer to their position, and she saw the entire Allirehem fleet approaching the harbor. The city had only five ships to defend itself.

How can this be? Katie wondered. Her heart began to palpitate, fearing for the lives of the soldiers and civilians on the ground, but there was nothing *she* could do to stop to the attack. Talia closed the door once she and her brother entered the room.

"Oh, don't worry. The hatch will close once we leave, but you'll still be able to see the battle through it," Christian told them. "Well, take a seat on the couch if you want. Accelron will be the one protecting you while we're out there."

Ethan sounded scared. "Are you going to destroy the city?" he asked.

Christian gestured for them to sit down and relax, and he didn't answer until they did. It looked like the city was only minutes away, and its defenses did not look prepared. Katie couldn't hear the sound of any aircraft engines, but at least the ships would be crewed. Katie just suspected that those five ships would get taken out quickly. What would the city do for its defense after that?

"No, of course not. Not entirely. Just enough to bloody their noses and make them resentful of the House of Lance. The Cromellas... well, they'll fight us for now. But we'll need them to be our allies one day when we return to these shores. And that is also why Accelron here is not taking part in the battle. Along with protecting you," Christian explained.

He and Talia had walked themselves over to their personal armory and began to load up. Christian grabbed several clips of ammo and a flashbang before he grabbed two pistols. He took ammo for his pistols as well, and then he walked over to his workbench where he began to fiddle with the assault rifle sitting on top of it.

In the meantime, Talia had loaded a short, semi-automatic shotgun, and then she grabbed a long pistol with a suppressor on it. She also had her glowing staff strapped to her back. Once that was done, the two of them grouped up next to their Eedon Rath-ni and shared one last embrace. They both hopped onto their Eedon Rath-ni a moment later.

"Just try to take the battle in, guys," Talia told them, looking back on Embar. "The two of you don't have to do anything this time but observe."

The two of them took off into the air and towards the top of the island. Once they were gone, the hatch closed, leaving a see-through window in its place. Katie watched two formations of numerous Dravens head in two separate directions. Christian and Talia led one smaller formation of six Eedon Rath-ni, composed of four ravens and two eagles, in the shape of a trident.

The two dragons that Katie saw when first coming aboard the ship, led the other formation towards the harbor. *Their names are*

Vishneuaira and Aushathrex. Two powerful dragons from the five lines, Sovereign told her.

Five lines of dragons? Katie asked.

I've already said too much, but I apologize. Maybe I will tell you more in a few years, Sovereign finished.

At that moment, there was a tap at the door to Christian's quarters. Katie looked away from the battle and watched Accelron walk across the room to open the door. Ethan couldn't pull his eyes from the battle.

When Accelron opened the door, there was a similar-looking soldier but with white skin and a nametag which read Glad-han. "There's been a call for you at the port turret bays. I'm to fall in as your replacement," said Glad-han, before he paused for a moment. "By order of Naliais himself."

As soon as Glad-han mentioned Naliais, Accelron broke form and began to leave the room. When he looked to Katie a moment later before striding out of the room, he did not look like he wanted to leave. It was more that he *had* to leave. Katie turned her eyes back to the battle.

There looked to be about twenty Dravens in the second formation. The airship began to speed up and moved to a new area, and soon enough, Christian's formation was out of sight, and they had a much better view of the harbor. The battle still had not quite begun. Katie wondered if Minon Cromella was just that unprepared, or they still didn't realize they were approaching.

Below them, Katie saw the entire Allirehem fleet beginning to encircle the harbor. Sirens began to ring, and the air vibrated to the sound of warplane squadrons. Finally, the city's defenses were waking up. The five ships defending Minon Cromella were composed of two destroyers and three battlecruisers. From above,

Katie watched the cannons of the Allirehem fleet flash, and then she heard their thunder a second later. The clangor of fire and splintering metal rang out all across the harbor and the city, but the Iishrem fleet was still in the fight.

Iishrem returned fire with a strong volley and scattered their formation across the bay, daring the resistance fleet to target the city. Allirehem obliged them but held back on their cannon fire. Buildings across the island still took significant damage from the gun turrets. Katie watched the barrels of one of Allirehem's missile cruisers suddenly begin to smoke before releasing its payload high into the air. The missiles went to several different locations all around the city, but they focused heavily on one of the Iishrem destroyers that was limping out of the harbor. Half a dozen missiles impaled the ship, with just as many explosions. As the formation of Dravens began to approach the harbor, Katie got her first glimpse of Iishrem's warplanes in action. Nine squadrons of them began to descend from the top of the island towards the harbor, well in front of the buildings.

The formation of Dravens and their Eedon Rath-ni rotated their ravens out to the front as the two forces neared. The warplanes began to fire on the Dravens. As the Dravens or their Eedon Rath-ni were hit, golden sparks sprayed off them. Then the Dravens on the conspiracy of ravens began to fire streams of blue sparks into the chain-guns on the warplanes, which caused them to temporarily jam. The Dravens who rode eagles, formed up to create an arrow formation, with the ravens forming direction, the eagles the line behind, and the two dragons just beneath the apex of the arrow.

The Dravens flew straight into the swarm of squadrons and began to pick off planes one by one with rifles, rockets, and dragon fire. There were several eagles who gripped long steel swords with their talons, and they performed gravity-defying aerial acrobatics moves to stab the engines of the planes, cut off their wings, or impale their pilots. The range Dravens provided several roles during the battle. Some of them sniped soldiers on the sinking ships or took out gun encampments across the city. Others sniped from the fleet itself, while their hawks took to the air to harass soldiers in the harbor.

All the while, the Iishrem Fleet defending the city was beginning to sustain more damage and become overrun. At the center of the harbor, there was a large door into the island, carved out of the earth itself. Katie wondered if there was a ship in there or if they were holding it back so that it wouldn't take damage.

Where is the rest of their fleet? It should be six times this size, Katie thought.

All just another clever trick of Christian's, Sovereign explained to her. *Phoenix feathers power these ships. They disrupt tracking hardware if you haven't noticed. And they were enough to ward off Eedon Rath-ni inside the Shrouded Sea.* How all of this had become possible was beginning to make much more sense to Katie. *No, it isn't. You still have much to learn!*

If you say so, Katie resigned while she resumed watching the battle. The ship she had seen struck by a dozen missiles before was making a run for it out of the harbor. The Destroyer had its engines forward, full speed, headed directly for the mouth of the bay, where perhaps it could escape to fight another day. Three Allirehem battlecruisers in that portion of the bay threw their engines into reverse, averting a collision by the narrowest of margins. The Allirehem fleet limited themselves to firing only their chain-fire turrets until the ship was clear of the city.

Once the ship was clear, one battlecruiser fired three piercing cannon shots into the limping ship. One in the center of the mid-deck, another one story above the engine propellers, and the last took out a significant portion of the top deck up front. The destroyer continued to limp out of the bay, leaning to one side, until it wrecked on large boulders jutting out of the water a few minutes later.

The battle was not going well for Iishrem. By the time another fifteen minutes had passed, the 5 ships defending the harbor had all been sunk, and the warplanes had been routed with the last remaining few flying off in various directions. Once that happened, turret fire from the ships ceased, and two battlecruisers began to fire several dozen missiles into various locations throughout the city, causing modest infrastructural damage to some buildings, roads, and transportation stations. It looked to Katie like Allirehem wasn't trying to be particularly aggressive towards the civilians.

It was another five minutes after that when the Dravens began to return to the *Valkyrie*. The Allirehem fleet provided them with any covering fire that they needed while they did so. A few seconds later, Katie could hear the airship opening its entrance hatch, far behind and below her. Soon after, she could see Christian and Talia returning on their birds, Anacarin and Embar. Suddenly, her brother jumped off the couch and sprinted to the back of the room.

"Um, Katie, you may want to grab something," Ethan told her. Katie panicked when she realized that she had forgotten about the hatch. She jumped off the couch and ran to the back, then she grabbed ahold of a railing before the glass hatch began to slide down. When the hatch began to open and the wind was not too violent, Katie relaxed. She felt a little embarrassed that she had taken it so seriously. Christian and Talia alighted in the room a few seconds later, and then the hatch closed again. The room darkened as the ship pulled a shade down over the hatch.

It took Katie's eyes a few seconds to adjust to the new lighting. "Holy shit!" Ethan stammered.

"Well, yeah, what the hell?" she felt herself blurt out at what had just happened. Katie felt only lucidly aware of the death and destruction that her perception had just been cut off from. Christian and Talia casually walked past them on their way to unpack themselves from the battle.

"You saw the restraint, didn't you?" Talia asked.

"I guess that depends on your definition of restraint," Ethan admitted.

There were a few moments of silence. "Worse things are happening this very moment in Ferrum. This is war, Ethan. Get used to it," Christian told him. The two of them were sent back to their rooms after that, and Katie's journey eastward to Allirehem continued.

Chapter 22
The Frantelli Crime Family (Brian 5)

KARDADIN, GALLIEM, ALLIREHEM

SUMMER, 1153, FOURTH AGE

*T*he next day, Brian woke with a sore, stiff back. He found himself seated on a bench in a local police department, within their drunk tank for people like him. Brian figured it was whichever station had been closest to Ambley's when he had gotten into his altercation with the bouncer. Something he barely remembered, and the headache he had frayed his mind and blurred his vision. He woke in a position with his legs stretched out across the three bench seats, which hung halfway off, and he had his back and neck twisted so that they just began to incline up the seatback before they stopped, where Brian rested his sweaty head just near the top of the chair. As soon as his vision was good enough, Brian saw that he shared the tank with several other detainees.

The two other men and one woman around his age all generally looked like him, well, like he did that morning more enough: greasy, beat-up, and poor. One more observation of the efforts the other detainees had taken to sit as far away from his as possible, and at one whiff of the air, Brian could still smell his soiled pants from his escape of Maish.

Brian grumbled and bowed his head before he sat up and then cracked his back, neck, and knuckles. He agitatedly hung his head and asked himself how much longer this would go on for, this sucked. As one relief, quickly enough, Brian got his answer.

"Prisoner, prisoner, wakie, wakie," began one voice that came from outside the bars to the cell. "Say, Stigson, which one is it we're looking for?"

Brian found his attention diverted from looking at the wall to looking at the door to the cell where two overweight cops were standing. Brian was able to see one of them held a mug of coffee in one hand with a clipboard in the other, while the other was forking a chunk of macaroni and cheese covered with barbeque sauce into his open mouth. Brian saw that Stigson was black and slightly taller than the other cop, but Stigson was also slightly fatter.

"It's Bringsly that we're looking for, Manno. Bringsly, which one are you?" asked Stigson while he let his clipboard hang in his hand to the side, and placed his coffee down on an end table, safely outside of the cell.

"He's the one that looks like he kicked up too much sand on the beach last night," Manno replied, observing each of the four detainees in the cell, still without resting his eyes directly on him.

"They all look like that, Manno. And they all smell like low tide," said Stigson laughing.

"Well not that one," said Manno, as he finished off his last chunk of mac and cheese, and then tossed the Styrofoam container into a trashcan a few feet away. "That one smells like he soiled himself. That's Bringsly."

Brian finally felt himself pointed at, and he rose off the bench as Stigson held a large chain of keys in his hand, then began to rattle one of them around to let himself into the holding area of the cell. Brian stepped up to the first of two doors that would let him out of the cell and waited.

Manno walked up to one of the bars on the side and looked at Brian. "You're lucky you've got a friend in the resistance. Otherwise, you'd be in here another 3 to 5 hours, and then you'd owe us taxes and processing fees," Manno told him.

Brian felt himself immediately roll his eyes. Mason had probably been one of the first to know of his arrest and bad behavior. He grumbled and then hoarsely said, "Yeah well I guess they know what a talent I could be when I get through with my boot camp that starts next week," Brian lied.

"Alright step in," Stigson compelled him, while he held the inner door to the cell holding chamber open for him, and then closed it behind him. The door to the rest of the jail was obviously still close, while Stigson annoyingly pressed him up against the bars of the cell and gave him a full pat-down.

"Sir, what would he be trying to take out of the jail," Manno asked in a jovial tone, while he admired watching what was being done to Brian. At that moment, Brian felt two fingers poke up his rectum, Stigson must have believed he was hiding something in his prison wallet.

"He's clean," Stigson informed Manno. He turned to Brian and looked him in the eyes before letting him collect himself, off the bars. "You're clean. I just like to watch them squirm. Their wonderful time in jail can't end quickly enough before they get back out to the public. That reminds me, this one needs a shower, a shave, and a fresh pair of clothes. Good thing his taxes and wartime provisions pay for such a thing. We want to help our city not remember there's a war going on two thousand miles away, and we can't do that with you looking like a bum or a refugee. Come on."

By then Stigson had finally put some handcuffs on him, and Manno had opened the outer cell door to let them both out. Brian was silent, resigned to do what he could to stay in their good graces, and therefore get released from the jail as quickly as possible.

"Alright, to the showers, boy. Get!" Manno prodded Brian forward, once he had walked by him in the hallway.

He had to say something now. "Don't touch me again, I don't even know where the showers are," he told them.

Again, he felt the sanctity of his own ass desecrated again, with the thumb of Stigson's nightstick encouraging him to shoot forward down the hallway. As if his ass had ever been particularly clean since he left Maish. Stigson jogged in front of him and gave him a look telling him not to test him for dicking him around with his nightstick. *When is this going to end?* Brian asked himself.

At last, Stigson led him through the police station to a shower room in the back. He held that door open for all three of them, and then each of them entered the spacious shower room.

"Strip," Manno told Brian, this time just giving him a gentle push towards the showerhead, which descended a few inches out of the ceiling in the middle of the room.

Brian knew just what kind of shower it was going to be, as he set about taking off his clothes. Once he was naked, Brian stood underneath the shower and waited for the water. He'd been through this before, but that didn't mean he didn't shudder when the cold hit him or almost slip when the water began to pool under his feet around the drain, and the spray of the water was so violent all he wanted to do was get out of its way. When Manno finally did toss him a bar of soap, it was a low lob and at the knees. Brian stumbled to his knees to catch it, and then that's when he heard the two of them laughing together while they each sprayed him with a showerhead of hot water on both his balls and ass. He stood up and stumbled back into the shower, and finally got the chance he had needed to clean his sack and ass. The two of them finally seemed to lay off him, after that.

The shower ended seconds after Brian got to that point, and he was relieved it was finished. At least now he felt clean, again, physically anyways. *Damn Rosa*, he thought.

"That's good enough. I'll watch him, you get his clothes. Remember, the special clothes," said Manno. While Stigson left the shower and returned a minute and a half later, Manno and Brian said not a word. When Stigson returned, he gave Brian the outfit and a simple black pair of walking sneakers. Graciously, they left him in peace to towel off and put on his new clothes. The outfit was a light orange shirt, and a very faded pair of black jeans, along with a pair of socks and underwear that *looked* worn, but once he groaned and put them on, actually felt quite clean.

Finally clothed, clean, and about to free of jail, Brian walked out into the hallway and was greeted only by Stigson this time. With a smile on his face and nice straight posture, Stigson led him down the hallway towards the check-out counter and said, "Best enjoy your day, sir. Stay safe out there."

He handed him his phone, wallet, and a phone charger for his phone he had never seen before. "You've got a good friend on your side. I wouldn't let that go to waste," Stigson told him before he slapped him on the ass and held the exit to the street open for him. Brian huffed and turned away from the asshole cop. He was finally free, but now he needed to figure out his next course of action. Of course, he was still reeling about Macie and his chopper, but if life wasn't going to end, and it seemed like it wasn't to, at least for the moment, Brian figured he might as well get on about something else. One check to his phone showed a full charge and a message from Mason.

Don't get in trouble again, I won't be able to bail you out again, as easily. The outfit I gave you is for your transformations. Wear it whenever you think you may transform, and it will help you still be clothed afterward. Brian didn't text back.

He felt ready to seek out his old career field.

From his own knowledge, Brian already knew the general layout of the city of Kardadin. He walked himself away from the touristy boardwalk and beach area of the city. Within a few blocks, he was in a drastically different portion of the city. The city was louder here. Instead of sun-seeking families and pleasure-seeking tourists, Brian heard Gallaeic spoken in different tones for different purposes. Brian led himself down an alley in between two roads with brick buildings on either side, full of various businesses.

Brian looked from side to side. He could see restaurant or market managers arguing with truck drivers about their morning deliveries, while several vagrants still slept underneath newspaper and cardboard. Typical sounds of construction reverberated through the buildings in this portion of the city. Brian could hear Gallaeic urban hip-hop being played loudly on several different speakers either inside or on someone's back patio. This district was the most culturally affluent section of the city, and its businesses, infrastructure, and products spread out from here to the rest of the city—and Allirehem beyond that.

So now that Brian knew he was in generally the right area of the city to find possible jobs from his old career field, he knew the first thing he would need to do is find a contact or a front. If Brian had wanted to find a contact quickly, he probably shouldn't have left the tourist section several blocks ago, because mafia contacts were most easily findable in bars near the water, run by the locals, but frequented by visitors for such a potential purpose. Since he wasn't close to any bars of note, in this section of Kardadin, Brian decided he needed to find a front.

A front was a building where mafia operations could be conducted, at least on a small-scale level. Normally the operations took place in the back of the building, thus the front was a legal business, which helped divert the eyes of the law, and could come in a range of disguises: like a flower shop, or a small fish market.

"Armando, where's your loyalty to my market. My customers demand the freshest ocean aashings in our waters, but now you're selling me fish that ought to be going to the restaurants on the water where tourists won't know the difference. Everyone knows this!" said the fish market manager Brian had noticed when he had strolled into the alley a few minutes before. Brian could see the man was a few inches taller than him, and he had a thick mop of brown hair which sat messily atop his sunburnt northern skin.

Brian grabbed his phone and quickly brought up some of the latest news articles on the Kardadin mafia families. From his past connections in Raegic, Brian had a good feeling that the man he looked at with brown eyes was a family member within the Frantelli crime family. It looked like Brian had been just lucky enough to quickly find where he needed to be, and spot whom he needed to speak to. To help his plea for work, Brian also opened several newspaper articles about his original run-in with Mason from several weeks ago on another internet page.

"We go through this each summer, Vraine. When the tourists start to come to town for the summer, the restaurants on the water are simply willing to beat your prices. Now that even more refugees have fled here from Maish, they're willing to pay double. After all, some of the refugees who have been lucky to escape this far do have money. These aashings are still plenty fresh enough for your market," Armando said to Vraine. Vraine didn't not like that, and his eyes and posture made him look like he wanted to fight the fish trader.

The two of them did not shake hands once they had concluded their argument. Vraine handed Armando a thick padded envelope, and Armando pulled two wooden crates filled with aashings off his truck. He put them down next to the market's back door. Armando retreated to his refrigerated truck's driver seat and was out of sight a few moments after turning the truck's engine back on.

Vraine still looked quite displeased, once the truck was out of sight. When he bent down to pick up the two wooden crates of fish, Brian knew it was a good opportunity for him to introduce himself.

"Let me help you with one of those," he suggested to Vraine.

"Who are you?" asked Vraine, who had just seemed to notice him for the first time.

"No one you know, but I couldn't help but overhear how your aashing supplier stiffed your market for tourist restaurants. Maybe I could have a talk with him on your behalf?" Brian offered. Vraine gave him an extended sullen look, which told Brian he was either going to tell him to get lost, or he was still trying to interpret exactly what Brian had meant. Vraine began to open his mouth for a moment, then he paused and held off on answering. He looked Brian over from top to bottom, judging for himself if he was physically intimidated by him.

"No, that's not what I need right now," Vraine told him. He picked up his two crates of fish from the cut-out handles on the bottom one, and then he had Brian take the one off the top for him. "Maybe my sister does, though."

Brian smelt the salty dead fish rise through his nostrils while he waited for Vraine to open the backdoor to his market. "I appreciate that actually. I'm new in town, but I have contacts in Maish and old references in Raegic from my time there," he told the man.

Brian and Vraine walked into the backroom of the market. In front of him and down the hallway, Brian could see the entrance to the storefront and the manager's office before that, off to the left. "I can't promise you anything yet. You'll have to prove yourself first," Vraine told him.

Vraine led him down the hallway and stopped at a thick grey door, which sealed off a refrigerated storeroom. Vraine slid the door to the side and walked through the thick shades, which held back some of the cool air. Brian wondered what he would have to do to prove himself to Vraine. He had a feeling he wouldn't like what he had to do, but he *had* to do it.

"What would I have to do?" he asked Vraine.

The man put down his crate of fish next to several others, and Brian followed suit quickly. "Tell me what you want first. I can tell you with the war coming imminently that we have a need of enforcers now. When Iishrem is here later, there could be opportunities for some of these enforcers to take on new, less violent rolls as insurgency coordinators, but they would need to be good at getting others to follow their lead before it resorts to violence," Vraine began to explain.

Brian felt his muscles tense while he shivered in the refrigerated storeroom. "I'm really just hoping to just be passing through. I'm looking for passage across the ocean to Maravinya. Anywhere close to Bentlion would be ideal, but I'd be happy to settle for Draxion City as well. There are trains," Brian finished.

Vraine began to laugh just after he finished talking, and Brian felt himself grow uncomfortable. He wanted to get out of the refrigerated storeroom, but oddly, he felt like he needed permission to leave first. He was speaking to someone inside a crime family after all.

"How exactly do you expect to manage to get there in a time like this?" Vraine asked him.

"A charter," Brian told him plainly while looking him directly in the eyes.

"That would require a lot of money. Iishrem might be here sooner than you could accrue it," Vraine told him after he had had a good laugh.

Brian wasn't discouraged, but he was beginning to grow impatient. "So. You said I would need to prove myself first in order for any of this to happen anyway?" he asked Vraine. There was barely a moment of silence between the two of them before Vraine charged forward at him with his arms out and pushed him out of the refrigerated storeroom.

Ahh, yes, a physical confrontation, of course, Brian thought as he felt his back bounce off the brick wall. He wasn't going to take this fight against Vraine personally, but he hoped he wouldn't have to hurt him too much for him to make his point. Brian ducked underneath a punch aimed for his jaw as he bounced off the wall. While Vraine's punch to his jaw missed high, Brian did feel a crunch to his ribs when Vraine's other fist connected with his mid-section a moment later.

Brian needed space, and he wanted to prove his point quickly before he took too much damage himself. Brian pushed his way into Vraine's mid-section with his elbows out and checked him back into the refrigerator door that Vraine had shut after the fight had begun. Brian threw three jabs into Vraine's stomach while Vraine guarded his face with his arms up. A few seconds later, Brian found out the hard way that Vraine wasn't fighting back just so he could kick him off his feet and tackle him to the ground.

Vraine was much heavier than Brian had suspected. It took a considerable amount of his strength and wrestling knowledge for him to roll over and get back on top of Vraine. By the time Brian was able to do that, the confrontation between the two of them had caused quite a mess and a ruckus in the back of the market. It wasn't until that moment that Brian noticed two other bulky male employees were watching their fight. They stood on either side of who Brian hoped was the sister that Vraine had mentioned before. He hoped that the three of them wouldn't join in the fight to help Vraine. Brian knew he was wrong when he saw the look in the woman's eyes. The woman had similar sunburnt northern skin, black hair, and brown eyes like her brother, but she was several inches shorter than him and wore her short hair spiked up at the front.

There had to be a better way for him to escape the war than this. Brian backed off Vraine and eased his way back to the exit. As he did so, the two bulky male employees walked after him, side by side down the hallway. Vraine got up and dusted himself off, then he stood by the woman who was just observing the entire altercation. Brian took another step back, then he acted like he had stumbled, hoping one of them would charge forward at him.

Brian's gamble paid off several seconds later, when he nimbly stood to his side and caught the charging man on the shoulder as he stumbled forward past him. Brian pushed that man down the hall and into a pile of empty cardboard beer cases while he waited for the other man to rush forward.

"Wait, wait. That's enough," Brian heard Vraine say a second later. Brian looked at him and saw no more fight in his expression. It was quite a relief to him. Vraine looked down at the woman who stood next to him.

The woman said, "He knows how to fight in small spaces and against greater numbers. We could use a man like him for a job Mom has coming up."

"Perhaps so. She'll have to be the judge of that for herself, though," Vraine admitted. "This is Bella, my sister."

The bulky man who stood in front of him retreated next to Vraine, while the one Brian had pushed away got up and walked back over to stand on the other side of the woman. The man gave Brian a dirty look while he passed him by, but Brian didn't care. Brian had something to say for himself. No one here knew who he was and what he could do—what he could offer them.

"I can do more than this you know," Brian told them, then he pulled out his phone and handed it to them. "I'm Brian Bringsly," he told them. He tried to relax and loosen some of the tightness in his muscles from the fight. There were a few more seconds of silence while Bella continued to study his phone screen.

"Not just Brian, but also the tiger of Maish," Bella told him. There were no hushed gasps shared between the other three men, but they each exchanged looks as though to say they already knew who she was referring to. "What're you looking for in return?"

Brian looked her in the eyes intently. "Passage to Maravinya—and citizenship papers for the country as well," he finished.

"Very well. We'll take you to Mother, the matriarch of our family. She'll make the final decision on whether or not you get this chance," Bella told him.

The job Brian received as his possible payment for passage across the ocean to Maravinya was a matter of territorial expansion that the Frantelli family wanted to go in their favor. A week after arriving in Kardadin, Brian found himself in a dark, smoky room within a mansion, several miles outside the limits of Kardadin. At first, it had surprised him that the family would be so willing to let him in and give him a job so quickly—even if they would just try to kill him if he failed—but the more he learned about the job and what *they* could gain from it, the more Brian realized that they *must* have been looking for a man like him.

Forty-five minutes into the meeting that Vraine and Bella had brought him out of the city for, Brian believed the matriarch of the Frantelli family was just beginning to get to why she needed a man like him for the job that she had in mind. The matriarch of the family was an octogenarian with shiny black hair in a short cut, which draped her bangs across her forehead to the left in a V.

Fray'la Frantelli sat behind her desk with an inquisitive look directed towards Brian as she sucked on a cigarette with pursed lips. She exhaled, putting her bottom lip out in front so that the smoke would go directly toward the ceiling, where a foggy cloud of it had formed—even though Vraine had boasted of the room's air-filtration system on their way over. She stabbed out her cigarette on a crystal ashtray that was sparsely filled with at least a half-dozen other butts. Next to the ashtray sat a glass of red wine, which was almost empty, and a bottle that was down to its last few ounces. She poured herself the last of it into her glass, against the wishes of Vraine who sat across from Brian.

Brian had to admire her robust attitude for a woman of her age and the way she commanded her underlings. It all seemed like a façade she was putting on to Brian, like Fray'la would be a different woman if he met her by chance, instead of within her home surrounded by her family.

"There exists a tenuous peace between the four crime families of Kardadin you see; us—the Frantellis—the Knots, the Carlins, and"—she paused for a second. Brian watched her body slightly stifle itself while she said the last name—"the Vornins. It's only existed for the past few years, as the four of us have all seen the war getting closer. The smaller three of us each know what comes for this city after the Resistance inevitably fails to stave them off—a full-scale occupation of Galliem by Iishrem."

"Ma, how do you know that's going to happen?" asked Vraine. "The fighting in Maish has been about fifty-fifty since it started."

"It has been little longer than a week, Son. Allirehem's partial control of the first but possibly most important city in the country is not going to last. Once the Resistance cedes Maish, the rest of their invasion forces will no longer have to force their way through a choke point to fight in the rest of the country. Iishrem will use Maish as a forward command post to launch their conquest of the rest of the country. And as to what could be the worst effects of Iishrem occupation, we only have to look at what is happening in Ferrum. A once beautiful city, t's just a husk of its former self. Sure, always directly in Iishrem's path, and the Resistance did it no favors. I'll not see that happen to my city," said Fray'la.

Brian was finally beginning to see exactly where she was going with this meeting. "What's your problem with the Vornins? Do they not see the same overarching threat you do?" Brian asked.

"A quick learner," Fray'la said out loud. "You see the Vornins hold the lion's share of the Allum Rock trade in the city. They move over fifty percent of the city's supply, geographically speaking. My family has worked tirelessly to chop into their chunk, cementing a very reasonable third of it. I'm fine with the other two families where they are. I'd even give them several blocks off the top if the areas aren't practical for us. But the Vornins need to be knocked down a peg. Hopefully, then they'll go under new management soon after." She took a long sip of her wine.

"Why should the Frantellis have the lion's share of the city? What makes your family so noble that yours can run the best insurrection against Iishrem?" Brian asked, and then he thought of one more important question. "And how does this all play out? I kill these people, take their territory, and a mafia war doesn't start the next day between the four of you?"

"It'll work because you won't be killing anyone, and who you will fight isn't a member of the Vornin. In order for us to take a lion's share of the city, you must beat their best fighter. You need to sneak into their warehouse and then subdue him. If you're able to do this, put him in cuffs," she said, putting a pair of handcuffs on the table in front of him. "And put a gun to his head. Then take him out of his office, and my men will come in and assist you. Some of the underlings may want to kill you afterward. The transition of the territory will be seamless and without blood spilt unless the other family wants it to go as such, which would only result in a slaughter of their men and perhaps one or two of mine."

"Once it's done, Bella here will take you to a ship of your own, and the captain will take you to Valeium, as per your request," said Fray'la. There was a pause in the conversation, and Brian leaned back in his chair, feeling like he actually had a small chance of outrunning the war. "But, Brian, if you should fail me or expose my plan to the Vornins before you can pull it off, I will have you killed."

"That doesn't matter to me. Perhaps such an ending would be more poetic for me than anything else. My payment for all the crimes of my past," Brian told her.

After taking another swig of her wine, Fray'la smiled and took a drag of another cigarette. She stood up and offered her palm out in contract. "It sounds like we have an accord, Brian."

Brian put his palm on top of Fray'la's, and their contract was set.

Chapter 23
Icon (Bailey 5)

ILLIAS, HAISHA, ALLIREHEM

SUMMER, 1153, FOURTH AGE

*T*wo days later, Bailey woke to the sound of a pouring rainstorm coming in through her hotel bedroom window. She wanted to sleep in. She had shopped, drank, eaten, and danced her way across the city for the last two days. She finally planned to return to Lampshire this night—after some reading in a park she had found several blocks away, and hopefully, a late lunch with her father. There was no reason for her to be getting out of bed this early. Then she began to hear movements in the living and dining rooms of the main suite. It sounded like her father was scuttling about the room, and several moments later, Bailey thought it was bordering on a commotion.

It quickly became apparent to Bailey that she was missing something. Bailey rose out of bed in the silk pajamas she had picked out for herself on her first day after arriving in Illias. She walked out into the living room and found her father packing his things, making his way out the door. How was she not surprised at all?

Bailey frustratedly tried to blow a few strands of her long hair out of her face, but she ended up leaving all of her bangs down around her in indifference. "I guess you're not staying much longer?" she asked.

Her words caught Clancy dead in his tracks, and he forced a wide grin across his face from ear to ear. "Bailey, I'm so sorry. I swear this is against all of my best wishes, but the fighting in Maish has gone quite south, and Mason needs my help," he told her. "With fall term about to start in just a few weeks, he simply needs my assistance—before he can possibly be off the Allaeyic mainland for seven of the next eight months. I was hoping to take you all the way to the academy myself, but I suppose this is the best I can do."

Bailey felt herself exhale in angst. "Would it really be so hard for you to ever finish something you've started?" she asked. "Do you just not really care about my overall safety?"

Clancy put his suitcase down and stroked his hair back as he walked over to the door. Bailey tailed behind him and saw there were several large packages sitting in the entryway. Knowing her father, Bailey doubted enough time had passed for there to be anything good in any of them.

"If we could speak at the table, please? For a moment?" Clancy asked.

Bailey sat down quickly and folded her hands, then she watched him intently while he made his way over to the small circular table, carrying some of the packages from the door. One of them was a long, skinny black suitcase. First, he handed her a small brown box, big enough for a phone. Bailey was actually quite surprised when she found herself looking down at a thick neon-green phone with a horizontal push-out keyboard for texting. She turned it on, and a few moments later, she was scrolling through a brief list of contacts with Corso and Ben already on it.

"Thank you, Dad. It's a start," she told him. There were many alterations and modifications she would have to make to it, but at least she would have access to some of what she needed in a limited capacity.

The next package turned out to be the drive shaft of her dirt bike. "It wasn't practical to try and salvage everything, but they'll be an assembly waiting for you in your spare time—once you arrive in Meinghelia City. At least this will give you the personality of your old bike," he told her.

Bailey looked down and clasped the dirty and partly rusted drive shaft like it was buried treasure. There was one final package. "How did you get all of this back so quickly? Thank you," she told him.

"I told you I would. At least I can do a few things right toward getting you to the Academy, but for now, I have one final gift," he told her from across the table. Bailey leaned back in her chair and reserved final judgment on what he was holding back to herself. The package was the long, black skinny suitcase, which turned out to be a weapons case. Clancy put the suitcase down in front of her, and Bailey quickly opened its clasps and pushed back its top half.

Inside the suitcase was the carbine rifle Bailey liked so much. The K-9 pistol she had given to Corso during the skirmish was also there. Bailey grabbed it gently and choked it back to make sure it wasn't loaded. It wasn't, and neither was the carbine. The guns felt solid in her possession now, like her shots would no longer fly astray. The guns were now hers.

"Be careful with them," Clancy told his daughter as he looked down at her. She nodded as she examined the cogs, screws, and mechanisms of the rifle. "But what do I need to tell you. You've always understood quite well how to respect your guns and keep them in good working shape."

Bailey put down the pistol, stopped fiddling with the rifle, and closed the case a moment later. She could run through the rest of her tests and checks once he had gone. "You've kept your promise to me—although you aren't seeing me all the way there," she admitted to him.

"It was the least I could do for you. I know how much of an impossible and difficult path you've had to take, without any warning, in the last couple of days alone," he told her. "I'm proud of you. Your mother would be too."

"I wasn't given much of a choice," she told him. Bailey stood up from the table, sensing that Clancy wouldn't be around much longer.

"Neither was I. You remember what happened," Clancy told her. Bailey thought about that day. Perhaps she should have known everything that would eventually happen to her, once that first encounter with Christian had taken place. Perhaps she should have just run away. Maybe Hector would have found her then. Instead, he was just missing and absent from her life, like he had always been. Perhaps the two of them could have escaped the war in its entirety and lived on one of the sparsely populated Heylaphine Islands.

But then what would be the point of us ever coming together? Hector asked her in her mind. Bailey heard it so faintly, it sounded like a whisper. She just ended up looking around the suite, wondering where the voice had come from while Clancy gathered the remainder of his belongings.

"Before I go, there is one last thing for us to talk about. Your Eedon Rath-ni. Hector you claim is his name?" Clancy asked in an unsure tone.

"Yes," she told him.

Clancy put his hand on her shoulder and looked down at her. He shifted his body so that he put just a little weight on her—only enough that it felt like an encouraging pat on the shoulder.

"You said you haven't heard from him much at all?" he asked. He let his hand off her shoulder, and Bailey turned away from him and put her head down a little. "I never had much of a connection to Raejen either. At least, before Christian showed up. It was a surprise to me too. Christian tells me Hector is a known hawk among others who have already joined the Resistance or enrolled at the Academy. There must be something to his absence."

"All I can hear is the occasional whisper or two. One just now, and one earlier not too far from here in the Lampshire District. I looked for an hour after that, Dad, and I never heard again from him that night," she told him.

"I think that's your strongest lead then, Bailey. You need to head back there today or soon. The fall semester at the academy starts in just over a month, and you'd be safest there, but first, you need your Eedon Rath-ni. Now, call me if you need anything—like if you think it's something that you can't quite handle by yourself. I have people that can assist you, but you need to think through a plan first. Don't forget that calling in back-up can often change the situation entirely—and not *always* in your favor," Clancy told her. "Now I should probably be going. Your stay here is covered through the first day of fall. If you need more time than that... well, we'll have to work through that together."

Clancy stepped towards Bailey to hug her, but she turned away from him and only allowed him to hug her side. "I'll walk with you to the roof," she told him.

Clancy recoiled from her and brought his arms back down to his sides. He grabbed his rolling suitcase by the extendable handle with one hand, and then he grabbed his leather satchel which he kept his more personal items in with the other.

The two of them walked over to the front door, where Bailey opened the door for her father first as he was carrying several things.

"Thank you," Clancy said with a brief smile.

Bailey closed the door behind herself and followed Clancy down the hallway towards the same staircase they had originally come down several days ago. She did not bother to open the door to the stairwell for her father, and so Clancy rested his satchel on the extending handle of his suitcase and opened the door himself. Their shoes clanked on the concrete staircase while they made their way up the two flights of stairs before they exited onto the roof a few moments later.

The rain had slowed up a bit. Of course, that didn't mean that the sun had come out. It all just made Bailey want to go back to sleep. This day was not conducive for finding an Eedon' Rath-ni, but Bailey wondered if that was really herself telling her that or something more malicious. Clancy walked over to Raejen, who had already been waiting for them on the roof.

Clancy gave her a warm embrace, then he pushed his suitcase handle back in and put it in front of her talons. Bailey noticed that Raejen's saddle already had the assault rifle and pistol that Clancy had brought for himself strapped to it. He put his satchel around his back, and then he stepped towards Bailey again for a hug. She did not stiff him this time but only lightly placed her hands on his shoulders.

He held out a key and gave it to her. There was a small piece of paper attached to it. "On the phone I gave you, you'll find the coordinates of my cabin outside of Meinghelia City programmed into it. After that, it's as simple as finding Hector and then plugging the coordinates into the phone's GPS." he told her.

"When will I see you again?" she asked.

"I don't know," he admitted worriedly. The two of them parted from each other, and then she watched him fly out of sight.

Bailey headed back to her room and went back to sleep for the next few hours, unable to shake the empty feeling inside—as if there was nothing else she wanted to do.

Seven more hours passed—six of which she spent in bed—and then Bailey finally couldn't find any more excuses to remain in bed rather than go and explore the city in search of Hector. Her vitality had been fully satisfied, and there weren't more any books or movies she felt like enjoying. Bailey hopped out of her bed and quickly noticed that she felt an extra spring in her step. She needed to eat something, though. She wanted to take it easy that night, so after showering and putting her hair into a simple ponytail and one thick bang which came down past her right eye, she dressed to blend in.

She dressed in a pair of loose rugged khaki shorts, which ended in a tight cutoff several inches past her knees and pulled up several inches past her waist. The pants were meant to exaggerate her legs and butt, which helped her feel like hers were almost average-sized.

Bailey set off from her father's hotel suite with her new phone, camera, and a small notepad and pen. She also took a pair of headphones and a pair of light blue aviators she could put on if the sun ever bothered to come out. At this point of summer, this far north in the world, some nights the sun was up until past 9:30 pm. Bailey grabbed a thin rain slicker from the closet before the door and stuffed it into her pocket before she left.

She descended via the elevator and strolled out through the classical old-world lobby, lined with marble floors and mirrors, into a cool, overcast day. It was no longer raining, but Bailey found out quickly that the city was still very much in the process of drying off. She put her aviators on for a moment, just to see how things would look, but took them off again almost as quickly because they began to fog up from the heat and rain droplets. That was annoying! Drops of rain wet the tips of her ears, and she felt water from puddles splash the short sections of her legs, which were exposed between the ends of her shorts and the tops of her boots. The streets that led her away from her hotel were brick and only wide enough for parking halfway on the curb, with one-way traffic to the side. Pretty brick or painted city homes lined the roads, rising as high as four stories tall, many of which had rooftop decks.

Bailey felt the wet, humid summer air in her lungs and listened to the quiet breeze. The rest of the city offered her the sounds of a passing storm. When she listened closely, she could hear the sounds of gentle revelry coming from the Riverwalk. She wondered how much the river's level had risen with the day's rain. Without looking at her phone for directions, Bailey set off to find her closest city thoroughfare. She found one that ran north to south and headed north on it, knowing eventually it would curve and lead her east to the Riverwalk.

As she walked, she kept to herself and listened to the conversations of locals, trying to pick up on more of their words—she had worked hard enough on it over the last couple of days. So much so that she could take a cab home and hold a light conversation with the driver if she wished. She felt less confident talking to youths her age, but that hadn't stopped her from dancing with several of them over the last couple of nights or ordering drinks with them and staring into their eyes. She had danced with both boys and girls, and generally, she had had better conversations with the girls, but she had also improved her vocabulary with the boys.

By the time Bailey made it to the Riverwalk, the day had cleared up completely. The sun was showing just enough that Bailey could feel its warmth as it set, far off in the distance. The city began to liven up, and Bailey exited the wide and busy thoroughfare, taking a cobblestone stairway down to the Riverwalk. Once she descended the stairs, she stood underneath a bridge that crossed the river in an archway, where she paused and looked up and down the river.

Both banks of the river were lined by the Riverwalk within the city limits of Illias. A stone promenade around 75 feet wide followed the river, with more buildings of brick and stone that housed shops, cafes, restaurants, and clubs. The river itself was lightly filled with motored boats sailing both upstream and downstream. Bailey saw a few personal boats and river vendors, but many more boats were filled with tourists or citizens enjoying the sights. There was even the odd evening cruise. Up and down the river, Bailey saw a multitude of crossings. There were more crossings closer to where she was at the moment than perhaps a mile and a half down the river to the northeast.

When Bailey thought about where exactly she had been when she had heard Hector's voice in her head, she struggled to recall much about it. Perhaps she could find it, but that would only take her more time, and Bailey didn't think there was anything particular about that exact location that would lead her to Hector.

She began to think about where Hector might be if he were hiding from her within the city. Was someone trying to hide him from her? What was blocking her connection from him? Bailey slowed her pace when she got into a section of the city that she had only heard about before—Brien'nia Street. The river was wide in that portion of the city, and there was even an island with a dense pine forest in the middle of it. There were fewer boats for tourists here. Most boats in the river now looked to be for pleasure purposes, but there were others that Bailey believed could have been intended for trafficking, protection, or syndication as well.

On the other side of the river, Bailey could see ships sailing up to darkly painted doors on the walls of the river embankments. There, the boats then stopped and turned directions, before sailing out of sight.

Bailey continued down the promenade and looked to her right, where a popular brothel rose three stories into the air. Out front of the three-story building was a patio filled with patrons surrounded by half-naked men and women at tables with food, cigars, and wine. There was plenty of cheer among all of them, but some of the couples at the back were clearly having sex. One of the women was grinding herself on top of her man while he drove himself into her. They still had most of their clothes on. *So, these are the love streets I've heard about,* Bailey thought intrigued.

She approached a three-story saloon and brothel. It had a line of patrons running up the block, each of them with a relaxed, grinning, or angsty expression. The line approached a gated entrance where guests were led into an outdoor dining area. Off to the side of the building, Bailey could see walls for stalls and groaning voices could be heard coming from that direction. She could only wonder at what was going on over there. The first floor was lightly filled with patrons and servers or the talent, and there was plenty of space for gaming like pool and also a few tables for cards and a dining area as well. When Bailey looked at the upper stories, she heard much more vigorous activities going on. Some of the windows were open. Bailey looked for a moment into one window, where she could see a couple of men having sex. One was white, the other black.

Bailey felt her eyes turn brown, and she began to understand some of the conversations in Haishian around her. She had only just stopped to look at the brothel for a few moments, and one middle-aged man coughed loudly at her and said, "It's rude to watch you know."

Bailey snapped out of her trance, then looked at him and laughed out loud. She thought about walking into the brothel in front of him. Bailey felt incredulous as if she hadn't accidentally walked in on people making love before or heard them in the act of it from hallways outside. This though was all in plain sight. She was old enough to enjoy herself there, and she likely had the capital, but she was not interested. Bailey turned away from the man after one more laugh and walked towards the patio of the brothel until suddenly, the window where she had seen the gay couple having sex shattered.

The sound of cracking glass pulled her eyes to the window, where Bailey saw a tan boy who looked a little older than herself with a short crew cut. He burst out through the window shoulder first, leading a girl with pale white skin and ginger hair along with him. They fell through the air, and the boy landed on his back with a thud. Then the girl landed on top of him. The girl was hurt. She quickly rolled off him to the side and lay on the cobblestone patio of the brothel, clutching at her side.

Somehow, how the boy turned over quite quickly and stood before gathering the girl back up. It took the boy a lot of effort and a complicated dance to get her up and talking to him, but quickly they began to make their way away from the scene. Bailey thought he was quite fleet of foot. In fact, he reminded her now of how she played paintball. Nimble feet and subtle movements, with the occasional jump or prance here and there. It was all a dance.

"C'mon, Cousin," said the boy as he knelt over top of the groaning girl who appeared a few years older than him. He put his arm around her shoulder and hoisted her gently into the air.

"Ahh, Icon, my stomach," she told the boy.

"It's just going to bruise, Brenna. It was just a twelve-foot fall, and you landed right on top of me. Give yourself a chance to walk it off. I am," he told her.

The girl, Brenna, looked at him with some spite. "But you are a range Draven," she told him, unable to keep her voice down.

As soon as Bailey heard Brenna call Icon a Draven, she found herself looking at his eyes, which were as green as a ripe lime peel. "I'm not anything without Ghel, and that fall with you on top of me still hurt me too," Icon told his cousin.

Bailey found herself utterly entranced with watching Icon and Brenna make their way from the scene. Brenna needed his help to limp the first couple of steps, but then she uncomfortably wobbled after him when he released her. The boy ran forward a few steps towards the promenade of the Riverwalk, where there was more space to make a faster getaway than on the sidewalks. Bailey then noticed that on either side of the river walls, couples could board two-person karts that hovered magnetically above the water at the level of the Riverwalk. There was an empty one waiting for them.

When Brenna passed Bailey, the two of them made eye contact but said nothing to each other. Bailey noticed the entry of a new party into the fray a moment later, when she looked back at the front door of the brothel. A short portly man and a tall, limber woman, both with pale caramel skin and black hair, came sprinting out of the brothel after them, wielding pistols and wearing trench coats. Bailey heard the soft ignition of an electric engine from behind her a moment later. She turned to see the cousins making their way from the scene in one of the karts and up the river towards the city limits and the mountains beyond that.

The man and woman chasing after them jogged on foot for a short distance, and then they postured for a shot, but eventually, they let them slip away uncontested as they had already sped several hundred feet away. Bailey looked at the man and woman and was quite surprised when she understood them speaking Gallaeic. She wondered if the two of them were intentionally speaking Gallaeic in the heart of Illias to avoid being overheard. Unless perhaps they wanted to be, by a specific person.

Police arrived on the scene and began to disperse the small crowd, which had gathered to watch the commotion. The police paid no mind to the pursuers, which Bailey certainly didn't mind either. She set her eyes on their backs and made her way into the depths of the city, following behind them.

The sun had only set a few minutes ago, and the remaining sun rays created an orange overcast sunset for her to tail them in. She followed them for several blocks farther up the river, where there was only one crossing in sight for at least twenty city blocks. Bailey figured her eyes were still brown because she could hear the conversation of the man and woman from far away. Bailey smiled as she listened to them talk, and she took her time wandering from vendor to vendor and admiring the city's fountains one by one.

"It's getting more and more difficult to keep the two hawks safe for their potential buyers with both of their riders now in town. How much did Lance promise us again?" asked the portly man.

The taller woman looked down at him and asked, "ĩ 75 million for the two of them? Is it our skills or our men you're losing trust in first, Shizen?"

Shizen stiffened and wriggled his back twice before he stroked his short beard. Shizen's long black hair was pulled into several ponytails. "It's the storage, Grenelda," Shizen told her a moment later. "This infrastructure we have is simply not conducive to hiding two Eedon Rath-ni underneath a city of this many people during the peak of summer. Especially since Bailey Triten just landed in town. But get this." Shizen pulled out his phone and keyed in a few commands to bring something up to show to Grenelda.

Grenelda's eyebrows eased soon after she began to read, and her shoulders slacked. "This is accurate? He's out of town just like that? He must either really not care about his daughter getting her bird, or he must be overly confident in the skills of a seventeen-year-old girl," said Grenelda.

Shizen smiled and huffed, then said, "She's nineteen now, but yeah. We're in the clear. If we can just make it through the next three nights and get past the auction, we should be able to get the two hawks out of the city to their buyers the following day. We ought to have plenty of men for a boy or girl."

"The boy knows where the birds are kept and how to get them free, but he'll never make it by himself, and the girl doesn't even know where they're kept yet. Just a few more days. Think of all the money we'll have. The beaches and neutrality of Dar'hi Rehem will be in our grasp for as long as we want!" Grenelda shook in excitement.

Hector, Bailey thought.

Bailey, follow them. Find the dark wet caverns of stone beneath the city. You'll find me there and one other. Free us. We won't be here much longer, Hector told her.

Her heart raced, but Bailey did not hear from her Eedon Rath-ni again. She picked up her pace and kept a keen eye on her targets as she closed some of the distance between them. She had to find out more! She needed to see where Hector was, discreetly. Shizen and Grenelda strolled down several more blocks of the Riverwalk, and then they took a right down a canal which split from the river. Now Bailey felt like she was getting somewhere.

The canal was wide enough for two lanes of personal-sized boats to sail through at once. There were two gunboats in various locations near the middle of the canal, and at the end of it, Bailey could see a riverboat that looked to be a few dozen feet wide with three decks. Bailey took cover behind the corner of a building several feet into the canal and watched Grenelda and Shizen trot down the rest of the canal. She did not feel comfortable following them any farther. Yet.

At the end of the canal, Bailey could see the water approached the beginning of a dark tunnel, that was closed off by a door where boats could continue through. Shizen and Grenelda entered the cavern through a smaller personal door on the side of the water garage door, leaving whatever was inside unrevealed. Bailey hoped this boy who had run away would know more about the sewer tunnels and underground waterways layout and how many enemies could be in it at once. At least, for now, Bailey would have pictures of all of it as she had been snapping pictures of everything with her camera every few seconds since she had started following the two of them. *I'll be back for you, Hector. Let me find us some help to break you lose,* Bailey thought to him, sincerely hoping that he heard her.

When she got back out to the Riverwalk, Bailey made sure to remember the location by marking it on her phone and taking more photos. After that, Bailey noticed her stomach rumbling again. She felt famished. Unfortunately for her, she had strolled out of the touristy section. This was, after all, a more industrial, shady side of the city. She took off at a fast jog. It was three blocks before she found herself a floating river kart of her own. Using one had not been in her plans at first, but with how hungry she was, Bailey felt she had no other choice.

She carefully hopped in, over the railing of the Riverwalk, and ran her resistance credit card through its terminal to get it started. Then she took off towards the nearest café she could find that was still open. She found a café that she liked the look of several blocks away from the brothel. It was in the direction Icon and Brenna had taken off in, about ninety minutes prior. The café would provide Bailey with a good opportunity to continue her immersion in Haishian, while also listening for clues on the whereabouts of the cousins.

Bailey walked into the café and stepped up to the counter after waiting in line for a few minutes. "What can I get for you, my dear?" asked the short, plump old woman with graying hair behind the counter.

"A turkey cheese, tomato, and avocado sub on a baguette please, with some potato salad and a soda," Bailey told the woman, feeling happy with her progressing fluency.

She paid with a card of her own this time, deciding to give the Resistance taxpayers a break, and sat down at a table in the back. She had gotten a replacement card for her personal accounts two days after arriving in town. The café was set up in a small box-shaped building, with the counter and the kitchen taking up two-thirds of the upper half of the building, with a quiet performance area to the right. The rest of the space was reserved for the café itself, which was filled with tables, chairs, couches, and coffee tables. There were even several bookshelves spaced out around the walls.

Bailey sat down at a couch, much preferring to put her legs up, kick back, and observe. She took her phone out of her pocket and placed it on the coffee table across from her. Then she took out her small padded notebook and pen and flipped it open. She began to take notes on any conversations she understood.

The first few conversations Bailey overheard weren't related to anything to do with the boy or girl. A family of tourists less fluent in Haishian than her sat around a table discussing their day of vacation while attempting to improve it. "The Raige'le aier Bridge was just magnificent," said a short, blonde-haired child.

The rest of the family began to talk around her, amongst themselves. "Turkey baguette," said a brown-haired female server that had snuck up on her.

Bailey smiled up at the sever and accepted her food. She ravenously consumed her food in a fury of crunching and chewing—and the occasional stabbing when Bailey wanted more of her potato salad. There were more conversations about the weather, the food around the city, and how business was going. Suddenly, Bailey heard a pair of familiar voices again, and she looked up from her dinner—which by that point was almost gone.

Icon and Brenna had strolled into the café, but not from the front door. Bailey whipped her eyes around the room to see where they were sitting. "I still don't know how exactly you got me out of the bath and into this situation," said Brenna. "I should probably just not be out in public, much less with you." Bailey saw the two of them sitting at a booth, which pressed against the wall in the small performance area of the café. Brenna ran a hand through her thin, curly crimson hair and looked around the stage room frantically to see if they were being followed. Then she looked at Bailey.

Bailey instantly looked away as they made eye contact, but it didn't matter. "Hey, I know you," Brenna said out loud to her in Haishian.

Chapter 24

Alyısay (Brıan 6)

KARDADIN, GALLIEM, ALLIREHEM

SUMMER, 1153, FOURTH AGE

t surprised Brian that *he* could see Fray'la's sedan approaching his position on the sidewalk he shared with Gelliem—one of her most annoying henchmen—long before Gelliem could himself. It was Gelliem, after all, who was supposed to be the lookout for her arrival. "I don't quite think you understand how dangerous this is to her safety, to bring her all the way out here, all to tell her something you could tell her on a phone," Gelliem reiterated.

"If she really believed seeing this, hearing this was that dangerous, I doubt that'd she'd come," Brian replied. He turned to his right and looked down at the short, thin man with a crazy-mad face, crow's feet, and wide eyes. "Besides, it looks like you could let loose a little steam yourself."

Gelliem looked up at him and sneered visibly before he turned back to the road in front of them and hacked out a loogie. He looked down the road to their left where Brian had just been looking and finally said, "There she is."

Brian looked to the west and saw her silver Marinclyade approaching their location from several blocks away—relieved that she would be there soon and hoping that Gelliem would relax. He began to wonder why such a trigger-happy fool had been sent to be her lookout for this meeting, but he couldn't worry about that now. He just wanted to talk her through his plan and see what she had to say. Hopefully, she would offer some insight or perhaps be able to make his plan easier for him.

"She'll be fine. Remember this is all just a walk in the park. She'll be safe at home with a glass of wine when I actually pull this off in three days," Brian told Gelliem.

Gelliem hooted. "And if you should fail, you'll be the only one to die," he told him with a grin. "Roar!"

Brian shrugged his shoulders and walked to an opening on the sidewalk with fewer people. When Fray'la's silver sedan stopped there, he was waiting for her just a few steps back from the curb with his hands in front of his stomach, one over the other.

Brian could just barely see inside the luxury sedan's tinted windows. Fray'la looked quite disgusted that Gelliem had not already opened her door for her. Brian knew he was playing his role correctly at least.

"Shit!" Gelliem exclaimed from behind him and rushed forward to yank the door open—somehow at an even pace.

Once Fray'la's door was open and Gelliem was in the process of helping her out of the car, the two other passengers of the sedan opened their doors and got out as well. It was Bella and another henchman that Brian had not met before. The driver remained in the car and pulled away a few seconds later.

The henchman was dressed in a casual suit and wore dark sunglasses. "Of course, you're bald and husky," Brian exclaimed at the henchman, over the apparent lack of irony.

"The name is Brayden," the husky man replied. Brian supposed that not *all* his hair was gone from the top of his head. Brian ran a hand through his slick, ginger hair.

"I don't care," Brian told Brayden.

"Brian," said Fray'la, putting her hands close to his cheeks. He allowed her to hold his cheeks, but she didn't keep them there for long. "Don't be mean to Brayden." Then she put her hands just below his shoulders.

"I know, Fray'la, I was just messing with him. Trying to lighten the mood. While we were waiting, it seemed like every five minutes Gelliem was going to have a conniption, just cause you're coming. Now you're here, I can't tell how he's handling it," Brian explained.

Brayden said nothing, and Gelliem looked dumbfounded. Bella didn't do anything except look at him and then Fray'la. Fray'la stood there with a grin on her face, and then she began laughing.

"Oh, good grief, Gelliem. It's the middle of the day, and Iishrem's Army is still no closer than two thousand miles from here. What could happen?" she asked.

Gelliem looked incredulous. "He does turn into an effing tiger you know."

Suddenly, Fray'la's expression looked both serious and afraid. She took off her sunglasses with her old but strong hands. She turned to Brian, looked up at him, and then said, "My bones are old and frail, they wouldn't crunch well. And there's barely a pound of meat on me."

There was some silence between the five of them while they huddled around Fray'la. Fray'la was wearing her nicest white pants, with a black blazer and a shirt that was spotted with different kinds of flowers. "It would probably be a waste of my time," Brian told her.

They all shared a laugh at Gelliem's expense, and then they turned to walk into an alleyway, which would take them off the main street. "Infamous Mafia Mom, Head bitten off by the Tiger of Maish. What an ending after over sixty-five years of professional experience in crime. I can see it now," Fray'la told the rest of the group.

Fray'la brought her red leather purse up to her chest and began to search through it looking for something. She pulled out a beaten and ruffled book. It looked like she used it as a makeshift personal ledger for exchanges and notes on the go. "Now, if we're all done laughing, perhaps we ought to get on with this. Church is out already, and I'd like to watch the Draxion City Assassins pound the Aceor Motormen tonight in Dargen," she told them.

"Yes, Mama. Brayden and I will spread out and scout ahead, while Gelliem keeps an eye on you both from behind. Sawl-en will be ready to pick us all up when this is all over," Bella told the rest of them.

Brayden was the first of them in the huddle to break off and walk ahead of them. Bella herself took the same pace behind him, and Brian and Fray'la began to walk forwards at a reasonable pace. Fray'la needed just a little help from a cane to walk. Brian looked at it and saw a thin black cane with several joints. It made it look like it could be whipped out or stowed away at a moment's notice.

For a moment, Brian watched Fray'la walk forward in front of him. She stabbed the uneven asphalt of the alleyway with the point of her cane and held it perfectly grasped in the palm of her hand. She would roll the cane forward, until just before her knees needed to catch up. She looked quite mobile to Brian. He found himself wondering if a vagrant would be at a disadvantage trying to mug her if all she had to defend herself was her cane. Brian figured she would go for the legs first.

"So, it's been eight days. What do you have for me?" Fray'la asked him.

Brian put his arms out to his sides and said, "Follow me."

Brian had spent the first two days after receiving the job putting his affairs in order. He wanted to have a hotel to check into and a train ticket to Bentlion when he arrived in Valeium. He had booked those and researched some potential Bentlion suburbs to live in from a public library. He had spent his nights in a dingy motel in the countryside outside of Kardadin, not too far from Fray'la's house, and they had loaned him an unregistered cheap piece-of-shit car to get around town in, just for a few days. It had served its purpose.

Brian put his arm out for Fray'la to take, and then he led her down the alleyway and over towards the next road. They would approach the Vornins' warehouse from the popular pedestrian market, which ran right up to the center of its southern outer wall, beginning several blocks away.

When they got to the sidewalk before the next road, the popular street market of Kardadin lay in front of them in the alleyway for the next five blocks. Brian could see the brick walls of the warehouse beyond that. When it was safe to cross, Brian, Fray'la, and several other pedestrians around them made their way across the street and into the market.

"When I was back in Maish, there was a woman I was seeing. We knew the war was coming, and I had a plan to get her out of the city," Brian began to tell her. Fray'la was silent. "They have this alligator that fights for them—Iishrem does. Calion Gordon is his name. He knocked me off my bike and skewered Macie with a claw right in front of my eyes. Even paid the manager at my favorite café to slip a laxative into my drink as we tried to escape from the city, as the first attack began."

"Why didn't you go to safety, and then try to leave later?" asked Fray'la curtly.

He sobbed once. "I suppose I figured that I wasn't being hunted, at least not particularly, not yet. I figured that would be our only real chance to escape the city, that they'd close off escape from the city and have civilians shelter in place from then on," Brian told her. *She would have been safe here if we could have made it together,* Brian thought.

"We can't change the past, Brian. If you really wanted to protect her, you should have ceased to have anything to do with her once you realized your Draven heritage. Iishrem will come for every Draven one day, living or dead, born in Iishrem or otherwise. If you aren't a card they can hold in their pocket, then you're a threat, justifying removal of such one in whatever way possible," Fray'la told him understandingly. She probably knew much of loss, war, and death, being a mafia matriarch. "But I also wouldn't hold yourself too responsible. She may well be dead if you had left her now anyway. At least you tried to save her."

Brian shook his head, wondering how it would have played out if Alyisay had shown up to save them. *Where are you?* he asked, not expecting a response.

You will see, he heard in his head, which came as quite a surprise. Brian stiffened back to attention and put his backbone into his stance. "I'm not sure my actions really made a difference," he told her.

Fray'la leaned forward, put her arms around his back, and said, "Brian, don't doubt your intentions or actions. Even unsuccessful acts of good and kindness cannot go unnoticed. They must not, that is the pathway to nihilism."

He did not expect that. In his mind, Brian heard Alyisay yawning. *Ehh, this is the boring part. Just wait until everyone sees me at the end,* she told him. Brian's heart quickened; where was she? He discreetly looked up and around the marketplace and couldn't see anything but blue skies above him. Brian nodded to her and said, "Yes, I suppose so."

"Come now, show me how this little expansion of ours will work," Fray'la said. Brian began to explain to her that there wasn't any easy way into the warehouse during the day, but there were slightly more possibilities during the night. Of course, this job couldn't be done at any other point of the day, and it would need to be in the dead of night too; he was planning for 2 am.

Of course, there would still be operations going on at the warehouse at that point in the night—but far less of them and much fewer people than during the peak of their operations. "They'll probably just be moving a couple of crates to their biggest distributors. There are several doors on the side of the building that look locked, but I wondered if any of them weren't. Over the past couple days, I've worked out that one of the doors is locked during the day, but then it is unlocked during the night and left relatively unguarded," he told her.

"A quick-fire escape," Fray'la said, seeming surprised.

Sounds like a reasonable plan, Brian. Sorry that you wasted your time coming up with it. Soon you'll be mine. I am your dragon, and I shall have you, Alyisay snared knowingly in his head.

Where are you? Brian asked as he looked at the sky in angst. He felt like he was going insane.

The joy in her voice made it sound like she was having fun putting him through all this. *Fun.*

Soon you shall see me. We dragons are like no other Eedon Rath-ni— just like you, Brian, are not like anyone else. You shall soon see my fire, and then we shall be together. But for now, finish your time with Fray'la, Alyisay told him.

A few minutes later, Fray'la felt comfortable with the plan he had laid out before her. They were two blocks south of the warehouse, but that didn't mean it was time for them to leave. Fray'la wanted to show him something. She took him to the right, off the market street, and led him a few blocks away toward the beaches, where the housing changed from condos and apartments to expansive multi-story mansions, cottages, and beach houses.

The two of them walked several blocks, and by the time they were just three blocks from where he could see the beginning of the dune cliffs, beaches, and ocean below, he had long lost sight of Bella, Gelliem, and Brayden. They approached a two-story mansion that looked to Brian like it had been built more than a century ago. It was well-maintained, and there were other houses like it around, but it certainly clashed with the newer modern homes and the tall hotels which rose over the beachfront. When they crossed the street and approached the house from the sidewalk, he saw the grey Marinclyade parked in its driveway waiting for them. Still, Brian did not see the driver. *Why is the car so important?* Brian wondered. Bella, Gelliem, and Brayden got out of the car there and grouped back up with them. Brian was sure they had never been far from him and Fray'la or had ever failed to have at least one set of eyes on her at all times. The Frantellis had many men, and some of them were tasked to blend in with the citizens.

When he looked at the old, expansive, rectangular mansion, which had a covered porch that ran all the way around its east and north side, he saw a few people outside drinking, smoking, and conversing. However, when he looked in their eyes, they looked whiter than usual. Like shades of it had penetrated their irises and slipped into their pupils. It was then that Brian knew just what Fray'la wished to show him. "I don't know for sure, so I'll ask just in case. Do you know the impact of Allum Rocks? Have you had any experiences of your own?" ask Fray'la.

Brian stifled, and he wondered if Fray'la was perhaps a bit too naïve or too cautious to make any assumptions. They came to the fenced gate of the property and entered the front yard, after Gelliem had opened it for them. As they approached the house, guests went about their enjoyments, not paying them any attention. He also spotted several stern-looking guards dressed like Brayden and Gelliem. One was by the front door, and another was patrolling the porch.

"A few, but it's been a while. A different portion of my life," he said quietly. Brian knew he had dabbled with some before, but he had lost most of his time under its effects sleeping.

When their party approached the front door, the guard with sunburnt northern skin and brown eyes regarded Fray'la with a nod, and then he held the door open for them. As soon as Brian stepped inside the mansion, his actions and intentions began to feel if they were not entirely his own, as if they were false. They entered through the lobby. The walls were wood-paneled, and a musical saranveina sat unattended in the corner. A saranveina looked a bit like a piano, but the keyboard rose and fell and was also disjointed in several places, instead of being flat and all together. There were also several levers that could be pushed up or pulled down tracts on the instrument's boxed lid, which sat directly below pipes that mimicked the keyboard at different heights and different directions. Saranveinas were quite popular in lounges or at weddings throughout Allirehem.

Before Brian and Fray'la continued in any farther, Fray'la ordered Gelliem, Brayden, and Bella to different rooms. Brian looked to his left and saw a sparsely populated dining room which led to a kitchen. The hallway in front of him had stairs to the second story, and there was a bathroom on either side. When Brian looked to the right, he quickly saw and heard what some of the house's guests were participating in. The two of them walked over to investigate.

Brayden was monitoring an orgy that was taking place, in an expansive dank sitting room. The room was dimly lit as the shades were drawn, and there were several naked couples making use of various corners, loveseats, ottomans, and a larger group that had spread out across a couch. There were several heterosexual couples, and a group of three men going at it together, but Brian couldn't stop himself from salivating over an entire harem of attractive young women all going about loving each other, some had toys or plastic imitations of a certain male body part.

Brian was tapped on the shoulder; he turned. "Champagne?" a white female server with red hair asked him.

"No, thank you," he said holding up his hand. Fray'la declined as well, and the server took her tray of champagne-filled tall glasses to attend to the guests participating in the orgy.

"A sudden heightened libido and the aspirations to try new things are what brings many of the youths to Allum Rocks, but there are several other purposes as well," Frayl'a told him. "Are you surprised by what you see going on here?" She pointed toward one of the sconces filled with the small amber and jade crystals which composed the drug. Allum Rocks were enjoyed by proximity to it, and it could be used to go through varying experiences.

Brian told her that he had not yet looked over the entire mansion, but he had seen enough of the orgy. He tried to ignore the sounds of sex as Fray'la led him away from the sitting room and took him to the back yard. Outside, the crystals were placed in the sconces and burnt to disperse the effects via the air. Brian passed by several lit torches and gently gathered some of the mauve wisps of smoke to him with his hands. The drug itself had the smell of a deep, musty cave.

A small crowd had gathered to watch a bare-knuckled brawl between a short and slender girl with black hair and a tall husky man with a scary face and a grizzly grey beard. Unsurprisingly, Gelliem had been sent to monitor the fight. Brian and Fray'la were able to see the fight well from an open spot on an elevated patio, which overlooked a back yard filled with more guests drinking. Brian also saw more Frantelli men walking around the crowd of people taking cash bets on the fighters.

Somehow, the small girl was winning. At that moment, the girl had draped herself on her opponent's back and had mashed and bloodied his face with her bruised and battered knuckles.

"That man is going to kill that little girl!" Brian told Fray'la.

"He won't. I've seen them fight several times before, and the Allum Rocks take care of us all. We just don't always know *how* exactly," Fray'la said nonchalantly, and then she turned away from the fight unconcerned. Brian followed suit. As soon as Brian turned away from the fight, a loud chorus of cheers erupted for one of the fighters. Brian turned back around to see the short girl with black hair in a boy cut. She was sitting on top of the big man's bare back with her legs crisscrossed and had her hands cupped and eyes closed. For a moment, her lips murmured too quietly for Brian to hear anything. She looked like she was trying to commune with some kind of deity.

"How did she do that?" Brian asked with his mouth hanging open. A blond-haired man from the crowd rushed forward to the small girl a few seconds later and nimbly lifted her up onto his shoulders. He then began to parade her around the room. The much bigger man was slowly helped to his feet.

"Come," said Fray'la. They left the backyard and walked back into the dining room through a glass door. They took some creaky steps to the basement where at last they saw what Bella had been observing. It was there that Brian saw the most sconces full of the drug. "Allum Rocks show us the memories of the dead—at least, the memories the dead would show us if they had a choice. Right now, you are feeling like you are not entirely under your own control. That's because until you leave the property, you're in a halfway state between life and death. Such is the only state of mind where such possibilities of human behavior can be shown to us, for what we can learn or enjoy."

Fray'la extended her arm and showed him what she had always meant to. The basement was lined with twin-sized beds that had chairs next to them. In each bed, there was one person asleep, while another sat in the chair next to their bed. All the people in the beds looked to be going through REM sleep. The other people sitting in the chairs next to the beds all had one of their arms interlocked by their fingers to one of the arms of the person in bed. While the person in the chair did that with one hand, they used the other to write down what they saw.

What Brian was most perturbed by, was the fact that all their eyes glowed like a bright magenta. "What could we hope to learn from them about the activities of the House of Lance, which they spent a thousand years hiding from their own people. It could help us win the war," Fray'la told him.

Brian said, "Yes, but at what cost?"—even though he did not totally agree with his sentiment.

Suddenly, the ground shook, and Brian felt something big hit the ground with a thud. Then he heard a thunderous roar, which snapped everyone out of what they had been doing and made for some very rude awakenings or awkward realizations. *Alyisay*, Brian thought.

There was a twenty-second pause as everyone just looked around and wondered what had snapped them awake. After that, several gunshots rang out from outside the mansion, and everything began to happen very quickly.

Here I am, Alyisay told him.

What have you done? What're you doing? Brian asked.

Come out and see me, my rider, she told him.

When the gunshots had first gone off, they were very recognizable—especially after everyone had snapped out of their actions. Fray'la seemed to know already just what was happening. She surged up the stairs as all the guests who had been sleeping began to violently wake. When they got upstairs, Bella, Brayden, and Gelliem quickly formed up in a circle around Fray'la in the kitchen to protect her, while all the guests haphazardly evacuated the property.

The ground shook again and again, and Brian heard screams coming from the street. The whole time, Fray'la glared up at him with ire like she already knew exactly who was waiting for them outside.

Once everyone had escaped, it seemed there was no other choice but to go out front. When the five of them got stepped out onto the patio, for the first time in his life, Brian laid eyes on his dragon. Alyisay was waiting for him in the middle of an intersection one block north of the mansion's lot. As soon as Brian and Alyisay made eye contact, she extended her neck out toward him and roared thunderously. She put her talons out, which were at the upper apex of her wings, and bore her wingspan to him like a peacock unfurling its feathers.

The road where Alyisay had landed had cleared of people, but that hadn't stopped her from smashing several cars. Brian did not see any charred bodies lying around him, and a few dozen daring city-goers were watching Alyisay from where they thought they could do so in safety.

Come over here and meet me, Brian, and bring your friends too—or you shall all face my fire, Alyisay told him. Brian didn't feel like he had any other choice and began to comply.

Chapter 25
To Free an Eedon Rath-ni (Bailey 6)

ILLIAS, HAISHA, ALLIREHEM

SUMMER, 1153, FOURTH AGE

As soon as Bailey saw Brenna approaching, she wanted to shrink within her skin. Her shoulders slouched over the coffee table, and she drew a long sip of her soda. She thought about running and even turned to do so. "Please don't run," said Brenna in Haishian.

Of course, once Brenna said that, Bailey felt suddenly like she had been trapped in place by a spell. Bailey forced herself to move an extremity and found she had no problem shaking her arms. She also shifted on the couch and found her legs and butt unimpeded.

Brenna and Icon sat down across from Bailey around the small round table. Bailey discretely pulled her food tray closer to herself, even though it was only lightly covered in crumbs.

"Ahh, you're a fan of their turkey sub, hey," Icon mused as he sat down. "I was thinking I would get the chicken salad myself. They shred the chicken here. No dicing it like Brenna likes."

Brenna turned to look at her cousin and snapped at him saying, "Icon!"

These two are quite strange, Bailey told herself.

They are, but they're good at what they do. They know what's going on, and they know where I am, Bailey, she heard Hector say in her head.

Very well. I'll work with them. But this won't make us friends with them necessarily, Bailey told Hector, desperately wishing she could just free him now.

"Why did you guys burst out of the window at a brothel? Why were you there to begin with?" Bailey asked with a raised eyebrow.

Both were dead silent for just a second, and then Brenna flushed and stammered, "No, of course, not for that. He was rescuing me actually," she explained.

"Rescuing you?" Bailey asked in disbelief. She looked Brenna over and saw a medium-built woman in her mid-twenties with ample curves and orange curly hair. Bailey imagined Brenna could do quite well for herself there if she wished to. Of course, then Bailey realized that perhaps that was the reason Icon had helped her escape. But then, who were Schizen and Grenelda, why were they chasing after them, and why did they just passively allow them to escape without so much as a warning shot? Bailey knew from her own past knowledge that if they had been shot at, it would have been far from the first time that someone had been gunned down in front of everyone on Brien'nia street for running out on a prostitution bill.

Of course, incidents of such violence were illegal, rare, and harshly frowned upon by the Haishian government for what impact it might have on the sex tourists that came to the city for just such a thing, but they still happened.

"I didn't want to become one. Don't you see?" Brenna told Bailey.

Bailey followed up on her strings of thought. "So, you were being coerced into prostitution? That's where Icon came in?" Bailey asked.

"I remember when we briefly made eye contact before we sped off on our kart. There was something about you," said Brenna.

"We don't need to tell her everything, Brenna," Icon said, finally chiming in.

Bailey felt her mouth hang open, and then suddenly her arm felt like it had been hit with the two ends of a snapping rubber band. "Oh, yes, you do need to tell me everything," Bailey told the both of them. "I know who follows you and why."

Hector, help me prove who I am here, she thought out to him. It made Bailey feel complete when he was there for her, even if only just in her mind.

I understand just what you need, Hector told her. Bailey felt her eyes glow brown, and then she looked at Icon with them.

"You're a Draven. Are you like me? Do you have a hawk in your mind?" Icon asked her.

Bailey nodded. "And I heard from a very good source that you know where he is." There was some silence between them, and then suddenly Bailey began to grow self-aware of the time. She wondered how quickly Shizen and Grenelda would be able to track down the cousins. What would they do to her when they found her talking to them?

"A month ago, our family came into the city to spend a week or two. I had heard from Ghel, my hawk, and then nothing, so we started to suspect something was up. While Brenna tried to find out more about the Hunters, as they're known, I was trying to figure out which environmental corporations had assisted then in the capture of our two hawks. Anyways, she went missing for a little over 2 weeks, before I was able to find her and rescue her, now we're here," Icon told her, filling in some gaps.

"We have some things to tell each other, and I don't think either of you is safe here. Why don't you two get yourselves some dinner, and then we'll head back to my place where Shizen and Grenelda can't possibly find us?" Bailey suggested.

"Fantastic!" Brenna said. "We barely know each other, but already you've been so generous to us."

"I'm merely playing my role," she told them. Bailey knew that *she* was no hero. Icon and Brenna looked like they didn't exactly know what she had meant. "Go and order your food, we'll bring it back to my place, and then we'll talk. You'll be safe there. My father is very important within the Resistance War effort. I'm going outside to make sure it's safe. Shizen and Grenelda don't know me, but I know what they look like. Here, you can pay with this card." She let them borrow her resistance credit card for their dinner.

Bailey turned to go. "There are many more of them beyond just Shizen and Grenelda. There's also a man behind the curtain who finances them," Brenna told her.

The plot thickened, and suddenly the task in front of her became even more difficult. What had they done to get themselves involved with people of the sort, and what had her communing with them gotten her into? She felt her eyes narrow with her pensive thoughts, full of frustration that any of this was easy in the first place. Then she carefully thought about her verb conjugations and said, "I know how they dress. I'll watches for them that way. Let's go. Best not stayed too long."

Icon and Brenna understood her well enough, and they rose to go to the counter just as a jazz band was beginning to set up for the night, and the dark black skies of the night were setting in. Still, it was muggy out. Bailey felt a bit little light-headed when she first got outside, and so she walked over to the edge of the Riverwalk and sat down on the wide stone walls that kept tourists from stumbling into the river two dozen feet below. A few karts with little headlights whirled by, causing little ripples on the water below.

Bailey looked out over the city then up and down the river and found herself surrounded by golden lights on the night sky. All around her, Bailey watched people walk up and down the Riverwalk, shopping, eating, drinking, or being entertained by street performers—or performers of another nature. Then she looked down at the river and saw its water sloshing below where she sat and thought that the water looked far too dark for how much light was around it. *What is going on here beneath the city?* she found herself wondering. She needed to find out, and Icon and Brenna would help her do so.

Bailey turned back to face the café and the Riverwalk and saw the cousins walk out of its front door several minutes later. She waved the two of them over. Brenna smiled widely and pulled a strand of her curly hair back down into the rest of her hair before she walked over, and Icon followed closely behind.

"So, where are we going?" Icon asked with a smile and gleaming eyes, both of which Bailey ignored.

"We aren't going far," she told them. By then she had learned her way around the major roads of the city, and even through some of the back streets. They could easily walk from here. The three of them got to it and set off for a brick staircase that would lead them up and away from the Riverwalk, back onto the main city level. Once there, the city was quieter and less crowded, but there were many more cars to negotiate around. The portion of the city they walked through had a plentiful selection of street-level restaurants with bands and rooftop clubs with dancing and strobe lights several stories up on top of some of the more popular hotels.

Bailey also saw several boutique casinos, where there was plenty of action going on at the sportsbook. Draxion City and Aceor looked to be approaching the end of a really thrilling game of Dargen. After that, close to 11 pm, Bailey finally saw her hotel rising high into the air.

"There it is," Bailey said, pointing out the hotel to Brenna and Icon.

"Ahh, the Visre-ion. Your father must be very important indeed," Icon told her from behind. As drizzling rain picked up again, Bailey led them off the street and into the grand lobby she had left a few hours ago. She was completely exhausted by then, and honestly, she just wanted to fall asleep. The three of them could discuss their plans in the morning.

Bailey led them over to the same elevator she had used earlier in the night and called it to her once again. While the three of them watched the floor level indicator for the elevator car decrease, Bailey asked, "I think we're all honestly kind of tired. I think we would all be better off if we just slept until tomorrow before we started going over everything. As long as the birds will still be where they are in the morning?"

Icon turned to Brenna, and she said, "Yes. They won't be moved anywhere tonight, and I'm quite tired too."

"It's so generous of you to let us stay at your father's apartment," Icon told her.

The elevator pinged behind them and then rattled open. They boarded together, and the doors closed with only the three of them as occupants. "Well, I need you two as well, you see. I need to free Hector. Are you going to the academy too?"

"I am," Icon told her.

"Who recruited you?" she asked.

Icon laughed. "An enormous ram, with an even bigger pair of testicles, named Von Din. He's one of the professors there," he told her.

Bailey laughed at Icon's joke, but Brenna's face contorted, and she scowled at him. When the three of them got out of the elevator, Bailey took them straight to her father's suite at the end of the hall. She pulled out her hotel key card, then shoved it into the slot above the door handle and twisted the door open.

Bailey held it open so that Brenna and Icon could walk through first. When she followed, she called their attention and pointed to a spare room key sitting in a wooden bowl on a console table, which was standing in the entryway. They nodded and walked farther into the suite. She watched both of their eyes widen when they saw all the equipment and electronics within. Bailey stepped in behind them and closed the door, then locked it for the night. Icon immediately began to admire the carbine, which Bailey had set standing up and next to the door. It was unloaded, but Bailey was pleased to see that Icon checked anyway before he picked up the gun and examined it further.

"Who is your father?" asked Icon.

Bailey wasn't sure if she should tell them. She wasn't even sure if she could trust them yet. Yet she felt she had to if she was going to rescue Hector.

"Clancy Triten," she told them. "Regal Commander of all Dravens allied to Allirehem, and Deck Lieutenant of the ARF Clancy Triten."

Both Brenna and Icon knew exactly who her father was. They each shared a round of beers and small talk around her father's coffee table in the living room with the news while Brenna and Icon ate their food. Then they decided to go to bed. Brenna took her father's king-sized bed, and Icon slept on the couch.

"Good night, Icon," Bailey said before she walked into her room.

Icon looked at Bailey, winked, and said, "Don't let the poltergeists haunt you!" Bailey turned around and casually flipped him her pinky finger pointed downward with her thumb stuck out. She then opened her bedroom door and slept with her pistol on an end table at the side of the bed.

She dreamt of herself dancing on the river, atop the water itself, while thousands watched from the promenades of the Riverwalk. Time slowed, and she looked out at the ends of her extremities to see they had been encircled by thin tendrils of shroud that all led upwards. Suddenly, she felt herself jerked off the water, outside of her will, and then she was thrown onto Hector. They began to fly over the river and under the bridges. In the meantime, Bailey looked at a man in the sky, who sat atop a dragon and controlled the shroud enveloping her with a marionette's grip. Bailey could not see any details about the man himself—just his outline and his golden eyes.

When she woke in the morning, Bailey woke to the smell of a hardy breakfast, even though she had not had any food in the refrigerator when they had gotten home last night. She opened her eyes, smelt the air, and listened to the sounds of the streets below. Her sheets had curled and contracted around her, and her beaded forehead let her know that it had been a hot night. Again, she was still tired and did not want to get out of bed.

She slipped out of her pajamas, and then she curled herself back over and burrowed into her sheets. Darkness was her world. Darkness and her naked body swaddled in sheets that she wanted to stay in for just one minute longer. A stimulant was introduced to the air. Bacon. Her nose caught it quickly, and she felt her legs tense just a little. She forced herself to close her eyes again. Several more smells were added over the next few minutes. The sloshing of ice and liquor in a mixer forced her out of her burrow and onto her pillows. When the news was turned on, *loudly*, Bailey knew there was no more fighting it. She rose out of bed and headed into the bathroom.

When Bailey finally stepped out of her room, fully dressed and ready to eat, Brenna and Icon were waiting around the table for her. The news was on. "Hey, there you are," said Icon.

Brenna got up and walked over to her to give her a hug. Brenna had a comfortable set of shoulders for Bailey to rest her chin on, and her hair was extra curly that morning. Icon stood behind Brenna with a smile on his face.

"The breakfast was on me. I'm sorry if I came off like a bit of a jerk yesterday. I went out early to get it, it was the least I could do." he told her.

"Thanks, Icon," she told him. Polite conversation versed out between the three of them from there. The turkey bacon was prepared just how she liked it, and the smoked aashing with fruit salad and buttered muffins really hit the spot. Icon had even prepared some libations of grape nectar and a cactus tequila. Several rounds of those made the news easier to consume. *Aceor defeats Draxion City. Casualties rise in Maish. Iishrem troops ravage Haishian Jungle Hinterlands, stripping land of wealth and resources. Haishian Senators Mull Call for National Draft. Ancient Ghost Infestation? Call Illias Poltergeist Defense Today! We're ready to believe you.*

Bailey turned away from it all, "Before we get started with our plan, I just have a bit of a question."

"What's that?" asked Bailey and Icon in near unison.

"Brenna, you were captured for near to two weeks in a brothel. Didn't they drug you? How many times were you violated, between now and then?" Bailey asked them.

The silence felt like it lasted an hour, as Icon and Brenna looked at each other, deciding how to answer. Bailey didn't think it was an unfair question. "We both knew what could happen when we came here to track down Ghel," Brenna began. "I've got a natural resistance to some drugs, so that's how we decided I would go after the hunters, and Icon would go after the corporations. When he figured out I was captured, he sent the rest of the family home."

"I'm incredibly resourceful. I can show you," Icon told her.

"Beyond that, recent legislation passed has put a real damper on how prostitutes would be treated in this city, if the brothel managers could do as they please. The brothels get audited by a government agency monthly. Any prostitute found with signs of physical abuse is released immediately and compensated. It's more about the mental aspect, how the brothel managers tried to control me, but I have a strong mind. I was only taken twice in the time. Honestly, they were both kind of cute though, and I was on Allum Rocks the whole time. I'll be okay," Brenna explained. Bailey was satisfied with their explanation.

"I'm so sorry Brenna. Truly. But if we can free our birds, maybe it'll be some nice revenge, so, let's go through it all. How do we get to the hawks and free them?" Bailey asked them, expecting to hear something well developed. She wasn't disappointed.

Icon pulled a square blue hard drive out of his pocket and held it in the air. He led them over to the command room per se and plugged it into the console desk. There were several files, but he opened one with a street map of the city, a map of the sewers and pipelines, and a map of the city's waterways. "The two of us woke up early and let you sleep in so we could start putting things together. You'll have the final call on any of the plans we come up with. These maps are what Shizen and Grenelda were after us for. I nicked this drive of sewer tunnels they were keeping the hawks in," Icon told her.

Bailey had three initial questions that she did not wait to ask: "What is the health of my Hector? Can our birds fly? And what're they being fed?"

"They're in good health, I can promise you that," Brenna told her speaking solemnly. "Elsewise they wouldn't be very valuable, would they?"

"What do they want with them? Why capture them and how without at least a dozen men lost to casualties each capture?" Bailey asked in disbelief. Was there something wrong with her Hector? Or Icon's Ghel?

Icon and Brenna answered her questions one by one. "Sail-eem. It has no effect on humans, but very debilitating to Eedon Rath-ni. Corrupt Haishian environmental corporations have been flooding the Illnayean River with it for months now. According to Eedon Rath-ni experts, the usual flight pattern for a hawk's first journey out of their suspected island home within the Shrouded Sea leads them down the Illnayean River. They stop to rest, get some water, and suddenly get weary, more docile. It makes it easy to sneak up on them. A hawk might cost them four or five soldiers each time if they don't have an Iishrem-allied Draven with them, but yours took out nine before they had him netted. He should fetch a rich buyer," Icon explained.

"Who are these buyers? What do they want with our birds?" Bailey asked.

"For themselves, of course. Eedon Rath-ni are an exotic rarity in the world if you can believe it because of this organization—the Hunters. The buyers are mostly oil barons and weapons manufacturer CEOs from the city-states in Selenia like Dar'hi Rehem and Darni-Sil. Iishrem's ships will need oil and better weapons after their embarrassing defeat a few days ago at Minon Cromella. The opportunity to buy our birds is a generous gift to all that would take their contracts," Brenna explained to her.

"So, you can see there is a mutual relationship there. Iishrem as an empire will not put their foot on the throat of the city-states that have a skill or resource to offer them—and are willing to offer it to them. Our birds are the gift to those who keep the relationship intact throughout the political strife," Icon continued.

There was still something Bailey was missing out on. "I don't understand. What can these rich oil barons possibly hope to achieve with our Eedon Rath-ni? They'll never serve them. They'd be better off just killing them," Bailey blurted out, her anger growing with this *Hunters* organization. She found herself eyeing her carbine across the room.

Icon finished with the Hunters' ace in the hole. "Oh, but you see what you don't understand. The birds will never serve them, but they'll always be fearsome to look at—if you have a cage big enough. Strong enough. Imagine the potential opulence of the world these cities could attract to their corner of the world."

Bailey was livid. "Our Eedon Rath-ni are not pets to be kept in cages. They are ours! I've waited for Hector to be with me for seven years, and now you're telling me he's about to be sold?" Her remaining breakfast had grown cold.

Icon cleared his throat. "But you haven't heard the good news," he told her. Bailey looked over and gestured for him to go ahead.

"There's an auction you could go to. I don't think your father could put up a winning bid for you, but it'll give you a chance to get some revenge and information. Let this organization know who they're dealing with. In the meantime, Brenna and I will find where they're keeping the birds, freeing them before they can be put on a ship to sail out of the city. If they make it onto a boat, the birds will be beyond our reach once they make it to the mouth of the river, and then they would pass into the bay via the canals."

"How can you know where Hector and Ghel are? Shizen and Grenelda must've let you walk away with your information knowing you'd be none the wiser. You weren't worth the trouble, and that's why they let you go," Bailey told them.

"No, no. I can deliver for you, Bailey. I've been shorting their Sail-eem gas reserves for weeks now. Like I said, the safest place to keep the birds at near full strength is the sewer system, but they can't drink that water. They keep them docile and netted with Sail-eem vented in through the pipes. Most of their men will be guarding the auction, but I know how to sneak into District Lampshire's Gas Pipelines building. I can cut off the gas flow to the sewers. The final effect of Sail-eem consumption is not being able to connect with your Eedon Rath-ni. Once I cut that line, it'll allow you to talk to Hector and me to deduce Ghel's sewer tunnel, based on my prior knowledge of them," Icon told her.

There was something Bailey was beginning to feel uneasy about. "This all sounds like it'll go too easily. What's going to happen when you get yourselves captured again, and I'm forced to watch you all become some kind of bargaining chip. Or worse, dead. Is there a man behind the curtain who runs this whole Hunters operation? Who's ultimately financing this?" Bailey asked.

The only answer she received from either of them was a silent pause. "Never was able to figure it out. The group has its investors, but the actual hierarchy is more like a council. This council is pro-Iishrem. It's just that simple," Brenna eventually told her.

"Mhmm, alright. So, how do we kick their asses and break out our hawks?" Bailey asked both.

"I was thinking you could go to the auction. It's open to anyone who looks the part and has the capital to get past the door. You won't be armed, but you can get your information for revenge later. Brenna and I will fly to pick you up on the boat, then we'll fly off. Hawks are the fastest Eedon Rath-ni. We can outfly them if we can just get clear of the city. Then we'll just fly to our home and lay low for a while until things blow over. Even have a little downtime first, before we get to the academy" said Icon.

There was one final question Bailey had. "Brenna, what's happening to you at the end of all this? Where are you going?" Bailey asked her.

Brenna looked at her and said, "Well, to Meinghelia City, of course. It's where I'll be safest. I'll just have to make it there on my own."

Bailey had something to offer her. Her father would *have* to accept it. "You can stay at my father's cabin until you get set up for yourself," she told her. "The both of you will always be welcome."

Chapter 26
Nahirehem's Fate (Ethan 7)

MONETIC OCEAN, NAHIREHEM, IISHREM

SUMMER, 1153, FOURTH AGE

everal hours after the conclusion of the assault on Minon
Cromella, Ethan and Katie were called down to the exit
hatch of the *Valkyrie*. *Come, come, Ethan. You'll be on my back
for the first time today, and then we'll fly together alone next!* Violet
told him excitedly. *It's time to leave this damned eggshell. Come...
come, let's get into the open air!*

I need a few more minutes, Ethan replied to her as he put the last
few of his belongings into a backpack Accelron had given him after
first arriving on the *Valkyrie*. Accelron had left about two hours
prior. The last he had seen of the man was him walking away with
Naliais, who had never been too short for conversations with him.
Ethan wondered if he would ever see Accelron again.

When Ethan reached the exit hatch on the *Valkyrie* five minutes later with all his other possessions in one lightly filled duffle
bag, Christian and Talia were already waiting for them on top of
their birds. Katie was already sitting down on Sovereign, in front
of Talia.

"C'mon, Ethan, let's get on with this. We still have a schedule to keep," Christian told him impatiently, sitting on top of Violet.

"Are we still not ready to be flying by ourselves?" Ethan asked.

Ethan, don't cause a scene. It'll only be this first time, and then we'll be free of him forever, Violet told him. *It'll be nice to have someone over your shoulder right now.*

"Of course not, Ethan. Talia and I are taking the two of you to Draxion City. Once we're there, the two of you will be able to fly the rest of your way to the Academy or not. But until we're there, you two are our responsibility—even in a flight as brief as this," Christian told him.

"Fine!" Ethan spat with an unamused grin on his face. He carried his duffle bag over to Violet, tossed it into the clutch of her talons with two hands, and Violet caught it in the air.

Ethan approached Violet for the first time to get on her back. She bent down and leaned forward for him, then looked up at him and waited. *Your boots aren't going to hurt me if you ruffle my feathers a bit. Sit down in the saddle,* Violet told him. Ethan was at least going to get on her by himself; he would have no one help him with that. Ethan put his foot closest to Violet into the stirrup, stepped up, and then swung the rest of his body around. He took a firm stand with his left leg to steady himself while he yanked his right foot up out of the stirrup. After that, he sat down for the first time and put his boots back into the stirrups the right way. Forward-facing.

The *Valkyrie's* exit hatch began to open in front of them, and Ethan felt a swirl of warm wind sweep through his hair. Then Violet began to stride forward, taking off into the air several seconds later. His heart lifted with her talons into the air, and he felt himself press the insides of his thighs against the sides of the saddle. His butt bounced off it several times, and then he felt Christian put a hand on his shoulder from behind.

"Just fly," Christian told him, and finally, Ethan relaxed. He sagged into the saddle as they left the exit hatch and the *Valkyrie* behind them. It was a clear, sunny day, and in front of them, far below, Ethan could see a small Destroyer group speeding away from the rest of the main fleet's formation.

"That's our boat to the academy. Should get us to Draxion City in another five days," Christian told him from behind.

"Is there a library on that ship? I never thought it'd take so long to travel all the way around the world," Katie complained loudly.

"You will read the books we supply you and like them!" Christian snapped at her.

A few minutes later, his ride atop of Violet under Christian's supervision was already coming to an end. Their approach had them land first by flying past the bridge and then quickly dipping down. After that, Violet ridged her wings like rudders and slowly flew in place while she matched speeds with her landing zone on the ship. When her talons were mere feet from the deck of the ship, Violet closed her wings, and they landed just with a little jolt atop the ship.

All too soon, his first ride on Violet was over. In front of him, Ethan noticed that Embar and Anacarin were flying several dozen feet off the port side of the upper deck. Ethan rose off his saddle and gently stepped off Violet. He walked over to her and pressed his head to hers. *Until next time*, Violet told him.

Ethan and Katie were led inside by a soldier to a shared bunk.

It was an uncomfortable first night shared between them. They both could have used several more feet between each other—and better privacy for changing as well. Katie also snored, which was not at all helpful. The two of them were on short nerves with each other by noon the next day, and the day had already not begun well for Ethan.

After getting next to no sleep at all, Katie had gotten the earlier shower slot, while Ethan had to remain in the room. While Katie was gone, he was able to get at least a little more sleep which helped. When Ethan heard a knock on his door, he rose to his feet and opened the door to find Talia behind it. She handed him a set of towels with several fresh changes of clothes. "Feel free to walk about the deck for an hour or two, but it's best to stay out of the way as much as possible. Head on over to the kitchen afterward, then Christian and I have something to show you later," she told him in Gallaeic.

"Deal," he told her smiling. Ethan really liked Talia. He looked forward to learning some magic from her once his training began. "What is it though? What are we seeing?"

"You will see," she told him, then she walked off down the corridor and out of sight. Ethan looked the opposite direction and noticed a few soldiers walking down the corridor to follow her. The corridors aboard the ARF Clancy Triten were only wide enough for two to walk abreast. Ethan waited for the soldiers to pass, and then he walked down the corridor in the other direction toward the showers.

The showers Ethan was instructed to use were little wider than a broom cupboard. There was a short wooden bench for his clothes and only a skinny grey curtain to protect them from getting wet while he showered.

His fresh clothes still got wet from his shower, even as he did his best to protect them while he showered and dried off. It didn't matter. It would be nice to have fresh air blow through his short blond hair today. He could even sit on the deck with his legs over the edge of the ship. Violet would fly by his side, and he would be able to think about Kiera. He missed her most of all, and it was worse not exactly knowing if she was alive or dead.

Allovein's words haunted him. "She isn't yours to know of any-more." Ethan sighed and set off down a corridor that would take him outside, standing to the side any time a soldier had to pass or walked in the other direction. Ethan didn't want to be in any-one's way.

When he got outside onto the deck of the ship, it was a dark and dreary day. The waves whipped the sides of the ship and sprayed him on the cheeks. He saw Violet and Sovereign flying in tan-dem above the coast. *This isn't Sovereign's first time here,* Violet told him. *He was here that fateful day—the day this city was killed.* Ethan thought about everything involved with magic that had led him to this point. Had Allovein been the bald man who had tortured him in his dreams more than a few times during his childhood? He hoped not. Ethan thought about the first time he had met Violet and the afternoon that had started it all.

What do you mean he was here that day? He watched the city get bombed, on whose, Christian's orders? Why are you telling me this? He looked all around him and saw ocean in all directions except one. There was an approaching curved landmass of forests and moun-tains on their port side. At this distance, though, Ethan could not make out much more. He put it out of his mind for the next few minutes as he continued to make his way around the ship and mull his thoughts over. When he looked again at the approach-ing landmass, he barely knew how to describe it, but it felt like he was approaching the literal form of truth in Rehem. His head felt clearer.

He watched it, the bombing, with Anacarin and Christian you see. Sovereign's not just any eagle, and Talia helped him visit Katie just before the assassination, and I visited you during, with the help of the same human, Violet told him.

So, Katie had known she was a Draven when he freely revealed his heritage to her, and she kept her status a secret! Ethan seethed and felt his hands quake.

What gives? C'mon, Violet, let's go find my sister, Ethan told his raven.

I'll hunt her shadow! Violet's voice rang in his head, and suddenly, Ethan felt his eyes turn violet, and Violet took her smaller form. She flew after him down the ship and landed on his shoulder, just like she had that very first day. *What are you going to do, Ethan?*

Ethan found Katie leaning over a three-level rope wire fence, where there were no steel barriers to keep soldiers from falling off the deck. Katie held a small, thin beaten book in front of her eyes, but Ethan wasn't sure if she was actually reading. Katie quickly noticed his presence and snapped back up, off the wire barriers. She stuffed the book in her side pocket.

"When did you first know you were a Draven? Before two weeks ago? I confessed to you. If you knew, why would you keep it from me?" he spat at her angrily. He felt even more upset that he had confessed to her earlier, and she had not come forward to him mutually.

Katie looked remorseful. She teared up and put a few fingers to the top of her head. "I'm sorry, Ethan, I wanted to tell you, but I just couldn't bring myself to when you gave me the chance. I held it out on you; I was scared. I wanted to move on and live a normal life, act like it wasn't a part of me, not obsess about it like you. But there's nothing that can be changed now," she told him. "I don't want to fight."

"Fight!" Ethan found himself dumbfounded. "Why do you think I want to fight you? I just want an explanation." Ethan felt himself curl a fist as the coastal land mass neared. Ethan began to smell smoke on the air, and then he heard a hallow whistle on it, like the wind blew through the landscape unimpeded as if it were passing through a city-sized windchime. Suddenly, he couldn't stop himself from rushing towards her. Violet leapt from his shoulder and flew off, cursing at him in his mind.

Katie ducked under him and hit him with an uppercut to the jaw that rattled his teeth. He stumbled past her and rebounded off a column that stuck up out of the ship. Ethan seethed. *That hurt.*

Ethan looked down at the crashing waves and influenced one, sweeping it up and into Katie, knocking her off her feet. To his detriment, Ethan had been overzealous, and Katie lost her grip and began to wash off towards the deck, while she ran a hand over her eyes, trying to get the water out of her eyes.

"Katie!" Ethan heard himself yell, and then he dove for the edge of the ship as Katie slipped under the rope and fell off the side of the ship. Ethan caught her with both hands, his eyes yellow. Katie weighed too much for him, and he struggled to hold onto her. He yelled, "Help!" at the top of his lungs over the rest of the ship.

Ethan heard an eagle shriek over the frayed concern that hung over the area of the ship they were in. *Ethan, let her go; Sovereign will catch her,* Violet told him. Ethan turned and looked to see that Sovereign was streaking down towards them. He pulled up and leveled out only a dozen feet above the break, then deftly guided himself underneath Katie and matched the speed of the ship.

Katie looked up to him with her yellow eyes. "It's okay, Ethan, this is what Dad made me take ballet for," she told him. Ethan let her hands go and watched Katie successfully kick off the side of the ship, then land on top of Sovereign. Sovereign caught her perfectly and did not shudder or sway when she first made contact. Instead, Sovereign surged upwards for just a second, so that she sat down on him quickly and firmly.

When Katie was safely back on the ship, Ethan saw Christian and Talia approaching. By then, Ethan could see the landmass in much greater detail. The ship was beginning to come around a short coastline, which hid the rest of the landscape beyond behind it. Tall, wide mountains with evergreen forests covering their bases rose all down the coast off the port side. Suddenly, Ethan knew just where they were.

We're sailing past Nahirehem aren't we? This is what Christian wanted to show us, Ethan thought. *A dark death.*

Oh yes, Ethan, Violet told him. *I can already see what remains from up here.*

Christian stood in front of them, looking down at them with disgust in his eyes. He held in a long rant for a brief shake of his head instead. "A shame. The two of you will never trust each other the same again." He paused. "But who am I to say this? Prove me wrong. For now, though, follow me."

Christian led them up the ship, all the way to the forward bow, where they took a good lean against the waist-high steel barriers. "Katie, your brother's quite good at geography. Don't worry, I just know," he finished, saying the last statement directly to himself. "Do you know where we are?"

Katie answered in a grave tone, "Nahirehem. What remains of it, at least."

Once she finished speaking, the bow of the ARF Clancy Triten passed the final piece of land which obscured their vision of the city. What the four of them saw beyond was darker than anything Ethan had been prepared for. He was at a loss for words as he knew the casualties. "Did you have to bomb the city this badly?" Ethan asked.

Christian did not look shocked at his question. "Oh, I didn't order that bombing myself. This was my home once. I just wanted to make a statement in front of a relic of a long-dead and long-forgotten past civilization. It always seems the harder you try and bottle something up—" he told them.

"—The worse it burns when it all steams out," finished Talia. "In fact, there is one more still there who shall be seeing us tonight—one last time." She gently put a hand on the top of her stomach, and then she looked down at it and smiled. While Christian pushed on with his proclamations, Ethan looked over what remained of Nahirehem. The city had several sections. Christian pointed out that the oldest portions of the city were the ones in the center that rose right out of the ocean in beautiful shelters and buildings hewn from stone. Many of them now lay in ruins, but they all led upwards towards a plateaued campus filled with stone temples that circled around a great stone dome which rose about 165 feet into the air from its stepped base.

The dome was cracked like an eggshell, with several large chunks missing, and it sat atop a spacious rectangular platform raised several steps into the air, which allowed Ethan to assume that the inside of the dome burrowed deep into the earth. Since the beginning of the war, Nahirehem was known as site zero. The city lay in silence, but Ethan swore he could feel eyes on him from everywhere.

"This was the council of Nations and Dravens once," Christian told them. "Well over a thousand years ago, Nahirehem and that building were the pinnacles of Draven and Eedon-Rathi-ni existence together. Eedon Rath-ni were born in the Shrouded Sea, and Dravens all over Rehem, but they all came here to train together. After that, they were sent out into the world with their power to make it a better place. But the Old Republic of Iishrem was too ambitious and over-zealous. That was how the House of Lance was formed. The council of Nations and Dravens trained too many who didn't deserve the power they wielded, and it was only a matter of time before they created Lance the 1st and sent him out into the world. He was the best of them, and then he found the Phoenix—thought to have been lost for the entire last age—and the reign of the House of Lance began. But we can correct all that, Ethan and Katie. We can usher in a brighter future for the world than any of us can imagine. One so bright that this will never have to happen again," he finished, pointing toward the city.

The oldest portions of the city, although now crumbling, had always been preserved historically. Beyond that, on either side, was what the city had been seven years ago. A dozen tall skyscrapers still rose into the air, a husk of their former glory. Ethan looked all around the cityscape thinking he heard voices, but he saw no people.

"What is in the city now?" asked Katie. "Why won't Lance the 13th or anybody repair the city and offer aid to those still alive?"

"Anyone left inside the city is now fully under the control of the House of Lance. They'd been indoctrinated and serve as nothing but expendable slaves for advancing the war machine." Christian paused. Then he looked back towards the crumbling Council of Nations and Dravens. "But don't worry. The indoctrination of the phoenix did not reach everyone in the city. One day, those who bombed this city and indoctrinated it will find a horrifying modification of human life they did not intend. They will have their justice for the war crime of annihilating Nahirehem—of course, that is only if you believe all that I have just told you."

Suddenly, Ethan felt a gust of wind blow through his hair, and he watched Anacarin and Embar land on the ship down the deck from their current position. Christian and Talia walked over towards their birds, carrying nothing but a single pistol each.

When the four of them reached a door into the ship, which Ethan knew was not too far from the kitchens, Naliais was waiting for them with several plastic containers of food. "I know you two are going to be back in the morning just fine but do be safe for me. Let the old man know I said, 'Hey'. Even though we've never met, you've told me everything about whom I owe my new life to," Naliais said. He handed them the containers and closed the door to the inside of the ship behind him. Christian and Talia both nodded, then accepted the containers.

Naliais walked over to the awaiting Eedon Rath-ni with the rest of them. He had his long, black semi-automatic sniper rifle strapped to his back, just like he almost always seemed to. When Talia got onto Embar, she turned back to Naliais while Christian kicked Anacarin into the air to scout ahead.

"Set Ethan and Katie up with some gun practice. Just pistols for now," Talia told him, eyeing his sniper rifle. "Wouldn't want them to dislocate something or anything worse."

Naliais nodded, then Ethan and Katie watched the two of them fly off toward Nahirehem until the ARF Clancy Triten sailed past another portion of the southern Iishrem coast that obstructed their view once again. At that moment, Naliais gestured for them to follow him. Ethan and Katie put their recent altercation behind them and followed Naliais into the ship, one after the other. Naliais took them through the thin hallways to the ship's armory.

The three of them stepped inside of the armory—a square room on the second deck down—and Ethan found himself quickly surrounded by the type of guns he had expected. The walls were lined with shotguns, assault rifles, SMGs, and weapons of all kinds. The ship's master of arms was a bald man who looked eerily similar to Naliais, but he was much taller than the sniper who was shorter than both Ethan and Katie.

"Ajax, a pair of beginner's pistols for the two recruits from Iishrem," Naliais told the man. Ajax regarded each of them with a quivering glare and then turned off to walk behind a portion of the office that Ethan and Katie could not see into. He brought back two standard-issue 12-shot pistols with eight magazines of ammo each, two pairs of protective eye goggles, and earmuffs. Ajax gave Naliais a small empty gun case, which Naliais carefully put everything into.

When the three of them left the armory, Naliais asked, "So, have either of you fired a weapon before?"

Ethan shook his head, then watched his sister naturally do the same thing while they both walked behind Naliais. A few seconds later, Naliais turned around and looked up at them annoyed. This time, they said "No," in unison.

Naliais smiled, then clapped his hands together and said, "Good. This'll be fun then. We'll get to see who is worse the first time."

"We'll probably both be pretty terrible," Katie told him.

"Speak for yourself," Ethan said, trying to help both take their minds off their fight from earlier. Katie replied only with silence. Naliais took them to the starboard side of the ship, which faced away from the rest of the fleet. His hawk, Eingeana, was waiting for them, flying in pace with the ship just behind it stern while they were halfway up its starboard side. Eingeana had a talon full of many thick acrylic balls with lights eight inches in diameter. She clutched at them with her other set of talons. Currently, they were all lit green in the center, but the balls would turn red if they were hit. They would also float along with the ship after being tossed, so they could be collected and reused later.

Ethan stepped up to a wood counter facing the sea where Naliais had placed the case and left it open. He took one of the pistols and pointed towards the open sea, then pretended to pull the trigger. Naliais smacked his hand hard with the end of a rod, causing Ethan to fumble the gun back onto the counter. He ducked with his hands over his head, closing his eyes, hoping the gun would not fire at him or anyone else. It did not go off. When Ethan opened his eyes, he scowled at Naliais, and Katie quietly laughed behind his back.

"Why did you do that?" Ethan asked him.

"Always check your guns to see that they're unloaded before you do anything else. Never put your finger anywhere near the trigger, unless you're ready to fire, and possibly kill someone. Most importantly, don't forget your safeties," he told them deliberately so that neither of them would again forget it. He cocked the gun back and showed them the empty chamber, confirming that the guns were, in fact, unloaded. Then he had them do that for themselves several times. After that, Naliais observed them both load their weapons, and then he told them each how to turn off the safety.

Once that was done, Ethan picked up his pistol for the first time and pointed it at the open sea. "Well, have at it," Naliais told them without any more directions. Eingeana began to hurl the large thick balls with lights parallel to the ships with varying apexes, heights, and arcs. They both fired their weapons repeatedly at each boulder, hoping to strike it just once in its center. Unsurprisingly, Ethan and Katie each had terrible accuracy scoring only a few hits each.

Their journey eastward towards Allirehem continued after that, and Christian and Talia returned the next morning.

Chapter 27

The Cliffs of Galliem (Brian 7)

KARDADIN, GALLIEM, ALLIREHEM

SUMMER, 1153, FOURTH AGE

When Brian began to grab for Fray'la's hand, she regarded him with a look of stern serenity and quickly pulled it back. Brian had misjudged her and watched in shock as her nimble hands quickly caught his wrist in the middle of the air. *How old is this woman, Brian?* Alyisay asked in his mind. Brian began to curl a fist, but Fray'la broke it with a swift smack to the back of his fist with the width of her cane. Brian felt a knuckle shatter, and an eye turned tiger yellow. Fray'la pulled him close by his arm, which she grabbed with her hand like a claw.

She whispered into his ear, "If you think I'm going over there to meet with that dragon with you are gravely mistaken. You are relieved of your services." Fray'la brought her cane up into his open palms, which she knocked back into his eyes.

Ouch, Alyisay thought in his mind. Brian felt like someone had poked his eyes in with a pool cue. He stumbled back, then tumbled down the several stairs that led up to the elevated patio, end over end, crashing all the way into some thick bushes before he came to a stop. Brian knew exactly what was going to happen as soon as he started falling. He felt his second eye turn tiger-yellow, and hair began to grow all over his body. Then came the tail.

Ummmmm... how did she do that? Anyways get up, Brian. Run to me. They will try and kill you now, Alyisay told him. When the transformation was complete, he stumbled out of the bushes and looked up at the group of Fray'la, Bella, Gelliem, and Brayden, who each stood on a particular stair—or somewhere else on the landing at the top—with pistols drawn.

"How convenient an escape option," Fray'la said down to him, she had a sneering look of revilement over what had just happened from the top of the stairs. "Kill him," she ordered, and weapons fired and flared.

Brian bounded out of the yard toward Alyisay as soon as they began to fire. His lanky body stumbled as his back legs bumbled their way along. Brian had to even out.

When he reached the road, the sound of more gunfire finally snapped his hind legs into form. Two Frantelli men dressed in suits were running at him with pistols drawn. Brian turned and ran towards Alyisay, but as he approached the driveway, he heard the Marinclyade's engine fire and then saw it come roaring out of the driveway. Its tinted windows were up and remained up, but then Brayden stood up out of the sunroof with an assault rifle. He aimed it at Brian and fired, sending him into the space between two parked cars.

When Brayden could no longer see to fire at Brian, he began to take potshots at Alyisay down the road. "You imbecilic!" Brian could hear Fray'la sneer from inside the sedan.

Are they really trying to harm me with nothing but a simple assault rifle? Well, they've got my attention; let's see what they're made of,

Alyisay snared in his mind. From the space between the parked cars, Brian watched Alyisay ascend into the sky. Brayden quickly ducked back down into the car as Brian watched the sunroof close after him. The tires of the Marinclyade screeched, and the sedan pivoted away from Brian and sped down the road in the opposite direction.

Alyisay hovered in the air for a few moments, letting Fray'la and the Frantellis escape a little as Brian could see their car weaving its way in and out of traffic down the road. Then Alyisay spat a wad of fire into the air as a volley. Several seconds later, Brian watched the ball of fire the size of a wrecking ball land on top of the fleeing sedan several blocks away. The roads had cleared, and everyone was watching all that was transpiring.

Oh my god, Alyisay, stop! Brian thought out to her. He didn't want her to kill Fray'la, not really.

Gunfire from pistols ricocheted around the cars and shattered windows from his two approaching combatants, driving him into the middle of the road. Brian feebly roared at the approaching mafia men who were following him out into the middle of the road. They were paying all their mind to him and no attention to Alyisay. *If she gets out of that, I'll leave her alone. And you'll have to be the one to deal with the consequences. Won't that be fun, Brian?* Alyisay taunted him, probably wishing to see a more complete demonstration of his abilities in his tiger form. *She's already wriggling her way out of the car, and the driver is putting out the fire. This lady won't feel my fire today after all.* There was much more than a modicum of respect in her voice about Fray'la.

Oh, I see you've still got these two to deal with, Alyisay teased. *Well, I'm not going to help you.*

The mafia men fired at Brian's feet, and the look in their eyes told him they would not miss the next time. Brian tired of this; he wasn't going to take this shit anymore. He innately crouched against his back feet and then sprang forward with his front legs stretched and wide claws bared. Before they could shoot him, Brian ripped his claws across their necks, bringing both to their knees as they clutched at their necks and gasped for breath. From down the road, Brian heard two engines revving. Tires screeched, smoke billowed, and then Brian saw two black muscle cars dangerously pass a pair of cars—one on the sidewalk and another in a left turning lane in the middle of the road, which caused a couple of close calls with both civilians and other traffic.

Might be a good time to run, Brian, Alyisay said to him. Brian did just that and darted to the left across the first intersection he came to. He trotted and pranced his way down the sidewalk, growling at people to get out of his way. Some of them required more intimidation than others, but Brian could not wait. He began to break through the stream of people, knocking several to the ground. Brian thought that breaking free of the crowds on the sidewalk would help him. Instead, it only raised his profile and created a bigger scene. The drivers wouldn't be able to track him as well, if he could just keep the civilians from getting upset.

At least it would buy him some time so he could figure out where to go. First, however, he needed to lose the cars. The drivers came around the corner of the street in a screech of rolling thunder. The two muscle cars deftly maneuvered through the intersection—this time with fewer close calls. The traffic was adjusting around them—the rest of the city seemed to know just who it was that drove the cars that followed him. Brian had to head north, up to the beaches. He could lose them on the northeastern edges of the city, where their territory ran out.

Brian knew a fast way to the cliffs and took a right, heading up the next road. Everywhere he looked, Brian saw people on their phones recording him. Still, Alyisay watched overhead. *Mhmm, here comes a car chasing you down. This ought to be fun to see,* she told him. He ran between two lanes of cars going in the same direction. All the while, no one dared to pass him or get too close behind him. In fact, many people just turned away onto another road when they got too close. That or they pulled over to watch. That made it quite easy for his mafia pursuers to catch up to him. Meanwhile, the other direction of traffic slowed to a crawl so they could rubberneck. Brian could also make out three police cruisers approaching him.

The first of the mafia cars neared, now just mere feet behind him. Brian looked to his right and thought about jumping into the crowd to lose them. *Oh, c'mon, Brian, let's see what you can do. Besides, there might only be more Frantelli men on the sidewalks with shotguns anyway,* Alyisay sang in his head. *Show them your black claws.*

Again, Brian heard the popping of a pistol several times from behind him, and he felt himself get nicked by one of the bullets on the inside of his back leg. The wound didn't hurt too much, but it did cause him to slow, which, in turn, allowed his pursuers to finally catch up to him in their car. Brian turned around and watched them get close. He wondered if they would attempt to run him over first. Instead of doing that, the driver pulled up alongside him so that he could shoot at Brian from point-blank range.

That was a mistake. The driver of the car brought his pistol up and pointed it out of the window, but before he could fire, Brian lunged for his pistols with his two front legs, while he draped his body to the side of the car to avoid being shot by any of the passengers. There were two of them he noted.

While the passengers clumsily tried to angle for shots, Brian ripped the pistol out of the driver's hands and tossed it across the road. He dug his claws into the driver's chest, and then ripped him out of the car through the open window. The driver when flying across the road, and quickly got entangled by several cars and a bus.

The car turned and skidded to a stop when Brian pulled the driver from the wheel. The impact knocked Brian to his knees and jarred both back doors open. Brian shook off his head and recovered, while the dizzied henchmen stumbled out of their seats. The one farther away had a shotgun, which was good for him because the closest one was only armed with a pistol. Brian pranced up to the first man who was bringing his pistol up to fire and ripped off his firing hand with his two pairs of front claws.

Then he jumped up and over the car, narrowly avoiding a shotgun blast to the side before he ripped out the neck of the other mafia man, the cool milky taste of blood in his mouth. Brian spat it out and ran again; a Rehem Rover was making its way up to him. He took off back into the road, and the SUV quickly approached him from the side.

Alyisay returned to him in his head saying, *So you can stop a car if you kill its driver, but what else is there around you? How can you stop a car with the environment of the city?*

It was a great suggestion. Brian turned onto a divided road that gently curved by darting through a busy intersection. As the Rehem Rover entered the intersection, it was nearly instantly clipped by an oncoming truck and sedan. The collision sent it tumbling over and over several times, before coming to a stop upside down, rendering the Rover out of commission. Brian tested his dexterity and reactions and made it through the intersection with ease. He could see the cliffs coming into view, just a few blocks away.

Brian heard two helicopters approaching. *I'll take care of these whirly birds. Get to those cliffs. That's how we escape*, Alyisay told him. Brian looked to the sky and spotted her several stories higher in the air than any of the buildings. He could see a blue police helicopter and a white media helicopter approaching her from the southeast and southwest. Alyisay deftly circled around in the air and then blew a thick stream of fire in between both helicopters. They peeled away and changed course to evade Alyisay, and then she flew after the police helicopter first, roaring at it.

When Brian turned to go, gunfire from a new party followed him. Three police cruisers had arrived on the scene, pulling across the intersection where Brian had lost the last of the mafia men. The police weren't very accurate, or they were shooting to miss because Brian was able to easily evade them without being hit again. Their perimeter had also left him an escape route down the next road.

He had a few seconds head start because the police had to get back into their cars to chase after him. Again, Brian bounded down the sidewalks where people were more afraid of him and would get out of his way quicker. However, by the time he made it to the end of that block, two police cars had already cut him off from the next one.

Brian heard a voice on a loudspeaker. "Stop or we will shoot to kill!" The policeman put down his loudspeaker and picked up a semi-automatic rifle, pointing it at Brian.

I've got this, Brian, Alyisay told him from above. He suddenly noticed that he could hear the two helicopters again. Brian watched a thick stream of fire come down from the sky where Alyisay flew in place above. The thick stream of fire hit the two hoods of the police cars, which the policemen had parked in the opposite direction to form a roadblock. Alyisay's fire quickly melted the engine block in each of the cruisers and sent the policemen diving away for cover. *Go, Brian. Through the fire; it won't hurt you.*

Oddly enough, Brian trusted her word, and he was happy a few seconds later after he had bounded over the police cruisers and no part of him had caught on fire or been singed. Brian looked ahead to see the boardwalk now only two blocks in front of him. He could feel himself smile on the inside as he bounded down the road towards his freedom. He could see the steep drop of the cliffs down to the beaches. There would be enough space for Alyisay to fly in place there, so he could leap onto her back.

Unfortunately, Brian found his hopes of freedom dashed before he could make it halfway down the second block. All at once, Brian watched five police cars arrive on the scene and block off his escape route. Four of the cars stretched out across the two lanes of traffic and sidewalks, and the last one remained behind them, blocking him from jumping over the hoods again. The other direction of traffic was completely clogged with traffic and frightened people. As Brian stood in the middle of the second block and stared down at the police blockade, he counted eight policemen armed with rifles or shotguns. They would have plenty of time to shoot him down if he ran for it.

Brian heard more screeching tires behind him, the three police cruisers he had left behind earlier were beginning to catch up to him. Brian was never going to make it across the ocean. He was going to get imprisoned in Kardadin again— and surely for much longer than just a night this time. He wanted to live for something—he *needed* to live for something—but Iishrem had already taken everything he had from him. His home, his Burcgetti, Macie; the loss of each of them burned within his heart.

C'mon, Brian, quit wallowing. Don't forget you've got a dragon on your side now. I'm sorry it had to happen this messily, but I needed to see what you could do. I had to make sure you were up to the task I have. Come to me, but you'll have to jump. I'll catch you, Alyisay told him.

Brian heard her roar again, then he watched her fly directly over him. The blockade of policemen opened fire at her while Brian heard a sniper rifle fire from behind him. There must have been a police sniper on the chopper. The policemen's rifles had little effect on the Alyisay—the shotguns didn't have enough range if any of them hit her at all, and the sniper's shot simply bounced off one of her scales. Like Brian had seen Mason's dragon do before in Maish, Alyisay burned a wall of fire eight feet high in front of the police roadblock. Then, Alyisay craned her neck around and spewed fire directly behind herself at the police chopper. Alyisay's stream of fire blanketed the police chopper for several seconds, until it began to smoke, descending rapidly and unevenly while the pilot looked for an emergency landing zone. Brian was clear.

Come to me, Brian, Alyisay said to him. *It is our time now. We shall show this world all that we can be!*

Brian growled and charged after her down the road while she flew toward the beaches. He could hear the police cruisers behind him speeding down the road to catch him. As he neared the fire, the sound of an engine revving made the short hair on his legs stand on end, but just before they could run him over, he jumped. Brian bounded up to the fire, then leaned back on his hind legs and jumped over the fire. When Brian landed on the other side of the roadblock, the wall of fire was already fading. He ran past the fifth police cruiser and then bounded over to the boardwalk. Alyisay began to fly in place before him with a wing stretched out for him. All Brian had to do was jump.

A rifle rang out at him from behind, and again Brian felt the inside of his right hind leg grazed by a bullet. The graze put him off balance while he made his jump onto Alyisay's outstretched wing, over the boardwalk railing. When Brian first felt his paws land on Alyisay's wing, he felt so strong. They made eye contact together, and Brian felt more complete than he ever had in his life. Then he stumbled and began to slip.

Shit, I'm going to fall, Brian thought as he looked down at the beaches far below.

You are not; I've got you, Alyisay told him. Brian blacked out once he slipped fully off Alyisay's wing, but she caught him easily with one of her talons and flew off.

When Brian woke several hours later, the two of them were sitting in front of each other on a deserted beach far away from the limits of Kardadin. Alyisay had laid him down on a bed of embers and ashes and left him to rest while he slept off the rest of his transformation, eventually turning back into a man. Her bed of embers had even healed his minor bullet wounds. Brian opened his eyes as soon as he felt his transformation back into his normal self complete. He saw billions of grains of sand laying on the beach in front of him, and he pushed his face off his charred, ashy bed and sat up.

He shook his body free of as much ash as he could, and then he brushed more from his hair. He looked at Alyisay, and only then did she begin to speak in his head. *You're awake; sorry about the ash.*

You were still a tiger when I got us away from Kardadin, and then I just put you down there and let you sleep it off, she told him.

Alyisay had her legs crouched, and her tail was curled around her body, stretching a few feet into where the waves finished crashing. Her wings were extended to less than half their full span, and she had curled them around him. *I knew the warmth would help you sleep better. I just had to burn a patch of sand in front of you, then roll you onto it,* she explained.

I've never had that much clarity during one of my transformations before. I was unstoppable once I was able to get going, he thought.

You were—once you were able to get going. It would have been interesting who would have had the upper hand in a full fight between yourself and Fray'la, she mused while she waggled her neck. *Left a few scratches on me too, so I shouldn't be too harsh on you. I did kind of throw everything on you at once.*

Why are you here, Alyisay? Why have you chosen now to take me as your rider and pull me into this war? Brian asked, feeling like he was somehow spitefully thanking her for doing what she had done at the same time.

For many years, I've lived in the far north of Haisha and watched over a remote jungle village because they've been protecting something for me that I can't protect myself. An egg. The village protected it for me, and I protected them from danger. But one night, a spineless man named Gi'les snuck into my village and recovered the egg. He escaped, and then he had his men burn the village down. By the time I rose to what was happening, there was nothing I could do that wouldn't destroy the egg itself, Alyisay told him. *I must recover this egg, Brian, and I need your help to get it done. This man, Gi'les, and I have a connection you see. But he isn't a Draven like you, so instead, he wants the glory of killing me for himself. He has spent the last five years hunting me with a band of well-*

armed men that I'd rather not have to deal with. Now he has what's most valuable of mine. But guess what… that dragon's egg is quite valuable to him too. He will wait for me to attack him, so he can finish me off for his own glory, and then he will be on his way. However, he will not know of you coming, Brian. I simply need you to sneak into his camp and get the egg to safety. Then I can finish him off for myself, and we can fly to the academy from there, Alyisay told him.

It was quite a lot for Brian to take in all at once. *So, you know where this man is?* he asked her.

I have a connection to him, like I said. And he will wait for me where he knows he has plenty of space to move around while he tries to kill me. It'll be easy, Brian, and then we'll show this world exactly who we can be together. Dragon and Draven, she told him. *What do you say?*

Brian needed next to no time to think about it. Just one last job, and then the safety of the seclusion from the war that Christian's academy would offer, the experience to improve his skills as a Draven, and the lifelong protection of his dragon. It was more than enough to make him agree.

Brian stood on the beach in his tattered clothes from earlier in the day and said, "Yes, Alyisay. We will show this world our fire."

Alyisay turned her neck and pointed her head toward the top of the cliffs, then she shot fire and roared. She stretched out her wings for him to climb on, and Brian got up to do just that. He stepped up to the end of her tail and grabbed one of her spikes to pull himself up. He did not have much of a problem, and Alyisay did not complain. While Alyisay began to turn around on the beach to fly out towards the ocean, Brian slowly made his way to the bottom of her neck. He took a seat on her scales, then put his legs around her neck, grabbing two of her spikes with his hands.

Riding Alyisay almost felt like riding his Burcgetti again, but his chopper could never crush tanks or shoot fire.

Chapter 28
The Auction (Bailey 7)

ILLIAS, HAISHA, ALLIREHEM

SUMMER, 1153, FOURTH AGE

The phone on the other side of the line rang. Three times. Then the voice of her father spoke. "Bailey, are you safe? What is it?"

She got straight to the point. She was sitting in the dining room of her father's suite, with Brenna and Icon at her sides. They were holding her hands to give her support. Bailey had never needed to ask her father for money before, because of his position. She needed to now, to save Hector. She wouldn't just be able to run this on his resistance credit card, it didn't work like that.

"I've met some locals, and one, named Icon, is a range Draven like me. Our hawks have been captured by a shadowy organization that pursues him and his cousin. He's offered to help me. The thing is, the both of them are being auctioned in two nights to anyone with a large enough bankroll to attend," Bailey began to tell him.

"What's the condition of the birds? Where are they being kept, and what's your plan?"

Icon answered after introducing himself and Brenna. "They're being stored underground in the city sewers. I know the layout and how to sneak my way in. I can also neutralize the only thing that's keeping our Eedon Rath-ni under their control in the first place. They are drugged on Sail-eem and have been underground for weeks. Once I can cut their supply lines, it'll restore our connections, and I'm sure they'll be ready for some revenge," Icon told her father. He said nothing, but Bailey could tell he was listening.

"We'll fly out to rescue Bailey from the auction as soon as we've got the birds free, and then we'll all hideout at our ranch, several hours north of Illias, but much closer once on the back of an Eedon Rath-ni," Brenna told him.

Her father had just a few questions. He was needed as well. "I've heard about that group. They've been a thorn in our side and hard to track, with so many potential cells and lucrative places to operate. I can give you whatever you need to attend the auction, but you're in deep, Bailey. I can't offer you any reinforcements to pull this off."

"Is this really a surprise to either of us?" Bailey asked him. "You're you, and it's Illias."

He grumbled at that. "Do as you will then. Text me the buy-in and I'll—" Clancy began to tell her,

But she interjected, "Charge it to the Resistance taxpayers?"

He hung up the phone. She needed $1 million to get into the banquet, and the minimum bidding began at $11 million. Also, she would need an alternate identity to disguise herself as—one who may actually be interested in purchasing them. She'd need a story and papers. The taxpayers of Allirehem would pay for it all.

***

The three of them set off across the lobby of the hotel and tried not to attract any attention. "Icon, stop nervously shifting the suitcase," Bailey told him from behind.

"Sorry," he apologized as they walked through the double doors to exit the hotel. She could see him looking at her strange mask, like it wasn't a dead giveaway of the event she was attending to anyone with well-connected sources in the city. What was different about her though was that beyond her mask, an oriole, she had dyed her hair bright blonde, jazzily styled it, and wore a black dress. She dressed to look like she was from Aceor—perhaps the daughter of the second of three marriages and fourth of nine children whose grandfather had built the family wealth on railroads. Or perhaps she was no one in particular at all.

When they arrived at the City Department of Gas and Water, it was just past 9 pm, and the building was dark, closed, and seemingly empty. Icon held up a small ring of keys and several lock picks. "Well, this is where we part for now. See you at about 11:30, just after the auction has concluded," Icon told her.

Bailey's hug with Brenna was brief and unremarkable. Bailey and Icon hugged for the first time after that. They were almost the same height. While they hugged, Icon put his head underneath her chin while she brushed his short dark brown crew cut just once. "Let's make them pay for what they've done to us and our birds," he told her.

"We will," she told him. Once Icon and Brenna were within the city building and out of sight, Bailey set off toward where she knew the auction was. She thought only of Hector while she made the brief walk to her destination.

Fifteen minutes later, Bailey found herself on a street a few blocks back from where she knew Brien'nia Street was. The buildings around her looked very historic. The infrastructure here had been incredulous to modernize along with the rest of the world. Bailey heard plenty of wall air-conditioning units running on full blast to keep the hot, stuffy air out.

Icon had given her an exact address on a sheet of paper, which Bailey had not looked at since beginning her walk. However, when she began to see a variety of fashions from different parts of the world, worn by people who looked very culturally affluent like herself, Bailey began to suspect she was headed in the right direction. Bailey fell in behind about a dozen people making their way to the same place.

"It's two hawks tonight, but two months ago they had an eagle and a raven for sale in Dig-la Teur," she understood a man behind her say in Maravinyian. Bailey forced herself to walk ahead of them.

All the streets in the area of Illias that Bailey was in were only barely wide enough for two lanes of traffic to move slowly across the cobblestone roads. When Bailey turned the corner, she looked down to the next intersection and found that access to the road she was on now had been closed off. Then when she turned to walk up the street, continuing to follow the stream of people, Bailey began to see more luxurious cars lined up on one road than she had ever seen in one place before. Not even while she was in Seems.

Bailey had to hold up her hand to keep herself from getting blinded by all the headlights as she got closer to the line of luxury cars, which now stretched farther up and around the block than she could see. When Bailey approached the intersection to turn left, where all the cars were headed, she had a chance to identify some of the brands of cars. She saw several sporty Fabershauts, a handful of Marinclyade sedans, and also half a dozen Rehem Rover SUVs—she even heard the unmistakable growl of a Burcgetti or two. All the cars had decadent rims, luminously colorful door lights, and heavily tinted windows, which were also more than likely bulletproof. Bailey wondered how many of the vehicles had reinforced roll cages to defend against Eedon Rath-ni attacks.

Bailey saw them pulling up to an opulent beige-stone building. Once the auction attendees were out of their cars, they walked up to the entrance of the building, which was just as well-lit and grand as the building itself. There they waited to be checked in.

Bailey wasted no more time and made her way to the end of one of the three short lines of people being checked into the auction reception. When Bailey was close enough, she could see the many ponytails of Shizen. His presence let Bailey know for sure that she was in the right place. Shizen would be the one to check her in, but Bailey was not scared.

"Curious choice of bird," he told her when she stepped up to him, stroking his chin beard afterward. He spoke in Haishian.

"Orioles magic; feel it happen," Bailey told him sportingly even faster. She only had to think about her answer for a split-second. Bailey handed him her ID passport, then gave him a small grin, which wasn't too wide and didn't last too long.

"What interest do you have in buying one of our Eedon Rath-ni? Is there someone you represent since you are by yourself? Where would we be delivering your Eedon Rath-ni if you are successful at the auction?" Shizen asked her. If Bailey could have told him just to shove it, she would have, but it was better that she used the answers that the three of them had come up with together.

"I represent my father, of course, the CEO of Cardinale Industries. He wants to build an aviary in Aceor. He has his four cages set up, and now he just needs one of each Eedon Rath-ni," Bailey told him, answering all of his questions at once. Shizen wrote down a few notes on a clipboard he held, and then he asked her one more question.

"Okay, it's Å1 million to get into the banquet," he told her. He pressed some buttons on his tablet and then held it out in front of her. Bailey grabbed her cell phone, went to her banking app, and held her phone directly over his tablet to transfer the funds. "Step forward and put out your arms."

Bailey did just that while she held her small purse in one hand so that she could be frisked. Bailey was very happy when Shizen called forward a short girl with black hair to frisk her, rather than do it himself.

The short girl with black hair nodded, stepped in front of her, and began to pat her down. Once the girl was sure that Bailey was unarmed and not wearing a wire, she asked for her purse. Bailey handed the girl her purse without complaint. A few seconds later, the girl with black hair pulled out a circular black device that was three inches in length and one-half in diameter. "What's this?" she asked.

"Lipstick," Bailey told the girl, who then twisted out a red stick of it which matched the color of her own lips. "Very well," said the girl, "you're free to go in."

"Thank you," Bailey told her, and then she quickly took her lipstick back and stored it away in her purse. What the young girl hadn't realized was that she could twist her lipstick inward to unsheathe a small ring of a knife around its outer edge, half as long as its case itself. It would be the one weapon she had on her person if things got ugly.

Bailey entered the building. Once she got beyond the lobby, which was filled with guests waiting to get rooms for themselves in the floors above or to check-in their coats, she walked into a banquet hall which was lightly filled with tables. There was just enough space that Bailey could easily slide past people while they milled about with hors d'oeuvres and cocktails.

The banquet hall had chandlers lined with gems, and in the middle of the room, there was a slain taxidermy of each Eedon Rath-ni. The dragon they had was forest green. It obviously took up the most space, and it had the most people milling about it. Bailey stepped up to the raven and felt like she wanted to vomit right in front of it. She forced herself not to. Bailey found herself wondering how all these people could possibly live with themselves. And she wondered how much of a difference each of the dead Eedon Rath-ni could have made in the war against Iishrem. Bailey forced herself not to think about it.

Bailey scorned herself when she thought about all the civilians who would never possibly be killed by any of these Eedon Rath-ni, because now all they were was some trophy kill in a banquet hall for the most despicable and affluent misers of the world. Bailey despised all of them, but she was able to keep a straight face after all her experience in Seems.

After Bailey finished reviling herself while she milled about the stuffed raven, she found herself a half-full table to sit at, so she could rest her legs. No one at the table paid any attention to her when she first sat down. While she could, Bailey looked out the back of the banquet hall and saw one of the river canals that ran through the city beyond a wide, dimly lit patio that was filled with guests smoking cigars.

"Ack heem," said a man across from her at the table. She realized for the first time that the five other people at the table, four men and one woman, were playing a card game, and they now expected her to play. Bailey was caught out of position. She wasn't quite sure what card game was being played—or what exactly was being wagered—but she was afraid that if she just got up and walked away, it would seem disingenuous and suspicious. It had been her fault that she hadn't noticed before.

"My apologies," she began in Haishian. "What game exactly are we playing? And what are the wagers?"

"We are playing Serven-pina. The player who takes the most cards before passing over a combined value of twenty-six wins the game. The minimum wager is Ⱥ 100, aces are always a 1," said the male dealer—the one who had 'ack hemmed' her just a few moments ago.

Bailey pulled out her own credit card and said, "Very well. I'll play a few hands. Ⱥ 5,000 out please." She still had plenty more than that in her own accounts, and she did not plan on losing that much.

"Wonderful," the dealer told her. This one part of the night, Bailey decided to be sensible and sponsored her play with Ⱥ 5,000 of her own. She exchanged the credits by holding her phone above his tablet. He smiled and wished her "good luck" before handing her a stack of thirty red Ⱥ 100 chips, and forty green Ⱥ 50 chips.

A new round of the game began, and talk began to circulate around the table again. The men and woman at the table each seemed to be from a different place based on their fashions, and they regarded her with the curiosity of a fellow competitor. They did not believe she was not a physical threat to them, but they knew that she was there to take their money.

"Where are you from, young girl?" asked a tall, ridged man with grey hair wearing an ape mask. He spoke with a wispy voice. He was wearing a blue suit, full of gold chains that ran from button to button on the arms of the jacket.

"Initial bets in please," the dealer requested sternly.

Bailey put in a single red chip, as did all the other players, before she answered the man's question. "Why is that any of your business?" she asked the man. The dealer dealt each player at the table two cards, face down. For her first hand, Bailey was dealt an ace and 3—both cards amounted to a score of just four. She was in quite a good position.

She would have guessed that the man she sat across from was from Darni-Sil. The man was not stifled or offended. "It's funny you should pose a question like that, as it is my company who provides some of the most high-tech gear that these *hunters*"—he enunciated in an ambiguous tone—"use." The gorilla then made an initial bet of ᴁ250, which she called quickly. A suitcase sat next to his chair with the emblem of Bailey's mother's past employer: Drev-Tech. *Now that's marginally surprising*, Bailey thought.

"You work for Drev-Tech, I see. Must get to travel a lot. Ever take any jobs in the region of Seems?" she asked him, getting straight to the point.

The gorilla leaned back in his blue suit and internally debated how he wanted to answer her question. She understood why he would do that. In the meantime, the player next to her—a woman with a koala bear mask, wearing a thin gray dress—bailed out of the hand, tossing her cards over to the dealer, face down.

"I hear Seems is quite beautiful during any time of the year," said the woman.

The final player at the table, wearing the visor of a knight also bailed out of his hand after looking at his cards. This hand would come down to either Bailey, the handsome man, or the house would take it if they tied. "Not for nearly thirteen years have I known of any jobs going on in or near Seems, but I must admit I cannot account for *every* region Drev-Tech might have operations in.

"Did you hear why they would have stopped operations?" Bailey pressured him.

Each of them was dealt a single card face up so that each other could see it. The handsome man was dealt a 7, Bailey a 6. "Why is that any of your business?" asked the dashing man, returning her the favor of a cruel irony.

"Just a curiosity really. The help our family could have used from a hawk's eye while we built our railroads. To find the best, most effective, and safest routes possible."

Bailey won the hand, and the man in the gorilla mask left the table somewhat perturbed, saying he had to attend to some personal matters. Bailey wasn't too fond of being distracted by the death of her mother at that moment anyway. Thirty minutes later, Bailey had made herself quite a bit of money—a nice gift to take home for herself, in addition to Hector, for her trouble.

When an announcement came over the loudspeaker of the banquet hall, Bailey knew it was finally time for her to leave the table and make her way towards the patio so she could board the riverboat. "Attention, all guests," rang a feminine voice over the loudspeaker system. "The auction sail around the Illnayean river will begin in fifteen minutes, lasting for forty-five. Patrons interested in bidding on our Eedon Rath-ni may now make their way toward the riverboat. For the rest of you, just lean back and enjoy a view of the auction."

At that moment, several projector screens around the banquet hall began to automatically unfurl. When they were all the way down, Bailey was granted her first glimpse at her future Eedon Rath-ni. The projector screens were filled with a live stream of Hector and Ghel in their restraints as they waited to be auctioned off. As soon as Bailey saw them, she pushed her chips over to the dealer and asked, "Can I color up?"

The dealer nodded and began to sort Bailey's chips into his bank, replacing Bailey's stack with a shorter stack of more valuable chips with the same overall value. Once that was done, Bailey left the dealer a chip worth A100 as a tip. Bailey quickly worked her way over to the cashier's office, which was near the lobby entrance. While Bailey stood in line to get credit for her winnings, she got a better look at Hector and Ghel.

Bailey looked at Hector on a TV and into his eyes. As soon as she did, Bailey could finally hear his voice in his head again. *Are you watching me through this camera they have pointed on me? Can you even hear me?* Hector wondered sadly.

Hector! Bailey thought as loudly as she thought she could in her mind. *I can hear you. Icon and Brenna are on their way to free you and Ghel. Stay calm.*

While Bailey stepped up to the cashier, Hector began to thrash around in his restraints that netted his wings and kept his talons on the ground. Bailey handed the cashier her stack of chips and the credit card she had cashed them out on. "Put all of it back on this account please," she told the cashier in Haishian while she held up her phone for it to be scanned and desperately tried to keep track of everything going on at once.

I must get out of here, Bailey. Where are you? Hector asked her desperately.

While Hector thrashed around, Ghel remained quite calm and serene with her wings tucked in and eyes closed. Guards milled about Hector on screen, but they did not whip him or use a cattle prod like Bailey would have expected. In fact, Icon had been quite true to his word about their condition. The two of them looked largely free of scars and were well-fed. However, they both looked quite dirty from having been in the water canals underneath the city, and Hector's feathers were quite ruffled.

As the cashier handed her back her phone, which she put into her purse, Bailey saw Ghel's eyes begin to glow forest green. All at once, Hector stopped thrashing and settled down.

Oh, I see, I see. The boy and girl I met before are right outside the door to this river tunnel, just waiting for the right moment to free us. Bailey, when do you think that would be best? Hector asked.

Bailey felt so relieved that everything was going according to plan. She turned away from the cashier's office and walked over to the patio exit of the banquet hall. When she stepped outside, the night was still warm and muggy, but it had grown a little windy. *Tell Ghel to inform Icon that the best time to rescue you would be after the auction has begun. I'll let you know when. Then just as it's ending, you'll arrive to pick me up, and we'll all fly off together,* Bailey told him, believing she had made the best decision possible.

Plenty of guests were milling about the patio, smoking cigars, sipping champagne, and eating the hors d'oeuvres. All the while, they took glances at Hector and Ghel on the TVs. Bailey got into the line for the triple-decker riverboat that awaited any of the guests interested in bidding on their Eedon Rath-ni. There were about a hundred and fifty people in disguise waiting to get onto the boat. When she looked back at the now just one-third-full banquet hall, she reviled them all, that they would just cosign on all of this with their corrupt money.

Bailey knew that she needed to keep all her personal vendettas out of her mind for now—or at least until she was riding away on Hector. All she could do was patiently wait in line to board the riverboat. That was when she first spotted Grenelda. She was the one letting prospective buyers onto the boat. After another minute or two, Bailey stepped up to Grenelda.

"ID please," Grenelda requested.

Bailey handed Grenelda her ID and picked up her phone, ready to transfer another ⅄11 million taxpayer appropriated funds so she could steal her hawk.

"Very well, and your credit of ⅄11 million for when the bidding will begin?" Grenelda asked her. Bailey attempted to smile as genuinely as she could at Grenelda. She held back her tongue, then they exchanged funds in the same way.

To Bailey's relief, Grenelda accepted her credit without a problem and then allowed her to walk onto the boat a second later. Bailey would have to do something nice for her father the next time she saw him. Bailey felt nervous as she walked over the ramp that would put her on the boat. She was one of the last to step on. *Okay, Hector, I'm stepping onto the riverboat now. Just hold off on the rescue a little longer.*

I'll tell Ghel to inform Icon to do just that, he told her. Bailey just hoped that she wouldn't fall off him at any point during their first flight together. Bailey felt a little motion, and then the riverboat began to move up the canal that would take them to the Illnayean River.

She immediately began to put an escape plan together. First, she began to count the guards that were on the boat. Bailey counted six stationed strategically along the railings of the first deck, while four more swept through the middle of it. All the guards were armed with burst action assault rifles, a single stun grenade or flash-bang, and a pistol. Bailey began to make her way up to the second deck of the riverboat, where she knew she would need to be for the auction itself. The second deck of the riverboat was a single square-shaped gathering hall with drinks and, of course, more appetizers. Bailey counted four more guards. The third deck above was the captain's quarters and the control room, so she assumed that there weren't any additional guards up there.

Bailey took a seat in the back of the auction hall, not planning to make an actual bid, next to a robin and a bright yellow star. She could see the man with the gorilla mask sitting one row from the front. Once everyone was there and settled, the riverboat turned left and sailed into the Illnayean River, making its way up the Riverwalk. There was a moderate amount of river traffic as the night approached 11:15 pm, and plenty of people were still awake and enjoying the night.

The auction began quickly once the boat began to sail along the Riverwalk. Just like in the banquet hall, two projector screens rolled down, and then they were filled with the live stream of Hector. He would be auctioned off first. As Hector's auction began, Bailey waited for the best chance for Icon and Brenna to start their rescue.

"We're going to start the bidding off at ₳ 11 million. Do I have ₳ 11 million?" asked the auctioneer.

"Here," said a man a few rows in front of her. Suddenly, the live stream of Hector cut out and was replaced by a hype video that The Hunters had put together to drive up the potential sale price of Hector. *Okay, Hector! Go! Go! Go! Tell Ghel to let Icon know that you can both be rescued right now!* Bailey thought in her head.

Hector heard her and responded quickly, *Roger that,* he told her. *I can't wait to see you. I'll keep you updated.*

Bailey felt herself begin to quake with anticipation. The video being played began to show clips of Hector's capture—including several of his kills. In the video, Hector landed on top of two soldiers, crushing them. Then he batted three more away with his wings as they approached from behind. After that, he used his wings to surge forward and grabbed two more soldiers with his talons. He crushed their chests and diced apart their bodies with his talons.

As the video continued to play clips of his capture, the value of his bids jumped dramatically.

"Do I have ♈30 million?" asked the auctioneer.

"Here," said a woman in the front.

Ah. Finally, I'm free of these restraints. Time for some revenge, Hector told her.

Keep it reasonable. Don't get yourself so hurt that we can't escape, Bailey told him.

You should see the spray of blood I just got from pulling someone apart with my two talons, Hector told her. Bailey smiled on the inside, fantasizing about having seen that in person.

That all sounds great, but seriously… we need to be escaping before your auction ends, or the entire organization will know at once, she told him.

Okay, okay, Hector told her. There was a momentary pause in the action. "♈ 35 million," rang a voice in the auction hall. *There we go. Anyone left is just running off for help. Icon and Brenna are getting onto Ghel now.*

Great, Bailey thought. She looked out the window to see where she was on the river. They were sailing underneath a stretch of several bridges, where the river began to bend northwestward out of the city. She relayed the information to Hector. *I need you both here as soon as possible.*

We're flying out of the tunnel now, Hector told her.

So that was it then. Bailey knew the rest of the auction didn't matter. *How long until you get here?* she asked him.

Thirty seconds, Hector told her after a brief calculation. *I can see your boat in the distance. Make your way towards the south side of the river and jump off the second deck and onto my back.*

Bailey pushed all her fears out of her mind and pretended like she was playing paintball. "36 million," rang a voice as Bailey observed the four guards. She stood up with her purse in her hands and began to make her way to the exit of the auction hall. There was a small landing before the stairs down to the first deck that she could jump from. She eyed the guard who stood closest to the door. The four of them looked attentive, but none of them had their rifles drawn. It was time to make The Hunters hurt for what they had put her through.

Bailey reached into her purse and pulled out her lipstick and began to twist it like she was going to put some on, but instead, she twisted it to the other side and then lunged at the guard watching the closest exit and stabbed him in the left eye with its blade. He cried in pain and stumbled back into the wall. He then bounced off it just a foot from having been blinded. Bailey wedged herself into the space between his back and the wall, unstrapped his assault rifle, and took it for herself. She also made sure to grab his two extra magazines of ammo from the straps on his belt as well. She stuffed them into her purse. After that, Bailey grabbed the scream-ing guard by the scruff of his neck just as the three others were beginning to react. The auction had ceased, and all the potential buyers watched in scared, stunned silence as they crouched down in between the rows of chairs. That was except for the man wearing the gorilla mask who had drawn a pistol and was aiming it at her.

"Oh shit!" Bailey exclaimed as she pulled the guard in front of herself. The room rang with gunfire. Bailey was not hit, but she felt many chips of shattering metal and glass. She began to pull the guard out the door with her. He had been shot several times, and he was starting to weigh Bailey down. Thinking quickly, Bailey pulled the pin out of his flashbang grenade and tossed it into the center of the auction room.

As soon as she heard the grenade go off, Bailey looked for Hector and saw him flying towards her at a moderate, consistent rate. *I see you. Jump when I say so… Now!* he implored her.

Bailey trusted Hector; it wasn't a decision. Before any of the guards could reach or shoot her, Bailey strapped the assault rifle around her back, ran forward, and lunged off the second deck. She landed on Hector's back, then sat down and took hold of a handful of his feathers. Finally, after all these years, they had each other.

Chapter 29

The River dance (Bailey 8)

ILLIAS, HAISHA, ALLIREHEM

SUMMER, 1153, FOURTH AGE

As soon as Bailey had landed on Hector's back, gunfire began to chase her from the riverboat behind. The felt the force of an explosion on her back from some unknown source. She heard bursting rifles in her background, and she instantly thought to duck down on Hector as low as she could, clinging to his back. *Don't worry, Bailey. I'll get us a good opportunity of our own. Just hang on*, Hector thought out to her. In the meantime, he looked up at her and met her gaze with a wink. Bailey was so happy to have him.

Sounds fair enough, Bailey thought. *Let's make 'em pay!*

That's more like it! Hector thought.

The two of them approached one of the many bridges over the river. *Tonight, Bailey. Tonight, we shall learn to fly*, Hector thought. Bailey tried to mentally prepare herself for the first of his aerial maneuvers. Hector's flight began by skimming the ceiling of the bridge and then performing a half loop, rising back above the bridge, before turning over right side up to land quickly on its stone railing. Hector perched there and bared his wings to the passing pedestrians—some of whom were backing up into the road. Cars swerved to avoid hitting the pedestrians, but not all of them were successful.

Bailey quickly got a chance to see where Icon and Ghel were. The two of them were circling around the riverboat, taking shots from several stories up in the air. She couldn't see them that well with her oriole mask on. Her time at the banquet and auction was over, and she was still disguised as some entitled youth from Aceor or no one at all, so she ripped off her mask and tossed it away. Bailey pulled the assault rifle off her back and cocked back its release. It was loaded, and the safety was off. *This is for Amanda,* Bailey thought.

This is for me, Hector added.

Bailey almost fell off him when Hector surged back into the air, pulling several large chunks of the stone bridge railing along with him. He flew her towards the boat. When Bailey looked at the first and second deck of the boat, six guards were waiting to fire at her again, while three more were on the other side of the boat harassing Ghel, Icon, and Brenna.

As Hector approached the riverboat, he did a rudder roll to the left to throw off the aim of the guards, while also releasing his load of stones—several large chunks of which struck two guards in their chests. Bailey popped up and fired five bursts at two of the guards. She missed with the first three but knocked a guard down with a burst to his shoulder and one to his stomach.

Again, the man in the blue jacket wearing the gorilla mask came out on the second deck of the boat and started firing his pistol at her. *What the fuck is with this guy?* Bailey found herself wondering.

He was likely to be my buyer, or so I heard, Hector thought in her mind.

That ticked Bailey off even more. She lined up a shot to the center of his stomach and hit her mark. The man in the blue jacket dropped to his hands and knees rocked there back and forth for a moment. He glowered at her and then put a foot back up. *Of course, he's wearing a vest,* Bailey thought. She would have to let him go. She reloaded.

Their revenge would be short-lived, as Hector and Bailey soon found out that the Hunters would not let them escape without a chase. From somewhere off in the city, Bailey heard a dragon roar. Such a sound instantly put fear in her heart.

Bailey, we need to get out of here. We hawks don't often fair well against dragons in a close fight, Hector told her dreadfully.

In the meantime, Brenna began to scream at the top of her lungs. She was hanging onto one of Icon's boots while he clung to Ghel with his two arms around her neck. *Okay, but we must get Brenna,* Bailey told him.

I can get her. Let me at her, Hector thought.

While the man wearing the gorilla struggled to his feet, so he could limp to the relative safety of the auction room on the Riverboat, Bailey pulled up underneath Icon and Brenna. "Jump! You'll be fine!" Bailey yelled out to her new friend.

Brenna looked down at her with fearful eyes, her hair flying all over the place. She looked back up at Icon. "I'm sorry," Icon said to her.

Brenna released her grip on her cousin, dropped down onto Hector's back, and took a hold of Bailey's shoulders. "Icon, we have to get out of here and away from these people. We can't take all of them on," Bailey told him.

"Yes, you're right. The mouth of the river is the quickest way out of the city, then we'll follow it to our home, deep in the rainforest like we planned," he told Bailey. "I'm sorry, Cousin."

"Let's just get out of here," Brenna told them.

That was when they were collectively blinded by a string of searchlights that were strategically set up to illuminate the river on both sides of the Riverwalk. It was now as bright as the middle of the day. While the three of them held up their hands to keep the light out of their eyes, a charcoal dragon lurked above. The figures of a shadowy man and woman could be made out on its back. The two of them landed on top of a skyscraper, around twenty stories high—one of the only ones around District Lampshire. The dragon had landed on top of the roof with a jolt and then stretched out its neck to roar at them.

The dragon's second roar over the summer night brought with it a sudden hushed chill over that entire portion of the city. Citizens and tourists were watching the whole exchange, ducking behind cover across both sides of the Riverwalk. The more intelligent people were just fleeing the scene entirely.

"What is this?" Bailey asked, quite out loud. All she could see of the man was his shadowy figure. That and he appeared to be wearing a mask with glowing golden eye shades. When she looked at the man's eyes, Bailey felt her eyes glow brown.

"You have taken what you believe to be yours," the man's voice rang out across the quiet district, amplified through its system of alarm speaker stations. "But these Eedon Rath-ni are not yours to keep; I will show you." Before the man took off, the shadowy figure of the woman stepped off. She was wearing a similar mask, but with glowing white eye shades instead.

Bailey fancied a trick of her own that she had just thought of. "Icon!" she yelled out. "I'd like my carbine back, please. Here, you can have this burst-action rifle."

"I'm not accurate enough to use this gun well anyway," Icon admitted. First, Bailey strapped the assault rifle around her back again, so she could first catch the carbine when Icon threw it several seconds later. Icon tossed the carbine to her, with a two-handed push that she caught easily. Then he tossed her a satchel of ammo. Bailey temporarily laid the carbine down on Hector's back, before she grabbed the extra magazines of ammo that she had for the burst-action rifle from her purse.

While the river was still brightly illuminated, she held the two magazines out in front of her for Icon to see and then tossed them to him. He caught both without a problem. Then she tossed him the burst action rifle with a two-handed push as well. He caught the rifle without struggle.

"Brenna, are you good?" Bailey asked her friend, looking back at her. Bailey saw that Brenna still had her pistol, which made her smile. Brenna nodded and then cocked the pistol back.

Bailey secured her carbine to the strap she had taken from the burst-action rifle, before strapping it around her back. *Okay, Hector, get us out of here,* she told her hawk.

Roger that, he told her, and then he surged back into motion. As the dragon roared closely behind them, Icon led the way north-westward towards the mouth of the river where the city ended and the jungle began. From Bailey's geographical knowledge of Haisha, she knew that if they followed the Illnayean River towards its mouth, it would then split into several others that stretched farther into the country, cutting through the jungles—or there was a solitary canal leading to the bay. If they followed the river in the other direction, it would take them through the city until it rose back up beyond the steep but short mountains that boxed in Illias against the coast.

"Brenna, you keep me updated on how close that dragon is," Bailey told her friend.

"Um… Bailey," Brenna said from behind her.

As Icon led their formation on Ghel under the first bridge which Hector had ripped several chunks from, Bailey flew on Hector's back just to their left. Bailey craned her neck as far as possible in both directions and could no longer see the dragon. *Hector, this dragon must be right on us, but I can't see him,* Bailey thought to her hawk.

As it turned out, Hector could swivel and rotate his neck much farther than she could. Hector turned his head to a near two hundred and seventy-degree rotation. When Hector saw the dragon, his pupils contracted, and he squawked at the dragon. *Hold on,* Hector told her.

Hector suddenly banked left harshly toward the other side of the river, keeping them underneath the width of the bridge as long as he could. Bailey felt the bridge shake above them; the dragon must have landed right on top of it. Tires screeched, pedestrians screamed fleeing, and fire erupted. Orange fire brightened the night sky around the Riverwalk.

A stream of fire shot out in the direction of Icon while he rode towards the mouth of the river. Icon dodged the fire, but it forced him all the way down to river-level, where he got caught up in some of the fleeing boat traffic. *Hector, get me a shot at this guy,* Bailey told him.

Right, Hector responded. When Hector finished crossing the width of the bridge, he was just a few feet from the beginning of the Riverwalk. He made a tight left bank into the first archway underneath the bridge, and then he rolled his wings over, pausing first at ninety degrees before completing his inversion. The three of them hung there in the air for just a second, and then Hector thrust his wings upwards and brought them on top of the bridge about a thousand feet away from the masked man on the dragon.

Okay, Hector. Nice and easy, Bailey thought.

Right. I'm too low, though. I can only glide for a few seconds. Better take your shots quickly, he told her.

As Bailey rode on Hector on a gradual downward glide, she rose on Hector's back to her knees and remembered all the practice of her life. She steadied herself on Hector's back like she was just riding her dirt bike with no hands. She grabbed the carbine off her back, cocked back the release, and then aimed down her sights. If this Draven was anywhere near as powerful as Zeren Wikes, then he must have shields. Her shots wouldn't kill him, but Bailey believed she could wound him. She then told Hector her plan—the trick up her sleeve.

Hector was a fan of the plan. It was a fantastic opportunity for them to strike while the dragon and the rider were only concerned with driving Icon from one side of the river to the other. Bailey took her first shot at the man from about four hundred and twenty feet away, but she saw no yellow embers crumble off the masked man. *Missed*, Bailey thought.

Keep firing, Hector urged.

Bailey felt herself exhale as she squinted at the now well-illuminated man. Bailey fired again, and again, and again, striking the man with one shot right to the chest. The shadowy man with the mask first noticed their presence above the bridge when Bailey was about two hundred and fifty feet away. By that point, the man had already lost. He had let them get far too close to his back, unnoticed.

Bailey fired one more shot right at the man's head, which struck the top of his mask and pushed it up before the bullet skimmed away. The impact of the bullet sent streaks of golden embers sparking everywhere and knocked the bottom of his mask up into his mouth, which also temporarily blinded him. When Hector flew right behind the back of the dragon, he reached out with his talons and sieged the man off the dragon's back. The charcoal dragon quickly reared its neck to try and burn them, but Hector flew off in the other direction.

Hector, don't crush this man, and then let's out-run this dragon. We need him alive. That way we can find out more about this organization. We're going to need information if we're going to take it down one day and prevent what happened to you from happening to any other Eedon Rath-ni, Bailey thought out to him.

Before they could get too far up the river, Bailey heard the man's voice from below. "Bailey Triten," he said in a computerized gargled voice. He had pulled his mask back down and over the rest of his face. He held up a frag grenade. He had pulled the pin out but held in the release. "Release me, or I will kill us all."

It was of extreme interest to Bailey, how the masked man knew her name, but when she hesitated, the man threatened her with the live grenade again. *Hector, release him, peacefully,* she reluctantly told him immediately. *Let's just get out of here!*

Bailey watched Hector drop the masked man into the river. She did not hear a grenade go off, but the dragon roared after her a second later. Bailey didn't think she was going to need her carbine again for the rest of the night, so she slung it around her back and threw her arms around Hector's neck.

"Brenna, put your arms around my stomach and hang on," she told her. As soon as Bailey felt Brenna's arms around her stomach and chest on her back, Bailey said, *Okay, Hector, show us how to fly.*

Hector said nothing in response, but suddenly he had a new look in his eye. "Bailey, are we going to be okay?" asked Brenna from behind her.

"Yes, I know we are," she reassured her friend. This time, Bailey felt the heat of the dragon's fire much closer to her back. The dragon was chasing after them, but Bailey could no longer look back.

Hector surged forward and then swooped into a brief but steep dive to build up speed. He collected Ghel into the wind of his wake and began to pull her along with him. Bailey heard Icon screaming, "Woooooooo!" from behind.

When Hector came to the first set of three bridges spaced out relatively evenly, he flew over the first one and performed a cork-screw loop to the left and under the next one. He then surged over top of the final one and made a violently quick ascension with his wings. As they were rising back up above the bridges, Bailey was able to look to the north side of the river and see Ghel had done the opposite maneuver they had. Icon ended up sweeping under the first bridge.

Then Hector's real flight began. The two of them formed up in tandem with each other again and began to pick up speed, building distance between themselves and the pursuing dragon. Whenever the dragon seemed to find a good opportunity to spray fire at them, Hector would perform more of his aerial maneuvers using the crossings for cover. Without its rider, the dragon wasn't able to track them as well, and it eventually left to retrieve its rider when Hector and Bailey were beyond reach.

A little later, the jungle grew before their eyes. They were finally getting away from Illias altogether. Once they were clear of the city limits and free of the dragon, Icon led them deeper into the jungle along one of the several smaller rivers that split from its mouth. They flew low to the water, which would keep them in the dark, allowing them to travel quietly. The ride became quite peaceful, and for the first time since leaving Seems, Bailey took in a breath of fresh air and sent all of it up into her brain.

Hector and Ghel flew as close to the river's surface as they could. *Watch this,* Hector told her. Bailey missed his gaze to look ahead at Ghel while she looked back at Icon and began to dip the tips of her wings into the river. Hector followed suit. The gentle breeze sprayed Bailey lightly in the hair and helped her relax and lean back on Hector for the first time.

She looked down at the water and saw large glowing orbs of pale whitish-yellow light rising to the surface. Then the water began to bubble and up to the surface came some furry, pudgy, koala-size bear-fish, with gills on their necks and a translucent, glowing orb of pale light for an ass.

What are they? Bailey asked.

Regashens, Hector told her. *They have quite a vibrant culture under the river and are borderline sentient. They believe to be killed by one of us will turn them back into magic in death, and from there anything is possible.*

A cast of them climbed out of the water on rocks and began to coordinate a way so that some would be thrown from rocks in the river to trees with branches that curved over them. The further they flew down the river, the more of them there were. Then Hector and Ghel ascended back into the air and the Regashens who had climbed onto the branches of the trees began to try and drop down onto them as they flew threw.

A few of them landed on Ghel's and Hector's backs. They began to posture over their feathers and then ripped several times at them drawing blood, while their faces contorted, their orbs turned a bright orange-yellow, and they hummed a tune like they were sucking blood from a straw. *We'll end this quickly*, Hector told her. Bailey trusted him and turned around to watch him catch one in his open mouth, which he then ate. Ghel caught one in her talons and then ripped in half, before dunking both ends into her open gullet.

Once that happened, all of them instantly calmed down, including any of the ones that had briefly attacked their Eedon Rath-ni. They all slipped back into the river singing, "Hunt us all, oh hunt us all, the magic Eedon Rath-ni after all. After death, we all become, magic once again, like we had always been, through it all!"

Finally, when things had settled down again, Bailey sat up on Hector and said, "Well, that was creepy as shit."

"And distracting. I mean why were they singing? And how did they come up with that song?" Icon concurred.

"Mother Nature?" Brenna suggested. They all laughed, and their hawks enjoyed their kill as they flew a few feet higher into the sky.

"That's our home you see. And no one who doesn't know where it is has ever found it yet," he told her in a boastful tone while pointing out an approaching homestead. Icon landed Ghel in the middle of a courtyard of short grass with a short brick fence around the yard. Bailey and Brenna landed next to them on top of Hector. "You were so nice to take me and my cousin in. It's only fair that I repay you. Come and meet the family. Well, what's left of it anyway."

That all sounded nice to her. The house was a dimly lit one-story rancher with a small second-floor loft. As Icon and Brenna set off toward the house, Bailey stepped off Hector and finally had a chance to put her arms around her Eedon Rath-ni in the way that she wanted to. She gave him a tight hug, and he squawked in her ear gently.

You rescued me, Hector told her. He looked away from her and down at the ground. *Perhaps I don't deserve this name, considering.*

Bailey pushed away from him and held up one finger in front of his eyes, then she formed an O with her fingers. *We are whole now*, Bailey told Hector. *And for the record, it seems to me like we all rescued each other. You and me, Icon, Brenna, Ghel, we all beat the Hunters, and after we rest up, we'll fly to Christian's academy. We'll train, and we can work our way to the bottom of the organization. That way we can keep taking down its other heads.*

Bailey was sure that wouldn't be the last she heard from the Hunters, but it didn't matter for now because she had Hector, and she never wanted to be without him again.

Chapter 30
Draxion City (katie 8)

DRAXION CITY, MARAVINYA, ALLIREHEM

SUMMER, 1153, FOURTH AGE

Katie had spent each waking moment of her day so far waiting to hear one specific sound. When she finally heard the sound, it came as an exuberant relief. The horns of the ARF Clancy Triten began to hum and snapped her out of a momentary stupor. She closed the thick crime novel that she had spent the last five hours reading. Then she swung her legs over the side of her top bunk in the closet-sized room which she had shared with Ethan for near to the last week. Katie looked down.

"Wait, wait, wait," Ethan said from below her while he rolled over and off his bunk. He then stood to his feet. "Let me out first."

Katie smiled at him and let him exit their shared living space first—it was only fair. She hopped down off her bunk as soon as she had the space to land on the floor without knocking her brother over. With her feet on the deck, it turned out that she was more enthusiastic to see land than her brother. Katie slid around Ethan a few moments later while they made their way down the corridor that would take them to the deck of Destroyer.

When she stepped out onto the deck of the ship, with Ethan right behind her, they found it was a drizzling, overcast night. The weather still felt perfect to her, and she couldn't wait to get off the damn boat. It had been far too long since she had last been on solid ground when she had arrived back at her parents after graduation. *Sovereign, are you seeing this?* Katie thought to her Eedon Rath-ni when she turned her vision to the stunning skyline that she saw rising in the distance toward the horizon.

Sovereign screeched from behind her and came streaking into view along the starboard side of the ship with Violet in tow. *Aye, it's quite a sight to behold,* Sovereign told her. *Another human forest that I'll get to cross off my scroll of ones to visit. The trees here run much higher than the ones in Imperium Aendor.*

Skyscrapers, Sovereign, Katie told her eagle. *Not trees.*

So you say, he replied. Katie saw the skyline of Draxion City coming into view off the bow of the ship. The sight of the city steadily grew closer and rose farther into the air as the destroyer and the group of ships that had supported their excursion east-ward with Christian and Talia toward the academy continued into the harbor.

A few minutes later, Katie could begin to see into the city itself. Christian and Talia also joined their viewing. While Christian stood on the side of Katie, Talia stood on the side of Ethan. As soon as they joined them, Anacarin and Embar joined Sovereign and Violet in their formation. "You know what city it is we're sail-ing into, Ethan?" Christian asked out loud.

"Draxion City," Ethan answered confidently. With the city at that point closer than it had ever been, Katie was able to see greater detail in the cityscape. Draxion City was built around the central edge of the Gulf of Maravinya. A river perhaps a half-mile wide at its mouth divided the city in half by north and south, meandering much farther into the country than the limits of the city itself.

"Just so," Christian said, confirming Ethan's answer. Katie had a good feeling that a question for her was coming next, and she had a good idea of exactly what the question would be.

"And what river is that, which cuts through the middle of the city, Katie?" Talia asked this time.

"The Meinghelia River," Katie answered.

Katie was correct. "That river will take you all the way to Meinghelia City if you follow it long enough. There you'll find what exactly on the opposite side of the same river?" Talia asked both.

"The academy," both answered in unison. Katie was quite confident in her brother's geographic ability to help her follow a river all the way up to a town of brick that laid on the side of a hill across from Christian's Academy. The Academy was on the doorstep of a small mountain—the only one in the area—and Katie was quite confident the large number of Eedon Rath-ni gathered peacefully in one area would be a huge giveaway as well.

Christian nodded. As the sun set for the night behind them, Katie saw that the city was chopped up into different sections based on use. Most of them looked to be dedicated to shipping. The south side of the city had mostly shorter buildings that looked residential, while the north end of the city housed its financial district—which had the most influential deathly market exchange in all Rehem.

"Very good," Christian told them. The ARF Clancy Triten destroyer blew its horn once more. That was good news. "That's fifteen minutes to port—better go and grab your things."

Christian waived them off, and Katie led the way back towards their room, through the narrow corridors of the destroyer. Ethan had been much more organized than her during their stay aboard the destroyer.

"Looks like you've already packed," she said to him when they arrived back in their room. Ethan turned to her and softened his eyes. The trip had been difficult on each of them— both from a lack of personal space and with each of them being in different grieving stages over the loss of their parents and past lives. Ethan had been taking his loss of Kiera especially hard.

"Yeah, let me just grab my backpack and duffel bag and I'll give you the room," Ethan said. He paused to grab his bags and then took one more look over the room to see if he had forgotten anything. He then looked to the small desk where there was just enough space to put an uncomfortable wooden chair behind it. He saw that he hadn't picked up the photo album Katie had put together for him yet. He gently picked it up, then said, "Thanks for doing this, you know. I wish I could think of something else to do on my own."

"You don't have to," Katie told him.

Ethan put a hand on her shoulder and held it there for a few seconds. He left the room without another word and closed the door behind him. Katie opened the small compartment closet in the room, which had just enough depth for her to stuff her empty duffel bag in. She withdrew the bag and tossed it onto the bed with all the compartments already unzipped. Katie engaged in an efficient fury of gathering, making the most of her time by grabbing everything of hers very quickly. She was even able to neatly fold and organize her outfits.

When Katie was finished packing her belongings, she finally left the compartment behind and did not look back. She joined her brother, Christian, and Talia in the middle of the port side of the deck. A ramp had been extended to the deck of the ship so that Ethan and Katie could disembark.

Before they could get off, Christian held up his arm and pulled them aside. "As soon as we get off this ship, no more speaking Iiasmaeic until you're safely at the academy. Understand? Your accents are fine, but not a word in your native tongue," Christian told them.

Ethan gulped, and his eyes glowed violet.

"Very well," Katie said in Maravinyian, then rolled her eyes and huffed.

Christian simply blinked at them, and then turned around and led the four of them over the ramp. When Katie first felt her feet step onto the concrete pier that stretched out into the river to meet them, she wanted to stop, drop, and roll all over it. She wanted to kiss the pier.

Katie began to laugh out loud at her thoughts but did not tell any of her party what she was laughing about when Ethan, Talia, and Christian stared back at her in dazed confusion a moment later. *What? I don't understand the premise of why this is funny at all,* Sovereign thought, quite annoyed in her mind. It all just resulted in Katie laughing to herself even harder.

When Katie had had her fun, she settled down and focused her mind back on the action as the four of them made their way up the pier and toward the city. As the four of their Eedon Rath-ni began to fly directly above them, it began to cause a bit of a scene. However, Katie had noticed that many of the locals recognized Christian anyway. Most of the citizens of Maravinya did not approach him, but they all regarded him with a certain air of respect and loyalty. The Maravinyian people stood tall with their shoulders high, like they weren't afraid of the war one day coming to their shores.

They were currently far from the front line and well protected, but somehow, Katie knew that the war would reach these shores one day. Perhaps these people would not be ready for it.

When the four of them reached the end of the pier, Christian hailed a cab for them. A minivan pulled up a few seconds later, then Christian turned to her and said, "Tell your birds that your hotel is the tallest, roundest building in the sky." Christian pointed to a tall, circular black building made of glass that rose higher into the city than any other. The building also had a square-sided exterior for one-half of its circular exterior. "They can land on the roof." The cabbie jumped out of the car and ran around to the other side so he could collect their bags and stow them in the trunk.

"Aren't you staying with us?" Katie asked, unable to think of anything else to say.

"No, we're continuing on to the academy tonight—like I told you both when we began this trip," Christian told her, speaking in Maravinyian.

Sovereign, did you hear that? Katie thought out to her eagle. She then looked to the sky a few seconds later. She saw him making some daring aerial maneuvers through the open spaces in some of the shipping cranes off in the distance. Violet was perched on top of one while she watched him deftly fly. Katie had noticed that Sovereign could often read her mind and pick up on what people said to her that way, but not always.

Sovereign looked at her with his golden eyes, and she felt her eyes glow in response. *Yes, yes, I see it. We'll head over there now. It's just nice to be flying back over land again, don't you know?* he asked her.

Katie nodded to him, stepped into the minivan that was waiting for them, and sat in the third row with Ethan. Christian and Talia each took a seat in the middle row, and then Christian told the cabbie the address of the hotel. Katie and Ethan sat in silence while Christian and Talia quietly whispered to each other like lovers. The cabbie programmed the address into his GPS and then began to follow the directions through the crowded city streets.

Katie noticed that the cabbie often took glances back at Christian and Talia, using his rear-view mirror. She said nothing of it because Christian noticed it himself almost as quickly as her. "Yeah, it's me," he told the cabbie slyly.

"Oh, I knew it. I knew it! What an honor it is to drive the most notorious terrorist Christian Knowles," said the cabbie in a joyous, high-pitched voice. "You know just before this I was driving someone who works at the tank factory just outside of the city. I've never seen so many tanks built so quickly. Hopefully, we'll never have to see them in use on these shores."

"Thank you, my friend. You're too kind," Christian said thankfully. He did not turn red.

"Tell me," Talia said to the cabbie. "I've never been to this city before. What do most people think about the war?"

"To tell you the truth, it isn't on the minds of most citizens unless they're involved in the industry itself," the cabbie told them, referencing those who built the materials which enabled the war machine to continue. "Some people talk about friends or family members who have enlisted. They worry about them, of course, but they are also thankful that there are those willing to fight."

There's something about these people, Katie thought to herself.

Most of them have never seen the true effects of this war except on TV. Perhaps they won't for several years, but I have a feeling Maravinya will have an important role to play before the war is over, Sovereign told her from somewhere above.

The only question that remains is whether they be ready for it when it arrives? Katie felt that was a better question left unanswered, and the conversation between Christian and the cabbie ended soon afterward.

When they arrived at the hotel, Talia slid open the van door and stepped out onto the sidewalk first while Christian took care of their fare. Ethan followed her out, then Katie stood up with her head curved to the side so she could exit the van. Christian joined them a few seconds later, and then the cabbie sprang out of the van, so he could grab their bags from the trunk for them. When everything was finished, Katie saw Christian hand the cabbie ₳50. The cabbie thanked him and then went on his way.

Before Katie could pick up any of her bags herself, a porter working for the hotel came out with a bag cart and insisted that he do everything for them. When all their bags had been loaded onto the cart, Christian handed the porter another ₳50 and then led them into the hotel. When they stepped inside the lobby, the first thing that Katie noticed was the fountain at the center of it—and the statue of Draxion the Bold in the center of that.

"This city was named after one of the founders of the academy—who you'll soon learn more about. Draxion the Bold, however, never quite made it to these shores in his lifetime, so the story for how the city came to be named after him is an interesting tale for another time," Christian told them. Katie looked at the statue of Draxion and admired his strong jaw and deep blue eyes, but she found all the places where knives were sheathed around his figure to be a little unsettling. How many did he need?

Christian walked them to the front desk of the hotel and took care of getting them checked in over the next few minutes. When that was done, Christian handed them both a room key each and then led them over to call an elevator down. When one arrived, the four of them stepped in and rode it up to the thirty-second of thirty-six floors. Christian and Talia led Ethan and Katie to their rooms, both of which were quite spacious, had a king-sized bed, and all the expected amenities of a 4-star hotel.

Katie tossed her duffle bag and backpack onto her bed. Ethan's room was several doors down the hall. Christian and Talia stored their bags temporarily in her room once she and her brother had settled in. For the first time ever, and perhaps the last, Ethan, Katie, Christian and Talia all ate together at the hotel restaurant. The restaurant consisted of the top two floors of the building, which had been specially modified to complete a panoramic rotation of the city every two hours.

Conversation was light between them. When they were finished with their dinners, it was time for Christian and Talia to depart for the academy. After the four of them briefly returned to grab Christian and Talia's bags, Christian led them over to a staircase that would take them to the roof. They ascended the stairs and then came to a ladder that had a hatch at the top of it. It had been left unlocked for their use.

Christian swung his bulky duffle bag over his back, and then he climbed up the ladder, opened the hatch, and stepped out onto the roof, walking out of sight a moment later. Katie heard Sovereign screech the moment he did, and it made her smile. Katie climbed up onto the roof after Talia and her brother. When Katie got up onto the roof, it was so windy she was almost afraid she would blow off.

When she looked across the square portion of the roof, she saw that it had a large open square for taking off, and stables had been erected with heating lamps and tanks of fish to eat for five

Eedon Rath-ni. In fact, all five stalls were full. Katie saw Violet and Sovereign underneath one stable with two stalls, and another two ravens and a hawk she didn't recognize in the stalls of the other stable. "Ahh, I see Ruth, Schenn, and Fantaine have already arrived. Ethan and Katie, you may want to go about fraternizing with some of your new classmates, while you have the time. As I understand it the complex of bars, clubs, lounges, eateries, and venues is an extremely popular destination to spend a few nights before making your way to Meinghelia City," Christian told them. "But be warned, not all of the venues in the complex will allow just anyone in or are so easy to get into. There're ways to figure out how to get in, of course, for regular people; but I don't think you two with your burgeoning abilities should have much trouble."

Ethan and Katie both looked at each other intrigued by that suggestion. Christian had already ushered Anacarin and Embar into formation toward the range of mountains that rose on the horizon and positioned them to follow the river that became narrower the farther it went from the city. Christian dropped his duffle bag in front of Anacarin, who took it with one of her talons, while Talia did the same with Embar. Christian and Talia had something to say to her and Ethan before they left.

"When you both rescued yourselves and then joined us on this journey, I told you we would only take you this far. I now leave the choice to come train at the academy with us—beginning on the first day of fall—up to each of you. Think long and hard before you make that choice, because there will be no going back afterward. A life at the academy will show you the true meaning of challenge, struggle, persistence, and strength. You look death in the eyes, and if you do not meet its gaze with one of your own more powerful, in turn, you'll be taken by it," Christian told them.

"If you decide not to come, then you each have your rooms until the first day of fall. Get jobs and live out the rest of your days here in Maravinya. There are papers of citizenship for each of you in your rooms, as well as a resistance passport. Live out the rest of your days in peace, until the war comes for us all—as it surely will," Talia told them.

Katie hugged Talia first, while Ethan and Christian shook hands. When Katie shook Christian's hand, she tried her best to grip his hand firmer than he hers. She still lost.

Christian and Talia waved and then took off. With just a few flaps from both Anacarin and Embar, they were soon out of sight, and Katie walked over to the stables that had been erected for visiting Dravens with Eedon Rath-ni. While the sky began to grow dark, Katie took some time to admire Sovereign and take care of some knots in his feathers. She picked up one of the brushes next to the combs and began to run it over him.

Thank you, Sovereign said while he eyed her. There was an open tank of aashing fish next to both Violet and Sovereign, and they perched underneath an awning that had just enough space for them to comfortably fit within. Several heating lamps were positioned there to help keep them warm during the night. Sovereign eyed one of the aashings, and then he wryly wriggled his neck into the tank and plucked one out with his beak. Such an action made Katie laugh. When she looked over at Ethan who was also brushing Violet, Katie saw Violet lift one out of the tank and into her mouth while her eyes glowed blue.

"Christian's right you know," Katie told her brother. Katie stroked Sovereign's feathers once more and then patted him on one of his wings three times. "We ought to get out and see the city.

We've come all this way and done nothing particularly fun since... well, you know."

Ethan exhaled, put down the comb he had been running through Violet, and looked up at her. He seemed tense. "No, you're right," he told her. "An hour and we'll go out to a dance club?"

"Sure," she agreed. They both said goodbye to their Eedon Rath-ni with a bow and a hug, and then they each returned to their rooms to shower and dress up.

When Katie was finished showering, she curled her hair and fixed up her eyelashes, then she put on a light base of make-up, figuring it might be a while before she got to look that nice again.

Christian had spared no expense when he had given them the option to survive on their own if they wished. Along with their passports and citizenship papers, Christian had also left her a new smartphone and opened an account for her with $10,000 in it. She could only assume that Talia had done the same for her brother.

Several outfits had also been placed in her closet at some point between arriving and now. She wasn't a fan of whoever's sense of fashion had put these outfits together, but they would have to do for the night. Katie pulled on a nice pair of light blue jeans and a tight black halter top. The clothes accentuated her curves; she wanted to impress. She was going out to a club after all—and meeting new people. Katie liked that.

Katie grabbed her room key off her dresser and left the room. She listened to the door close behind her, and then she waited for an elevator down the hall. One arrived a moment later. When Katie finally left the elevator, after having to let a gaggle of Maravinyian tourists off in front of her, Ethan looked relaxed and happy to see her. Before heading out into the night, Katie suggested that they each make a small purchase with their new cards to make sure they worked. There was a gift shop in the lobby of the hotel. Katie brought herself a Draxion City Whalers Dargen cap, and Ethan bought himself a pair of frayed gloves with finger openings.

"Rad," he said, looking at her hat. He held up his gloved hands in front of her.

"Wizard," she told him, pointing to her cap.

After both of their purchases went through without fail, they left the hotel and set about the city. Thankfully, like Christian had suggested, the bustling complex of clubs, venues, eateries, and lounges was only a handful of blocks away, easily seeable from street level, as it all rose a dozen stories into the air, with apartment and offices above.

Ethan and Katie giddily walked up to a directory and decided they would each pick one venue to visit, and then they could each go their separate ways, or go back to the hotel for the night. Ethan selected *The Veralin Lounge*, which was up several floors and over-looked the bay. The two of them climbed the staircases to get to the lounge and then stopped not too far from the door to get in.

When they approached the door, Katie saw Ethan's eyes turn violet. "What is it?" she asked him. "Do you think this is one of the particular places Christian referenced?"

Ethan surveyed the venue. The outside of it was a brick façade with a patio dining area, with wide-open widow doors to which Ethan could see the inside of a sports bar with not a lot of open space, thanks to overcrowding. Ethan could also see that the major-ity of the TVs were showing the ending of a thrilling Dargen game between Raegic and Dig'la Teur. Raegic was leading by 4 with just a few minutes to go. There was also a long line to get in at the front door, but Ethan told her he saw a side entrance. He pointed it out to her, and sure enough, there was a side entrance with a couple of people randomly milling about. Some were in pairs or threesomes. One pair stumbled up to a black-clad door on the side. A slit near the top slid open, and they both heard the couple say something before they were admitted inside a moment later. Katie couldn't hear what they had said, but Ethan had overheard it with his magic.

Ethan smiled at her and said, "C'mon, let's go.

"What's the passphrase?" Ethan was asked when he stepped in front of the door. Katie could see a pair of brown eyes behind the open slit on the door.

"Get it, Bombhead!" Ethan said, out loud.

Katie had a question, "What does that mean?"

When they came out of the hallway, which contained access to the kitchens and bathrooms, Katie quickly discovered they had entered a speakeasy. There weren't many people around, perhaps three dozen in the whole venue, including the employees, but conversation was light, the venue was lit by many candles, and there was cigar smoke, live music, and revelry. Katie certainly couldn't see any other pairs of glowing eyes amongst the crowd yet.

The two of them each ordered a glass Repanòs Whiskey and a Cárlales Escapaño cigar while they enjoyed themselves in the lounge. They would stay for an hour. The two of them went off by themselves for a little while, and while Ethan went to go finish his cigar outside, Katie stayed inside and attempted to observe some of the patrons without attracting too much attention to herself. There was something about this one young patron with dyed gray hair. She was only a few years older about herself, but something about her high cheekbones reminded her of someone else famous she had once heard of. However, her face did not look familiar, and even when they both made eye contact for a brief second, they both just looked away embarrassed a moment later.

Several minutes later, Ethan met back up with her. They were both ready to leave the lounge. The two of them went back outside and Katie found another directory of the complex, then looked it over. *There* was a club named *Stenatos*. Katie could already see the line waiting to get into it winding out of the complex several stories down, and it was moving relatively quickly. "That's my choice," she said pointing it out to Ethan.

"Fair enough," he told her.

The two of them quickly figured out that *Stenatos* was another difficult venue to get into. However, there was clearly no side entrance to the dance club, and all its anxious patrons were lined up in a queue outside, so it was obviously not another speakeasy. However, what Katie did see outside the entrance determining who could get in was a test of strength. Groups were admitted by a determining factor of whether or not one representative from each party kick an oblong Dargenball through uprights, which had been erected, from 20 yards away. The two of them got into line and waited for their turn.

When they were close, Ethan pointed out a party of three, each with glowing eyes. The group of three selected a tall black girl, Ethan's age with blue eyes. She stepped up onto a strip of turf in provided in front of the uprights. She was offered a pair of cleats to put on, but she declined. The black girl simply walked up to the location to kick from, with the Dargenball in hand, and then pretended to punt the ball.

The black girl held the ball out vertically in front of her, and then let it drop to where she would have kicked it, if she had moved her leg at all. Instead, Ethan noticed that her eyes had turned ruby red, and watched the ball go tumbling end over end through the center of the uprights. Their party was admitted without contest. "They look like fellow students to me," Ethan told her.

"We should talk to them when we get in," she told him. Since Ethan had gotten them into the speakeasy, it was clearly her turn to get them into the dance club.

Katie also declined the pair of cleats offered to her, already feeling right at home in her sneakers. Katie had practiced punting Dargenballs a few times in her life. She had no trouble punting the ball through the uprights as well. The two of them were admitted, and they quickly ended up finding the table the black girl with glowing blue eyes and her two friends had gone to.

The two of them quickly ambled over to the party around a tall round-top table and introduced themselves, breaking the ice. "Ethan, you say your name is? It's a pleasure to meet you," the black girl, now with ruby red eyes told her brother. "I'm Ruth," she said.

Ethan smiled at her and failed his first test at fitting in with Maravinyians—or at least Maravinyian women. Maravinyians did not shake hands, they offered their palms to each other—one to place on top of another for just a few seconds. A tall, slender man looking around thirty stood next to Ruth. He began to giggle to himself, "You must not be from around here, friend. And who is this" he asked Katie.

Katie placed her hand over the table, palm up, and said, "I'm Katie. Sorry for my brother. We're still getting used to all the customs, you know. Just arrived here from Raegic." Katie was trying to disguise her accent like someone who had learned Maravinyian growing up on the crime-ridden streets of the politically corrupt city.

"Schenn," said the man with olive skin. He smiled at them, and several wrinkles appeared on his face.

The last of the strangers arrived at the table. "No, I don't think that's it at all. I recognize an accent like that without mistake. They're from Imperium Aendor. Never fear, Ethan and Katie. You have nothing to fear from us. I'm Fantaine," said a frizzy blonde-haired girl with a curvaceous body. "I only know because my father is high in Resistance command and had strong suspicions that Christian embarked on his journey through the Shrouded Sea for more reasons than one."

"Well, Fantaine," said Ruth as she pulled back a strand of her hair and then opened up her purse which she had been holding in her hands before, "a bet is a bet." Ruth handed Fantaine ₳ 50 and then stowed her purse away again.

"There must be quite a story behind getting recruited by Christian within the heart of Iishrem, Imperium Aendor. The three of us could probably learn a few things from you," Schenn postured.

Several rounds of beers and shots were ordered by the group over the next two hours and there were several extended sessions of dancing. Both Ethan and Katie had many things to tell. "So, you both *are* going to the academy for training on the first day of fall, right?" Ruth asked them. Katie thought of Sovereign at that moment, and somehow, she knew that Sovereign was thinking of her too.

"Sure am!" Katie exclaimed with a smile.

"Of course!" Ethan said in competitive spirit.

They paid their tabs and headed towards the exit. It seemed to Katie like the five of them were going to be great friends.

Chapter 31

The Egg (Brian 8)

FARLIN-TAL NIAI, HAISHA, ALLIREHEM

SUMMER, 1153, FOURTH AGE

rian would take no chances of anyone in the Frantelli crime family following him or trying to kill him again, so he and Alyisay flew directly northeast without delay. They would arrive in Zapfhreon after a two-hour flight. They'd spend the night there.

So, what is it that's so important about this particular egg that it would have ever been entrusted to you in the first place? Especially if it was a known fact that you could crack or shatter it at any moment? Also, how did you get it to the jungle village, and how did you communicate with them? Brian asked her, hoping that she would quickly decide to answer all his questions and tell him everything. Brian quickly found out that such was simply not meant to be. Not with Alyisay.

Woah, you cut right to the chase, don't you? Alyisay thought in his head, reprehending him. She craned her neck all the way around to look at him while she continued to fly onward. Then she gave him an inquisitive look by squinting her eye at him, as if she were staring into his very pores. Brian seethed and pouted when she turned around and did not answer all his questions.

She did allow him a few facts. *It is perfectly possible for me to protect the egg by myself, at least for a short time. It's just not a long-term solution,* Alyisay began to tell him. The sun had long ago set in the distance, and Brian thought he would enjoy a long night's sleep when they arrived in Zapfhreon. *You may not know it, but there are ways for man and Eedon Rath-ni to communicate with each other without being connected. Old ways; esoteric ways. You see the uncontacted tribe I had protecting my egg was one of the last such in the world. They had never quite lost their faith in the Eedon Rath-ni in our large-scale absence of over a thousand years. My protection and my faith in them were a gift, but I failed them; now a man who hunts me holds what's dearest to me.*

Yes, I know, but why is that? Brian pressured her, trying not to be deterred by her balking at his earlier string of questions.

It's an egg I've been tasked with protecting until the time comes for it to hatch. We recover it, it goes to the academy, and it's no longer your problem. Then you've got my loyalty for the rest of time, Alyisay explained to him in his head. When he harrumphed out loud, she could tell he was not quite satisfied with her answer. *Look, if you can recover this egg for me then I'll owe you the truth one day. Until then, perhaps it's better that you do not know the potential impact of failure.*

Very well, Brian told her while he gritted his teeth.

He was not cold while he rode on top of Alyisay. Once he sat on her, he noticed that her scales around where he sat began to warm him. When Brian and Alyisay passed through Zapfhreon the city, they flew high above it without stopping. Brian couldn't see much of the city other than the street lamps and car lights on the roads below. One thing Brian did notice was that the buildings were remarkably short and spaced far apart, considering the amount of open space and people living in suburbs around the city he saw. He wasn't quite sure what to make of that. *What a polarizing population density*, he thought.

Several minutes later, the two of them began to descend in search of a roadside motel where, hopefully, their presence wouldn't attract much attention. Perhaps they could even work their presence to their advantage. Brian spotted a long, straight, thin route that led out of the city and was sparsely lit by cars. *Let's follow that road there*, Brian told Alyisay.

Once they were close enough, Brian was able to make out a roadside sign for a nice hotel several stories tall. It appeared to be the nicest one around. Brian flew right past that one, and they continued for another two minutes or so before landing at a roadside motel which looked like it had seen its prime around fifty years ago. The roadside neon vacancy sign was even malfunctioning, but Brian saw only three cars parked around three separate one-story motel buildings. The night manager of the motel stormed out of the motel lobby and charged right up to him before he had much of a chance to look around any further. Brian just wanted to rest; he didn't want any trouble.

Brian did not understand the artful, subtle language of Zapfreni, but he did recognize the universal language of 'Please don't kill me or burn down my motel!' The night manager of the hotel—a portly woman with frayed brown hair, crow's feet, and light brown skin with freckles—grabbed at his arm and tried to stay directly in front of him while Alyisay sneered at her and twisted her neck for a better angle if things got violent.

Ought I to just dispense with this one, Brian? Alyisay asked him. He was so tired, that Brian half-considered her proposition, if only for a moment. He did not respond to her directly, trusting that his precedent set with Fray'la earlier in the day would stand for how he wanted engagements to go from now on. Brian saw a sign in the window of the motel. Even if he couldn't understand Zapfreni, he could still read a sign on the door for the price of a room for a week. It was ᴁ 250.

Brian reached into his wallet. Fray'la had lightly filled his pockets, while he had briefly worked for her as an extra investment towards his ability to succeed—beyond his own expertise and desire to leave the shores of Galliem. Brian reached into his wallet and withdrew ᴁ 100, then said out loud, "One night?" in Gallaeic.

As soon as Brian spoke in Gallaeic, the night clerk snapped out of her frantic pleas and spoke softly in broken Gallaeic. "It's your dragon, right? It protects my motel while you stay; you sleeping free," she told him. She pushed his hand back over to him when he tried to extend her the money. She began to walk off, away from Alyisay, and then she called on him to follow her into the lobby with a wave of her hand.

Brian followed her and then turned back to look at Alyisay while he continued to walk towards the motel lobby backward. *Just go rest over there*, Brian thought to her, looking at a large clearing in the parking lot. When the night manager brought Brian into the motel lobby, it was dimly lit and looked peaceful. It had two padded high-back chairs which sat next to a short table of breakfast appliances including a toaster and a bagel slicer.

The night clerk went behind her desk and began to check him in on her computer. Brian asked for a room in the wing of the motel that Alyisay had flown over to. She gave him the key for room 24.

"There are Iiasmaeic troops in the area, and our army is slow and incompetent. Come back anytime," she told him and then sent him on his way.

"Thank you," Brian said and then left the lobby. He walked over to room 24 and looked in the window and found it to be exactly what he expected. A comfy bed and clean room, which just didn't look particularly appealing. Such was perfect for him. Brian stuck his key into the door and twisted it open, then said he good night to Alyisay before he went inside.

See you in the morning, my rider, she told him.

Brian smiled at her and slept well that night. When he woke in the morning, he showered and took his only outfit of clothes to the laundry machines that were offered in the back room of the main office. He had to walk there in just his towel and some shower slippers.

"Good morning," said the same manager from the night shift. "Ha-ha, ohh."

She eyed his slender, almost naked body and did not complain while he walked right past her and into the laundry room. She followed him in and paid for his load with a laundry token.

"Thank you," Brian told her. He didn't mind that she was eyeing him. She reminded him a little of Macie, and somehow, that brought a short grin to his face. "Did you have any trouble last night?"

"I listen to their movements on a radio. Sounds like they spotted your dragon moving in for the night and buggered out of the region. Might even give our shitty army a chance to fortify their positions," she told him. Brian manipulated the laundry machine to wash and dry his clothes in the right way, then he walked back out to the lobby to grab himself some breakfast. He sliced a bagel, toasted it, and then covered it with cream cheese. He also scooped up some scrambled eggs and bacon onto a plate.

Brian turned to go, but the manager caught his attention, one last time. "Next time you come back maybe stay a bit longer, I'll serve you lunch," she told him, toying with a curl of her hair while she stared at his groin.

Brian grinned and humored her. "I'd be happy to let you ride my dragon by then," he told her, and then he returned to his room to wait out his load of laundry. In the meantime, he ate his breakfast.

How is it I ever got stuck with a bum that has no home and only one set of clothes? Alyisay questioned him as he ate his breakfast.

I'm an outlaw, Brian told her.

And I am a dragon, she told him. *An Eedon Rath-ni like no other.*

Brian finished waiting out his laundry by watching the news and taking in some of the ads. *Population in Illias swells amid sporadic skirmishes in Haishian hinterlands. Want to deter your home from Draven or Eedon Rath-ni attacks? Buy the Zòrnentná X9000 homestead missile defense system. Guaranteed to deter even dragons or alligators.* Brian would have to take the ad he was watching at their word for that last claim.

An hour later, when Brian's laundry was finished, he returned to the hotel lobby still wearing only his towel. There was a new manager there, but thankfully she had already been briefed by the last one why there was an orange dragon waiting in the parking lot—and a man with orange hair walking around the lobby in just a towel. Brian retrieved his clothes and put them on back in his room. He then checked out of the motel. He was ready to get on his way to Northeastern Haisha, so he could get to work on figuring out how to retrieve Alyisay's egg for her.

The two of them took off towards where Alyisay claimed the man, Gi'les, was waiting for her to strike at him. It was somewhere far in the northeast corner of Haisha, where a cruiser group waited for the man to collect his trophy and leave. Once Gi'les had claimed Alyisay's head as his trophy, he would apparently embark on a journey back to Taerit to sell the egg to the House of Lance, but the two of them could not let that happen. Brian preferred, if possible, that they kill Gi'les in the process as well.

When the two flew above the dense jungle of Haisha, Alyisay followed the course of a river before descending. *What're we doing, Alyisay?* Brian asked.

Alyisay flew just a few feet above the peaceful river, which was surrounded by the jungle. Brian looked into the lush jungle and saw signs of men. Not men of material wealth, but just simple men, living in a simple society. *It's nice down here you know. Peaceful. No one bothered me if I didn't bother them. We were even able to live together for quite a while. In harmony,* Alyisay told him. *But soon there will not be any places like this left in the world.*

Alyisay pulled back up into the air and began to crab her flight towards a solitary mountain in the distance. When they got closer, Brian was able to see that what they flew towards wasn't a mountain at all. Instead, it was a hollowed-out, archaic volcano. Alyisay flew them directly over it, and Brian was able to look over her neck and into the cavernous volcano below. *This was my lair once, and there was my village.* Brian felt his eyes turn tiger yellow, and his vision snapped to exactly what Alyisay wanted him to see. A mark on the jungle.

Brian saw a clearing in the jungle with the charred remains of a village. The farther Brian looked out into the forest, the more brands he saw on the jungle floor. They almost looked like they were ripples on a pond. One day the entire jungle could be one contiguous ripple if Iishrem rained hard enough. They flew on through the jungle and passed out of it shortly after noon. North

of the great jungle of Haisha was the hinterland plains and grass-
lands—a land where people survived off their own passion, persistence, or craft. Lawlessness and tribalism were rampant; there
was such little national unity in Haisha. Often, troops from Iishrem
would bypass the plainlands entirely and head for the potential
riches of the jungle.

The density of the jungle and the mountains that surrounded it
would keep cities like Illias safe for a time—at least until Iishrem
got its northern fleets into shape. Farlin-tal Niai stood in the
middle of a largescale grassland's region, with very few suburban
offshoots. In terms of Haishian infrastructure, Haisha's hodge-
podge geographical features lacked the unifying characteristics to
make the country whole. The Zapfreni region in the south was
cut off from the rest of the country by mountains. It often postured on independence or rebellion and acted with the mentality
of a little brother with a chip on their shoulder. Illias had become
one of the most economically diverse and powerful port cities in
the world because of being boxed in against sharp mountains and
dense jungles.

Tribes still in the jungle had been left historically *uncontacted*,
and the northern plain regions kept to themselves. There was one
single metropolitan corridor that forged its way across the entire
country—from Zapfhreon to Illias—and then it spindled its way
into the jungle like a solitary lightning strike on an otherwise
peaceful, clear night. If viewed from high above, which Brian was
just beginning to do, the highway looked like it just barely penetrated the northern grassland region, before slowly building back
up again into a city. Alyisay and Brian flew past all of that and
landed near to the coast, in a region of Haisha that was unpopu-
lated almost entirely before the beginning of the war. Now it was

rife with Iishrem troops, and the only native population in the area was not incredibly quick to violence over land and resources they had no use for anyway.

Brian suddenly felt Alyisay snap his vision into place again, showing him exactly what she wanted to. The Iiasmaeic cruiser group loitering off the coast like it was out of place, even during a wartime invasion and occupation. *We're close*, Alyisay told him.

Alyisay took him down to the roof of the forest below and then told Brian to do something he was not entirely ready for. *Duck down and hold on*, she told him.

What? Brian thought. He barely had time to react as Alyisay plunged into the trees. She did not shoot any fire, and her body began to harden around Brian so that they could crush through the trees during their crash. Brian felt himself jostled all over the place, but Alyisay turned her wings in around him and swaddled him like a kangaroo's pouch. It was at that moment that Brian finally knew exactly what was going to happen and how it was all going to play out. All there was to do now was to just let it all happen.

Brian felt his eyes turn tiger yellow, and by the time their bodies came to a skidding halt, ending their crash, he was already a tiger. *I've never felt this alive before.* He stood and looked across the lightly decimated forest around them, looking first directly toward the coast to see if they had attracted enemy attention.

The base Gi'les protected himself inside was designed like one that had meant to be temporary. One which had long since become too cramped and congested to protect anything valuable—like an egg. If Alyisay had attacked directly, it would have gone terribly for all three parties involved.

Alyisay perched in front of him, hidden within the forest. The two of them looked out toward the base together. By the time they did, suspicions were arising, and troop movements within the base were beginning to click into action with the marching beat of boots on the ground and rifles drawn in the air, waiting to be fired.

This is where we part, Brian, Alyisay told him. *If we should come out successful on the other side of this, I'd be happy to be your dragon for the rest of our lives together. What do you say?* Alyisay asked him.

He felt his eyes narrow. *Sounds perfect, I am going to show you exactly what I can do,* he told her. Brian inhaled from as deep down in his body as he could, then he roared.

Chapter 32
First Flight (Ethan 8)

DRAXION CITY, MARAVINYA, ALLIREHEM

SUMMER, 1153, FOURTH AGE

After a few more days of touring the region around Draxion City, it was quite exciting to Ethan to know that he was going to make his first flight to the academy, with a small band of his new friends. He quickly found out that their flight there would be far from the first anywhere for Ruth, Fantaine, and Schenn. That fact made Ethan much more comfortable when he woke up thinking about it. His day began with him standing at Katie's door, using his magic to make Katie think someone was knocking on her door until she was forced to open it. This revealed that she had brought some Maravinyian hunk back to the hotel the night before. Off one of the mirrors in the room, Ethan saw a thick, white male ass with the rest of a naked body sprawled out across the bed.

She stood at the door in front of him with her golden eyes and looked at him spitefully. "What is it you want?" Katie's harsh voice pulled him back to attention.

"The party is raring to go within ninety minutes. Are you going to get rid of your piece of ass and join us, or are you going to fly to the academy by yourself?" Ethan asked her. He had been quite adamant about her curtailing some of her more zestful foreign activity over the last few nights while she partied it up. Now Ethan felt like she had gone and jeopardized their entire cover within this city as they waited to make their flight to the academy. *I can't understand how it is she's so confident in her abilities to fit in,* Ethan thought to Violet.

Ehh... well, you know, Ethan. Your sister's always been very direct and to the point. Always able to get what she wants—despite whether or not it actually means anything to her, Violet told him.

Katie brought her hands up to her face and pulled her eyes down. It looked like she was attempting to stifle herself from lashing out at him for invading her privacy. Katie succeeded, but her tone with him was sharp, and she sounded quite exasperated.

"Yes, I'll be there. Now get out of my face," Katie told him. She shut the door to her room with a bang. Ethan shrugged his shoulders and walked back to his room. When he got there, there was a text waiting for him on his phone from Ruth. *Want to try out some real moves before we have a long, straight, boring flight?*

When Ethan arrived at her room several minutes later, Ruth opened the door to greet him wearing jeans and a sizeable gray sports bra.

When Ruth opened the door in front of him in such attire, it was obvious to him she wasn't ready for him to be there. Ethan did his level best not to take any subtle glances at her bodice. "Yes," Ethan told her. "I would love it if you could show me some real flight moves, before a long, straight, boring flight to a place we already know we're going to."

Ruth said nothing, playfully putting her hands on his chest, gripping his shirt, and pulling him into the room with her. "Get the door," she told him, before she turned away from him to get a loose, long-sleeved T-shirt to put on. Ethan kicked the door closed with the back of his boot, and then took his one chance to admire her bare back and round ass while she walked away. By the time Ruth had turned back around to him, Ethan had finished his observation, and he turned his vision towards her computer browser. Ethan began to wonder if there was any safe-space he could be looking without possibly giving off the wrong impression, but he wanted to be there in the room with Ruth, and she had let him in, then not said a damn thing about anything yet.

"Do you want a beer and to watch TV or something while I finish up?" Ruth asked him, with an inquisitive tone and eyeing glance. He nodded, then said nothing. Ethan lay down and put his head back against her bed frame. She dug into the mini-fridge in the corner of the room and tossed him a can, which he caught. Ethan popped open the can of beer and it fizzed and threatened to overflow, so he had to start drinking it quickly—too quickly it seemed, and Ethan spat up a little of it, to Ruth's laughter. Ethan sat up and smiled at her, then he raised his beer. Ruth gave him a quick look over, then grinned and went into the bathroom. A few moments later, Ethan felt his eyes glow violet. He wondered if Ruth's were glowing ruby red as well.

Are we going to fly soon? Violet thought in his mind, with a snare in her voice.

It was a relief to Ethan when Ruth came out of the bathroom wearing a Dargen cap for the Farlin Tail-Niai Rangers Dargen team. The two of them were now ready to go. Ruth led Ethan out of her room and let the door close behind them. They walked to the elevator bay without a word, while they each postured on some piece of potential flying advice to the other.

When they reached the roof, they found Violet and Ruth's raven, Wraith-wen Al, already saddled up and ready to fly. The hotel had a renowned Eedon Rath-ni handler on call, and he had visited last night.

The mortality rate of such a career over a twenty-year span is about 4%, so says the deathly market, Violet informed him. Ethan wondered how she knew that. *It's a raven thing. They don't call a flock of us a conspiracy for no reason.*

The wind blew through Ethan's hair and percolated through the frayed cotton of his gloves. He would have been afraid to lose a hat he valued riding Violet, but somehow, he figured that Ruth had probably taken *enough* precautions to keep hers around throughout their ride.

The pair hopped onto their birds and took them on a ride through the city. A spire which looked like a twisting cathedral of deathly sorts stared at Ethan and Ruth from the horizon. The actual Deathly Market which they were currently flying towards was, of course, made of actual material. It just happened to rise and swirl up, out above the rest of the city, with several spindly fissures made of material that looked quite ethereal.

"What is this place?" Ethan asked Ruth, not knowing if she would actually know any better than him. Before they got there, Ruth was 25 feet in front of him to the northeast. She turned back to him and said, "A gateway into Hedeth'rehem herself. A place where the living go to bet on the ways others will die. Drowning has great odds, in the wake of the assault on Minon Cromella. Disintegration is trending up in Ferrum."

Ethan looked below and saw hordes of people heading through the tall arched doors. "What happens there? What is it like?"

Ruth took a grimmer tone. "Well, some people call it a ladder, others a tunnel. A place of all your fears and your dead relatives left behind. You'll find anything you want there or nothing at all.

"How dark," Ethan told her.

"But that's why we're not going inside, Ethan. Don't worry; it can't hurt you unless you walk in the front doors. Just follow my moves and try not to hit it. Flying is a dance, Ethan. When we go into combat, it will become vastly different. Try to follow my moves and path."

Her flight path wrapped its way around the closest fissure in a counterclockwise loop. While Ethan watched her, he could see pedestrians on the city level watching her flight with passing interest. When Ruth approached the bottom of that fissure, she shot herself around the outside of it, and then she dove back into the spaces between the Deathly Market.

The Deathly Market had a central tower that rose out of the ground like a spire. The other fissures all came directly out of that, which curved and spiraled around it somewhat like an octopus. Ruth continued her intricate flight with an aileron roll as she passed in between two fissures pitched at a ninety-degree angle. All the while, she rode low to Wraith-wen Al's back.

Ethan flew Violet in motion around the back side of the market so he could continue to watch Ruth's maneuvers. She continued through the two fissures, then she performed a half loop upwards into the air and had Wraith-wen Al correct their inversion. Then, to cap it all off, she did a full loop and followed that into a steep descent, spiraling counterclockwise. Ruth pulled up just before she would have flown into one of the fissures, and then she had her raven extend his wings fully over the extent of the same one.

When Ruth finished her flight back over to him, she had an expectant look on her face, waiting to see what the two of them could do. *Alright, Ethan,* Violet told him. *Let's show this potential mate of yours what we can do.*

What? he thought in his mind, that was off-putting at a moment like this. Ethan felt his eyes turn violet, and he saw the peripherals of his vision begin to fade black. Violet flew him towards the Deathly Market with several flaps of her wings, and then she began to repeat the flight pattern that Wraith-wen Al had taken. When Violet flipped him inverted over the top of the first spire, the vision of it looked like his dreams.

Ethan began to stare into the material of the building itself. When he investigated the grey, beige, brown, and black-looking ethereal material, Ethan began to see faces. Violet flew too quickly for Ethan to get a good enough look at any one face, but he might have recognized some if he had. Ethan didn't need to help Violet repeat Wraith-wen Al's flight pattern as long as it wasn't too intricate. When Violet completed her aileron roll through the same two fissures, Ethan looked down at the city and saw people recording him. He smiled at them for a moment while Violet pitched him through the fissures at a two hundred and seventy-degree orientation, instead of a ninety-degree one.

Violet had to take several more flaps than Wraith-wen Al to correct her inversion after her half-loop. When Ethan felt fully inverted again at the halfway point of their full loop into a steep descent, he began to scream his ass off. Ethan put his hands up in the air and pressed his thighs to Violet's saddle while he screamed, laughed, and flew.

When Ethan was finished and had grouped back up with Ruth, it was time for them to head back to the hotel so they could check out and fly out with the rest of their party. As Ethan was jogging back towards his hotel room door, he saw the boy Katie had brought back with her that night finally walking away from her door and down the hall. Ethan pressed his room card into the card reader and opened his door a few seconds later when the indicator on the door had flashed green twice.

There was not much to pack, and Ethan looked forward to getting settled in at Meinghelia City with three days to spare before the beginning of fall term. He put on a loose hoodie that would help keep him warm during his flight. He had purchased it from the hotel lobby two nights ago. When Ethan was finished packing, he checked out of the hotel by inserting his room card into a chute for them on the wall. There was nothing else to do after that but climb to the roof.

When he reached the top of the hotel with his duffel bag full of his belongings, Schenn, Fantaine, and Ruth were already waiting for the two of them to arrive. The four of them and the five Eedon Rath-ni would continue to wait for Katie for a while longer. When Katie finally emerged onto the roof in the tightest fitting jacket that Ethan had ever seen, it was finally time to go. The five Eedon Rath-ni had lined up in an arrow formation. Schenn would lead the way, with Fantaine and Ruth behind to the right and left, and then Ethan and Katie would be behind each of them.

Just before they took off, Fantaine stepped off her raven and grabbed her wand off her saddle. Her eyes turned yellow, and then a second later, 4 yellow sparks shot out the end of her wand and hit each of them in the chest. Ethan felt a cool windy feeling sweep over his body, and then he looked down and saw a few golden stars dimming back to nothingness over his arms. When Ethan touched his arms, he felt something jelly on his skin, but he could see nothing there. All the same, he felt much stronger.

"Shields," Fantaine told the two of them. "For confrontations, you know. They won't last forever, but we'll make it to the academy with them, and then you'll learn how to produce your own soon after."

Their formation took off and headed for the mouth of the river at a descent of about ten degrees. When they pulled up to the brim of it, they were quickly approaching the edge of the city. "Hold firm!" Schenn boomed from out front of them. "There's something coming. Something that deigns to be seen." Ethan watched him abjectly wave his arm about the sky as a thick storm cloud formed above them. In the overcast early afternoon, the city cast a chrome overtone over the entire scene. The clouds pulled in together around them and spun a tendril out to reach them like the one Ethan had flown into on the back of Anacarin once long ago. But this one meant to hunt their flight and knock them to a fall if possible.

"Look about the water!" Fantaine yelled to the group from ahead. Ethan obliged and looked down into the murky water. While the river was certainly water, Ethan saw a murky substance that lurked below, which was not quite the same as the ghostly ethereal building material he had witnessed at the Deathly Market earlier in the day. This substance looked like it was thick enough to hide something from view completely, unless something was so bold as to come above the surface.

Ethan studied the water long enough to see that something was approaching. Suddenly, a pack of silvery animals with the bodies of dolphins, faces like apes, and wings like that of a snow owl over their fins came ascending out of the water. In an arching motion, Ethan saw them leap out of the water and ascend into the sky only narrowly clearing the immediate flight path of the entire group.

"Oh wow, what're those?" Katie asked immediately, crouching down as close as she could to Sovereign's back soon after.

"Grimadorphes," said Ruth pointing to the gray creatures that flew out of the water and into the cloud tendril that was approaching them from above. Ethan saw approximately five of them, but perhaps there was a sixth he had glazed over in the spectacle of them bounding out of the water.

The animals looked to have a scroll attached to one of their wings, while an extended feather on the other looked as if it was used as a quill. The leader of the cast of grimadorphes gathered his band into what resembled a jagged sword, which then plunged itself into the depths of the storm, dispersing it immediately. When the clouds had cleared and the scene had settled, the grimadorphes, and all their silvery nature, were nowhere to be seen. They flew on.

When their group was entirely out of the city, they continued above the thinning river, while mountains approached in the distance. A handful of them had summer snow coating their peaks. As Ethan began to pass directly over the range of mountains on Violet, he got this feeling from over her shoulder that someone was stalking him, but when he turned around there was no one behind him. Just the open sky. She ignored it. Suburban towns were mostly around them, with some solid tree cover, and a single railroad made its way into the mountains along the riverside. A massive forest rose beyond the mountains and spread around them, and mining towns with irrigation access for shipping their goods into Draxion City via the river were dotted between the branches.

For miles, Ethan could look down to the river and see multiple thin, flat riverboats shipping various materials. The farther their group flew past the mountains and up the river, the fewer riverboats that there were. The population of Maravinya was thinner here. Where there were towns, they looked more like large homesteads, which had been carved out of the forest. Roads from those towns led back out to a regional freeway, which generally followed the river back towards the mountains, crossing it in several locations.

When the freeway they followed thinned out and combined into a single two direction road with space for three lanes, Ethan had a feeling that their group was getting close. There it was again, that feeling of being watched. This time when Ethan looked behind himself, he could see Katie but no one else. She nodded at him, then said nothing else. Schenn had led them at a rapid pace towards Meinghelia City, not allowing much time for dallying if they were each going to keep up. The moment when Ethan could finally begin to see a town of brick buildings sloped on the side of a hill where the river's path curved from running north to east, he knew something was different for each of them.

Ruth was a first-year student like himself and Katie. The sun began to set in the west as their formation approached the town from the south. She had long ago put on fashionable sunglasses with black and brown oblong shades that went far above the top and bottom of her eyes. Ethan thought they had looked a little bit ridiculous when she had put them on, but he had seen several other Maravinyian youths wearing similar ones over the last few days.

Ethan quickly got bored of flying all the way at the back as they got close, so he flew up into the middle of Ruth and Fantaine. Sovereign squawked at Ethan when he did that, which forced him to look back. Katie gave him a nervous glance as if to tell him not to forget about her. Ethan didn't plan on forgetting about his sister, but first, he wanted to watch Fantaine look at several points of interest that approached them in the city. When Fantaine began to do that, Ethan couldn't help himself from noticing her voluptuous curves for just a few seconds that he savored.

Schenn began to sing a melodic tune on his hawk, just loudly enough that Ethan could hear it. "Winding riv-errrr, Maravin-yaaaa. Mountains rising, whispers from the Shrou-ded Sea-eee. Though the pines there, a town of brick on the rive-aaa, full of magic and some Eedon Rath-niiii. We fly on-nnnn, to our home." Schenn paused. "Little mountain. Meinghelia City-yyyy. Maravin-yaaaa! Wind-swept Dravens. Lead us home, bring us in," he sang.

"What was that?" Katie asked him from far behind, making the most of the fact her voice could boom when she wanted it to.

"Just a little song I thought of. We should be able to see it soon—just there, over the horizon," Schenn said, pointing northeast. Suddenly the loud crack of a sniper rifle rang out from behind them. Then again, and again, shots rang out across the sky. Ethan felt a bullet whiz past his ear, but he was unharmed. He also looked to his left and saw Ruth with a frayed expression dip into a brief dive before completing an Immelmann turn. That put her just about even with Schenn and Fantaine who had been leading the formation. When they heard the shots fired, both of them turned back around as quickly as they could.

Ethan flew Violet into the middle of their formation where the four of them collected and assessed the situation. "Schenn, can you see anything? Where did the shots come from?" Fantaine asked him from his side.

"Reyszn says she smells an unfamiliar hawk in the area, but I can't see anything, and the horizon is clear. She things whoever fired at us was just following and wanted to give us a scare," Schenn told them.

Ethan realized he had a bad feeling in the pit of his stomach, just then. Where was Katie?

From below, Ethan heard a scream. It was his sister. As soon as Ethan heard her screams, he looked over the wings of Violet and could see her falling. "Guys, help!" Ethan yelled to Fantaine, Schenn, and Ruth. They had not yet heard Katie's screams. Ethan and Violet pulled up, then banked into a steep dive and did a barrel roll to help them catch up to Katie.

Katie had fallen off Sovereign, who was in a full-tilt swoop trying to catch up to her as she fell towards Meinghelia City from high above. She was beginning to fall over the sloped portion of the city, with still enough room to be caught, but that gap was closing quickly. While Sovereign tried to reach her with one of his talons from directly above where she fell, Ethan and Violet flew to Katie from above as quickly as they could. When Sovereign just grasped her with one set of his talons, Katie wasn't able to hang on, and then began to fall end over end. Violet told him, *Ethan, there's not much farther I can go. You have to use your magic!*

Ethan felt his eyes glow blue, but he had no idea what he could do. The hard roof of a campus building was rising quickly to meet their descent. Ethan did not have long left. First, Ethan put his hand out in Katie's direction and was able to steady her tumbling. Katie thanked him with a soft expression and golden eyes.

The rest of the formation began to close in around them. The roof of the building that Katie would hit was coming up fast. *Ethan, do it! Use your magic to manipulate the wind around your sister. Make a swirl that will blow her back up into Sovereign's talons,* Violet told him. Sovereign was still right there, reaching for her as best as he could, but Katie always seemed to be just an inch out of reach. As Ethan once again focused on his magic to save Katie, many things happened all at once.

Ethan felt his eyes turn violet, and the roof of the building came into his vision. They were no more than fifty to sixty feet above it. Then Ethan saw a tall, hulking man with brown hair and copper skin. He was standing directly underneath where Katie would land. Ethan saw a bronze dragon on top of the building to the left of the man. As Ethan used his magic to push Katie up into Sovereign's grasp, the man with copper skin turned into a ram the size of a minivan, and the dragon stretched out its wings across the top of the building. One wing stretched upwards to break Sovereign's fall with Katie then safely in his talons still screaming, of course, while the other stretched out towards the end of the building where the ram had positioned himself at the edge.

Once Sovereign had Katie safely within his grasp, he tucked in his wings and began to roll down the dragon's wings, end over end, like a boulder down a hill. When they rolled onto the ram, the ram used his position to roll them off the building and back into stable flight, but Katie was still not yet safe. They would still need to land in a hobbled manner so that Sovereign wouldn't squeeze her to death unintentionally within one set of his talons. Violet pulled up to stop their descent, quickly after they passed beneath the roof of the building, centered over a busy city street.

The building that Katie and Sovereign had rolled off was only six stories tall. Sovereign flew towards the closest road below him, which was filled with cars. The cars didn't look like they were going to go anywhere for him. Ethan knew this wasn't going to be a pretty crash, but before that happened, two more instructors at the academy revealed themselves to Ethan and the rest of the group. A woman with flowing purple hair appeared out of thin air with eyes of the same color on top of a raven. She pulled a short black wand out of her coat pocket and aimed it towards the set of talons Sovereign was using to hold Katie. Orange sparks shot out of the end of the wand and hit Sovereign's talons. He dropped Katie.

"That's Carra Richen," Ethan heard Ruth say from behind him. "Don't worry; she's got this now."

"And I think there's one more coming too," said Fantaine from behind him. "Tober Law."

Carra's eyes changed color to silver as Katie fell through the air towards the ground again. Suddenly, wispy grey streams began to shoot out the end of her wand, forming a thick cloud. Katie came to a rest atop of the thick cloud, which then carried her safely to the ground. Katie landed on the sidewalk, got up, and dusted herself off after the cloud dissipated back into thin air.

Where Katie stood up on the sidewalk, a short, white bald man, who looked to be over fifty years old, stood next to her. Ethan figured that man was Tobler Law. His eyes were a burgundy red. Ethan looked away from him to watch Sovereign struggling to land. He was headed right for a busy intersection. Just before Sovereign landed in the middle of the intersection, which would have crushed several passing cars, a hawk came streaking into view. He flapped his way into the intersection and pushed two cars which were beginning to drive into the intersection out of the way so that Sovereign could land safely in the middle. Ethan could also see that the traffic lights for the intersection had all turned red as well—the ones that he could see, at least.

Once Sovereign was safely on the ground, the man who had originally broken Katie's fall—the great ram with the help of his dragon—called out to their formation wherever they were in the area. "You escorting a couple of freshmen, Schenn?" asked the man.

"I'm sorry, Von Din. I should have been more vigilant. We were fired at, three times. Did you hear?" Schenn told him.

"Yeah, yeah, Tobler alerted us first. There's plenty of space for everyone on top of this building here. Let's have a talk about that, maybe we ought to be more properly introduced," Von reasoned. With a wave of his hand, he called each of them over to land on the rooftop with him.

Chapter 33
Meinghelia City (Bailey 9)

MEINGHELIA CITY, MARAVINYA, ALLIREHEM

SUMMER, 1153, FOURTH AGE

O nce Bailey had watched Hector glide over toward a large clearing in the yard next to Ghel, Icon led her and Brenna inside the homestead. Bailey noticed only one window had any light to it. When they got inside, they quickly found out that the rest of the family was already asleep. Icon insisted on not waking them, and Brenna went along with it. They would be there in the morning Icon had told her. Bailey rolled her eyes at that but went along with it quickly enough all the same. It was time for her to rest.

Icon led the two of them up the stairs to the second-story loft. The stairs rattled under her feet, and Bailey felt better than she had since this had all begun. The hot air rose with them as they finished walking up the stairs, but several fans and air conditioning units helped keep the expansive, open loft cool. There were three full-sized beds spread out across the loft, with end tables at their sides and lamps on top of those. There was a large TV in the front of the room, with a Saek-a Rehemcast game system plugged into it.

It looked to Bailey like the three of them were going to have some kind of slumber party. Bailey would have been excited, if she didn't already know that she was just going to pass out as soon as her head hit the pillow. By that point in the night, Bailey had sweat through her entire ensemble. While Brenna began to settle in, Icon left the room. Bailey took that opportunity to finally strip down and step into the shower. She would appreciate a fresh feeling while she slept that night.

She did not shower for long—only long enough that she could get her hair somewhat back to normal and stifle some of her fever adrenaline. When she had finished toweling off, Bailey opened the door to see that Icon was in the process of leaving her a pair of pajamas. Bailey smiled at him, standing there in a towel, and then asked him, "Any chance of some ice water?"

"Duh," he told her. "I was already going to get that for all of us here anyway."

Bailey picked up the pajamas and put them on back inside the bathroom. When she stepped out, she got into the open bed beneath the fan at the back of the room. The mattress and sheets underneath the fan made a special combination for Bailey. She slept well that night. All that woke her was the joyous celebration of Brenna's return, which she overheard take place downstairs at about 7:30 am.

Bailey met the rest of Icon's family one by one and enjoyed herself at the leisure of the day. Icon brought the girls breakfast in bed while the three of them sat around the TV listening to comedy podcasts. Several hits from a bong full of Hurinst's plant were also shared between them, which only served to intensify their laughter.

Ramos was Icon's little brother. The youthful sprite came bounding up the stairs in the late morning, and Bailey and he talked about the stars and regashens on the river.

It was shortly after that when Bailey finally got out of bed to go walk around the homestead. Raver-a, the matriarch of the family, was a stern-looking woman with caramel-brown skin and a weathered expression. She was staring into the eyes of Hector when Bailey first approached her outside in the open homestead which sat on a mostly open plot of land of several acres. Raver-a had no fear of the Eedon Rath-ni and showed it. Bailey wondered if that was out of respect for their intelligence, or indifference. Raver-a seemed to love the hawks. "Icon is not exactly my son, but I do consider him one. He told me how they captured your hawk, what they could have done to him, and exactly how it was allowed to happen," Raver-a told her.

When Hector saw Bailey talking to her, he had been in a stalking and squawking match with Ghel. They were circling around each other in the yard, but then both of them flew over. The hawks landed on either side of them and then spread out their wings in a circle around them.

There was once a time when hawks could sing symphonies on the wind that their riders would be able to hear wherever they were, Hector told her. Bailey turned towards his beak, which was pointed down at her, and looked him in the eyes. She tried to stand up taller, but when Hector saw her do that, he only returned the favor.

What happened? What took away the symphonies? Bailey asked.

Hector did not answer her at first, but then his eyes began to glow red like she had never seen them do before. *Why the phoenix, of course,* he told her. There was darkness in his voice of hatred and revilement, but then a light of begrudging respect as well.

That evening, during dinner, Bailey sat at the table with Icon, Brenna, and the rest of their family. She had not been allowed to help prepare it—much to her dismay—by the patriarch of the family, Brigleios. "I can help cook you know," she had told him a few minutes after meeting him for the first time in the kitchen.

Brigleios was not a tall or strong man. He had a round belly, but he was not too fat. He had a scraggly beard and thick, greasy black hair that was just beginning to gray. "Now I wouldn't want you to have to do that," he told her. "You only just got here. Just have a beer and watch TV. The Raegic Brigadiers are playing the Dig'la Teur Ocelots."

"But I don't care about Dargen," Bailey said out loud. The patriarch of the family turned away from her and held up his hand with his first two fingers generally pointed upwards, to wave her out of the kitchen. Bailey left the kitchen for him after she couldn't think of anything else to say. *At least you can still insist on setting the table*, Hector told her.

Bailey nodded and accepted that as an accord. She walked into the living room, where streaks of dusty, dank sunlight stretched over the room. A large TV hung on the wall facing away from the kitchen. She grabbed the remote to turn on the TV and switched it to the Dargen game. She sat across from the TV on a comfy couch. She thought about going upstairs to play the Saek-a Rehemcast but decided to just stay downstairs because dinner would be ready within ten minutes anyways.

Bailey lay across the couch and pointed her head towards the TV. She watched Dargen for a few moments, but before she could get into the game too much and understand how it was played, she began to tire from all the excitement and exhaustion from the last few days. Maybe it was a better sport to play in person rather than watch on TV. It would provide nice background static for her to fall asleep to for a few minutes.

"Dinner's ready," came Brigleios' voice from the dining room down the hall a few minutes later, snapping her out of her stupor. Bailey was quite hungry. Around the table were two final family members that Bailey had not yet met. Raver-a stood up when she entered the room and snapped her niece Pris-tien into action—she had been texting on a phone. Pris-tien had dark caramel skin, long black hair, and deep brown eyes but with somewhat strange teeth.

Pris-tien spoke in a way that suggested she was trying to hide her teeth with her lips which were not quite big enough to do so. "It's nice to meet you. I just wish you rode a dragon or a raven. Anything else but a hawk," she told her.

"Pris-tien!" exclaimed Brigleios.

Um, what did that girl just say about me? Ought I destroy this ranch? Hector thought jokingly.

Bailey laughed to him inside her mind and out loud at Pris-tien's insult of Hector. "That's n-not what I m-mean," she stammered. "It's great to see another hawk, you know. I just wish I could see all the other ones too. All I ever seem to see up here are hawks, you know?"

"It's alright," Bailey told her. "I'll explain to Hector that it's nothing personal."

It was after that moment that the final member of the family full of strange relations deigned to be noticed for the first time. A young baby in grey clothing sat in a highchair at the end of the table. That was Jillian. Jillian could cry and scream quite loudly, but Raver-a was good at getting the baby to quiet down with a goofy look or embrace. Their dinner began with a round of soup, salad, and rolls. After that, the main course was a kangaroo shoulder roast, with fried kale chips and roasted potatoes. Cooked jelly bugs were served as a crunchy but sweet delicacy to top everything off.

When Bailey went back to sleep that night, she thought she would be ready to head to the academy the next day, but that didn't quite happen. Again, hits of Hurinst's Plant from the bong were passed around the three of them and Pris-tien—who decided to join them for an hour. Ramos wanted to smoke some too, but he was denied by Brigleios. He was too young. It wasn't until 2 am that the three of them finally stumbled their way up to their beds. They slept in again until 11 am the next morning.

In the afternoon, Bailey gathered Icon and Brenna in the loft so they could discuss their flight plan to Meinghelia City. The three of them agreed to leave the morning after next. They listened to the news for an hour to hear what they needed to be aware of. The Illias city government was conducting a full-scale investigation into just how the Hunters had been allowed to operate so brazenly in such an important city within the Allirehem Resistance. Her father's voice also came over in the air in a statement, condemning the corrupt environmental groups that had been linked to the organization. He also issued further warnings to be vigilant against similar future events.

"Illias was lucky to get away with only a handful of civilian casualties. As was my daughter just as lucky to escape with her hawk and her life. But why was the luck necessary?" Bailey remembered hearing his voice on the radio. She felt like she could see his face wrinkling as he spoke through the radio waves. "Who are these people? And how many potential Allirehem-allied Dravens have they taken off the field forever? This must cease. The Eedon Rath-ni are not a commodity to be bid over."

Bailey had obviously already talked to him on the phone after successfully rescuing Hector. She didn't need to hear anything else that he had to say. Brenna tuned the radio to a classic rock station, and the three of them poured over the map of Allirehem that they had spread out across the coffee table. It would not be a terribly long flight, and it was only longer than it had to be because the three of them had agreed that they wanted to stay over land as much as possible, giving Illias an extra-wide berth when passing by.

Then she thought of Amanda for a moment, and she finally figured out a text to put together to Corso and Ben. She wrote to Corso: *Corso, it's Bailey. I'm safe, and I've rescued my Eedon Rath-ni—a hawk named Hector. I'm so sorry to hear about Amanda, and if there's anything I can do to help, reach out to me. I'm here for you*, Bailey sent the message.

She wrote to Ben: *Ben, it's Bailey. I'm sorry I ever had to put you through something like that. I'm so sorry we lost Amanda; she was a life-long friend. I never meant for any of this to happen—it's just the sad reality of what Dravens and the war have done to our family. I'm thinking of you.* She sent the message a moment later.

Once that was done, there was not much left to discuss about their trip to Meinghelia City. The next day, during the afternoon, there was a peaceful moment between Bailey and Pris-tien, while Pris-tien carried Jillian in her arms.

"I'm really glad that you came along at this very moment for Brenna," Pris-tien told her, looking over at her and then beyond her. Bailey turned her vision to where Pris-tien was looking, and she saw Brenna walking around, reading a book next to one of the barns. "There are many women in that city who offer themselves up to that industry, but others are coerced, and the corrupt city overlooks it for the tourism."

"Well, I really needed them too," Bailey told Pris-tien blushing. "All I could really do was offer them a safe place to stay and trust them. I would have been hopeless in finding and freeing Hector if we had never met."

Pris-tien smiled at her, then embraced her warmly. The seven of them went out for crocodile that night in town. It was even more succulent than the kangaroo had been two nights previous. When they got home that evening, there was no bong swapping or late-night comedy podcasts. The three of them fell asleep in their beds quickly and woke up early the next morning. Bailey woke to the smell of a hearty breakfast. Much to her delight, Brigleios and Raver-a allowed them to eat in the loft. Pris-tien and Ramos joined them. Breakfast was a hearty helping of potatoes with deer bacon, buzzard eggs, and bagels with goat cheese.

When they were finished eating breakfast, it was not long after that, that Bailey, Icon, and Brenna would leave for Christian's academy.

"The winds are a bit strong today," warned Brigleios from behind her after they had finished packing. Hector stood directly in front of her. This time *she* would lead the way. With her duffle bag around her back, Bailey walked up to her Eedon Rath-ni while she gripped her carbine in her left hand. Her pistol was holstered at her side. Raver-a had not gone lightly, giving them weapons for their own protection during their trip. She had given Icon an automatic assault rifle, which he had slung across his back.

Brenna walked with a pump-action shotgun strapped on her back, wearing a sun-cap on her head. She wouldn't be doing any falling off Ghel this time. Raver-a had called up a renowned Eedon Rath-ni handler, and they had custom fitted a double saddle onto Ghel. She had also spared no expense in buying Bailey a saddle of her own as well. Bailey walked up to Hector and embraced him around his neck. *It's time*, he told her.

Bailey nodded at him and held his gaze for just a moment. After that, she shed the duffle bag off her back and put it in front of Hector's talons. Once she was free of that, she strapped her carbine around her back, hoping that she wouldn't need it as much as last time. After that, it was time for her final goodbyes. She walked over to Raver-a and Brigleios, who stood together by themselves. Icon, Brenna, Pris-tien, and Ramos were all chatting amongst themselves several feet away, and Jillian was sleeping inside.

"Thank you for the hospitality," Bailey said to the both of them, after a brief hug with each.

"We were quite worried, you know, when Brenna went missing. We sent Icon out for her because of his connections and resourcefulness, but if you had not come along for him," Brigleios began, "I'm afraid by now, we would have had to say goodbye to both of them."

"It's just the country we live in," Raver-a told her. "Perhaps this war will change it for the better—just not by the hands of Iishrem I hope."

"Come back anytime," Brigleios added with a wave.

Bailey smiled at the two of them, and then she walked over to the youths. "You'll be such a cutie in a few years when you're all grown up," Bailey told Ramos, giving him a kiss on the cheek. "Try and treat the girls nicely for me."

"I will, if they're good to me," Ramos told her with a devilish grin. Bailey, Pris-tien, and Brenna all laughed together while Icon scowled.

"You seem very persuasive and resourceful," Bailey told Pris-tien when she walked over to her. They kissed, once on each of their cheeks lightly. "You could make a shrewd politician someday. Maybe fix some of these problems you see."

Pris-tien looked at her and grinned. She didn't bother to hide her teeth. Bailey didn't think they were *terrible*, they could just use a little straightening. "A revolutionary I think would be more interesting, personally," Pris-tien told her.

While the two of them hugged, Bailey hoped that Pris-tien would be careful and make sure to keep herself well protected if she ever took that route. "Don't ever lose your keen perspective," she told Pris-tien.

With the exchange of goodbyes finished, there was nothing else to do but jump on Hector. As soon as Bailey put her first boot into one of Hector's stirrups, she knew she was going to feel much more secure while riding Hector from then on. *I hope not to have to do much more jumping or other risky maneuvers until we're more acquainted with each other*, Bailey told him.

Slow and steady, Hector replied while she finished turning herself around on Hector to face the front. She then slipped into both of his stirrups in the correct orientation. The padded leather saddle warmed her butt quite nicely as soon as she sat down. She leaned back against the short backrest, which rose halfway up her back. "Ready to kick off, Bailey?" Icon said from beside her.

Bailey pulled out her phone and punched in the coordinates her father had given her for his cabin outside of Meinghelia to the phone's GPS app. The imaginary flight path lay right in front of Hector's beak. "Ready!" she told him.

"Bye!" sang the rest of the group.

Bailey turned to give each of them one more look and a wave, then she felt Hector kick off into the air. She was able to watch them get smaller for a moment, but Hector's flight soon pulled her back to the direction he was flying in. When Bailey looked below as they flew on, the dozen-acre homestead that Icon's family owned soon just became a blip on a spindling tree of suburban townscapes, which led towards Illias, shimmering beige and white in the distance. It was only partly visible due to the jungle and mountains.

Brenna and Icon rode on top of Ghel to her right just a few dozen feet or so behind her diagonally as they crossed the closest section of the Illnayean River. Their formation continued to put a large buffer between their flight path and Illias until they were well beyond it. Their flight over the jungle portion of the Haisha was quite peaceful and serene until they passed over the solitary metropolitan corridor that burrowed its way through the jungle, all the way up to the plainlands of the north.

After being in the air for about two hours, they began to approach the Allaeyic Straight, an extension of the Allaeyic Ocean which narrowly divided Haisha from Maravinya in more a *regional* perspective. Their flight over that took another hour or so. To pass their time, Bailey began to tell Icon what she knew from her father about life at Christian's Academy.

Dravens enrolled at Christian's Academy would be trained for three years, over the course of two eighteen-week-long semesters. There was a winter break of about a month between the end of the first and second semesters of each year.

Bailey would enroll in classes to gain an education that would make the most of her unique skill set. She would be trained in her skills but also have them diversified so she could be even more versatile in the battlefields of the future. Lastly, there would be the boot camp element of the academy, where she would be pushed by her instructors to compete against her fellow first years for incentives like weekends off, monetary rewards, or travel passes. However, none of those prizes would ever come easy. *I really can't wait to get there*, Bailey thought.

Soon enough, we'll see it right there over the horizon, Hector told her.

Their formation flew onward and soon began to fly over land again. Their flight path took them within sight-seeing distance of Bentlion, a city of tall, intricate, elegant glass skyscrapers wedged between the coastal plains of northwestern Maravinya and the Barela-tin Mountains. Clancy had not told her much about that city specifically, and none of them really felt like stopping for lunch after such a big breakfast. Her father had promised them that the kitchen at his cabin would be stocked with food for dinner when they got their anyway.

It took their formation another hour to make it through the mountains and the forest. They were approaching Christian's Academy from a general north-northwest direction. After that, it was not long before Bailey spotted the solitary mountain that rose out of the forest. The academy would be on the south side of that mountain, but her father's cabin was on the eastern side.

"Alright, we're about ten minutes out; follow me," Bailey called back to Icon and Brenna. They were still a little behind her. Bailey held up her phone in front of her, which had an arrow path that she just had to have Hector follow. Where she looked Hector flew. The application instructed her to begin her descent, and then it gave her several options for landing strips.

Once the cabin was in sight and Bailey had picked out a good landing strip, she said to Hector, *Alright, Hector, take us in.*

Roger that, he replied while squawking out loud. Hector led Ghel in behind him at a nice gradual descent, and then they came to a running stop and peeled off to the right of the open yard around her father's cabin. Ghel came to a running stop after peeling off to the left.

Bailey was desperate to stretch her legs, so she jumped off Hector as soon as he came to a stop. When she hit the ground and looked around, Bailey heard the carbine clicking around on her back. She looked to Icon and Brenna when they had each safely reached ground. Bailey took a deep breath and let the Maravinyian air fill her lungs. There was something different about the air in a new place so far away from the one she had once called home, but Bailey knew that this place was her home now.

If it was not always her father's cabin, then it would be Christian's Academy or Meinghelia City beyond that. Bailey was home, and she had beaten the trials of escaping Seems and rescuing Hector from the grips of his terrible hunters. However, she knew it would not be long before she found herself embracing the new challenges and trials of life as a Draven, fighting in the Great War for Allirehem, Christian, and all else that she held dear.

Chapter 34
The Other Professors (katie 9)

katie couldn't believe that after years of wrestling and gymnastics, she had fallen off her eagle so easily, but then it was her first time flying. Even if she had been shot at. When Katie had first shot, she ducked down as quickly as she could. She had tried to look around to see where her attacker was coming from, but when the second shot came a few seconds later, it grazed right over her knee. She saw the bullet dissipate through her shield and turn into yellow sparks, but her flinch and expectation at possibly being shot were exactly what caused her to fall in the first place.

As soon as she fell and turned body down towards the approaching town, Katie couldn't hear anything over the sounds of her own screams. Even as Sovereign spoke to her calmly in her own mind, while he tried to catch her from above, and the rest of her party was never far from her fall, she could hear only the sounds of her own screams in expectation of her own death. Then, somehow miraculously, she was saved, and their attacker had apparently just retreated from the area.

When she had dropped down onto the cloud, it caught her like a comfy mattress that faded away gradually until there was nothing left, and she was safely on the ground. At the offering of a hand from Tobler Law—the short, bald man with a grey beard—Katie was able to pull herself up and stand without any searing injuries.

"Are you alright?" Tobler asked her. He took by her elbow and looked into her eyes. "We all can fall, even the best. But not everyone can get back on afterward. If you are ever going to get back on that regal bird again, then *I* must see you. You must believe in yourself, and it must be now."

Katie shook her arm away from him, and he let it go without a fight. They were not at the academy yet, and he was not yet her instructor. "I'm alright, a bullet just grazed me. I'm never going to fall again," she told him.

"One of Lance's favorite female wrestlers in Iishrem, and she vanished right from under his nose in the night. A woman like you I'm sure has many things to show us," Tobler jested with her.

Katie glowered at him, and then she spat off to the side, not saying a word. Tobler reacted expressionlessly to her spitting. Katie wondered what he would have done if she had spat on his boots.

Katie dusted herself off and began to walk down the two blocks that separated her from where Sovereign was—still, in the middle of the intersection. Sovereign and Tobler's hawk took up the entire junction. First responders were arriving on the scene and assisting the drivers and passengers out of the two cars that Tobler's hawk had pushed out of the way so that Sovereign could land safely. The civilians around her were used to similar events, but they still watched *her* with a captivated interest.

Katie felt her eyes turn golden. When she passed by other pedestrians on the sidewalk or had them pass by in the other direction, they tended to regard her like they knew exactly what she was and gave her some space.

When Katie stepped into the intersection and walked up to Sovereign, he turned to her and thought, *It'll never happen again.*

Sovereign, she thought to him as she stood in front of him, *after everything we've been through together, you don't have to think like that.*

Katie surprised herself with that sentiment, and then she climbed back into Sovereign's saddle. Tobler was not far behind her, getting onto his hawk. It was a brief ride up to the top of the university building, where everyone else was waiting for them. Sovereign kicked off into the air with a few flaps of his wings, and Katie held on tight. He flew her up the slope of the town until they could round the building at the next corner. All the while, Sovereign rose to the top of the brick building using the natural wind currents and just a bit of gentle flapping until it was time to land again. The roof was filled with patches of dirt surrounded by gravel that had shrubs and small trees growing out of them.

I've never seen human trees do this before, Sovereign thought to her while he sniffed the shrubs.

There was not quite enough room for all of the Eedon Rath-ni and their riders to fit atop the roof at once, and so Von Din's dragon had retreated to another one, all by his lonesome, while each of the ravens was in their smaller form somewhere around the building. Violet and Wraith-wen Al were both perched on the shoulders of their riders. Fantaine's raven perched on the top of her staff, with its eyes glowing sky blue like the gemstone of the same color. Carra's raven perched on a utility box on the other side of the building, which left *enough* space for Tobler's hawk, Reyszn, and Sovereign.

"A good thing we all happened to be here for the new girl from Iishrem," Carra said to Von Din and Tobler. "Schenn, Fantaine, they didn't know where they were going, but you two are much more experienced Dravens than any of them."

"I know," Schenn offered to the three other professors of the academy. He held his palms out in front of him, asking them for leniency. "At least we all had shields up?"

"Just so," said Carra. She turned to Tobler, "Who could have been firing at them?"

"It's troubling me, indeed. As soon as things are squared away, I'll return here and do some investigating. There must be something to this confrontation, but now that we're in Meinghelia City and all of our future students are safely on the ground, I think we can relax, just a little," Tobler explained.

"Mhmm, still, the brother did prove himself quite well in his improvisation to help save her," said Von Din. "Would you agree, Katie, is it?"

Katie flushed; she had not been prepared to suddenly find herself in the spotlight. "Thanks, Ethan," Katie told him. "I'm glad you were with me." And she was sorry for having been so harsh to him earlier in the day. It was true, perhaps she should have gotten rid of... *what was his name last night?* Katie thought.

Are you serious, Katie? Sovereign questioned her inquisitively.

You know, I really can't remember what his name was. He lasted a while, though, Katie slyly.

"And yet, they all worked together to save her and learned some important lessons as well. First years, what did we learn about physics and geography today?" Tobler asked Ruth, Ethan, and Katie.

Ethan didn't have to think long before answering, "It's important to use what's around you in flight and fight. See where you need to be and how it could offer to help advance our goals," Ethan began.

Tobler's expression became one of exuberance. "That's right, son," he told her brother. Katie rolled her eyes and put one of her hands on her hip. That question had been too easy.

"But what else needed to happen? Ruth, why couldn't Ethan have just taken a better angle, if he were better trained, and caught her all at once? Or Sovereign?" Carra asked the girl a few years older than herself. Katie could swear she had already heard Ethan fawning over her.

Ruth answered this time. "There would have been internal injuries to Katie. Or he could have mistimed it easily and knocked her off course horizontally and out of reach," she told the group.

"And why could that have been unfortunate?" asked Von Din last of all. He directed his question directly to Katie. She was not surprised.

"The increased potential collateral damage," Katie told him. She looked at Sovereign and wondered about the carnage he could inflict on an unprepared populace at close range, during a crash. "Who knows how many cars Sovereign could have taken out in his descent."

"Oh, yes, just so," said Carra. "Perhaps this group of three first-years *are* indeed ready for a life at the academy."

"Perhaps these first years would like to lay their eyes on the academy for the first time and get settled into their dorms," Tobler posited.

The conversation nearly came to a halt all at once when Tobler said that. "Looks like you struck a nerve there," Carra noted.

Katie could tell her expression had eased, and she was quite ready to settle in at her new home, under the assumption that it would be a while before she ever traveled as far as she just had again. Katie was back on top of Sovereign quickly after that. One more time, Katie lifted her left foot and put it into Sovereign's left stirrup. She surged upwards and pulled herself onto him with her arms, and then sat back down. She inserted her boots into the stirrups, and then Sovereign kicked off into the air again.

Katie had Sovereign circle back around to the other side of the building as the rest of the group hopped on top of their Eedon Rath-ni and took off in various directions. Tobler stayed behind above the building for a while, looking for any signs of their now fled attacker. Von Din would lead their formation this time, but he wasn't about to let another incident happen. "Ethan, Katie," Von Din began, "you'll fly at either side of me this time. A line of three behind them, Ruth, Schenn, and Fantaine, and then, Carra and Tobler, you'll bring up the rear halfway in between each of them."

The two-pronged arrow formation quickly took form. Once it did, Von led her and her brother on, out of the town and over the river. The short mountain where Christian's Academy sat at the bottom of the southern edge, rose on her horizon. When Katie saw the campus for the first time, she leaned back and thought about her parents briefly. The two of them would have been proud of her and her brother for making it this far. It wasn't on her mind to avenge them, but one day she wanted to find their grave and bring them flowers.

The campus of Christian's Academy was laid out before them. There was a lake on the far northwestern edge where all the stables for the Eedon Rath-ni were located. South of that was the dorms. There was a separate dorm for each year. Beyond that, there were the mentor suites and instructor accommodations. After those, were the educational departments and separate colleges of the academy. Katie also spied a large square building at the base of the mountain, which was labeled, *Mess Hall.* That was self-explanatory.

In the center of it all was a small oblong Dargen pitch with a bowl of stands around it with enough capacity for several thousand fans. Off to the eastern end of the campus, Katie could see the shooting range and an obstacle course. A paved asphalt track ran around the entire campus, ending at a dirt trail, which led up and around the mountain. There was a building at the top of it, which was considered the final building of the campus. The Mountainlair it was called.

Naturally, there were also buildings for administrative purposes, such as Allirehem Resistance Headquarters. When their formation was near enough, Von Din took them in on a gradual descent, bringing them all to a running stop just past the Dargen pitch, near the administrative suites and the first-year dorms. Katie stepped down off Sovereign and embraced him warmly. *We made it,* she told him.

Together at home, at last, Sovereign admitted. He then rested his beak on top of her head and pushed down on the back of it with the tip of his beak. Katie closed her eyes and focused her mind on Sovereign's thick beak. Katie thought back to the moment in her life when she had first seen him, all those years ago, deep within the subterranean levels of the Imperial Spire. She realized at that moment, that it had never been just her or Sovereign in all of this. Carth had pushed her in the direction of her natural skills and honed her fighting style, but Marleigh had taught her well in the use of détente as well.

Katie realized that it was her meeting Sovereign that had given her cause to fight. It was the loss of her parents and her home that would keep her moving forward. Through it all, from the beginning to the end, there had always been Christian and Talia. They had always been there—somehow seeming to manipulate her life and her path when they wanted to, when the impact of the war on her was always peaking for herself or her brother. She couldn't help but wonder *why?*

Here they come now, Sovereign proclaimed in her mind. Katie's eyes were open instantly, and Sovereign backed off to give her some space. Katie turned around, then watched Talia and Christian approach.

It'll be good to see them again, even if it's only been a week, Katie thought. *I wonder how differently they'll act, now that we're on their turf.*

Good chance to find out right here, Sovereign agreed.

"New Dravens, fall in," Christian said sternly as he approached them with his arms behind his back. Katie understood that appearances were important since she was now on campus, even if the semester hadn't entirely begun yet. She was ready. Katie neutralized her expression and stepped into place with her arms at her side. Ruth beat her to the point; her brother was a little slower. They each remained silent. "Fantaine, Schenn, Von, and Tobler, you're dismissed. We'll speak later on. At ease, Dravens." Those dismissed walked off.

Katie felt herself instantly relax and exhale. She moved her arms from her sides and crossed them behind her back, with her fists unclenched. Christian and Talia stepped up to speak with them and were joined by Carra. Katie soon realized that each of the instructors was going to induct one of them into Christian's Academy. Carra stepped up in front of Ruth on her left, and Talia stepped up in front of Ethan on her right. Christian stood in front of her, with a piercing gaze.

"State your name?" Christian said to her first. Once he did, Carra and Talia began to follow his direction with Ruth and Ethan.

"Katie Campbell," Katie said out loud. She did not think she had been too loud or too meek.

"And the name of your Eedon Rath-ni?" Christian continued.

"Sovereign," Katie said out loud.

"What is it you came here for?" Christian asked her.

Katie did not answer quickly. "I wanted to make my *own* decisions about my fate. I wanted to see the world, not be a disposable weapon to be harvested by Iishrem. Not after what *he* did," Katie said in reference to Allovein.

"Why did you complete your journey? You've now set foot on this campus. There is no turning back now," Christian told her.

"I've got a chance to be one with someone that I've waited to be for all my life. We'll be the greatest fighters you've ever met," Katie told Christian.

"That's a good answer," he told her. Almost as quickly, Katie was sure she could feel Ethan and Ruth glare at her out of his apparent favoritism, although she did not turn to look. "Kneel."

For the first time, Katie noticed that Christian had a sheathed rapier at his side, as did Carra and Talia. His had an elegantly weaved handle, but Carra's was a little bit more ornate. Talia's handle was a simple carbon black, with a single amulet that shimmered dark navy-blue. Katie knelt.

"Katie Campbell," Christian began, "do you swear to at all times give your training, education, and success at my academy your all?"

"I swear," Katie told him. Ethan and Ruth both swore as well.

"Do you promise to always love and cherish your Eedon Rath-ni as a part of yourself and treat them with the respect they deserve?" Christian asked her.

"I promise," Katie told him endearingly. *As long as we're together, we can beat anything this war throws at us,* Katie thought to Sovereign.

I promise to always love and cherish my Draven as the soul of my story, Sovereign thought to her. *I will never again let anything happen to you, which I would not go through myself. We are one.*

"Will you, here and now, swear your allegiance to the Allirehem Resistance, to fight for them and myself until the war is over or your death takes you?" Christian asked. Katie didn't take long to answer, but she wished he would have been a little more elaborate about his intentions with his question.

"I swear my allegiance here and now," Katie told Christian, looking up at him with her two golden eyes. Ethan and Ruth swore their allegiances with violet and ruby red eyes.

The sound of three silver rapiers being unsheathed emanated around them. Christian tapped Katie with the tip of his rapier, first on her right shoulder and said, "By the power vested in me, Christian Knowles, I induct you into the Resistance Draven Training Academy of Allirehem. Rise." He finished his induction by tapping her on the left shoulder, and then on the forehead. The tap on her forehead was with the center of its shaft, not its tip.

Katie stood back up, along with her brother and Ruth. "Well, welcome, welcome," Christian told the three of them. He clapped his hands deliberately in front of his chest, and then put them behind his back as if he were hiding something. After that, Carra and Talia each took one step back around him. In one fluid motion, Christian projected his arms directly out at the three of them. There were about eight feet of open space between them. Out of

Christian's hands at the end of his motion, came a genderless ghost whose ethereal form began about a foot off the ground and ended at around Ethan's height. The ghost was cloaked and had a veiled expression. All Katie could see were its non-expressive lips that spoke its mono-toned voice.

"I am the dean of the academy," the ghost proclaimed in a wispy voice. It began to cough a moment later, and then it hunched over and brought up a fist to punch its chest. It turned around to look at Christian, and then it looked over his projective pose which he had held since apparently bringing the dean into form. "Oh dear, Christian, have I not asked you to stop doing that to first years?"

Christian broke his pose with a smile and then began to chuckle to himself. The dean turned back to face the group of first years. "He doesn't control me as if I'm some kind of poltergeist. Never fear. Any Draven can summon me if they have me in their minds and know the proper method. I just may not always be able to appear exactly where or when you need me to," the dean explained.

"Well, teachers, I do believe it's time for the three of us to do teacher things. Let's go!" Christian snapped Talia and Carra into motion with his words. "Do enjoy your two free nights. Commencement and the great feast of fall starts at noon in the Dargen stadium. Don't be late. Dean, please show them to their accommodations."

Christian led Talia and Carra away with the order of his words. "Come, young Dravens," the dean told the three of them. He moved out in front of them and began to lead them away from the Dargen pitch to the dorms while they walked on a paved sidewalk.

Katie regarded Sovereign with one last look, before heading off towards the dorms with the dean. *You brought me so far,* she told him.

We carried each other, he returned. Then he turned away and flew off with the group of Eedon Rath-ni towards a spacious lake in the distance where many others had gathered.

"You may notice that this sidewalk is quite easy to walk on. You'll soon find out just how this academy is different from any boot camp or university campus. In this case, it's nice to have something easily walkable when we may want to attract some dignitaries or guests. A fair word of warning: the instructors will be harsher to you in front of them but also fairer."

Katie followed the dean, a few steps back from him. She looked back to see Ruth behind her, and then Ethan was just a little farther back. Katie caught him looking down at Ruth for just a moment, then he snapped his eyes away.

"There are some things you will notice on our brief walk. A full tour can be given later, but I will call your attention the first of these statues that we pass," said the dean. He had stopped next to the statue of a shirtless, portly bald man with a round face and a bow on his back. The engraving upon the base of the statue read, *Gabel the Rich.* "You'll notice his name and a *defining* attribute. What is it you notice about his statue that is related?"

Katie saw several ancient coins sitting at the top of the base of the statue, and then she noticed that Gabel was holding an empty pouch in his hand. "He's lost his money," Ethan noticed.

"Excellent," said the dean. "Ethan, perhaps you could return them to him."

Katie watched her brother nod, then bend down and pick up the three brown coins. He placed them into the pouch that Gabel held in the palm of his hand, and quickly after that, the statue came alive. "Damn you for summoning me at this very time," said Gabel's ghost, which had stepped out of the statue and was standing next to it while he berated them. "Do you have any idea the trouble you've just caused for the Deathly Market? This will take months to balance out! Booooooooo! Boo!"

Katie watched in shocked fashion along with everyone else at the ghost who milled about in front of them. "I'm sorry, my founder. Is there anything I can do to correct this?" the dean asked his apparent ghostly creator.

"No, but I will be quick. One last time, please stop summoning me during market hours!" Gabel told the dean. The dean began to hold up a hand to respond, but Gabel cut him off with a wave of his arm and a sneer. "Well, first years, I'm Gabel the Rich. As the last of the alliance of Dravens allied to a free republic in Iishrem were realizing we were fighting a lost war, I set out and financed this whole campus. Of course, when they were built, the technology of the time was entirely different, and, of course, Christian never came along for over a thousand years. So, what you'll find now are the original buildings, mostly, with massive retrofitting for today's technologies—provided, of course, at the expense of Allirehem taxpayers. What a good use of *their* money. Now, carry on." Gabel disappeared with a wave of his arm, and Katie was relieved when he was gone.

She felt her mouth hanging open as the dean turned back around to them. "You'll have to forgive Gabel; he is quite a miser, after all. Quite an old one at that," he said to them. Once that was finished, the dean wasted no more time in completing his journey to the first-year dorm building with them. Of course, the dean did not wait for them to open the door for him. Instead, he passed right through it and continued onwards, leaving the trouble for a dutiful Ethan.

When they got inside, the dean took them to a key room and had them each select a different room key. "That's really all there is," the dean told them in parting. "Go up and get settled. I can't wait to know each of you better, man." The dean then vanished.

The three of them left the room with their keys and belongings. Eventually, Katie said goodbye for the time to both Ethan and Ruth. When she unlocked her room, she found it to be about what she expected. There was space for two, but only a single bed had been set up for her. There was a desk, a dresser, and a closet with plenty of space. Katie even had a shared bathroom with the next room over. She dropped her duffel bag and thought about getting unpacked, but instead, she grabbed the crime novel she had put away when she had left the ARF Clancy Triten. Now she had the time to finish reading it.

Chapter 35

Coastal Confrontation (Brian 9)

When Brian finished roaring, Alyisay took off into the air immediately. He watched her rise into the sky from beneath the trees. As soon as she crossed the boundaries of the forest and the open air, the base raised its alarm. Its annoying sound relayed exactly what its message was to its allies. Brian would have to be efficient. The sound of the alarm had rallied the loitering cruiser group off the coast into action. They would be sending reinforcements to the base, while Gi'les went on his merry chase of Alyisay, and Brian recovered the egg.

Brian began by skulking into the tall grass in front of him as Alyisay approached the base. He took his time prowling his way through the tall blades of grass, which parted for him when he walked through. Brian thought up to Alyisay as he monitored the base in front of him. The movement of Gi'les and his men had taken on a faster pace. In addition to that, the base had a complete Zòrnentná X9000 missile defense system. Brian cursed himself for having seen that dumb ad on the TV earlier in the day. There were two towers with rocket-launching stations, with four pods each that surrounded the front gate on either side.

Brian heard the unmistakable snuffing sound of three rockets being fired one right after another from the first tower. *Alyisay!* Brian exclaimed in his mind.

Brian! Alyisay screamed back to him in his mind, while she streaked back into his vision. *Calm down. No stupid missile defense system is going to kill me that easily. Watch this.*

Brian watched Alyisay divert the path of the three missiles by flying right in between the three of them as they closed in to hit her. Two of the three rockets exploded into each other, but one managed to loop back around and follow Alyisay up into the air. Alyisay followed up her first aerial maneuver with a wingover, and then she flew back away from the base at the bottom of the loop. The final missile exploded into the missile tower that had fired it, and Brian watched three soldiers get flung off the platform with the resulting explosion.

A voice boomed out on a loudspeaker. "Stop! Stop! Stop! She cannot possibly obtain what she wants by herself! That's what she is—all by her lonesome! Chase her!" boomed Gi'les' voice over the base's loudspeaker. And chase her they did. Brian heard the rattling of chains, and then he watched as the front gate opened and seven armored Humvees came rolling out of the base. Each of them had a manned machine-gunner post, and all of these began firing at Alyisay once they cleared the walls of the base.

To the disadvantage of Gi'les, their vehicles had to exit through a choke point. Two missiles fired from the only remaining missile launcher left, directed at Alyisay from right in front of her. Alyisay was still not deterred as she closed her wings and absorbed the impact of both and did not take much damage. With her close-range distance to the last two Humvees, Alyisay had no trouble bathing them both in flames. The rest of the Humvees continued to fire at her, causing generally inconsequential damage.

When that was finished, Alyisay flew over the base and then banked westward to draw Gi'les away. *I saw him get into one of Humvees, Brian. Go now; the gate is closing*, she told him. Brian reared back and pounced into motion. *You'll make it. Trust in yourself and your power*, she told him.

Brian knew that if he had just been his normal human form, he would have stood no chance of sneaking into the base before the front gate closed, but he was just so much faster as a tiger. Brian remained hidden from the Humvees by using the tall grass around him, and he scampered through the closing gate a few seconds later. He just made it.

Brian ducked into some hidden cover once he made it inside the base, where he could still worriedly watch Alyisay's confrontation a few seconds longer. The Humvees continued to drive away, chasing Alyisay around the wide-open plains. The clangor of chain-turrets rattled the landscape, and the snuffing of rockets being fired at Alyisay was followed by the fiery explosions of timed detonations. She thought nothing to him while she fought, but after watching her evade turret fire by rising into a nearly vertical ascent, Brian was no longer quite as worried about her.

While the Humvees swarmed around her like bees on the ground, Alyisay kept her eyes on them all and used the limitations of their firing angles against them. Brian also saw that several soldiers had jumped out of the Humvees to fire more rockets. Alyisay left the area where she was flying in place and dove into a circular roll. She then began to light the tall grass around the rocketeers on fire.

Suddenly, from behind him, Brian felt eyes and rifles clicking into place. The splinter group of guards left to protect the egg while the reinforcements arrived had spotted him. Brian snapped out of his cover and bounded away from the gate. He looked up at the three guards in front of him who had bulletproof vests and moderate armor on for protection. Brian would have no trouble working his way through their armor, so long as he held his form as a tiger, but he wondered why the soldiers weren't already firing at him.

Brian remembered from his flight over the jungle, that Haisha had thriving populations of big cats in its jungle regions—and some smaller more sporadic ones in its northern ones. Perhaps they had not yet made the connection that he was Alyisay's rider. The three soldiers began to circle around him and put away their rifles. The three of them each withdrew a stun baton that had been attached to their legs at the hip. Brian could also see a sheathed knife at the top of their chest armor as a weapon of last resort. As long as Brian could keep plenty of them around him, they wouldn't use their rifles or pistols on him—except as a last resort.

Brian knew that he had the best chance not to get mortally wounded if he generally avoided conflict as much as possible—and he attained the egg quickly. Brian knew finding the egg would be easy. It would be in the center of the most heavily guarded building left in the base. Brian began his search of the base with a sashay towards the guard directly in front of him, who had foolishly tried to encircle him with his other two companions.

Brian intentionally acted in a non-threatening manner, stretching his back legs out towards the two other guards that were circling around him. He fawned up to the guard directly in front of him and growled lightly at him after moving his legs into place to look like he was sitting. Brian curled and swayed his back from side to side, closely watching the guard nervously twitch his arm while he held the stun baton pointed out at him.

Brian then saw his opportunity to strike, but he thought about not taking it. He wondered what would have happened if he didn't attack these men. Would they allow him to walk right up to the egg itself? Brian knew they would never let him do that. His attempt to trick them would be up once he tried. He knew he would only be able to use this trick once. He had a decision to make.

Brian took his chance when it presented itself to him. Brian closed his eyes and continued to sway like he was just going to fall right over, but before he did, he struck the guard in front of him and dug his claws into his chest armor. Brian felt the cool, milky feeling of blood underneath his claws, and he opened his golden eyes to look up at the man. He had drawn blood. Brian rolled himself over and pulled the man along with him.

Brian began to ravage the man's chest, pulling at his armor to rip it off. As soon as he did, the composure of the other two guards broke. They screamed at him from behind and approached rapidly. Brian turned his head around to look back at them while he ravaged the screaming man's chest one more time. Out of the corner of one of his eyes, Brian saw the downed guard begin to reach for his knife. Brian pinned down his arm before he could grip his knife. Brian also saw that the two guards mere feet behind had left their chests wide open while they lunged at him with their batons.

Brian realized that he would probably never quite have enough time to finish any of these men off entirely at this point. He would need to run after this last move. He realized he was about to be shocked by the batons and prepared for it as best as possible. The shock came. It jolted him awake, and all at once, Brian kicked the guards in their chests with all the might that he had. The two guards flew back into a trailer and left two huge dents in its side. They did not get back up.

Brian stormed off through the base, keeping to himself and evading the guards that knew of his presence as best as possible. The whole base soon knew of his entry after his escape from his initial altercation. However, there were still plenty of raised buildings and troop transport vans to hide under, plus a lack of general interest unless he was entering into an area with a higher concentration of guards. Brian drew one unlucky guard into a pavilion filled with picnic tables, which Brian used as cover to close the distance between himself and the man. Then Brian bounded up and over a table and upwards into his prey. He looked the screaming man in the eyes and then ripped out his throat, revealing the salty, murky taste of the man's flesh, tissue, and blood.

Of course, as soon as Brian did that, guns were brought back into play. Brian finished the unlucky guard off and quickly took cover again underneath a raised building. He had found where the guards clustered the most. *Alyisay, how's it going on your end? Can you see the troop reinforcements coming in from the sea?* Brian thought to her.

I've neutralized the rocketeers, and I've worked my way down to the last Humvees, but, Brian, I've seen no sign of Gi'les yet. He must be in one of these last two Humvees, Alyisay told him.

Carry on, he told her. *I'm approaching where they're storing the egg now.* Brian was crouched on his knees underneath a square-shaped mess hall. In front of him stood a building that resembled a chapel. There was a wide square-shaped roundabout in front of it. The church had a large patio, and it was filled with six guards who were armed to the teeth and standing perfectly idle. In front of the raised patio at the bottom of the steps were four more guards. It was clear to Brian they were waiting for him; it was a trap. Brian wondered if Alyisay had known. He would soon find out. Brian sprung the trap by stepping out of his cover and into the roundabout in front of the chapel.

At the moment that he did, the rest of the trap closed in around him. The guards that he had left alive and uninjured enough to fight closed off his exits. None of them drew their guns or batons on him. They each just stood at attention, as if waiting for something. Something then began to happen. The trusses of the chapel began to rustle and shake. Something was awakening. Something for him. A man named Gi'les waited to meet him on the inside of the chapel.

Brian heard the splintering of wood and saw the doors of the chapel lurch forwards as if they had been pounded outward from the inside. The front doors stayed closed the first time, thanks to a strong metal frame.

By the time the doors came flying off a moment later, Brian was already quite sure exactly who had been behind it in the first place. Without being able to talk, Brian growled at his future attacker. *Hey, Alyisay, Gi'les isn't in any of those Humvees,* he thought out to her. *He's still in the base, and he has the egg.*

Gi'les had stepped out in front of him, wearing an armored exo-mech mining suit. The suit had no guns; it had never been designed for projectile weapons. "You like my suit, rider?" asked the man. Gi'les walked out onto the patio and then stepped down into the courtyard. The ground shook with each step. "You see, being from a region so close to the dragon's home island in the Shrouded Sea, naturally we've had the most experience dealing with them. But it was never the arrows that felled the dragons we dealt with. No, our dragons came from the ground itself. So, we bore our way into it to fight them on their terms. Or at least that's what Drev-Tech would tell you for about $6 million. All the same."

Brian watched Gi'les clench his fists, and the suits mining-based weapons came to life. In one arm, Gi'les held a two-ended rod shaped like a boomerang, and in the other, he held a short, ribbed drill that could stab Brian and rip through his flesh.

For a moment before Gi'les began his attack, he knelt in front of him. The egg was safely protected within an armored box on the back of his suit. *Alyisay, did you know the fight was going to go like this?* Brian thought out to her.

He could tell she was not yet returning to him. Instead, she was flying off towards the approaching reinforcements, having finished off the last of the Humvees. She flew past the base and growled at Gi'les before flying out towards the approaching landing vessels, which were two fan-propelled hover boats with either more rock-eteers or a turret gunner as either passengers or ordinance. They were protecting an amphibious landing vehicle, filled with another twenty to twenty-five troops. *Are you sure you would have agreed to go through with it if I had told you?* Alyisay asked him. *I'm sorry. The offer still stands. I will be your dragon if you can finish this. C'mon, we're almost there!*

Alyisay roared and blew a river of fire from her mouth to the surface of the water, engulfing the two hover boats. That left the landing vehicle as a sitting duck. At that rate, she would be finished with her work long before him! She was making it look easy, and Brian couldn't accept that.

He planned to make this fight his quickest win ever. He would fight like a tiger and think like a human. He would use his sleight of hand and his knowledge of hand-to-hand fighting to take Gi'les down in just a few short moves. Then perhaps Alyisay could help him with the rest of the soldiers after he killed Gi'les. Brian waited for Gi'les to attack.

"The suit admittedly doesn't do all that well against dragons out in the open, but it should work just fine against you for my purposes here," Gi'les said. "As soon as I finish you off, I'll have that cruiser blow her clean out of the sky. It's not a matter of men as to when she'll die, it's just a matter of myself."

Brian growled. He watched Gi'les rev his drill, and then he let his instinctual moves take over the dance. When Gi'les lunged at him, Brian reared back with his tail in the air, and he let the drill stab the ground in front of him. Brian pounced for the tip of the drill while it was on the ground to try and scurry up the arm to maul Gi'les in the face, but Gi'les caught him across the face with the boomerang-shaped rod. Brian felt blood in his mouth for the first time that day and stumbled back.

When Brian stumbled, Gi'les pressed his attack with his spinning, ripping drill. He lunged it at Brian, driving him away toward the circle of soldiers that surrounded them but did not help either party. Brian stumbled up against the legs of the soldiers and felt shredded rocks spray all over his body from Gi'les's drill while he stabbed it onto the gravel. Then he jumped for Brian and landed close.

When he did, the soldiers backed away quickly to give Gi'les more space to operate in his armored exo-mech suit. Gi'les swung his boomerang rod at Brian and took out his legs, flipping him on his back. Then he jumped over the top of Brian. Gi'les began to rev his drill to stab Brian in the chest, but Brian clawed him in the face severely before he could and then kicked him with both of his hind legs. This sent Gi'les stumbling and lurching backward.

Gi'les then took a new approach. He walked his way forward toward Brian, waving the boomerang rod low to the ground in front of his path. He held the drill in front of him, ready to use it at any time. Brian allowed Gi'les to direct his movement around their fighting space with the rod, waiting for an opportunity to strike when Gi'les would think he had him cornered.

Brian was sitting perched like a cat in a window as Gi'les lunged for him. Brian ducked under the drill and jumped over the rod in one fluid motion. Then he bounded around the corner and jumped onto the back of the suit. When he began to fly, Brian felt himself start to come out of his transformation. It was now or never. Brian latched onto the back of Gi'les exo-mech suit as firmly as he could.

"Hey, stop it!" Gi'les exclaimed from in front of him, while he dug his claws into the back of his legs through an exposed area on the suit. Gi'les grimaced and fell to one knee. Brian looked at his hands and saw them turn back to his normal ones. He used his nimble hands to open the power box on Gi'les' suit. He could disable it if he could just cut all the wires. Such an action would also instantly release the egg to roll out of its protective case.

Brian put the epicenter of the massive tangle of cords in his vision and bit it out with two of his tiger teeth, as his face had not yet transformed back into normal. He released Gi'les and stumbled off him, back in his normal body again and wearing his raggedy clothes. He watched the case protecting the egg split open at the bottom, dropping the egg toward the ground. Brian dove and caught the egg with his two hands, cradling the brittle egg with his two arms like a baby and bringing it as close into his chest as possible before tucking in his legs and beginning a forward roll.

He rolled to a stop at the end of the steps that led up to the patio in front of the chapel. *Alyisay, I think I'm going to need some help here,* he thought to her.

Just keep the egg protected. My fire can't burn you, remember? Alyisay asked him.

I do now! he thought. He curled up and watched Gi'les approaching him with a knife after he had been forced to exit his mech since Brian had shut it down. The rest of his soldiers had their rifles pointed at him ready to shoot. None of the soldiers were able to pull their triggers, though. Brian saw a wave of fire crash into them, disintegrating all of Gi'les' reinforcements into ash, leaving just the two of them in a duel. Gi'les was his to finish.

Brian had nothing but his arms, legs, and teeth. "I'm not a coward," Gi'les told him. "What is it she's told you about me? That I stole what was most valuable to her and murdered a bunch of savages to make a profit and claim her head? I am but a man. I cannot breathe fire or crush people with my feet. Look at what I've done." Gi'les tossed him a knife similar to his, and he caught it without trouble. Brian picked up the egg and put it behind him, then he charged forward at Gi'les.

Brian swung his knife for the face of Gi'les who merely leaned away, and as Brian missed to the side, Gi'les punched him in the stomach, sending him to the ground. Brian stopped himself from landing on the gravel on his stomach but stumbled to one knee. Brian quickly looked back and saw Gi'les bending down to stab him in the heart. He grabbed his arm with his hands as Gi'les showed it in front of him and then shouldered himself into it, flipping Gi'les into the ground. Gi'les dropped his knife when Brian flipped him to the ground. Suddenly Brian felt his legs kicked out from under him. His vision inverted and he felt his back and head hit the graven.

Brian held onto his knife when Gi'les kicked him onto his back. Gi'les turned around to go and grab the closest available assault rifle, that wasn't too close to the charred bodies of the burnt soldiers. If Brian let him get to a gun, he didn't anticipate Gi'les tossing him one like he had a knife, and he would also be able to shoot the egg to pieces. Brian leaned up, and as Gi'les was bending down to pick up an assault rifle, he threw his knife into his back. Gi'les shuddered and groaned, but then grabbed the gun and began to bring it around. Brian saw all of this and gathered himself to his feet, then dashed for Gi'les and lunged for the knife. His nimble hands found their target as Gi'les fired several shots in haste, missing everything. He held onto the knife, and the assault rifle was knocked out of Gi'les' hands when he turned around to fire at Brian.

The two of them engaged in a brief struggle standing together, their eyes looking deep into each other. Brian yanked the knife out of Gi'les' abdomen causing the man to shudder and groan again, and then he plunged the knife into Gi'les' stomach again. Gi'les spit up blood and punched him in the ribs, trying to just get an inch of space away from Brian for a respite, but Brian held onto the knife and then drove it further into him. Gi'les' eyes shot up; he wouldn't last much longer now. Gi'les staggered back just far enough for Brian to stab him in the heart. Finally, Gi'les gave him one last look, and then fell over, dead.

Alyisay landed not far from him in the roundabout not long after that and waited for him. *We really should go now; I don't like my chances in a prolonged fight against that cruiser group. Iishrem will just have to come after this prize again on another day,* she told him. *C'mon.*

Brian gathered the egg from behind her and placed it gently in a burlap sack he found lying next to one of the dead soldiers. Alyisay burned Gi'les' body and his exo-mech suit while he did that. She thought nothing to him about the death of the man they had come all this way for, but they were successful in their mission, and now it was time for them to go. He sat down on her back, grabbed onto the two spikes he had used before as handles, and watched her kickoff into the air a moment later.

The two of them quickly put the cruiser group and the rest of Haisha behind them. Brian wanted to do nothing more than get this all over with and secure his place at his new home, wiping away his chances of possible involuntary and untrained experiences with the war. Never again would he let what happened to Macie happen to anyone else he loved, without having something to say about it first.

Alyisay knew the way to the academy—as she had always told him before. She flew him there in several hours with only a stop for dinner and some relief in the middle. It was almost midnight by the time they descended into the academy. Alyisay brought him to a running stop in the middle of the campus and made enough of a ruckus to rouse Mason. He was there by the time Brian stepped off Alyisay and finished saying goodbye to her for the night. *We did it,* Brian thought to her as he watched her fly off towards a lake that was surrounded by Eedon Rath-ni.

And our next trials await us soon, she thought back.

"My sources are good after all," Mason said out loud. "The Tiger of Maish has joined with his dragon. I can't thank you enough for the safe rescue of the egg."

At the parting of his hands, two resistance soldiers walked forward from where they had been standing behind him. They took the egg from Brian and put it into a padded suitcase, which they then locked. The soldiers began to walk off towards a nearby building with a tall radio tower on top of it. "A word," Mason requested, "before you get settled in?"

Mason took him under his wing, putting his arm around his shoulder and leading him towards the first-year dorms. "I saw to it that Macie received a proper burial—once you left," Mason told him. He reached into his coat pocket and pulled out Macie's necklace—the one she had been wearing on the day they had tried to escape Maish. "She was wearing this. You should have it. I think it would mean something to her."

Brian cradled it in his arms knowing it was fragile. It was the last piece he had of a woman he had loved many times. He'd failed in saving her, and more doubly even felt somewhat responsible for it. He began to cry, before he stifled that to sniffing and put the necklace around his neck.

"Thank you," he told him. Mason patted him on the shoulder for just a moment in solidarity. Brian looked down at the necklace for the first time. It was light, but when he looked down at the moon and dragon encased by it, he could feel the weight of Macie's life and memory now connected to the path he had taken to get here—and the path he would follow moving forward. Her death would not be in vain if he was able to grow from the experience.

Mason led him up the stairs to the first-year dorm and unlocked it with a key. He took him into the lobby of the first floor, and then he headed behind a check-in desk to grab a room key. Brian got room 24, again. "You've got one free day to rest up before your next set of trials begin. How are you going to spend your leisure time until then?" Mason asked him.

Brian took the key from his hands quickly. "Well Mason, I'm gonna go up to the bathroom in my bedroom and take an enormous shit I've been holding in from Haisha. It'll be nice to have a regular toilet and bed again."

Chapter 36

Beatrice the Prophet (Ethan 9)

MEINGHELIA CITY, MARAVINYA, ALLIREHEM

FALL, 1153, FOURTH AGE

*T*alk was quiet and light among Ethan and his fellow first-year Dravens as they stood underneath the middle of a concourse that led onto the dargen pitch contained within the small stadium on the campus of Christian's Academy. It was not an awfully long concourse, because the single-leveled seating bowl only had about twenty rows. However, the steps which led up to the seats were steep, allowing spectators to easily see down onto the playing field below. As the semester had not yet begun, the dargen course had not yet been put together, but Katie could see the two level goals on either end. Katie twitched behind him, wearing a tight, thick pair of combat pants.

"I don't mind the look of them," Katie said out loud, turning herself to look at her backside while she wore them, "but could they not have picked a better material?"

Ethan opened his eyes and felt them turn violet like they had been when he had watched the assassination of Sax Drugren from the top of the Calanor Stronghold. The texture of his combat pants didn't bother him. A soft, young voice from behind Katie said, "It's not about the texture of the pants. It's what the material can do for you. Hi, I'm Bailey."

Ethan turned around to look past his sister, and he saw a young, smiling face, full of cheer. Ethan liked Bailey's messy dirty-blonde hair, which came down in several different thick strands around her head. Ethan noticed the top of her head only came up to the middle of Katie's neck. Bailey held her hand in the air, waiting for Katie to smack it. Katie softly touched the bottom of Bailey's palm with the tips of her fingers several seconds later.

"Well, that was a terrible high-five," Bailey exclaimed assuredly.

"High-five?" Ethan asked.

"Sorry, you caught me off-guard. You're not from Maravinya?" Katie asked their new friend.

"Seems, Middle Rehem. I had plenty of styles of greetings to choose from when I was growing up! But your pants... well, it's one of the first things they're going to teach us about. They're Shed'lieos pants, and they'll help deaden the impact of bullets if such attacks progress past the natural magical shields you'll start to produce—once they teach us. I can see your eyes are golden. A strength Draven?" Bailey asked Katie. Ethan noticed several other first years were beginning to take notice of their conversation.

"Your shields will be up for as long as your eyes are golden. And who are you?" Bailey asked him.

"Ethan," he told Bailey, whose cheery attitude he thought was encouraging. He went in for a hug. Bailey didn't hug back at first, but she stood there and did not push him away. Ethan was not too close to her, he supposed. A second later, she put her hands around the bottom of his waist and held them there for a moment, then she backed away.

"Your violet eyes," Bailey remarked, noticing his magic, which he had just felt activate.

"Like my raven," Ethan told her, taking care of answering her potential next question.

Bailey thought for a moment. It would not be long before Ethan naturally pulled a few more of the first-year students into the conversation. "It's all got something to do with your peak color," Bailey told the two of them. "At least, that's what my father tells me."

"Your father?" asked a tall older man with a weathered expression. He had spiked up orange hair and a slender body. When Ethan looked over at him, he couldn't believe how wryly his arms looked. At the moment they seemed to be naturally resting below the bottom of Katie's waist, but Ethan could have sworn they were significantly shorter before he was able to bring him into the conversation. "Name's Brian."

Brian offered each of them his palm, like all tactful citizens of Allirehem should have. Ethan wondered, *Mhmm, I don't trust him.*

Ethan, said Violet in his mind. He looked around the tunnel and found that his fellow classmates were of all ages. He believed he saw one older than forty, and perhaps another in her younger teens. Ethan wondered how quickly word of his nationality would spread throughout the class. *Everyone will know within a week or month. Even the upper years. Ethan, it will be a focal point on which you will be judged moving forward. Not everyone will be as welcoming as those we have met so far. In fact, I suspect this one may be hiding baggage.*

Ethan accepted Brian's greeting as quickly as he could. He needed friends before rivals and allies before enemies. "Ethan," he said out loud again for a second time.

Another boy almost as old as him entered the conversation from behind Bailey, snapping out of a momentary stupor. He had been texting on his cell phone just before. "Hey, name's Icon." He greeted the group with a brief salute, not asking for physical contact from anyone upon their initial greeting. "I've got a rough past, but I don't let it get me down. Every day could just well be my last, and I try never to forget that," he told them.

Ethan noticed Bailey's eyes fray in anguish at the end of that statement, if only just for a second. "It's nice to meet you, friend," said a new voice. Ruth had entered the conversation at last. She introduced herself to the rest of the group as the pace of the scene around them began to liven.

For the first time, Ethan was able to look around the tunnel in front of him and observe a few more than a dozen of each type of Draven. There were several defining attributes that he began to observe acting themselves out in natural patterns among his group of fellow first-year students. Ethan suspected that he and his sister were the only ones from Iishrem, but he could clearly see that nearly all the other significant nationalities, creeds, and skin-tones from Middle Rehem and Allirehem were represented.

At the playing of a wooden flute, the range Dravens like Bailey and Icon—with each of their unique skill sets—began to make their way out into the middle of the dargen pitch. A cauldron of hawks was waiting for each of their riders to step up and approach. The ceremony was beginning.

Naturally, at the leaving of one portion of Ethan's future classmates, he was pulled along with them in motion as he watched. The range Dravens walked out onto the pitch and stepped up to their hawks, who had each landed interspersed within the stadium, somewhere on the dargen pitch.

While that was happening, Ethan was able to notice for the first time those who sat in the stands beyond the dargen pitch.

The rest of the attendees for the commencement ceremony lightly filled up several sections of seats in the stands. Classes of almost as many second-year students sat in the section directly center left of the stadium tunnel that the first years were exiting out of, while a noticeably smaller class of third-year students sat in the section that was to the right of that.

In the section beyond that, Ethan could see the instructors, along with second- and third-year mentor Dravens. In the section to the left, Ethan could see a group of guests, representatives, and dignitaries. He knew a few of them on sight. A man with a scar over his right eye and grey hair named Penn Bastion was their contact with Resistance HQ. A tall woman with thick hips and bushy black hair named Natalie Waters was their representative with Allirehem Resistance Fleet COMM. A man who sat by himself at the top of one of the seating sections was armed to the teeth with several heavy weapons. Ethan knew that man's name was Colt Rotator, and he was the Master of Arms at Christian's Academy.

The final group of attendees for the ceremony beyond that were the staff members of the academy. "Future students, Dravens, teachers, and Allirehem soldiers and allies," said Christian's voice, pulling Ethan's vision temporarily back to the proceeding ceremony. "We gather here today to induct a new class of Dravens who will fight for our collectively free future."

A new voice began to boom over the bowl of seats. Naliais had joined Christian on the dargen pitch, in the middle of a clearing of the hawks. The wooden flute that had sounded over the stadium before was tied around his neck. "As the Range Draven instructor, I, Naliais Mackeen, can't wait to get to work with Dravens with such diverse skill sets as these. Nevertheless, they'll all have to learn how to shoot, fight, and scrounge together every bit of compromising information on the enemy as they can to be successful."

Naliais paused, and half as many staff members as Dravens on the pitch walked up to the students carrying large square-shaped boxes. In addition to Naliais, Ethan also noticed for the first time that Varly had rejoined the two of them at Christian's Academy after drilling them through Gallaeic and Maravinyian in a handful of days. Ethan would begin working on his fluency in Haishian and Rehemic soon, while he continued to improve in his fluency of other the other languages. Ethan had not yet heard anything about having to start Zapfreni or Selnian.

Varly was the flight instructor and mentor for the Academy. As such, she was currently flying in place in the air on top of her hawk, which had a white underbelly with many small brown spots. When each of the future range Dravens had been handed a box, Christian called down one final instructor to join him on the pitch. It was Talia, his wife. Talia walked down a flight of stairs, out of the stands, and down onto the pitch with her long staff in her hand.

Ethan watched Talia step up to the side of her husband with her forest green eyes, and then she turned away from him. Ethan could see Talia's eyes change colors to orange before an orange burst for each student shot out the end of her staff. Ethan watched the balls of orange sparks each hit the boxes that the range Dravens held in front of them. The boxes fell apart, revealing various designs of square-shaped riot shields.

"You're right. These shields may not entirely have a purpose to you students," Naliais began, "but as long as we teachers have our rapiers, you shall have your shields. Huzzah!" Naliais drew his rapier and pointed it high into the sky. That was the signal. At the playing of his wooden flute again, the range Dravens sprang into action—only this time, the group of them hopped onto their hawks and took off into the air after they had put their shields around their back.

When all the hawks had flown out of the stadium, the next type of Eedon Rath-ni began to land. "Here comes the congress of eagles," said Katie from in front of him.

The group of eagles approached in silence and maneuvered their way into separate landing spots around the playing field in mesmerizing fashion over the next few moments. Naliais left the field of play and walked back up towards the stands of attendees. Christian was the instructor of the Strength Dravens.

Ethan put his hand on Katie's shoulder and asked, "Okay, are you ready?" before Christian called her and her fellow dozen or so strength Dravens out onto the pitch with him.

Katie put her hand back on his opposite shoulder. "I'll see you up there at the end of this all. And we'll get started on it all again together," she told him with a smile. Katie let him go. Ethan watched Katie and several other men and women somewhat around her physical stature and composition walk out onto the field. Ethan hoped that Christian wouldn't directly call attention to their shared heritage.

"As some of you may know," Christian said boomingly, "There are those in this class of new recruits that really did come from all over."

Ethan cautiously restrained himself from groaning out loud. Instead, he thought out to Violet, *So, he'll address the rumors but not point us out directly. How indecisive.*

Violet told him, *Be mindful of how he treats you now in front of your peers.*

"And yet, I believe this class of strength Dravens have it all. Fantastic combinations of prowess, fortitude, and spunk. Myriad potential in each will be of the least of your needs once the semester begins tomorrow," Christian said.

When his introductions were over, the same staff members that had brought out the shields before this time returned with suitcases. Christian had given each of his students a rifle of their choosing to customize and grow familiar with. The rifle that Katie was handed became a part of her as soon as she took it. For a moment, Ethan marveled at the strange choice of assault rifle she had made, compared to her fellow classmates.

She had told him it was the A5H4T, otherwise known as the asshat. "It may not be the prettiest," she had said in front of him a day earlier when she picked it out, "but it's undeniably reliable in close range confrontations, and its iron sights are bliss in their simplicity."

While the strength Dravens each put their rifles around their backs and prepared to board their eagles, a staff member brought Christian an instrument of his own. They dropped a rectangular suitcase at Christian's feet, and then he opened it a moment later. He pulled out a golden alto saxophone. While he played a short tune, Ethan watched Katie and the rest of the strength Dravens hop onto their eagles and fly into the air.

The eagles left the stadium and joined the group of hawks who were still flying directly above it. The entire first-year student body would take a synchronized flight from the bottom of the academy, around the mountain, and then each would land at the Mountainlair near the summit. There they would partake in a great feast for the fall semester.

There was a short break while Ethan began to track the ravens as they flew into their places. Ethan saw Violet streaking down towards him from the northern end. As the last raven to land, Violet alighted in the center of the pitch with a few flaps of her wings. None of her fellow Eedon Rath-ni intimidated her, but Ethan had felt the eyes of some of his fellow classmates on his back. Of course, dragon-riding Dravens were going to be the last in the ceremony to take off.

"I guess I'll see you guys up there. It'll be good to see how the rest of you all drink, especially together. Whenever we first get the chance," Brian told Ethan.

Ethan heard Ruth's voice behind him. "Hey, c'mon, it's almost our turn," she told him.

The class of magic Dravens separated themselves from the remaining group of beast Dravens, and Ethan and Ruth walked out onto the field. In the middle of the formation, Carra and her purple hair was Christian's instructor for magical Dravenry. With his duties temporarily played out, Christian left Carra some space on the pitch. She had called them out to her with a lovely tune played on a violin.

"See you up there," Ethan told Ruth when they parted a few seconds later and walked over to their respective ravens.

Carra had a different sort of gift for her magical Dravens. "You know it's really the founders that made this academy what it is. What it was," she told the crowd of observers. "I don't believe we should forget them."

Carra spread her arms out in front of her and pulled them up around herself. As she did, a handful of ghosts rose out of the ground with her. Of course, Ethan quickly recognized the Dean, and Gabel—still, he complained about the deathly market—but it was a different ghost that glided over to him to give him his gift. Ethan watched her approach.

The ghostly woman looked his age but dressed in more of a more feudal manner. *Kiera?* he thought; the ghost had a striking resemblance to her.

"No, I'm not who you think I am," the ghost told him off the bat, quickly assuaging his fears.

"Then who are you?" Ethan asked her readily.

"One of the founders of the academy," the serene female ghost told him. "I was called Beatrice the Prophet. For years now, I have seen the coming of you and your sister to this academy."

Beatrice paused and turned away from him while Ethan heard Carra saying something, but he didn't care to listen to exactly what it was, unless it was time for him to get onto Violet. He looked over at Violet and wondered if there were ghost Eedon Rath-ni. "Is there something you have to tell me?" Ethan asked her.

"Not anything, in particular, that you want to hear," she told him. "But there are many events in your future I could tell you about."

"How about one or two?" Ethan asked, putting up his hands, figuring it couldn't hurt to ask a ghost about his future. Now one that was already right in front of him, quite openly anyways.

"Well, how about this?" Beatrice said as she broke into a short pace back and forth.

"Beatrice, do go on and tell Ethan his information. We have a schedule to keep to, even you ghosts must abide by," Christian said to her from across the dargen pitch. While Carra went back into her vamping for her incoming class of first-year magical Dravens, Beatrice told him the information she offered.

"Well, you have a look of destiny you see. People will follow you—but not always to the best of ends. Your sister, though, I have seen her too. *She* has the look of a wanderer," Beatrice told him.

It was exactly as she had told him before. Beatrice had told him a thing or two that he had never particularly wanted to know, without knowing if her prophecies were generally accurate in the first place. "Well, thank you," he told the seer ghost. "I'm sure I'll learn lots of great news from you over these next few years."

Beatrice did not laugh at his joke and vanished back into thin air a moment later. *C'mon, we don't need her predictions. Let's kick off into the air one more time,* Violet told him.

Ethan looked away from where he had seen Beatrice vanish and over to Violet next to him. She bent down and stretched out her wings for him. Just like he was back on the *Valkyrie*, Ethan stepped into Violet's stirrups and sat down on top of her saddle, ready for another ride.

After he gripped the handles on her saddle, Violet kicked off into the air and ascended from the stadium with a few flaps of her wings. Ethan stayed with his proper flock of Eedon Rath-ni—the conspiracy of Ravens—and flew toward an open portion of the northwestern quadrant over the dargen stadium. At the sound of several low-pitched growls and moderate roars, Brian heard the handful of dragons approaching from the lake.

Of course, because of their size, it took the weyr of dragons the most time to land safely on the dargen pitch, but Mason and Von both worked quickly, bringing their students up to them to give their gifts and having them get onto their dragons. Ethan didn't care to pay particularly close attention to what Mason said to Brian when he approached him, but he watched him walk over to his big orange dragon and get on her all the same. The gifts for the beast Dravens seemed to be miniature statue representations of the forms they took during their transformations, so naturally, Brian received the statue of a small orange tiger.

When Ethan saw Brian kick off into the air, it looked like he wanted to join him in his area for a moment, but Brian didn't end up doing that. He stayed in formation with his fellow dragon riders, while its cluster over the southeastern quadrant of the dargen stadium grew lager.

Once all the first years were in the air, four final Eedon Rath-ni joined their flock. Ethan heard a thunderous roar. A green dragon approached the dargen stadium from the northeast. It landed in the center of the pitch and picked up Mason with ease. After that, Ethan saw a tree seem to shake itself loose of a massive hawk. It was an Eingeana, and she picked up Naliais. Carra's raven picked her up having been perched on top of one of the Academy department buildings. Finally, Ethan heard a piercing screech from behind and saw Anacarin streak into the stadium to pick up Christian.

Christian brought the four of them in formation into the center of the massive flock of Eedon Rath-ni. Just before Christian began to speak, Ethan had a chance to observe the entire scene. The sun had risen high in the sky and was shining brightly on his cheeks while he sat atop of Violet. Several dozen other Eedon Rath-ni watched the entire commencement from various locations across the campus of Christian's Academy. Ethan smiled for a moment and thought sadly about his parents and Kiera.

His parents were gone, Ethan knew he would have to accept that. However, Allovein had been mum on exactly what Kiera's continued livelihood was. *She could still be alive*, Ethan mused to himself.

"First years!" Christian exclaimed, bringing them all to attention one last time. Ethan listened and pushed everything else out of his mind. "Not a single one of you had an easy or simple path here. For some of you, your connections to your Eedon Rath-ni linked you to the effects of the war and its most pivotal impacts. For others, your magic was a childhood brand or a skill set that made you an outlaw, a runaway, a spy. But what about the rest of you. What about all of you?"

"What stories of the past will you tell your fellow Draven classmates in the dawning future? I now pronounce this fall semester of the year 1153 in the Fourth Age commenced," Christian said, looking down at his watch. "What stories of the future will you bring into being as this great and terrible war plays out all around us? Come, follow me, and never fear, for Rehem is meant to know of the strength of Dravens, and the phoenix should come to fear the magic of the Eedon Rath-ni. Now go on, fly!"

Christian thrust his sword in front of him and sent his legion of Dravens and their Eedon Rath-ni around the small mountain and up its side. With his eyes wide open, Ethan flew onward towards the Mountainlair and his future training as a Draven. Ethan knew he could face down anything, as long as he believed in his magic and had Violet at his side.

_ End of Book One _

Appendix

1. PLACES

    a. Iishrem – A collection of 9 states united under the rule of the House of Lance, with a combined population of around 3.7 billion.

        i. Dusk – The largest, most populated, and most central state of Iishrem. Grows most of the food for Iishrem, has bountiful oil reserves, runs mostly on wind power, and is responsible for constructing a large portion of Iishrem's war machine (vehicles, weapons, supplies).

            1. Imperium Aendor – Although not technically part of Dusk, the capital of all Iishrem is entirely encompassed by it. It has been the center of the House of Lance's power since beginning of the 4th age and fosters many of the nation's brightest minds and most influential persons.

            2. Malin Harr – A city built upon a lush river valley and the longtime home of the Aleium branch of the House of Lance. Located within the valley at the center of the city is Iishrem's Center for Draven Abilities, or CDA, where Iishrem trains its newest Dravens, in the wake of the successful assassination of Sax Drugren.

            3. Mos Marron – A city in the southern marshy regions of Dusk near to the coast. Has a strong cultural, regional dialect, one of the only ones permitted within Iishrem under the rule of the House of Lance. The city excels at weathering its constant storms and exports dishes the rest of Rehem devours.

        ii. Falclaine Islands – A collection of islands located due south of Dusk. Authority has remained with their longtime rulers the House of Cromella, who pledged fealty to the House of Lance at the beginning of the 4th age, to retain their position and not have a war. Responsible for the building and development of Iishrem's Royal Navy as well as its warplanes.

            1. Minon Cromella – The capital of the Falclaine Islands and seat of power of House Cromella.

        iii. Reyvula – A sparsely populated region of Iishrem defined by two geographical features, each with one population center in its relative center.

A dense forest and the city of Rune, and a range of sharp mountains with the city of Beratile atop of a spacious plateau, accessible by climbing, or several tunnels. Reyvula subsists largely on hunting rare game and mining rare valuable minerals.

iv. **Fuet** – A largely arid and cavernous region of Iishrem. Stylers (giant spiders, some the size of apes) roam in wild packs. Iishrem tests a lot of new techs here as well as stores a large population of its political dissidents in its large swaths of open land. The population itself largely keeps to itself.

v. **Castainya** – A largely forested state within Iishrem and home to some rare snakes among other rare species. Taerit, a city built on the north side of a lake out of the mammoth trees themselves is the location where Iishrem trains most of its special forces.

vi. **Councillia** – A cultural birthplace of Iishrem's lore, mythology, and conspiracy, and the shelled remains of a long dead and long forgotten civilization. After the bombing of the Council of Nations and Dravens, the remaining population of Nahirehem becomes the largely mindless dregs of completing large scale projects for the House of Lance. Although the Council of Nations and Dravens is largely only cosmetically damaged in the bombing, members of the house of Lance refuse to set foot on its campus or even the city for shrouded reasons, and little is known of what has happened to the population of the city that was within the Council of Nations and Dravens at the time of the bombing.

vii. **Rhollian** – Not much is known about this largely forested state within Iishrem at this time.

viii. **Gazsamine** - More remains of the Long Dead and Long Forgotten civilization lay deep within the rainforest jungles of this state of Iishrem, with good potential for ancient technologies to be redeveloped for modern uses. The House of Lance controlled these ruins for hundreds of years after their rise to power near the end of the third age, but recent civil strife with some of the local leaders over the way they are by the House of Lance has led to small scale skirmishes, and weakened their grip on some of the more influential relic sites.

ix. **Kafari** – The population of this state largely reside in two coastal cities, whose main exports are seafood and pearls. The population also excels in sailing and is home to the building of some of Iishrem's more unique warships.

b. **Middle Rehem and Other Governments not Associated with Either Iishrem or Allirehem**
   i. **Saventaul** – A thorn on the arch of Iishrem's crown, this island-based city has long eluded annexation by Iishrem thanks to its choppy, polar waters, magnetic disruptions making it hard to find, and a collection of competent pirate navies that are good at regularly coming together to fight greater foes than themselves. Always in need of great surgeons.
   ii. **Middle Rehem** – The region between Iishrem and Allirehem with no particular allegiance to either. Estimated combined population of any place mentioned within this section is 0.6 billion
      1. **Selenia** – A collection of four city-states that have a loose alliance with each other, which have allowed them all to prosper and remain free of Iishrem since the dawn of the 4th Age. The cities have always been a place of military might, technological development, and bountiful resources other nations covet. Resources like Petrol which will be hugely influential in the war to come. Vrainemark even has a burgeoning space program.
      2. **Haerlin Springs** – A thriving city built atop a large desert oasis. One of two cities where the world of Rehem travels to gamble or bet on the Deathly Market. Because of its location and importance to both sides, an uneasy truce exists which has kept it largely free of damage.
      3. **Ferrum** – A once pristine city nick-named the gateway to Allirehem, by the end of the first book it has been officially annexed by Iishrem, most of its population enslaved, deserted, or depleted, and large portions of it has been razed. Once the construction of The Long Road reached this city, the Allirehem Resistance did its condition and population no favors, by largely retreating without much of a fight. Iishrem now uses the city as a forward operating base for launching ground attacks into Galliem.
      4. **Seems** – Another neutral city-state a tentative truce here exists between both sides because of the collective interest of the global elite. Home of Rehem's tallest mountains, many nature parks, gambling, and winter sports.
   iii. **Heylaphine Islands** – A sparsely populated collection of Islands in the southern Allaeyic Ocean between East Rehem and Maravinya. There are a handful of maritime based communities but no centralized govern-

ment, so while it may be in Allirehem, it is not recognized as an official state or part of the Allirehem Resistance.

c. **Allirehem** – A collection of four nations united Christian Knowles and their combined opposition to the expansion of a cultural hegemony by the House of Lance. This alliance is very newly formed and long running historical rivalries between its four nations are not easily forgotten or washed away. The estimated combined population of its four nations is 2.3 billion.

    i. **Galliem** – The first country of Allirehem to face a ground assault by Iishrem. Known for a fairly libertarian government and several powerful crime families that run drug trades, and often buy politicians to exert their influence.

    ii. **East Rehem** – An expansive island continent in the southern Allaeyic Ocean. Raegic, while a picturesque city, is often plagued by riots and revolts thanks to its well-known and well-documented government corruption. Sen Rhêt Hill a city that rises up a hill and out of an expansive lake is the capital of the country and has produced may famed artists over history.

    iii. **Haisha** – Another island continent in the northern expanses of the Allaeyic Ocean, with a hodgepodge of geographical features, peoples, and cultures. Little national unity exists because of this. Also, home to the last "uncontacted" populations of humans who reside deep within its dense, lush, jungle rainforest largely reachable only by walking or water.

        1. **Illias** – The capital of Haisha and one of the most economically powerful cities in Rehem. Human trafficking and other groups like The Hunters, and The Fool's Fleet influence its governmental powers while corruption is rife, money buys power, and those who speak up must regularly fear for their lives or that of their families.

    iv. **Maravinya** – Perhaps the most powerful and well protected country allied to Allirehem currently fighting against Iishrem. Its government is "clean", its people united, and there is great wealth and resources to supply Allirehem well for a long war with Iishrem. However, the country is relatively unproven in war, as well as handling invasions at home, and its newer navies are fairly green.

        1. **Draxion City** – The capital of Maravinya and location of the Deathly Market.

2. **Meinghelia City** – A secluded and protected city where Christian secretly trains his new Dravens at his academy before sending them into the war against Iishrem. Its location may well not stay hidden, for long.

2. IMPORTANT NON-POV CHARACTERS & GROUPS OF PEOPLE

a. **Tamil Kun** – The first Draven known of, and all in current existence descend from him through some relation.

b. **Dravens** – Special soldiers normally specializing in one unique art of Dravenry with a strong connection to an Eedon Rath-ni corresponding to their specific art of Dravenry.

   i. **Magic or Stealth Dravens** – Dravens who specialize in combat with magic who have the unique ability to turn invisible. Paired with the Ravens of the Eedon Rath-ni.

   ii. **Strength Dravens** – Dravens who specialize in hand to hand combat or with magically enhanced armor, shields, or weapons. Paired with the Eagles of the Eedon Rath-ni.

   iii. **Beast or Dark Dravens** – Agents of chaos with the unbridled potential ability to turn into a huge beast to fight enemies for short periods of time. They are often as uncontrollable and unpredictable as their counterparts, the Dragons of the Eedon Rath-ni.

   iv. **Range/Informational Dravens** – Dravens who specialize in fighting enemies over range and distance, often using information against their opponents. Paired with the Hawks fo the Eedon Rath-ni.

c. **The Eedon Rath-ni** – The Lords of the Sky who are just beginning to re-emerge from their homes within the Shrouded Sea to fight a war they exist for.

   i. **Ravens** – The most magically gifted of all the Eedon Rath-ni with the ability to kill their enemies with a simple stare or control the minds of men, which is only surpassed by that of the Phoenix. They are typically the smallest and slowest of the four species though.

   ii. **Eagles** – The strongest and fastest of the Eedon Rath-ni, their unique attacks and defensive capabilities make for a powerful, yet controllable combination, along with their Dravens who fight in a complimenting fashion.

iii. **Dragons** – Untamable beasts and hoarders of riches, these beasts only emerge from their home within the Shrouded Sea to fight with Dravens worthy of their skill set, who compliment their personalities. They quickly rise to anger, and while significantly faster than Ravens, they often lack their agility because of their size, although within Dragons there is the most significant potential for size variation. Dragons often have one of several potential unique abilities to be shown in greater detail as the series progresses.

iv. **Hawks** – Although they are usually the weakest of the four types, these Eedon Rath-ni have great potential to preside and exert their influence over battles because of their unmatched swooping and ability to soar to the greatest altitudes of any. Their connection with their Dravens is unmatched over a great distance, and they remember well.

d. **The Phoenix** – There is only one. An immortal bird of immense power that has been under the "control" of the House of Lance and their descendants since the ending of the 3rd age. Can produce fire waves, has the ability to indoctrinate mass populations of men, and its feathers are used to unleash great magic of wide varieties and applications, which would otherwise be unachievable by even the most powerful Ravens and their magic Dravens. Their capabilities never lessen until they are utilized, which will make the use of them hugely consequential in determining the outcome of Christian's war.

e. **The House of Lance** – The ruling house of Iishrem. Have been in power since the beginning of the 4th age.

i. **Sax Drugren the 12th** – The Emperor of Iishrem at the beginning of the book. Dies by assassination at the age of 260.

ii. **Lance the 13th** – The Emperor of Iishrem at the end of the book. Rises to power upon the death of his father at the age of 25 and is 34 at the end. A most powerful Draven who as an Eedon Rath-ni of each type, and the excels in the application of each art of Dravenry.

iii. **Tagros Aleium Lance** – The brother of Queen Regent Reialya and head of the Aleium branch of the House of Lance. Has great influence over Lance the 13th because of his position and the value of his sister's marriage. Still youthful, late into his eighties.

iv. **Queen Regent Reialya** – The sister of Tagros. She is beautiful, vibrant, and adorned by the general population of Iishrem.

    v. **Iel-Shland the Eldest** – The oldest son of Sax Drugren the 12th from a long passed an unknown marriage. Has the genes of longer life and is very regionally powerful in his seat of power, Montal.

f. **The Keepers of the Sword** – A cult of esoteric and reclusive men and women who have lived in the shadows for the entire 4th age, hoping to one day launch a war to free Iishrem from the grip of the House of Lance. Their seat of power is the ruined remains of the Council of Nations and Dravens as well as the academy Christian opens.

    i. **Christian Knowles** – The Infamous Terrorist Draven who starts it all, brings magic back to Rehem, and gets the Eedon Rath-ni to re-emerge from their slumbers within the Shrouded Sea to fight for or against their cause. Mentor of Strength Dravenry at his academy.

    ii. **Gal'gatha and his three daughters** – The family that Christian finds after his fall including his future wife Talia. They are the descendants that Draxion the Bold left behind, who waited patiently for the right time to strike. Their full role in the series remains to be seen.

g. **Iishrem Allied Dravens**

    i. **Allovein Camnair** – A dark wizard with a murderous raven. Recruits for the Center for Draven Abilities in Malin Harr and the instructor of Magic Dravenry there.

    ii. **Calion Gordon** – The sharpest tooth of Iishrem's first jaw of attack. A wrecking ball made or claws, armor, and teeth, resulting in easy wanton death and destruction, wherever Lance pleases.

    iii. **Zeren Wikes** – A sturdy pen of Iishrem. Zeren knows where to make his mark and how deep. Not too proud to retreat, so that he may leave his ink somewhere else on Rehem again someday.

h. **Allirehem Allied Dravens**

    i. **Clancy Triten** – The father of Bailey Triten and Regal Draven Commander of all Dravens allied to Allirehem. Perhaps an even more powerful strength Draven than Christian himself, although they fight on the same side

    ii. **Mason Black** – Turns into a bear as his alternate form. The mentor of Beast Dravenry at Christian's academy.

    iii. **Naliais McKeen** – The best sniper the Allirehem Resistance has on its side, as well as the mentor of Range Dravenry at Christian's academy.

    iv. **Carra Richen** – The mentor of magical Dravenry at Christian's academy.

i. **The Hunters** - Mercenaries for hire with a penchant of hate for the Eedon Rath-ni. A few Dravens trained by Iishrem mixed within. Controlled by a shadowy council, which has been bought off by the House of Lance.

j. **Academy Founders** – There are 10 known founders of Christian's academy. Although not all of them ever made it there in their lifetimes, the ghosts of each can be summoned by any student or professor. They are: Draxion the Bold, Bentley the Wise, Gabel the Rich, Archam the Furious, Acentrina of the Stars, Ecalypsa the harsh, Jason the Brave, Salomon the courageous, Lenore the Enchantress, and Beatrice the Prophet

3. **FEATURES AND OTHER**
   a. **Shadow** – Pure black nothingness that drips and pools together like water.
   b. **Shroud** – Gray wispy clouds, a physical form of death itself.
   c. **Oceans**
      i. There are three recognized oceans on the planet of Rehem, the Monetic Ocean, the Eldeic Ocean, and the Allaeyic Ocean.
   d. **The Shrouded Sea** – The shrouded home of the Eedon Rath-ni. Not much is known about this area which covers roughly half of the planet, by the humans of Rehem. All expeditions into it have failed miserably, with the exceptions of ones led by Tamil Kun and Christian Knowles.
   e. **The Long Road** – Selenia and Middle Rehem's price to pay for largely staying neutral in the coming war was the construction of this road, as no such land connection between Iishrem and Allirehem existed before hand. Represents a bloody and seven-year prelude to the actual war itself largely commencing.
   f. **Languages** – There are several languages spoken widely throughout Rehem. Some are outlawed but still practiced in small pockets of society, and others are dead, known only by those with the esoteric knowledge of them.
      i. **Major Languages** – Iiasmaeic, Rehemic, Selnian, Haishian, Gallaeic, Maravinyian, Zapfreni
      ii. **Esoteric** – Old Calanorian
   g. **Currencies** – There are three currencies widely used throughout Rehem. Selnians $\mathcal{S}$, Allies $\mathcal{A}$, and Iagmites $\mathcal{I}$.
   h. **Dargen** – Dargen is the premier sport played throughout Rehem, for perhaps 1000 years. Regularly played on a square grass pitch of 120 yards long by 60 yards wide with a top level of play made up by a series of intercon-

nected bridges and platforms. Normally, teams have a goalie for each goal, two defensemen for each level of play and three forwards on each level of play making play 11 on 11, with seven available subs to use throughout the games, which last 60 minutes and are played in 3 20-minute periods. Each period starts with a forward from each team standing 10 yards from the ball while it is laid in the center of the bottom field in the first and third period, and the center of the top level for the second. At the sound of a whistle they charge into the center to retrieve an oblong football. Grappling is allowed but striking or kicking is a foul and automatic possession to the other team. Once a team takes possession of the ball, they have as many as two passes to transfer it to another player on their team on the other level successfully. When the ball is on the bottom field of play it must be passed by kicking and then thrown to a player on the level above. Self-passing is allowed. When the ball is on the top field of play it must be passed by throwing and then kicked to a player on the level below who catches it in the air or otherwise regains possession of the ball before the other team. By kicking the ball into the bottom field goal, a team will score four points, as is the same for throwing it into the goal from the top field of play. However, throwing the ball into the bottom field goal, or kicking it into the top is worth 6. Fouls are awarded for overly aggressive or physical play and result in extra-man advantages for the team fouled for a short duration of the game.

    i. **Known Dargen Teams** – Raegic Brigadiers, Dig'la Teur Ocelots, Aceor Motormen, Draxion City Assassins, Farlin-Tal Niai Rangers, Reyvula Mountaineers, Seems Orioles

i. **Brands and Drugs**

    i. **Vehicles**

        1. **Marinclayde** – Sleek sedans with tinted windows. Luxury at its finest. Perfect for secret dealings on the side, and a reliable quick getaway for a crew of up to five. Comes standard in Charcoal gray.

        2. **Burcgetti** – The most coveted of choppers in all of Rehem. Wide handlebars for true cruising. Comes standard in black.

        3. **Fabershaut** – Comes standard in red, with the quickest acceleration of any street legal car in Rehem. Fireproof exterior for brief encounters with dragons because you can outrun them with our speed.

4. **Rehem Rover** – A classy versatile SUV for your whole crew. A reinforced roll cage for bouts against eagles. Comes standard in dark green.

ii. Drugs

1. **Allum Rocks** – For normal humans, a gateway to the memories of the dead, the most significant memory of their past, if they had a choice in it. Crystals of amber and jade, inhibited by proximity and a willing mind to its affects.

2. **Hurinst's Plant** – Acrabiniz, a paper wrapper, and a spark of magic. Inhibited by inhalation. Used to forget your troubles and to laugh.

iii. Products and Companies

1. **Relnás** – The lighter of choice for those who live boldly and to be remembered. It just takes liquid, a wick, and a flick.

2. **Repanòs Whiskey** – Amber luck, cooked in fire, served with salt, and enhanced by hard ice.

3. **Cárlales Escapaño** – Smokey goodness, with hints of oak, cherry, and cedar. Will not produce shroud.

4. **Saek-a Rehemcast** – Arcade developer of the Glare of Ravens, and Rehem's predominant video game console, in the wake of Sax Drugren's assassination. Our games will make you throb with dark emotions.

5. **Zòrnentna X9000 Missile Defense System** – The complete missile package for protecting your home or base from Dravens and Eedon Rath-ni. For just $400k you'll get our turret launcher with 4 pods, and your first four missiles are free.

6. **Drev-Tech** – A technology firm based in Selenia. Makes a wide array of devices for seeking out artifacts from a long dead and long forgotten civilization.

On Development

The rebirth of this novel I believe, is the ultimate example of persistence and triumph in the face of controversy and trial. This book that I hope you love had to persist through a horrific head-on car accident, on the date of 4/13/13, then suffer a much maligned first release, and finally a contrived and painful process of bringing this ultimate version into being. I've reached the day where I can say all the work, hurt, and struggle I went through was worth it, for those of you who read this.

What I mean to say with this section is: If you don't succeed at first, try again, and don't give up. The greatest teacher, failure is. Endure. Persist. Win!

About the Author

B.A. Ellison grew up in southern Maryland and began writing stories on his father's computer from the age of eight. When he read *The Raven* by Edgar Allen Poe in high school, it would become his inspirationand place the spark within him to begin writing what would become *A Tale of Shadow and Shroud*. Work began on 1/10/2007.

It was a dream of passion and persistence from then on, throughout college and his life afterward. When he was ready enough to take a shot at it all, it became a craft.

Our dreams lay before us. If we can but make them real.

Thank You

I really hope that I have started something here, with the release of this novel. If you enjoyed reading this, please consider adding a review to this book's page on Goodreads, Amazon, or wherever else you review books. Please also feel free to check out my website baellibooks.com and follow me on Twitter @baellison4. A new fantasy series like this one, can only hope to be as popular as its fanbase is rabid. An aspiring author needs proper feedback, support, and input from his fans and readers, else it is hard hope to do this again, much less learn and grow. Until next time,

-B.A. Ellison